Dreamers

Also by Elaine Feinstein

NOVELS

The Circle
The Amberstone Exit
Children of the Rose
The Ecstasy of Dr Miriam Garner
The Shadow Master
The Survivors
The Border
Mother's Girl
All You Need
Loving Brecht

POEMS

In a Green Eye
The Celebrants
The Magic Apple Tree
Some Unease and Angels
Badlands
City Music
The Selected Poems of Marina Tsvetayeva
Three Russian Poets

BIOGRAPHY

A Captive Lion: The Life of
Marina Tsvetayeva

Lawrence's Women: The Intimate Life of
D. H. Lawrence

Elaine Feinstein

Dreamers

MACMILLAN
LONDON

First published 1994 by Macmillan London

a division of Pan Macmillan Publishers Limited
Cavaye Place London SW10 9PG
and Basingstoke

Associated companies throughout the world

ISBN 0-333-59840-7

1 3 5 7 9 8 6 4 2

A CIP catalogue record for this book is available from
the British Library

Typeset by CentraCet Limited, Cambridge
Printed and bound in Great Britain by
Mackays of Chatham plc, Chatham, Kent

For Martin and Marina

Acknowledgements

The author would like to thank Dr Miklos Teich and Professor Alice Teich for their help in exploring Vienna. She would also like to thank the Authors' Foundation for a grant which enabled her to complete this book.

Part One

1848

Chapter One

IT WAS A FEBRUARY morning in Vienna. The wind was blowing savagely from the east and a little snow was settling on the domes of green and bronze in the First District. There, surrounded by bastions from the days of the Turkish siege, stood the houses of the rich, their restaurants, cake shops, milliners and coffee houses. Those who ministered to the rich were already hard at work preparing food, washing clothes, wiping marble floors. The young girls of the Graben were sleeping. The Emperor lay in bed in the palace of the Hofburg and was not to be disturbed until noon. On Ballhausplatz, where Prince Metternich conducted the country's affairs in the Chancellery, the day's work had just begun. The Imperial Chief Minister was already at his desk and this morning he frowned at the news from Paris that lay before him.

Beyond the Graben, close by the Cathedral of St Stephen's, stood the solid town house of Natan Shassner, the banker. It was a building that had once belonged to a baron, and it was still decorated with elegant gilt vases, trailing flowers and figures that recalled the heraldic insignia of the former owner; Shassner had left the façade in place while refurbishing the rest. Now there were white lacquered chairs with goats' feet, inlaid cupboards, curtains of Chinese chintz and baskets of plaster fruit in the fine drawing rooms.

In a pretty breakfast room on the first floor, Minna Shassner was enjoying an extended breakfast with her son Anton. On the table was her favourite porcelain; the cup hand-painted with small green leaves, the sugar bowl with a garland of roses. The porcelain came from the Herend pottery which had recently begun to flourish in Hungary, and the milk jug carried a portrait of one of her uncles.

Minna was a graceful woman with fair hair and steady grey eyes. Her family had wide connections all over Europe and was one of the few allowed to reside in Vienna when Jews were forbidden there. The line ran back to Samson Wertheim, for whom it was said ten of the Emperor's soldiers stood outside his home on guard at all times. Her immediate family had been much less astute; indeed, her father's lack of enterprise had been treated with some impatience by his sharper brothers. All his daughters had absorbed his own love of music and dancing. For all the gaiety of her manner, however, there was a sadness in Minna's face. She had been a quiet and serious child, a little shy in the salons of her more important relatives, though proud enough to claim the celebrated Fanny von Arnstein among them.

Natan Shassner had decidedly bettered himself in marrying the eldest daughter of his employer. A handsome man, broad-shouldered and sturdily built, he had come into Vienna from one of the Eastern provinces of the Habsburg Empire with no more to advance him than a quick brain, a knowledge of languages and a punctilious honesty. As a young man, he had dealt in whatever goods were needed: coral, feathers for village beds, tobacco, horsehair and poultry. Now he owned a banking establishment.

Minna's way of life was not very different from that of her fellow Viennese citizens. Several members of her close family, including her own sister, had converted to Christianity. She liked plays and concerts, and had a gentle musical aptitude of her own. All she wanted for her son was the life on offer to the children of those who could choose their own way.

Anton, at seventeen, was a slight young man in golds and browns, the silk of his cravat glinting with the same russet tones as his hair. His face had an olive glow, and his small features echoed those of his mother. Yet, for all this charm, there was an awkwardness on the left side of his body; a hint of paralysis along his left arm which was the result of a childhood illness. He customarily kept his left hand concealed in a pocket.

When a chambermaid in silk shoes came in bearing an urn of hot water, Natan Shassner entered the breakfast room a few steps behind her. Anton looked up with surprise and a sense of intrusion: his father usually took morning coffee in his study. Minna, too, was surprised, both at Natan's unexpected entry and the severity of his expression. Her hand went up instinctively to correct the shape of her hair.

'Something is wrong,' she guessed.

'Revolution in Paris,' said Natan, briefly. 'Barricades have gone up in the streets. Royal troops have fired on the crowd.'

'And will it spread here?' Minna cried.

'No need to be frightened,' said Anton quickly. He had meant mainly to reassure Minna with those words but, as his father's brooding gaze swung over to him, he could not resist adding, 'Metternich's police will see to it the Viennese go on dancing.'

'Don't be so clever. The Viennese are great imitators,' said Natan sharply. 'However, you are right to say the police will be concerned. They will be particularly interested in your hot-head student friends. Best stay away from them.'

'Do you mean I should not go into the University?' asked Anton.

Natan hesitated. The last thing he wanted was to quarrel

with his son, but he knew well enough that Anton already spent far more time reading novels and poems than attending his lectures at the Law Faculty. Minna broke across his thoughts in a troubled voice.

'We should go to the Tyrol. It will be spring soon. We could walk in the mountains, drink the fresh water.'

'Of course. If you would like that.'

'I mean we should all go.'

'What would I do in the mountains?' Natan asked her.

'Anton will be safer there.'

'He could be perfectly safe here, if he had more sense.' Natan turned to his son. 'Don't spend so many hours in the cafés playing billiards and gossiping with Rudolf von Mayerberg.'

'Now why do you object to von Mayerberg as a friend?' Minna frowned. 'His mother is close to the Archduchess Sophie. Surely Rudolf is no radical?'

'He's a waster,' said Natan contemptuously. 'An old, unmarried goat.' He turned to his son with some puzzlement on his face. 'Why are you so attached to the fellow?'

Rudolf von Mayerberg was the middle-aged son of a great Austrian family long since impoverished; his claim on Anton's interest lay in two plays written some years before but still popular. None of this much impressed Natan Shassner.

'Well,' said Natan, 'well.'

He took out his fob watch. He was already late for a meeting of the charitable board of which he had recently become the chairman. This morning they would discuss the increase in poor immigrants to Vienna.

'Be as sensible as you can,' he said. Then he bent to press a glancing kiss on his wife's pale forehead and left.

As soon as he had gone, Minna anxiously observed the elation in her son's face.

'Anton,' she reproved him, 'your father has the interests of society at heart.'

'But does he care about freedom and justice? I don't think so.'

'Please, Anton,' she begged him, 'don't listen to the words in the street. I have heard them all my life. In the end revolution is all killing and no change for the better.'

Anton shook his head and stood up.

'You can't want to shout "Vive la France",' said Minna.

'Why not?' he teased her. 'What other country has fully opened its doors to us as citizens?' He smiled at her anxiety. 'But I won't rush into the street. In any case, look outside.'

He put an arm affectionately around her shoulders and they looked out of the window together. Below them a burgher in his top hat was helping an elegantly wrapped lady to descend from her carriage.

'In the street everything is as usual.'

There were not many Jews in Vienna's First District; bankers like Shassner had paid a heavy tax for the privilege. Outside the walled city, however, where suburbs were crowded with less fortunate citizens of many nationalities, there was a small community who wore beards and caftans and sometimes Hasidic earlocks. Most of them came from the farther reaches of the Habsburg Empire for the Great Fairs, and remained in hope of a better life. As yet, few had found any opportunity to improve their condition. Times were hard, jobs difficult, and Jews unwelcome; even now, if they could not produce the correct papers, they were subject to deportation. A few streets near Taborstrasse had begun to take on a raffish air very different from other poor areas of Vienna.

There were market stalls near Leopoldgasse selling trinkets and secondhand goods, and exotic smells of hot potato cakes and sour pickles. For all the poverty, there was energy everywhere and the eyes of the many children were dark and alert. The police watched the neighbourhood with particular suspicion. Students sometimes lodged there because rooms were cheap; Efraim Jacob, the son of a provincial Jewish merchant, was studying law at the University and had chosen to live in Taborstrasse itself. There were rumours that he involved himself in politics.

On Haidgasse, in two large rooms on the first floor of a house built round a courtyard, lived Joseph Kovacs, a child violinist who played at the Hungarian café. That morning, Joseph woke early under a heavy rug to hear his mother and father arguing in bed. It was dark and cold, and he could not make out the words, only the angry voices. The sound hurt him. He loved them both and wanted them to love each other, but most of all he loved his skinny, gallant mother.

His mother Hannah had ginger hair and sallow skin, and what her face lacked in regularity of feature it made up for in animation. She came from generations of women who had run mills and workshops, while their menfolk dreamed and studied. Joseph was the only child she had carried to term, and she was inordinately proud of the boy. Her husband Peretz was a melancholy man with heavy features and a querulous expression, as if always suspicious he was insufficiently loved. His brother had been an itinerant musician, and Peretz himself had some musical talent, though he had no aspiration to follow in his brother's footsteps. What he most wanted was to learn a decent trade. His spare energy went into reading and thinking.

Joseph heard his mother get out of bed to set about the chores of the day. With a flicker of excitement, he remembered how the previous evening a well-dressed gentleman had come up to him in the café. The Hungarian café was a dank, low-ceilinged inn, in which strolling musicians had played without much ceremony for many years. There were usually a pair of violins, a cello and a zither. Joseph played waltzes for the most part; the kind of music people liked to dance to, though there was little enough room for it. But, of late, people had taken to throwing money and asking him to play the tunes they called out to him, and once or twice he'd risked playing pieces he loved himself, lent him by the other violinist, who had a passion for Mozart. Sometimes he earned whole silver coins and applause.

The gentleman who had come up to him had been dressed in silks and velvet, all green and gold as the child remembered him; his skin fresh and seemingly without pores, although he was not young. He had bowed to Hannah, but it was to Joseph he had spoken. And the words remained with him: 'Where did you learn to play so finely?'

Joseph had stammered something about his uncle, but the gentleman had only shaken his head and smiled.

Yet what else could he say? The first sounds Joseph remembered were those of a rooster outside a village inn on the road to Debreszen, sitting on his mother's warm lap and looking at the pool of light in which his uncle played a violin; the melody had been so beautiful that when the sound stopped he found his cheeks were wet. His uncle had been playing for himself then, with half-shut eyes; composing or perhaps recapturing some piece of music he had learnt on his travels.

From that time on, Joseph had wanted a violin. Somehow his mother found the money for one. It was his father, though, who taught him to read music, pointing to the notes on a stave in turn so that he could imitate the sounds with his voice. His uncle carelessly took for granted that he could pick up how to play. At the beginning, merely holding the violin at arm's length seemed problem enough. Where the left hand should form spirals round the neck of the instrument, Joseph's pinned it between thumb and the base of his forefinger. He was perhaps six or seven before he mastered vibrato. By then his uncle had begun to listen to him with troubled admiration.

His father only worried about him. As he lay under the heavy rug that morning, an old resentment welled up in Joseph. Peretz could be kind, but that kindness could not be relied upon and sometimes he fell into a blind rage. Once Joseph had brought home a little white bird, given to him by one of the patrons of the café, and Peretz, in a furious mood, had taken it out of the child's hands, ignoring his beseeching cries. The bird had been sold, no doubt for rent or food, but the touch of hope which the green and gold stranger had brought Joseph was a little like the tenderness he had felt for the bird. He was apprehensive that Peretz would have no sympathy for it.

The table on which Hannah was peeling vegetables had a rocky leg, under which a pad of paper had been impatiently positioned. A smell of chicken fat, onions and roasting carrots that she was preparing for the evening meal came from the small oven.

Soon Joseph heard his father get out of bed and begin to prepare for the day, pulling on his old trousers and humming as he set out the ribbons and lace. As Hannah worked, she listened to that gentle humming and kept her eye on her husband cautiously. Presently, he picked up a Yiddish paper from one of the piles that lay about the room and sat down to puzzle over it. 'The gentiles are up to something,' he announced.

The gentile world was unpredictable and merciless. He didn't understand it, and had no wish to try and enter it. Hannah felt differently, though to please her husband she covered her hair chastely with a handkerchief like the other women of the neighbourhood. It was Peretz who had chosen, cautiously, to live where there were other Jews; it was not

why she had come to Vienna. With the intention of mollify-
ing her husband she brought him a glass of hot tea with a
lump of sugar, and, as he looked well-disposed, she returned
to the question she had tried to raise earlier.

'The man who heard Joseph play at the café yesterday. He
offered to give him music lessons.'

Hannah spoke crooningly in Yiddish, the language of her
childhood in Galicia. Peretz spoke little else, but Hannah
spoke reasonable German when she needed to do so.

He had taken a drink through his whiskery mouth, but he
paused at his wife's words.

'Lessons?' He rolled his eyes as if to an invisible audience.
'The woman's out of her mind. She sold two rolls of ribbon
and a few feathers yesterday, and out of this she wants to
buy lessons.'

'He said the boy had talent. Perhaps more.'

'What is that supposed to mean? Let him learn to use
machinery, sewing machinery. That is where the future is.'

Hannah said soothingly, 'The man was not asking us to
pay right away. We will find the money.'

Joseph flinched at the phrase that he knew was more likely
to madden Peretz than any other. Peretz's experience had
taught him to fear optimism. Joseph's heart burned with
pain, as Peretz reacted furiously.

'From where? Where will it come? Is there some cache of
gold I don't know about? What are you expecting? Isn't this
what you said when Aunt Sarah needed clothes for her baby?
And then we hardly found the rent?'

His mother answered patiently enough, though sometimes
Peretz broke in before she finished her sentences. The main
point she wanted to make was that Joseph's talent brought
in a significant proportion of the rent.

At last, she said exactly that. For answer, Peretz lunged at
her like a bear, his face red with anger and resentment.

'Is it my fault?' he demanded. 'They don't allow Jews into the trades here. I do all I can.'

Hannah knew that he did. She did not blame him. He was not by temperament a pedlar. He altogether lacked the wish to please. His natural intelligence was that of the scholar; his greatest pleasure was to go into the study house and argue there on Saturday afternoons. There was a pathos in his enthusiasm, for he had so little chance to acquire the learning he admired. It was his pathos, more than his offer of protection, that had led her to marry him. For his sake, and for all her scepticism, she kept the rules of the kitchen as well as any woman in the street; separating meat and milk and salting and soaking meat, whenever they could afford it, according to the laws. There was much pain in Peretz, but no malice, and Hannah was unperturbed by his anger.

'We had to help them: some things are a duty,' she rebuked him.

At this, Peretz began to speak his native Polish, of which Joseph could only make out a few words here and there.

Hannah replied angrily, and for response he slapped her. Against all his intentions, and against his mother's strict instructions, Joseph jumped out of the bed to her defence. He saw that her lip had caught on her teeth and that a few drops of blood ran down her chin.

'It's nothing,' she said, and put her arms around the boy to soothe him as Peretz turned to stare down at Joseph.

At first he smiled engagingly, as if trying to persuade Joseph that nothing serious had happened; that he had not raised his hands against his wife. He did not believe it himself. It could not be the case the Peretz, whose soul was as tender as any man alive, could do such a thing. And so he stared almost pleadingly at the boy, who glared back at him with wide-open eyes. Before their black reproach, Peretz's own gaze fell.

'What does he think, this little pisherkeh, that he is the man in the house?'

Hannah put both her arms around her son to protect him.

'He is a child,' she said. 'He doesn't understand. Be still.'

Joseph's heart beat fast and wretchedly. He was too small. Too thin. He could do nothing but look up at the fierce man who stood over them both. But, as he stared upwards, Peretz turned away.

'Don't look at me like that. I'm not an animal,' he said.

Hannah caressed her son's head. 'Run to the shops for me,' she said to Joseph. 'Here—' And she took some money from a jar.

'That's it. Let him run off and spend money,' said Peretz heavily.

So Joseph pulled on the heavy clothes, conscious that the mood had changed between these two unpredictable, worrying creatures who decided his life. He felt his mother press his shoulder reassuringly. It came to him, mysteriously, that his mother knew the point would be won. All this he understood, and yet there was still a pain in his heart as he went off obediently to do as he was asked.

'Things could be worse,' said Peretz as Joseph left. 'In Paris there is blood on the streets, and here it is quiet for the moment.'

There were many poorer people than the Kovacs family in the district of Leopoldstadt. Hannah, after all, had a market stall, and Peretz was healthy. In the same building where they lived, in a single attic furnished with little more than mattresses and lemon crates, lived Clara and her brawny Aunt Rebekka. No one knew much about them.

Aunt Rebekka went out at odd hours of the day and night, and did not discuss where she went with anyone. It was generally assumed that she and the child were illegal residents who had chosen not to register as required by law.

Aunt Rebekka was a fearsome woman with a broad, coarse face and little green eyes, whom no one was inclined to question if she did not wish to be questioned. There were rumours that she ill-treated her niece Clara. The child had a sweet face, with black eyes widely set apart and thick lashes; her hair stood up in curls all around her face. Despite a certain dreaminess, she was clearly lively and intelligent. Indeed, if she had been a boy, there was a rabbinic elder or two who would have intruded to insist on the child being taught to read and write, but they did not intervene for a girl. As it was, Joseph's mother once gave her a storybook from her stall when she saw the child puzzling over the pictures, and Joseph had easily taught her the alphabet on a rainy day a few months earlier when he had found her sitting on the stairs near his flat.

That February morning the windows of Clara's attic room were thick with rime and the child lay in a heap of coats on the floor, careful to keep her hands and feet tucked deep inside them. The clothes had an indeterminate sweetish odour, but they were warm and, as she rose towards wakefulness, she huddled down into them again. From across the room there was a sound of stertorous breathing that paused and whistled at the sound of each indrawn breath.

The deep snoring came from Aunt Rebekka, who slept late on cold mornings, particularly when she felt ill. Last night she had been out until past midnight and had arrived home singing; there had been no supper for Clara, and Rebekka had collapsed into bed without thought for the girl. Now Clara lay where she was and dreamed of a fine white table, with candles and a plate of fried fish. There was a gentle woman with white hands who stroked her hair and urged her to eat. Someone was singing.

When she woke, only the hunger remained. Nevertheless, she had no wish to wake Aunt Rebekka, because for as long as Rebekka slept there was time to do what she wanted, instead of what her aunt demanded. It was a freedom that was not hers at any other time of the day. The child watched the breath go in and out through the purplish lips and pulled on more warm clothing very quietly.

Rebekka rolled over. Her breathing once again took on an even rhythm. Her mouth, as she lay back in sleep, fell inward over two missing teeth, and this gave her a certain pathos. The child held her breath, but her aunt did not wake.

Clara knew what she wanted to read: the book she had been given by the lady who sold ribbons from a market stall. Slowly, and concentrating all her efforts, she made out the story. Meanwhile, her aunt fell over heavily on to her back, her eyelids flickering. Clara hardly dared move in case she might squander her few moments of freedom. As she puzzled over the words, Clara forgot all about the cold. The world of the book became as real as the room in which she knelt. Indeed, the room had little solidity for her at any time. She had no clear idea of how she came to be in Haidgasse. She could not have said for certain how old she was, or remember her own mother or her home, or anything that had happened in her life before Rebekka found her. It was as if her whole life had begun a little over a year ago in an old house by a canal, when Rebekka had appeared to claim her as a niece. As she thought of their first meeting, there was always a smell of wet wood and the taste of thin, grey porridge and a kind of bewilderment because no one had cared enough to resist Rebekka's claim, or investigate on what it rested.

'Clara?'

'Yes, Aunt Rebekka?'

Her aunt muttered the next few words into the pillow as

if still lost in her own dream, and unaware that she was not speaking aloud. She often behaved in this way when she had been out late the evening before, and Clara was unworried by the mumbling. She guessed her aunt's breath would be sour and that her temper would be short.

'Is there anything you'd like?' she asked, as she felt the small green eyes on her.

'Nothing,' said Rebekka. 'Except another hour's sleep. You woke me.'

Clara was wise enough to make no denial.

'My head aches,' Rebekka announced then. 'I want a glass of tea.'

'Yes, Aunt,' said Clara.

'My leg aches,' said Aunt Rebekka, fretfully. 'I slipped in the street. I must have done myself an injury last night.'

She put one fat leg out of bed and stared down at the red and swollen ankle, which looked much as it had on any other morning. Rebekka suffered a great deal with her legs.

'Where are my shoes?' she asked. 'I shall freeze in this room.'

Clara lit the little stove, and cowered gratefully over the pitiful warmth it threw out. She had not dared to light it unbidden. Rebekka forced on her shoes and sat up slowly, her green eyes flickering over the child to see what she was up to.

'I shall have to go to the Board today,' she announced then, yawning.

Clara had no idea what the Board was, but Rebekka usually returned from it with enough money to buy a loaf of bread. Once there had been a fowl. She looked up therefore with a little hope in her eyes.

'You can come, too,' said Rebekka. 'There will be potatoes to carry.'

Chapter Two

THE NIGHT BEFORE JOSEPH'S first music lesson was spent in vigorous preparation. A brown velvet jacket was sorted out for him from Hannah's stock: the buttons checked, the seams and corners of pockets stitched. And Joseph went with his father to the local bathhouse. There Peretz thoroughly scrubbed him from head to toe, washing his hair with a rough hand and towelling him briskly, before unexpectedly giving him a kiss on the top of his head.

Once home again, Joseph set himself to practise a new piece he had been lent by the cellist from the café. It was a sonata in G minor by Giuseppe Tartini, written more than a hundred years earlier but published only recently. It was a demanding piece, and he had taken some trouble to learn it well.

While he was practising, the concentration kept his excitement at bay; Joseph felt calm. It was only as he put the instrument aside and tried to make himself ready for sleep that his heart began to pound, and he realized again how very much he wanted something to come of the adventure.

What did he want? He did not know. He was ten years old, and more at ease making music than doing anything else. But that wasn't all. In his fantasy he was moving away from narrow alleys and dark rooms into a world where anything was possible, a world where Peretz's gloomy predictions, so often accurate, no longer came true; a place where people devoted themselves to making beautiful things and talked of nothing else.

The following day was sunny. Hannah left a friend in charge of the stall for the afternoon, gave Joseph a boiled egg, and they set off. At the corner of Taborstrasse, they stood in the afternoon sunshine to wait, since the gentleman who was called Herr Becker had arranged to send a carriage for Joseph. Hannah had been determined to accompany him, even though it meant giving the Polish woman from the neighbouring stall a share of the afternoon's takings. Joseph suspected it was because she did not quite trust either the gentleman or the messenger.

As they stood in the early March cold, stamping their feet, Hannah fell silent. In her mind were high ceilings and fine furniture and her son on a platform receiving applause. She tried to still such thoughts. There were so many talented young musicians in Vienna.

Herr Becker's carriage was drawn by two grey horses. A surly, tufty-haired man helped them into it. The interior was neither so fine nor so clean as Hannah had hoped. The red silk of the seats had frayed in several places. There was even, she observed, a wine cork on the floor. She pursed her lips but said nothing to Joseph, who was oblivious to such matters.

Nevertheless, when they arrived at the narrow lane where Herr Becker had his apartment, the stairs were wide, there were plants in pots and the servant who received them asked for their card with a formal bow.

'We are expected,' said Hannah grandly.

A burst of laughter came from the room upstairs.

'Don't worry. There can be no mistake,' she reassured Joseph, whose thin lips had closed into a stoical line and who already feared to be sent home.

'Come upstairs,' said the servant. 'Herr Becker will be back soon, and it will be pleasanter to wait for him there.'

In the room into which they were ushered three young men in their early twenties were leaning against a piano. They were dressed in a casual manner which Hannah had not expected; their shirts were unbuttoned and their hair loose. She looked round the salon disapprovingly. It was as full of objects as a cupboard of Peretz's wares: Chinese vases, leather puppets, glassware, silver boxes. Books and music lay open on the floor. There was a good deal of dust in the loops of the green velvet curtains and the cushions on the carved chaise-longue were torn in several places.

One of the young men came over civilly enough to Hannah. He had a dark face, with deep laughter lines in his cheeks, and his eyes glittered with a kind of knowing humour.

'I expect you're here for a lesson, aren't you?' he asked.

His voice had a kind of insinuating slur as he spoke to Joseph, a worldly tone which suggested that he had already seen through Joseph's hopes and had thought little of their chance of success. It was a habitual tone, however, Hannah decided, picking up at the same time the hint of a Budapest accent.

'My name is Hans Rubin,' the man introduced himself, smiling. 'Things are in disarray. You will understand? It's the news from France.'

'What news is that?' asked Hannah, without particular concern.

The young man standing over her took in the stiff lace of her collar and the poor black cotton of her dress. Hannah felt the colour coming into her cheeks under the insolence of his assessment.

'Haven't you heard? The King has fled to London and there's going to be a Republic,' said Rubin.

'And what is that to us?' cried Hannah.

His friend Hellman had far more delicate features than Rubin; his eyes were shaped like those of a faun; his narrow lips formed every word carefully. Joseph liked the directness of his gaze as he spoke to Hannah.

'When times change,' he said, 'it's difficult to know what things mean. Or even what to hope for.'

'Then you do think it will affect Vienna?'

Joseph watched animation return to his mother's tense face. He continued to sit uncomfortably upright, with one hand on his wooden violin case. It was to the boy that Hans Rubin addressed himself. As he stared down at the serious young face, he thought he had never seen such black eyes.

'Do you enjoy Becker's music?' he asked.

'I didn't know he was a composer,' mumbled Joseph, startled out of his silence.

For answer, Rubin sat down at the piano and began to play a lively march.

'There,' he said. 'That's one of his tunes.'

'Very charming,' said Hannah, looking up from her own conversation and nudging Joseph to show appreciation. He did not know how to respond.

'We teach perforce, all of us,' said Hellman, smiling and trying to decide if the child was sullen or frightened.

'Do you want to tune your instrument?' called Rubin cheerily. 'Save time later.'

Joseph nodded slowly and opened his case. With the violin in his hands, he approached the piano. He felt better.

'No need to be shy,' said Rubin, rather put out by his silence. 'Have you brought some music?'

Joseph nodded again.

'Let's see.'

The two young men bent over the pages he had brought, and Hellman whistled, turned his grey eyes on the boy, and said in a low and gentle voice, ' "The Devil's Trill". That's a piece for a virtuoso.'

'He's an ambitious fellow, you can see that,' said Rubin, winking at his friend.

With a little flourish, he began to play the piano part.

'Do you want me to play now?' asked Joseph, a little upset. 'I think perhaps I should wait for Herr Becker.'

Rubin made a diversion into a jolly waltz with a shrug.

The third young man, who had so far said nothing, took this as a signal to begin singing in a deep and lugubrious baritone; it was obvious that he, and probably Rubin himself, had been drinking quite heavily.

'Don't tease the boy,' said Hellman, kindly. 'I should like to hear the piece.'

'It's a damned tricky piece,' said Rubin, pouring himself a glass of wine from the decanter that stood on the piano.

All this was so very far from how Joseph had imagined his first encounter with serious musicians, that he could easily have burst into tears of disappointment. He was determined, however, to give no sign of this.

'You could play to the gentlemen. Why not?' suggested Hannah tactlessly. It always made her happy to hear Joseph play, and she was sure he would be admired by the other gentlemen once he began.

Joseph was far from certain this would be the case. Hans Rubin might be a little drunk, but his fingers had flown casually over the keys with an accuracy that no one at the Hungarian café could have equalled. Altogether, he was rather sorry to have brought so showy a piece.

There was a pause, with all the eyes of the room upon him. Joseph realized that he had no choice other than to lift his violin under his chin. He knew he held it awkwardly and, if he had doubted it, the glance interchanged between Hans

Rubin and Hellman would have told him as much. Even so, as he played, the sadness went out of him. The room had good acoustics and his violin resonated richly. He had never played better, he knew, even though he could not guess what these unpredictable young men might expect.

There was a little silence when he had finished. Hannah, who had hoped for applause and congratulations, could not read the silence, and looked anxiously from one face to another. Hellman's faun-shaped eyes opened, and his thin lips smiled. Then Rubin turned abruptly to the boy. 'How old are you?'

'Ten,' said Joseph, with a note of defiance in his voice.

'Where did Becker find you?'

Joseph explained.

'It's not my business, of course, but how much is he charging for his lessons?'

Hannah said, 'I'm not sure Herr Becker's business terms should be discussed with you.'

At this point, Rubin let out a mild but unmistakable belch.

His friends laughed. Joseph guessed it was a common joke between them. It came to him quite suddenly that these men, for all their education and skill, and for all they could afford to send a carriage from one side of Vienna to another, were not so very different from the old musicians he played with at the Hungarian café. He smiled with the relief of that discovery. They responded to his relaxation at once.

'You took the last section too fast,' said Hellman. 'Don't you think so, Hans? That it was too fast?'

'Nonsense, we were perfectly in tempo,' said Rubin. 'You like to slow everything up so you can drag the last ounce out of your vibrato.'

'Listen,' said Hellman to Joseph. 'Some of those fast passages are better played with the bow jumping off the string. Let me show you.'

But, before he could do so, Herr Becker bustled into the room and came over directly to Joseph.

'I'm so sorry,' he said. 'You must think me very rude. However, I see you have made the acquaintance of some of my friends. Dear lady—' He bent over Hannah's hand. 'Forgive me. Things are not as usual. Not in the least. And yet, Art must go on, whatever shakes the world outside.'

Becker was a man in his forties, dressed in green velvet with a carefully tied cravat, which he undid as he collapsed on the torn chaise-longue.

The light was going out of the day, and the servants had come in to kindle tapers and draw the curtains so that the blackness did not become oppressive. Already they had been away far longer than Hannah intended, and nothing was arranged. 'Herr Becker—' she therefore began.

But the young men had clustered around Becker, and clearly felt their own needs should take priority.

Becker frowned at them. 'The French tour is cancelled,' he said straight away. 'It can't be helped, and it's the least of our worries.'

'Never mind that,' said Rubin. 'Do you have *any* money?'

'No. I'm sorry, but that's how it is. France is in uproar, there is absolutely no point belabouring me about it. I can't pay you a penny.'

'Listen, Becker,' said Rubin, his eyes darkening and the lines in his cheeks deeper in the candlelight, 'you owe me a good deal which you haven't yet paid. I don't mean to be difficult, but I have debts of my own.'

Becker lay back on the cushions and smiled. 'It will be all right,' he said. 'I have a plan. Young man,' he said then to Joseph, 'come at the same time on Thursday. You will have lessons twice a week.'

Hannah made a startled noise.

'Don't worry, there will be no charge. None. Twice a week. Did you hear him play?' he asked Hellman.

'Yes,' said Hellman, a little reluctantly. 'He is surprisingly good for his age.'

'For his *age*?' asked Becker, with a perceptible edge of irony.

Hannah stood up. 'We must go soon,' she said.

'The carriage will take you home,' said Becker. 'Please don't concern yourself. The boy must have his lesson. Oh yes, the boy must have his lesson. Look—' Suddenly and briskly, he was on his feet. 'Play me your piece.'

Joseph complied willingly. He knew now: the young men had said little about his playing not because he had played badly but because he had played well. The hopes that had been shrinking away suddenly rose and swelled into certainty.

'You see, you have to learn to make different colours of sound,' said Becker. 'Let me show you. You can play the same phrases on different strings.'

Joseph listened gravely.

'Take those fast passages with short bow strokes on the upper half of the bow. That way you can hear the melody.'

Joseph imitated Becker precisely and immediately.

At the end of the lesson, Becker sent him off to practise the trill section as slowly as he could.

'We must make it secure. Come back next Tuesday.' Becker looked solemnly at Hannah. 'We shall make something extraordinary of the youngster. Eh?' He put a hand on Joseph's head to caress the black curls affectionately, so that the sweet smell of his skin and his lace brushed over the child's face.

'Your face is too stern, though,' said Becker. 'We shall have to teach you to laugh a little if you are going to join this profession.'

*

Joseph did not often stand behind Hannah's stall, but one Monday morning a little after this she asked him to do so. It was a frosty morning but bright, and he was cheerful as he thought of his afternoon's lesson. He had to sit on a high stool to make himself tall enough to oversee the goods, and to be certain that no one was stealing from the boxes of lace and buttons that had been set out near the street. The box with small change was kept at his side, under a heap of coloured shawls.

All round him there was a bustle of shoppers; women turning over velvet jackets and starched shirts, arguing with neighbouring stall-owners, talking and laughing as if they were in a village market place. Most of the other stall-owners knew Joseph, and privately thought Hannah over-indulged the child. He should study, certainly, for that was the way to make a way in a hostile world. But music? Hannah deluded herself, they thought. And he might be a nice child, but he had no business sense. Even now, when he should have been urging and persuading the customers who turned over the second-hand clothes on his stall, his thoughts were obviously elsewhere. And when customers were few, he could be seen trying furtively to read one of Peretz's old books.

Joseph was indeed so deep into a story that he did not at first hear Clara's soft voice when she called to him, and she had to come round to his side of the stall and pull at his coat.

He looked up then, startled and guilty. He did not mean to neglect what he was doing. Timidly, she repeated herself:

'I brought this back. It's for your mother.'

Clara had finished the book Hannah had lent her. He looked at it and asked, 'Did you like it?'

'Oh yes,' she burst out eagerly. 'It was so exciting. The girl marries the prince and they ride away together to safety.'

'Hmm,' said Joseph, unimpressed. He no longer read

children's books, but Clara, he thought, though only a year younger than he, was after all only a girl. For a girl, indeed, she was easier to talk to than the others, who were only interested in dressing themselves up and giggling, and after a while, since she continued to stand there, he asked her, 'And did you understand it? All the words, I mean?'

She took the book back and found a page in it.

'What does "inarticulate" mean?' she asked him. Her eyes were open and trusting; her small face serious.

He shook his head and grinned, because he did not know either.

'It must be something about not being able to talk,' she said. 'Because if she could have told the prince who she was, the whole story would be different.'

Joseph read the sentence and agreed that that made sense.

'Here, Joseph,' called the Polish woman from the neighbouring jewellery stall. 'You've got a customer.'

A woman who was clearly not from the quarter was fingering some of the materials. She was well dressed with groomed hair, a neat, head-hugging hat and brilliant blue eyes. As he watched, she turned her attention to a tray of pearl buttons. Clara perched herself on an upturned barrel nearby, swinging her legs and waiting for him to finish what he was doing.

'Haven't you anything bigger than these?' asked the woman.

'I might have,' said Joseph, climbing down from his stool and walking round to the front of the stall.

He found several larger buttons but, as she could see at once, they did not match. The woman shook her head impatiently.

'These are no good. Not in the least. Haven't you anything else?'

'No, we haven't,' said Joseph, disliking the woman's bad

temper. He began firmly putting the buttons she did not want back in their box.

The woman frowned. She was used to a more ingratiating response.

'Aren't you going to look, at least?' she exclaimed. 'I expect better treatment where I shop.'

'You could try the stall along there,' he suggested.

The woman fixed him with her brilliant blue eyes. 'Don't you be insolent to me, little boy.'

She was a tall woman, slim-built but formidable, and she seemed to tower above Joseph as she wondered how to respond to his impudence. The stallholders on either side were even more dismayed by Joseph's behaviour. He is just like Peretz, they muttered among themselves. They disapproved strongly. It was one thing to lack trading skills, another to confront potential customers with rudeness when they had diverted their steps particularly to this street.

'Buttons and thread,' called a woman a few stalls away. 'Pearl buttons. All sizes.'

Joseph would have liked to lower his gaze from the blue stare in which he was caught, but he found it impossible to back off until the woman turned with an angry and impatient shrug and moved away herself.

Joseph went back behind his stall. His heart was pounding. He had almost expected the woman to hit him. She had not, but he wasn't sure anyone would have defended him if she had. She was so evidently a member of the local bourgeoisie, and no one would have liked to provoke an incident. Indeed, the Polish woman at the next stall came over to give him a piece of advice.

'Listen,' she said, 'that's not how you treat a customer. You tell a story. You laugh a little. You'll learn how to handle it. You can't afford not to.'

'I know, I know,' he said, hanging his head a little. His

mother would have joked with the woman until she had bought material and probably buttons as well. He didn't want to do that. To Clara, who had hung back to see the outcome of the encounter, he spoke more openly. 'I hate it. I wish Mother didn't have to do it.' Clara did not understand.

'But your mother enjoys standing here.'

Joseph thought about that.

'She would like much more to have a smart little shop with polite customers,' he decided. 'I shall buy her one when I'm older and can earn some money.'

'Will you now?' laughed the Polish woman, moving away to her own stall. 'We'll all buy shops, then. Why not? If they let us.'

Clara remained, as if there was something else she wanted to talk about.

'I heard you play at the café last Saturday,' she said.

'I saw you there,' he said.

'Not for long,' she said. 'They make you have something to eat if you want to sit down.'

'There are other places you can hear music,' he said. Information he had acquired from his new musician friends made him bold. There was something immensely flattering about her gaze. Of course it was only Clara, but he was pleased that she so evidently admired him. When she smiled, her face was so pretty. If there were not something unkempt in the clothes she always wore she would be the prettiest girl in the quarter, he thought to himself.

'When the weather is better I will walk you into the town and show you. You need only have a glass of lemonade.'

Her face shadowed at the mention of a purchase.

'I'll buy you one,' he offered. 'We'll go together.'

'If I can get away,' she promised him. 'If my aunt will let me.'

'Do you want another book?'

She nodded.

'Here,' said Joseph. 'Since you like fairy tales.'

She continued to look up to him. It crossed his mind that to have a girl who would look up at him like that, only perhaps with bright blue eyes and neatly groomed hair, would be a gratifying experience. To Clara, however, he only said, carelessly, 'You really ought to have a dictionary. You can't keep asking what words mean, can you now?'

'Where will I get one?'

'Oh, we have them at home,' said Joseph. 'They come in secondhand, but there's always a demand for them. I'll take one, if you like.'

She bent over the book and brushed her hair back from her face to see better, and he suddenly became aware there was a bruise at one side of her face.

'What's happened there?' he asked her.

'It's nothing,' she said, confused.

'Did you fall over? You should have bathed it: the skin's broken.'

'No, I didn't fall,' she said.

Chapter Three

THE SNOW fell heavily in Vienna and the air was harsh on the skin. Students meeting all over the city were talking in whispers of tyranny and injustice and what happened in Metternich's prisons. There were clerics and doctors who joined the meetings, and brave men who spoke from balconies. It was impossible to ignore the rising excitement. One morning, Anton found himself in a café on the Graben with a group of student friends and the playwright Rudolf von Mayerberg. A marvellous, rich scent of coffee filled the air and the elaborate cakes for which the café was famed stood on a table by glass-mirrored walls.

Von Mayerberg had a calm, rounded face with pale blue eyes, and he spoke in an untroubled, ruminative voice.

'Vienna doesn't produce philosophers,' he observed with a melancholy smile. 'Not one since Marcus Aurelius wrote his book in Vienna. And it isn't just philosophy we lack.'

The young medical student, Efraim Jacob, though a regular member of the group who hung about von Mayerberg, listened to these reflections with barely controlled irritation. He was a fierce, narrow-featured boy who had come from the provinces to study and who had to live with extreme frugality. The signs of poverty burnt in his deep-set eyes.

'Have we time for all this? Haven't you heard? We have a newly elected Reichstag. Things are changing. It may be that freedom means no more to you than having an extra scene or two in a scurrilous play, but I'm interested in the people who can't eat in the Sixth District. I'd like them to be able to ask for more wages without being pushed into gaol. Once they know it's possible, no one will be able to stop them.'

One or two of the students looked round uneasily at this. Metternich was said to have ears in every café in the city.

'Didn't you listen to Fischof and Jellinek? We shall soon have the freedom to say what we think without looking over our shoulders,' said Jacob.

The waiter, who had been in the act of clearing away a few dirty plates that were making the table look untidy, now dropped one into Anton's half-eaten cherry pie. Von Mayerberg, faintly amused, began an anecdote which bore upon the avarice of a certain well-known courtier and the difficulties of his poor victims, who struggled to service his sexual needs. The story was delivered with von Mayerberg's usual panache, the intonations of his voice exactly echoing those of his formidable mother. His voice seemed to reassure the waiter.

'And so he went home with blood in his trousers,' von Mayerberg concluded.

'You cannot speak of suffering without laughing at it,' said Jacob contemptuously.

'Except my own,' said von Mayerberg. 'I'm serious enough about that. You must surely have heard me grumbling about it.'

'Nowhere near the Court, I hope,' said another voice.

'Oh, the Emperor doesn't mind grumblers,' said von Mayerberg, smiling. 'While we are grumbling, we are safe enough. It is only when people fall silent that they are dangerous.'

At this point, Max Kallman arrived in a bustle of energy and laughter with two young women from the

Kärntnerstrasse. One woman was a blonde with a vivacious
face and brown eyes, the other less striking but voluptuously
built. Max could well afford to enjoy life since his father was
not only a professor at the University but also a member of
a distinguished aristocratic family.

'I have just seen your mother,' he told von Mayerberg,
'getting into a carriage with as many bags as if she were
moving house.'

'She's going to her sister in the Tyrol,' said von Mayerberg.
'She thinks she can hear tumbrils rolling in the streets. I tried
to persuade her the Viennese are too lazy to do her any
harm, but I couldn't convince her.'

Max gave a gentle, intimate pat to the buttocks of the
darker girl, who sidled off round the table and took a seat at
Anton's side. The boy helped her take off her outer garments
and could not resist staring at the whiteness of the flesh she
revealed. When she caught his eye, she smiled.

'Is it time?' Max asked Jacob, one hand carelessly on the
neck of the prettier girl.

'Soon.'

Von Mayerberg did not enquire into their appointment.
Instead, he smiled, and rose to his feet.

'I am meeting the director of the Theatre on the Wien,' he
said. 'I shall not be with you on this occasion, gentlemen.'

As the young men left the café, the laughing blonde girl
carelessly bumped into a waiter and knocked over a pile of
cups on a tray he was balancing. The dishes fell to the carpet,
and one or two broke against each other. With a sudden
burst of temper, the waiter turned furiously upon the girl,
his face red and his language coarse. The girl stammered an
apology.

'You saw that rage?' said Jacob to Anton when they were
out in the street. 'That is what makes revolutions. That
waiter looks tolerant and mild enough most of the day, but

inside he hates what is done to him. The Viennese will snap, when the time comes.'

'But how do you know what they will do then?' asked von Mayerberg.

As yet Haidgasse was untouched by any excitement. Joseph and his mother had gone for the afternoon lesson, and Clara was helping her aunt to put on her shoes.

'I want you to come with me today,' said Aunt Rebekka. 'Come here. I want to comb your hair.'

'Where are we going?' asked Clara, approaching obediently.

Aunt Rebekka tugged her comb through the thick black curls without much care about the pain she was causing.

'Don't jerk about so, and for goodness' sake stop snivelling,' she told her niece, as she saw tears coming to the pretty brown eyes. 'We are going to see an important relative. A sort of relative. If we can. And if he'll see us.'

'Where does he live?' asked Clara, her eyes opening wide. 'I didn't know we had any relatives in Vienna.'

'Well, we do,' said Aunt Rebekka firmly. 'Sort of relatives. Now, is there anything you can wear that isn't torn or dirty?'

'I could mend the grey dress,' suggested Clara, 'but there aren't any buttons on the bodice.'

'We shall have to do the best we can,' sighed Aunt Rebekka. 'Hurry up now. It's a long walk and my legs are killing me.' When she was dressed in her brown ruffled coat and a shawl, Aunt Rebekka looked an awesome figure.

For all her complaints about her legs, she walked at a pace rather faster than the child, who had to hurry along at her side to keep up.

It was indeed a long walk and Aunt Rebekka pulled her arm as she marched silently and purposefully through the old walls into the First District, which Clara had never visited before. Rebekka, too, seemed uncertain, looking at a piece of paper from time to time, and put out by soldiers who turned her away from the route she had intended.

Along the cobbled Graben they went, and the child stared up at prosperous top-hatted burghers with heavy watch chains, their ladies all feathers and lace. She was pulled impatiently out of the way of brilliantly lacquered carriages with their liveried coachmen. She stared up, too, at a white and gold stone column with a praying figure at its base and what might have been angels tangled at the top.

'What's that?' she asked her aunt.

'I don't know,' said Rebekka crossly. 'For goodness' sake, stop dawdling. We haven't got all day and we shouldn't have come as far through the town as this. We'll have to turn back through Herrengasse.'

On Herrengasse the houses were adorned with gilt flowers, plaster cherubs and the statues of graceful women. White stone figures carried the weight of every doorway. Clara craned her neck to make out those that stood far above her on the highest balconies. Aunt Rebekka was silent, perhaps because her legs pained her. Clara, too, found that her feet hurt and that she had little desire for conversation.

At Ballhausplatz, they found more soldiers and a crowd of people.

'These stupid soldiers,' Aunt Rebekka grumbled. 'We've come completely wrong.' She was taller than the soldiers blocking her way and tried to push past.

'I need to cross the square,' she insisted. 'Is there something wrong with that?'

Evidently there was, and the presence of more soldiers made it clear. Aunt Rebekka fumed helplessly as she was made to wait.

'We'll be late,' she said angrily to the child. 'And it's important. What's all this to do with us?'

For something unusual was going on. As Clara watched, an orderly procession approached the Chancellery at the far side of the square.

'Students,' said Aunt Rebekka with a sniff. 'Riff-raff.'

And indeed there were many young men, but there were also grandly frock-coated professors and top-hatted gentlemen. The crowd waited to see what would happen.

'Do you understand what is going on?' demanded a gentleman with a heavy watch chain and a silver-headed walking stick.

'Lord knows,' said Aunt Rebekka, impatiently.

There were others who were interested enough to tell her.

'It's the petition,' said one, importantly.

'For what?'

'Freedom of the press, and more participation.'

'What's that?'

Looking through the gaps between the soldiers' legs, Clara could see that a purple-robed gentleman had handed a scroll of paper to one of the guards on the gate. The scroll disappeared inside the palace doors. There was quite a crowd of curious spectators now. And more soldiers.

'We have business of our own,' said Aunt Rebekka impatiently to the nearest of these. 'What's this palace to us? I'm looking for Kohlmarkt.'

'I'm sorry,' said the soldier. 'You can't walk in front of the Hofborg.'

'Then we'll go behind,' said Rebekka, meaning to cross the square and leave at the other side of it. She pulled Clara to follow.

Those who had presented the petition were waiting hopefully, looking up at the fine windows, talking among themselves. The sun had come out brilliantly from a gap in the clouds. One of the fine gentlemen was laughing aloud when the first volley of shots, from the windows of the

Chancellery and aimed just a little above the height of a human head, took everyone by surprise.

There were cries of anger and a confused bustling retreat into which Metternich's guns fired again. This second volley of shots wounded several, including one of the professors who stood looking down in bewilderment at his shattered left hand until he was pulled away by his colleagues.

Not everyone managed to get away, however. Aunt Rebekka, caught by a random shot, lay on the cobbles. Clara looked down at her incredulously. All the impatience had gone out of her face. The green eyes stared, but without any light in them. And there was a red, bleeding hole in her temple just above the right eye.

As Clara stood where she was, a soldier, touched by the child's stunned expression, put a hand on her shoulder.

'She's dead,' he announced briefly.

Clara did not seem to hear the words. She fell to her knees on the cobbles, still silent but tugging frantically at her aunt's clothes as if she could attract her attention. Rebekka's arms were spread wide and her legs lay open as if she were grossly asleep. This, more than the blood covering her face, convinced the child. She had seen dogs lie dead in the street.

Clara let her hands fall to her side and began to cry without any thought in her head. If there were more shots, she did not hear them. She sat back on her heels and cried. Her weeping was not exactly for her aunt, or even because she was now alone in the world. Thoughts of that kind would come later. It was the evidence of death itself that appalled her: sudden, ugly and mysterious.

The soldiers lifted her weeping body away from the corpse, and turned her head so that she should not see her aunt thrown on to a cart with the other victims of the shooting.

'Where will you go?' one of the younger soldiers asked her.

Her mind was white with shock. The soldiers stared at one another over her head. Whatever charitable plan they might have conceived, however, was prevented by the orders of their superior officer.

'Get a move on! We're needed in Stefansplatz.'

Obediently the two young men left the child to her fate.

Clara stood where she was on the frozen street. She was numb with what had happened, but at length she roused herself. She was shivering. Could she find her way home? She wasn't even sure where home was, or what she would do when she returned there.

There was snow in the wind and an acrid smell of gunpowder. Church bells were ringing insistently. As Clara turned into Stefansplatz, she saw many people, some in elegant jackets and top hats, gathered about a pyre of brushwood. The effigy of a human being, made out of rags, was being hoisted high above the pyre and, as the figure reached the top, there was a moan of satisfaction from the crowd.

Clara paused and stared up at the rag doll. It was dressed in torn velvet finery, an old-fashioned white wig askew on a featureless face. The arms were sewn to the trunk in a gesture of distress. As Clara watched, a young man with a torch approached the pyre, and in a moment flames set the dry wood crackling; the wetter branches began to steam. An excited cry went up as the fire took hold—

'Let him burn! Let Metternich burn!'

Clara's eyes were fixed on the rag doll. The clothes caught first, and the flames ran up the body. When the stitches connecting the doll's head to the trunk burnt through, the head fell to the cobbles. Clara shivered.

The wild scene was hypnotic, yet she drew away. In Neu Markt, a coachman called out an irritable warning to her as his grey horses went too close, but she barely changed her path.

The light was gone as she turned into Haidgasse. The street was unexpectedly quiet. The Jews from Galicia and Poland had shuttered their windows and there were few lights to be seen through the cracks. Where were the ragpickers, the cobblers, the stalls of broken furniture? Where were the street pedlars selling their delicious potato cakes? They were hiding. Where were the stalls of old clothes? The lanterns? Taken indoors for safety. In the blank, blind windows there was not so much as a flickering candle. Behind them, the people she knew huddled in terror of their lives. Would anyone let her in? And if not, where could she sleep?

As she walked down the suddenly unfamiliar street, she became aware of a heavy shuffling behind her. Turning, she made out the lumbering figure of Joseph's father. He was wearing a greatcoat, which had fallen open over his pear-shaped belly, and he was carrying his pedlar's tray folded under his arm. When he came up to her he recognized her with a start.

'What are you doing out on the streets?' he accused her.

She was too frightened to answer. He stared down at her, his sad face touched with curiosity. His wife might call him mean, he told himself, but in fact he was only hemmed in by the unhappiness of his own life.

'Come with me,' he ordered.

Clara bit her lip and hesitated.

'Joseph and his mother lead me a dance,' he grumbled. 'They've gone over to some musician's house in all this upheaval. I walked as far as I could looking for them. Why did I ever come to Vienna?'

To reassure the child, his voice became friendly and he smiled. Clara could see he had good white teeth. She followed him.

'Back home in Poland people knew me,' Peretz confided, encouraged by what he took as her trust. 'Here I could fall in the gutter and die like a dog and no one would care.'

As he unlocked the doorway, he paused. 'What happened to you? Where is your aunt?'

The question brought new tears to Clara's hot, dry eyes as she explained.

Peretz was much affected by her grief. 'You see? We older folk have our uses,' he said gruffly. 'We seem harsh, but when we're gone, you see us more clearly. Don't cry.'

He fumbled in his huge pockets for a rag, and Clara took it, though it smelled of mint and snuff and made her sneeze.

'Joseph and his mother understand nothing about this town,' he said then. He spat contemptuously in the courtyard and looked up at the windows to see if there were eyes judging him. The sly movement displaced his skull cap, and Clara glimpsed the pink skin of his scalp. 'You can have a bowl of soup,' he said. 'If it isn't all eaten. My wife thinks of nothing but her son.'

That night Clara slept on the floor in Peretz's store-room. She had walked so far that, in spite of the confusion around her, she fell into an exhausted sleep. Peretz was more restless. He was worried about his wife, in spite of his anger with her, and the mixture of emotions maddened him and made sleep impossible. Once or twice, still dressed and carrying a candle melted into a saucer, he went in to look at the child. For all the tear marks on her unwashed cheeks, her skin was marvellously fine in texture, and she breathed sweetly. Her black hair curled all over her closed eyes. She was lying where Peretz usually flung his goods: all around her lay piles of bonnets, caftans, bits of fur and uncarded ribbons. Peretz muttered and turned away. There were still shouts in the street, and a sudden flurry of feet running along the cobbles far below. Out of habit, as he waited, he began to sort cotton and buttons with nimble fingers.

An hour or so before first light there was a knock on the door. Peretz nodded to himself. It was too tentative to be the police, if indeed there were any police in this new Vienna. Opening the door, he saw his wife on the threshold and, anxiety relieved, his anger flooded out.

'Where do you think you have been, you stupid, selfish bitch?' he shouted furiously.

Hannah looked haggard from her long walk.

'My God,' she said, leaning against the door. 'You know where I have been. The boy is safe, if you have enough humanity to care. The musicians are keeping him.'

'Are they? For how long? And what about his work at the café?'

His wife made a noise of bitter exasperation, as if she had predicted this irritable reply. Peretz suddenly felt very tired.

'Let's go to bed,' said his wife. 'We can talk in the morning.'

'The girl Clara is here,' he remembered to tell her as they climbed into bed, but his wife had been up all night and, if she heard him, she made no answer. They fell asleep with their arms round one another.

Clara was woken early next morning by a single shaft of sunlight which broke through a hole in the torn curtains. As she sat up, she made out the raised voices of the pedlar and his wife from the next room.

'Don't preach at me, you silly woman! Who brought her in, I'd like to know?'

The next words, uttered in a soft voice, were lost to Clara.

'You don't know any more than I do,' said the pedlar. 'Why do you pretend to be so wise?'

'With Joseph away,' pleased his wife, 'what room does she take, poor little thing. Like a doll.'

'I was a fool to bring her in. I know your softness. The Board will have to help her. That's their job, isn't it? Looking after widows and orphans. You and your son have to understand. We can't do everything we want in this life. We're poor Jews, and lucky enough to be alive.'

'You are right,' said his wife, craftily. 'Let her stay until the Board can do something for her.'

Clara could not make out the pedlar's reply, but she decided it must have been favourable, as the wife turned the conversation adroitly.

'They say that there is going to be freedom for everyone. Even Jews.'

'They? Who are they?'

'The musicians,' she said. 'The fine people in their house. They say it is a glorious revolution. Now, let's wake the child.'

With a bowl of hot water and a thick-toothed comb, she soon bustled Clara into the room that contained all the family belongings. These lay about in an extraordinary confusion. On an unmade bed lay clothes, music and piles of old and broken books. Overall hung a smell of soft-boiled carrots. Clara was given a piece of rye bread and a little milk, which she drank gratefully.

'Pretty thing, aren't you?' said Hannah. 'Nice little locket you're wearing.'

Hannah lifted the chain in her hand, observing the engraved shield of David.

'I'm told it was my mother's.'

'May I?' She snapped the locket open. A sweet, hand-painted face smiled out at her.

Peretz came over to inspect the pretty object. The poor did not often own such things. If they did, in a time of need they sold them.

'She must have been a sweet woman,' said Peretz. His voice sounded wistful.

'We'll find you a job soon enough,' said Hannah. 'Can you sew? Can you cook?'

'I can read,' said Clara.

'I suppose your mother taught you that?'

'I don't remember my mother,' said Clara.

'There, there,' soothed Hannah, glaring the while at her husband.

'I remember my father telling me I had a good head on my shoulders,' said Peretz, 'but what chance have I had?'

At this, Hannah threw a shawl over her head and briskly left, while the pedlar continued sorting through his goods. There were several books he had picked up on his travels, and Clara poked through them curiously.

'Can you read Hebrew script?' asked Peretz.

She shook her head.

'I like to puzzle over the old rabbis, but my wife has no time for it.'

'Can I look at this?' Clara picked up a German book doubtfully.

'Look. Take,' he insisted. 'Whatever you want.'

The Charitable Board of the synagogue in Seitenstettengasse did what it could to help Jewish orphans in the city, and about ten days later a job had been found in the kitchens of Natan Shassner. Clara set out for her new life. If Haidgasse had paused in alarm at the violence of the revolution, life had now returned to the street. Shops spilled heaps of second-hand clothes and household goods on the cobbles. Artisans were once again setting about noisy repairs to broken tables

and chairs. There was a general euphoria in the eagerness
with which things were being bought and sold.

At the far end of the street, however, a wagon with wide,
heavy wheels and dangling buckets waited to take Clara to
the First District. Clara climbed in with the books Peretz
had given her wrapped in a scarf. The cart made for the
ramparts that enclosed the inner city, and through them to
the salubrious streets where trees grew to shade the walks of
the rich and powerful in summer and where monuments of
generals and emperors sat at their ease.

The baroque frontage of Shassner's house alarmed the
drayman as much as the child. Clara's heart beat furiously.
At the servants' entrance, a fair-haired girl with blue eyes
and a flowered scarf round her hair led her along into the
kitchens. These were rooms larger and higher than any Clara
had seen, and she stared about nervously. There was a smell
of freshly baked cinnamon cakes, and everything looked
scrubbed and clean. Copper pots and pans hung from hooks
on the walls on each side of a fireplace. At a white-wood
table sat several young girls, not much older than Clara. One
was methodically sifting flour, another rolling dough. All
were taking instructions from a huge woman whose domain
the kitchen appeared to be. Heavily muscled and taller than
any woman Clara had hitherto laid eyes on, she wiped her
hands, and strode over to inspect her new employee. Her
hair was completely covered, as if she concealed a shaven
head, and her cheeks were fiercely crimson. Round her waist
hung a huge bunch of keys.

'So, you are an orphan? Without any relatives?'

'There's nobody,' said Clara.

'How old are you?'

'Nearly eleven,' said Clara.

'Have you ever been in service before?'

'No,' Clara admitted.

The cook dismissed this. 'I was in service before I was twelve, but that's no matter. The Shassners have instructed me to take in a few extra staff among the orphans of the city. The Board sent you.'

'Thank you,' stammered the child.

'Can you prepare vegetables? Do you know the laws of cleanliness, at least? The mistress is very strict.'

Clara said, 'I can read.'

The cook laughed. 'You won't have much time for that. All right, Lily—' One of the girls at the table stood up and smoothed down her apron. 'Take her and wash her and bring her down again,' said the cook. 'She can peel potatoes, I should think, though she looks a bit dreamy.'

That night, in the small attic room where she was to sleep alongside Lily, Clara felt unexpectedly cheerful. She had eaten potatoes with a tasty, meaty sauce. She had a clean bed with white sheets. The moonlight came in through the tiny window. Lily, who was soundly asleep long before Clara, had hung a piece of glass that served for a mirror, and Clara scrutinized herself. Her eyes were still wide and scared and too big for her face.

She looked out of the window. She could see the cathedral, with its huge, steeply pitched roof of yellow, green and black tiles. Lily, turning over, released a gentle snore. Solemnly, Clara unpacked her books and set them out in the window niche. Then she climbed into bed.

Chapter Four

THE MORNING AFTER the uprising, Natan Shassner sat in his study and worried about his son. The
book-lined room, the heavy Biedermeier furniture, brought
him no sense of security. He glared at the servant who had
come to lay another note before him and the servant returned
his look warily. A Jew from Galicia who had served Natan
for many years, he was alarmed at the sight of a single vein
beating visibly in Natan's left temple. Natan was a man with
an unusually large frame, and his face was heavy-featured.
His expression was usually humorous, but today he looked
black and threatening.

'Will you be needing your carriage today?' asked the
servant.

'No,' said Natan.

He seemed to be hesitating before he asked his next
question: 'Has my son returned?'

'He is in his mother's room,' said the servant. 'She has
asked for hot water to bathe his cuts.'

Natan's expression did not change, though his worst fears
were removed by this intelligence.

'These are troubled times,' said Natan.

Then he looked again at the note on the silver platter
before him, and waved his servant away.

The note was sealed with a seven-pointed coronet and

three plumed helmets. It was the personal heraldry of the Baron Salomon Rothschild. Natan opened it carefully.

'Uncle,' the message read, 'will soon be in London.'

Shassner understood the code. Prince Metternich, it seemed, had fled Vienna.

The news reached the cafés and lecture halls later in the day, and euphoria gripped the students who had made the revolution. It seemed that victory was theirs and had come at little cost. Within a few days a funeral was organized for those who had fallen; Catholic priests and the rabbi of the synagogue in Seitenstettengasse spoke quietly of new days and new hopes; an ecumenical act which itself signalled a stunning change. Soon after that, the Court left the city: von Mayerberg, too, though protesting the boredom of the countryside, went to join his mother in the Tyrol. Shassner, though a good deal less enthusiastic than his son about the new government, stayed where he was for the moment.

On the Saturday after the uprising, he walked thoughtfully to the synagogue on Seitenstettengasse, for he had remained stubbornly loyal to the faith of his fathers. He enjoyed his visits there: it was a hidden world, turned inward from Vienna, built inside the courtyard of a community house, since it was forbidden to build any non-Roman-Catholic building fronting the street. The synagogue itself was a large, oval building, with twelve pillars of yellow marble supporting a blue-painted dome. Gilt rays spread out from the only window in the ceiling, as if to imitate the light of the world outside, denied by the laws of Vienna.

Though far from a mystical man, Shassner had a strong sense of connection to the community from which he came. He recognized men in it who reminded him of his old father whom he had loved, and women who called to mind his mother as Minna never had. He had been generous at the time of the synagogue's building more than twenty years earlier and, though he was not altogether comfortable with the new rites and their mix of Hebrew and German, he enjoyed listening to Sulzer, a cantor with a more than usually fine voice. Even Minna, on a rare visit to the place, had grudgingly admired Sulzer's musical abilities.

The familiar prayers soothed him. And, since the old stetl habit of talking through services had never died out for all the decorum of dress and manner, he soon found himself in conversation.

'So, what do you think, Natan?' asked his neighbour, a goldsmith who worked for the Imperial Court. 'There may be Jewish deputies in the new Reichstag. We have to support them, don't we?'

Natan agreed to that.

'One of them could be Rabbi Mannheim,' said his neighbour. 'I wonder he still finds time to preach here.'

'It will be interesting to hear him preach today,' said Natan thoughtfully.

Natan listened solidly and without expression as Mannheim spoke fluently of the important role of Jews in the Revolution, and begged his audience to remember that they had been able to stand side by side with their Viennese brothers in the same struggle. 'We have the same aims. And they know we will be free together or none of us will be free. These are happy hours for our community.'

'Stirring words,' said Shassner's neighbour.

Shassner nodded, though he was in two minds about the wisdom of such an open allegiance.

Afterwards, as the service wound to its close, Shassner's other neighbour, a banker from Berlin visiting Vienna, voiced one of his anxieties.

'I hope your Viennese neighbours always remain so brotherly.'

*

Minna had not wished to accompany him to the service. She was unwell that morning, having been visited the day before by some of her grandest relatives.

'My cousins have now left with the others. Did you know that?' said Minna.

'The other nobility, do you mean?' enquired Shassner with some irony in his voice.

Minna lifted her head proudly. 'Yes, certainly that is what I mean. Why not? They are noble, after all. They have gone off with the rest of the Court.'

'I heard something of it,' said Shassner.

'They were sorry for me. They said you were obstinate, and I should try to persuade you to leave,' said Minna with a certain pathos, as if she had little belief in her ability to do any such thing.

'Please, Minna, let me decide what is best to do,' said Shassner, kindly enough.

He knew Minna felt uneasy in the presence of her relatives who had converted to Christianity, and he disliked their manner towards himself. But he guessed Minna's uncertainty had another source. From childhood, that side of the family had been lighter, more frivolous, less serious than Minna, yet she had always thought them superior, even while pretending to think of them as superficial. This made Shassner impatient with her rather than sympathetic. Most of the wealthy bankers of the First District had left, of course, but then they were men who felt their interests lay altogether with the ruling class. Shassner simply could not feel so. He remembered the ghetto life of the east too well, and some part of him responded to the rhetoric of the preacher in the synagogue. Moreover, Minna's Christian cousins in the role of prophets annoyed him. What did they know? What had they ever done for themselves?

'We shall be living in a city under siege,' said Minna,

pulling nervously at her pearl necklace. 'The barricades will go up and we shall be on the wrong side of them.'

'Things are quiet enough for the moment,' said Shassner.

'But you can't believe the Emperor will just yield to all these demands?'

'Metternich has gone,' said Shassner. 'The Emperor is in Innsbruck. I don't know. He has already agreed to a good deal.'

'Don't you know that Anton's friend Efraim Jacob is stirring up the factory workers?'

Shassner frowned. 'I must talk to Anton. That could be dangerous,' he admitted.

Chapter Five

ALL SUMMER the Emperor Ferdinand remained at Innsbruck. There were uprisings in Hungary, Bohemia and Lombardy; his whole empire was collapsing. Vienna went about its business good-humouredly enough, but there were fewer people needing musicians in the inner-city ballrooms. Herr Becker, whose finances were uncertain, took on extra pupils, including one or two matrons from the suburbs, to supplement his falling income. He might well have begun to regret his offer of free lessons for Joseph if the boy had not shown such talent and aptitude. As Joseph progressed through that year of troubles, a scheme that might help to finance his own ambitions began to crystallize in his mind.

Becker gave Joseph the music of Mendelssohn to study. He had known Mendelssohn slightly, and could gossip to the boy about the ways in which the mood of his music had changed the meaning of the word Romantic. All this Joseph absorbed easily, just as he learnt music by heart without apparent effort. Once, as Joseph played the heart-rending Concerto in E for Becker, the boy looked up and saw his teacher had tears in his eyes.

'You will be a virtuoso,' said Becker gruffly. 'Trust me. I will make a celebrity of you.'

Becker was not a good businessman, however. Joseph could not fail to observe creditors, who called for payment and who had to be fobbed off with less than they demanded. Becker had no commissions for his own pieces, and Rubin was impatient at the few engagements he had arranged for the autumn season.

'Wait,' said Becker. 'When the boy is ready, you will see.'

'And who will pay my rent till then?' asked Rubin.

He was not the only one to worry about the likely fruits of Joseph's efforts. Peretz had watched the family earnings dwindle all year as sporadic alarms reduced the casual trade on which their market stall depended.

'What does he earn? What can he earn? Lessons and food, that's all he gets,' Peretz grumbled.

This was not entirely true, for Joseph was often given silver coins by those who heard him play at Becker's apartment, and he gave most of the money he earned in this way to his mother.

The newly elected Reichstag controlled Vienna, and had set up a National Guard to protect its authority. Yet the supporters of the Emperor had by no means abandoned the city, and there were still outbreaks of street fighting. To the east of the city the Imperial Army was regrouping its forces, and in the First District there were many who confidently waited for the situation to be reversed. Those who supported the Revolution were apprehensive.

One hot day in August, as Joseph came back along Taborstrasse, he was challenged by several working men armed with staves who looked as if they had just come through the factory gates. Among these he was fortunate to recognize a glazier who happened to live in the same house as his parents.

'What's happening?' asked the boy.

'There's an army all round the city,' said the man, impatiently. 'Just waiting for a chance to fire.'

'Whose army is that?' asked Joseph.

'The Imperial Army, stupid,' said the glazier. 'Students and workers don't have an army.'

'We can only defend the Revolution if we stand together,' said a boy in a leather apron, a few years older than Joseph and from the same quarter. He was thick-set and round-faced and in his time had been something of a bully. Now he was willing to give his life for Freedom.

'Not much bodies can do against cannon,' said a fainter spirit.

'Even Napoleon didn't fire on Vienna,' said another.

'Maybe not, but there's a prince and cannon waiting to fire on *us*,' said the glazier.

'So the barricades must go up,' cried the boy in the leather apron.

And, indeed, men with farm implements and staves of wood in their hands had already begun to throw old chairs and branches of trees together.

'Let the child through, then,' said the glazier to Joseph's relief. 'He lives round here.'

Joseph was glad to run up the stairs and be back home, even though he arrived to find Peretz setting off to join the workers in the street.

'This is all going to end badly,' said Peretz, kissing Hannah as he left. 'Mark my words.'

'Be quiet, you'll frighten the child,' said Hannah crossly.

When he had gone, though, she stared out of the window in silence with her hands clenched into fists, and made no offer to produce food for Joseph.

In the early evening darkness, Imperial guns began to shell Vienna. They were inaccurate and haphazard in aim and many of the shells fell in the poorer districts. One set a house close by Haidgasse alight, and the people who lived there had to rush shrieking into the streets.

The bombardment changed the mood of the Revolution.

At the corner of a square near Taborstrasse, a house was burning and furniture was being thrown out into the street. There was a crowd of about five thousand, including stevedores, brewers and tanners from other districts, and an atmosphere of drunken excitement, even though the bodies of those injured or killed lay on the cobbles. Suddenly there was a huge explosion, and the crowd was showered with stones and tiles. A paint shop had gone up in flames.

In the First District the situation was no calmer. Shassner set an armed guard around his house and Minna was close to hysteria.

'We shall leave as soon as things quieten down,' Shassner tried to soothe her. 'We are safe enough indoors.' To his son, he said, 'Keep out of the streets. You can do no good there.'

Nevertheless, Anton slipped out of the house, against his father's wishes, to join Efraim Jacob in Am Hof Square where people had gone to protest the use of cannon against the city. On the way Anton saw a fashionable carriage which had been trapped by the crowd and overturned in the fray: one of the horses, with its legs broken, lay on the ground shrieking in terror. He could not see what had happened to the people, or their coachman.

Am Hof Square held the yellow stucco houses where Mozart played his first concert. It was an ancient, baroque square with a column at its centre to celebrate the end of the Thirty Years War. Crowds of angry citizens of all classes, alongside mutinous soldiers, filled it now. Anton and Efraim found a place near St Mary's Column to watch the confrontation with the men who had been willing to collude with the murderous bombardment.

It was hard to see what was happening. Above the Armoury were two elegant classical figures holding a golden globe; from the doors beneath, a group of men pulled an older man savagely behind them. A great roar of hostile excitement greeted their arrival in the square. Climbing on to the ledge of a column in the centre of the square, Anton could see two soldiers down on the cobbles, whom the crowd were kicking and mauling with their farm implements. An older man, still alive and struggling, was hoisted by a rope and strung from the street light at the corner of the square.

'String up the Count! Latour! Kill Latour!' yelled the crowd.

Count Latour went on kicking even as he hung there from the rope, and Anton suddenly felt extremely sick. All excitement had evaporated and he bent away from his friend to vomit on the pavement.

'I'm not a hero,' he muttered, more to himself than to his friend.

'Look over there,' said Jacob suddenly. 'To the south side.'

At the other side of the square a few soldiers who had failed to rescue Latour were now at the windows of the Armoury. There were puffs of gunsmoke and a howl of fury from the crowd.

'This way!' said Jacob, with the same suddenness as he had spoken before, pulling Anton to run away down Nagler-strasse. But another crowd met them in that old, narrow street. The protest had become a riot. For a moment the young men took shelter in an open doorway under a little golden image of two tender figures with a child between them. The savagery of the crowd pushing past them up the street belied the charming gesture.

The stone that caught Anton on the side of his head was thrown by a grinning boy in ragged clothes and was intended for the soldier who had come up behind him.

Anton woke to the sound of a single, insistent bird at about five a.m. He could feel his mother's gentle hand on his forehead and the familiar scent of her perfume rose from the grey lace and satin of her nightwear. It was like being back in his childhood.

'Thank God,' she said.

Gradually, his memory came back to him and he tried to sit up, but she would not let him.

'Lie still,' she soothed him. 'There's nothing to worry about.'

'I must know the outcome,' he begged.

Suddenly, she burst into tears. 'There've been many deaths. I've been so alarmed,' she confessed. 'Forgive me.' She wiped her eyes and smiled. 'When you were brought here last night, you asked to be brought directly to me.' Her head raised with pride. 'If you like, we will tell your father nothing.'

He was puzzled. He had no memory of wanting any such concealment, but he was not displeased to avoid his father's sharp examination.

'I can keep a secret.' Her voice was eager. 'You have kept secrets for me. When you were a child. Do you remember once, when you found me crying and I begged you to say nothing?'

'I do remember,' he said, surprised.

It was a vivid memory and not one they usually mentioned, but his present state was very much like that afternoon long ago, when he was a child of seven, in bed with a high temperature. There was the same sense of bodiless suspension, the same uneasy faintness and floating. He tried to focus his attention. It must have been during convalescence, after the sickness that had crippled his arm. That was when he had found his mother sitting in a window, mysteriously tearful as she looked out at the street. Remembering, he asked Minna:

'I have often wondered what was wrong. I kept my word, but you never told me why you were weeping.'

'Oh,' she laughed, 'I was a young woman. I cried so easily.'

'It is the only other time I can remember seeing you in tears.'

Now his curiosity was aroused, it came to him that it was important, that perhaps she even wanted to tell him about it.

'Why were you crying? And why did you ask me to tell no one?'

'These times,' she frowned, 'how can anyone bother about such private grief?'

'Was it something to do with Father?'

'Not exactly. Perhaps. I loved him so very much,' she said evasively. 'And I was jealous. Such a pitiful creature,' she laughed. 'My cousins were so much prettier.'

'You were the only one who thought so,' he smiled.

'In those days there was so much I didn't understand. Now I do. You are safe and that is all that matters.'

Anton suspected there was more to the story than that, but he felt disinclined to press for it. He closed his eyes. He felt a little sick and his head throbbed. His mother placed an icy handkerchief smelling of lavender water across his forehead. As he went off again into sleep he thought he might well like to keep the whole adventure a secret from his father's sardonic gaze, but he doubted the possibility.

A few days later, when he was almost restored to health, his father came to pay a visit to his sickbed. Anton saw at once that, however discreet his mother might have been, his father knew exactly what had happened to him.

'These are stirring times,' Anton said, by way of introducing the topic.

'Well, Vienna still has a government of the people,' said Natan mildly. 'We shall see what that means.'

'It means we shall have liberty and equality,' said Anton.

His father nodded, as if he had expected some such comment.

'You were with Efraim Jacob, I hear,' said Natan. 'I know his father slightly. He is a good, old-fashioned wine merchant. An Orthodox Jew. Much distressed by what has happened.'

'What *has* happened to Jacob?' asked Anton.

'He is in gaol.'

'But if Metternich has gone?' asked Anton, puzzled.

'The police defend their own,' said Natan. 'Your own role, by the way, has not been much noted.'

Anton digested his father's exasperating sense that nothing much had changed.

'Surely,' he began, 'you must hope the old regime will not be restored?'

'You had better think of other ways to work for Jewish emancipation,' said Natan phlegmatically. 'Don't excite yourself: you suffered a nasty blow to the head. For my part, I am sorry so many Jews were involved in the uprising. It will be remembered.'

'Who will remember it?' asked Anton.

Natan leant forward and patted his son's hand with an uncharacteristic show of affection.

'Rest. Take things calmly. Your mother was very worried. Let us see how things go. And tomorrow we leave for the Tyrol.'

Minna had come up behind Natan and urged anxiously, 'Your friend Rudolf is already there. And his mother. It is only sensible. I wish we had gone months ago.'

It was in December, over supper, that Joseph heard his parents discussing the thirteen Hungarian Generals who were to be shot, and the bloody justice likely to be exacted in Vienna.

'Does that mean the Revolution is over?'

'Of course it's over,' said Peretz, glumly.

'Does that mean I can go over to Becker's house next week for my lessons?'

'Listen to the boy!' exploded Peretz. 'He thinks of nothing but himself.'

Hannah said, 'Did you hear what happened to Jellinek, the brother of the famous rabbi?'

'What did he do?' asked Joseph.

'He wrote pamphlets supporting the Revolution. A hero. They've executed him. They say he was still talking calmly when the soldiers raised their rifles. A hero,' she repeated.

Peretz was deep in his Yiddish newspaper and did not hear this. Lifting his head, he reported, 'The Hungarian Prime Minister is dead. His widow has put a curse on the new Emperor.'

Hannah smiled. 'We shall have to see if it works,' she said.

Chapter Six

BY THE FOLLOWING SPRING, Becker was
ready to make use of Joseph's talent at a performance he
and his group were to give at the palace of Baron von
Arnheim. A stubborn man, the Baron had not run away to
the Tyrol with the rest of the aristocracy. Now that order was
re-established, he decided to celebrate his diamond wedding
anniversary in his own house and in the style to which he
had always been accustomed: the wine was the best from his
cellars and the tables were spread with the finest white linen.
The shine of polished floor and chandelier was dazzling.

As the banquet was served, there was little enough attention paid to Becker's group. Joseph played a movement from
Mendelssohn's Concerto in E. After this, the host brought
one of the guests to speak with Becker. Joseph watched the
gentleman with some curiosity. He was dressed in a flowing
blue coat with silver buttons cut away at the waist. Joseph
marvelled at the silk waistcoat embroidered with alpine
flowers, and observed Becker's unusual deference. Every so
often Becker glanced over to Joseph and smiled as if with
pleasure, but he did not offer to introduce the boy. On one
of the gentleman's wrists, Joseph made out the glint of a
narrow gold bracelet.

That night Becker brought Joseph home to his own
apartment, where he slept late. When he woke, there was

sunshine streaming in through the window. From somewhere close at hand he heard a burst of laughter. In a
moment, Becker appeared at his bedside with a steaming
bowl of hot chocolate and a sweet roll.

'Wake up. You can't lie in bed all day,' said Becker.

He was looking unusually pleased. The grandfather clock
on the other side of the room showed it was nearly eleven
o'clock. Joseph sat up and stretched.

'Hurry up.' Becker threw him a towel. 'We have an
appointment in half an hour. Get washed.'

Becker himself was dressed with unusual care for the hour
of day; his grey trousers clung tightly to his legs and floppy
lace cuffs dangled from his sleeves. Joseph's eyes took in this
unusually stylish dress.

'Are we going to perform?' he asked.

'Not exactly.'

Joseph hurried himself to dress as quickly as he could.

'You'll need some fresh linen,' said Herr Becker, frowning.

'Then I must get some from my mother,' said Joseph
doubtfully.

'No need to cross town for linen,' exclaimed Becker. 'I'll
send out for something.'

For all Becker's generosity in many matters, such an offer
was unusual.

'Where are we going to play?'

'For Herr Strauss.' Becker said this with a kind of reverence. 'He heard you at von Arnheim's last night and he may
want to use you. I will arrange it. Trust me.'

'To be with his orchestra all the time?' Joseph could not
believe this.

'For a special occasion,' said Becker, smiling.

Johann Strauss the elder had been found dead in a ransacked
room of his mistress's house earlier that month. Everyone had
gone to the funeral. Natan Shassner and his family, with all

the other important Viennese citizens, paid their respects in the great cathedral. The new dripless candles transformed the darkness of St Stephan's into golden brightness; the high-vaulted nave gleamed like a ballroom ceiling. Thousands of people filled it. Stefansplatz itself was crowded with respectable citizens, and far out from the inner city along the funeral route Peretz and Hannah and the other denizens of Leopoldstadt also stood waiting to pay their respects. Now his son, Johann Strauss the younger, who had spent so many years of his life at loggerheads with his father, was conducting a Requiem Mass for him. At the audition, Johann Strauss put a gentle hand, with a glint of gold at the wrist, on Joseph's black head and smiled. 'You will do well, young man.'

'I have plans for him,' said Becker importantly.

Not everyone enjoyed seeing Joseph treated with so much respect. One day, when Becker was late for Joseph's lesson, Rubin was shown up unexpectedly, looking surly. He asked Joseph if Becker had a decent bottle of wine in the house. His eyes were brilliant, and his face was flushed as if he might be running a fever. Joseph was reluctant to choose a bottle among those that stood in Becker's corner cupboard, and suggested Rubin might do so himself. Rubin brushed his clothes carefully. He was impeccably dressed in a deep maroon frock coat and light trousers.

'*Don't* make me kneel on Becker's filthy floor, Joseph. Do it for me, can't you?'

'Will you tell me which bottle, then?' asked Joseph. 'He keeps some of his wine for important friends.'

'*Important* friends? Thank you very much,' said Rubin, forgetting his clothes and falling to his knees so that he could make his own choice. 'Very nice, from a boy of ten.'

Rubin was already very much more intoxicated than usual, and he had some trouble finding a corkscrew.

'Well, come on.' He glared at Joseph after a time. 'It wouldn't kill you to give me a hand. Can't you see what I need?'

'I don't know where it is,' said Joseph, without moving, although he had registered Rubin's mounting hostility.

'Don't you?' asked Rubin. He began throwing newspapers off the table until he found what he was looking for. 'There. Good. That's something.'

He succeeded in opening the bottle, and poured himself a glass without ceremony. When he had drained it, he turned his attention to Joseph.

'I shouldn't get too cocky if I were you,' said Rubin with an edge of menace in his voice.

'I am not—' began Joseph.

'What you don't realize is that you're like a performing dog, or something in a circus. It's not so much you're a genius but that everyone is surprised you can do it at all. That's why people help you.' His eyes were cunning and malicious as they searched Joseph's face to see if the words had gone home. 'The rest of us were prodigies in our day. But you'll also get older. Then we'll see.' He loosened his cravat and drained another glass.

Joseph shifted in his chair. He was more alarmed by the baiting than he wanted to appear. Rubin had shown his envy before, but that afternoon he looked likely to turn violent. Joseph had seen Rubin come to blows with Hellman when he was drunk, and he wished Becker would arrive.

'Well? What have you got to say? Let's hear something from you,' said Rubin. 'Can you put two sentences together, or are you going to sit there dumb all evening?'

'If Becker isn't going to appear,' began Joseph, 'I think I might go home.'

He stood up and looked about for his violin case. It was by Rubin's feet and Rubin picked it up.

'May I have my violin?' asked Joseph politely.

'You won't be needing a rubbish instrument like this much longer,' said Rubin, standing up with the small case in his hands. 'I should think you'll be getting a Stradivarius soon, the way you are going. Why don't I just speed the process up a bit?'

He approached the window with the case in one large hand, and threw up the sash with the other.

'Please don't do that!' said Joseph involuntarily, though he had tried not to respond to the teasing.

'We're not very high,' said Rubin. 'I shouldn't think much damage would be done.'

The window was, indeed, only one floor up, but Joseph bit his lip at the thought of the case breaking open and the instrument falling on the cobbles. Rubin was very satisfied with the effect he had made.

'Come and get it, then,' he suggested.

Joseph went forward cautiously as Rubin laughed and held the violin case out over the sill.

'It's yours if you dare to reach for it,' he said.

Joseph hesitated. Was Rubin drunk enough to drop the instrument? It was impossible to be sure. As he approached the open window, Rubin laughed again and held the violin beyond his grasp.

'Look out,' said Joseph, seeing how ill-balanced Rubin was. At this, Rubin brought himself drunkenly upright, rather shaken, and made out his near escape. He backed away from the window, tired of the game.

'Here you are, dolt,' he said.

Joseph took the case gingerly from him, just as Becker arrived.

'What the hell is going on?' he demanded.

'We were only playing,' said Rubin, rather sheepishly.

'Yes? Well, I've got some news,' said Becker. His face was

glowing in triumph. 'I've got a solo engagement for Joseph. At Baden. I'm hoping something will come of it.'

So it was that Becker, far from an extraordinary musician and by no means a well-connected promoter, became the first business manager of the young Joseph Kovacs.

Joseph spent the next month practising the Bach D minor Partita, particularly the double-stopping in the Chaconne. As he imagined what might come of the Baden concert, he was both apprehensive and excited. Then a week before the performance, the left side of his face began to swell ominously. He found it difficult to open his jaw, and impossible to swallow the chicken soup which Hannah prepared for him. His head was hot and ached horribly, though he put the pain out of his mind and went on working at the phrasing of the Bach Partita. The next day it was as much as he could do to get out of bed.

Afraid that he might have an ear infection, Hannah dressed the child in layers of warm clothes and helped him to stumble along the street to a doctor's surgery in Taborstrasse.

There, two well-dressed women with appointments to see the doctor sat in the comfortable waiting room and watched Hannah in her working clothes beg the doctor's secretary for Joseph to be seen that morning. Joseph slumped in the stiff chair. Through his fever, he heard his mother's voice; first tentative, then angry. His jaw ached fiercely but even sharper than the physical pain was the fear that he would be unable to play his best in Baden. He might even have to cancel the performance. It seemed bitterly unfair. If there was a just God, as Peretz claimed, why would He maliciously put obstacles in Joseph's way when he was trying so hard? Through his fever, the voice of the doctor's secretary sounded shrill and unkind as she explained that the doctor had little time for new patients.

'Can't you see the boy is ill?'

'People who come to a doctor's surgery usually are. Sit over there. I'll see what I can do.'

'It will be all right,' Hannah said to Joseph, pressing the child's hand as she sat down at his side. For all her tenderness, he could tell she felt powerless.

The doctor received them without particular warmth. He was a tired and busy man who had troubles in his own family. This practice is going steadily downhill, he thought, wrinkling his nose at Hannah's poor clothes. As he listened to her account of the boy's aspirations and his concert the following week, he frowned. Evidently the child was badly spoiled and should be helping his family by getting down to ordinary work.

'Is there some medicine?' asked Hannah. Her fingers felt for a leather purse under her coat. 'I have brought money to pay you.'

'There is very little I can do,' the doctor said dismissively.

'Please. There must be something. Is it his ear?'

'No. A tooth is infected.'

'What can be done for that?'

'He must gargle with hot salt water. When the inflammation goes down, have the tooth taken out. Don't make such a fuss,' the doctor told Joseph.

Back in Haidgasse, Joseph, his face sallow and his eyes glazed with fever, gargled and spat his salt water into a bowl. He was still shivering and wretched when Peretz returned in the evening.

'You will feel better after a sleep,' said Peretz, patting the boy's hand and worried only about the boy's health.

'But I shall have to cancel,' said Joseph, forcing the words out between clenched jaws.

'Does that matter so much?'

Hannah tried to explain: 'What's the use of playing as well as he does if no one important ever gets to hear him?'

'There'll be other concerts,' said Peretz. 'And if he doesn't become a famous violinist? Would that be so terrible?'

Joseph closed his eyes at the sensible, unwelcome words.

As he lay on his bed in delirium that night, he imagined the rest of his life turning on a single moment of time, as if there were two ways ahead – one uphill, which glittered in the warm sunshine, and the other down into a stony wilderness where he would be outcast and forgotten. All through the night, Hannah sat over him, listening to his voice and trying to make sense of his scattered words until at last she fell into a fitful slumber at his side.

When she woke, Joseph's forehead was cool and his face less swollen. The doctor, for all his manner, had clearly prescribed the right remedy.

'Drink the hot soup. You will play brilliantly,' she told her son.

Joseph smiled, and went away to practise. Peretz's relief was tempered with more general reflections.

'What kind of a life is it that depends so much on what people think of you? On a single occasion?' he demanded.

'He will have a triumph,' Hannah said.

Peretz grunted. 'You fill his head with too many *meshuggenah* ideas.'

Chapter Seven

CLARA, TOO, WAS LEARNING the ways of a new world: the preparation of food in the Shassner house was a matter not only of lavish quantity but great delicacy. Every vegetable had to be scraped and washed in salt water; lentils, rice and wheat grains had to be sluiced with water to remove any contamination. Clara's role was menial. She did what she was asked with careful thoroughness. In the same spirit, she mastered the Jewish dietary laws to which her aunt had given only the most cursory attention. The separation of dairy products from meat was practised in the Shassner household with as much fastidious care as could be found in the ghetto, with its skull caps, curling sidelocks and traditional Polish dress. A whole separate kitchen with its own implements and pans was set aside for the preparation of meat dishes; it was there that fowl were drawn with expert hands and turkeys prepared for the oven, and the unclean quarters of lamb and beef set aside for the Viennese poor.

Overseeing the operations of both kitchens was a man to whom even the cook was deferential, and Clara counted herself fortunate that she had no occasion to speak to him. Monsieur Lafitte, as he was customarily addressed, took great pride in having trained in the kitchens of the Palais Fouche under the great chef Carême, who had once cooked for Alexander I of Russia. There, in Paris, while working for the Baron James de Rothschild, Lafitte had learnt to combine the art of French cuisine with the arcane laws of the Jews. Immaculate in white-starched apron and hat, he moved from the dairy kitchen to the meat kitchen with total authority, tasting, modifying and deciding everything like a great artist.

Lesser minions were under the direct control of the cook, and of her Clara was often afraid. There was a kind of controlled rage in the woman which sometimes escaped in blows. Lily, who was given to giggling and talking to Clara about a young man she had met on the back stairs, was scolded soundly for letting her attention slip from the task in hand.

Only once was Clara asked to work in the meat kitchen, to help prepare the stuffing for a goose's neck. Usually she worked in the dairy kitchen. There she learnt how to roll pastry, and how to bone a carp. She did everything she was told, yet she was often in trouble with the cook. Once, when she was chopping fish, she chopped her finger by mistake and ruined a whole basin of fish with her blood. The cook was on to the waste in a flash. 'Reading at night again?' she jeered at the girl, cuffing her head as she passed. Clara flushed, and regretted that Lily had ever been allowed to observe her interest in books. She shot her a miserable look and Lily, more a chatterer than a spy, bit her lip as she recognized the betrayal.

Clara had sought Lily's complicity, because she needed candle light, and Lily was willing to help her find candle ends, though was puzzled at her passion.

'They taught me to read, too, but it made my eyes hurt,' she said.

Clara tried to explain that the books opened a magic door to a different life.

'Princes, princesses, that kind of thing?'

'Sometimes.'

'You mean love, that's what you mean,' chortled Lily, and began once again to explain how exciting it had been when the messenger boy caught her on the back stairs and pressed his body close to hers.

'He put his tongue in my mouth,' said Lily, still delighted at the thought of it. 'And such a sweetness, Clara, you cannot imagine. A sweetness went all through me. Do you know the feeling? I'd only ever felt it in dreams before.'

Clara listened seriously to Lily's words, though she had not yet become a woman. She could not believe the longing aroused in her would be appeased by the clutch of a messenger boy, however sweet his tongue.

'I suppose you'd prefer to be loved by a prince?' teased Lily. She was a little envious of Clara, who was becoming a beauty. When she smiled shyly now, an elusive dimple appeared in her cheek.

'They aren't all love stories,' Clara objected.

Lily, however, was only interested in the lovemaking, and for a few nights Clara read passages aloud to her that dealt with the union of lovers, though Lily always fell asleep before they were over.

It was a misfortune for Clara that she made an accidental enemy of the cook at the time of the worst riots. Many of the staff had fled the inner city altogether then, but Clara and Lily had nowhere to go. Outside was all the ugliness of a mob on the rampage. Among the buildings ransacked were Rothschild's headquarters on the Renngasse. The windows of Shassner's palace were also broken. From their attic room, the girls could hear the noise of breaking glass, and shouts from the street: one night they crept down to the comfort of the familiar kitchen, where they thought to bolt themselves in the dairy pantry. Cold as it was there, the heavy-doored room felt safe and, wrapped in blankets, they slept there till morning.

They were woken by the noise of barrels being rolled purposefully across the stone floor, and for a moment they feared the mob had entered the house. Then, alongside the noise of men coming and going, they heard the peremptory voice of the cook. Peering out of their hiding place, they became the accidental witnesses of an amazing act of thievery.

The cook was supervising the removal of sides of beef, crates of eggs and whole salmon. It was Lily who understood what was happening.

'She's selling them off,' she whispered indignantly. 'What a nice pile she must be making for herself.'

'Ssh,' said Clara.

Lily had spoken softly enough but the cook, made nervous by her exploit, paused in her arrangements and looked round uncertainly as if sensing their presence. In a panic, Lily tried to draw across the inner bolt to their cupboard. That was a mistake. The scraping sound drew the cook's attention to the pantry.

'There's somebody here,' she said, and advanced on their hiding place. With her huge arms, she easily wrenched open the pantry door, which the bolt had failed to latch, and pulled the girls out on to the stone floor.

'Let's have a look at these spies,' she accused them.

Clara was for a moment so frightened of the huge, angry face above them that she was silent, but Lily spoke up smartly enough.

'Don't you complain at us! You're *stealing*! We can see you!'

In response, there was a blow of the cook's muscled fist round Lily's face.

'You've seen nothing,' she said. 'Do you hear? Nothing!'

Lily, her nose bleeding and her eyes wet and blubbery, agreed.

The cook surveyed Clara's frightened face for a moment, and nodded.

'See that's all you remember!' she said.

After this, the cook often looked at the girls thoughtfully, as if she was not altogether satisfied she could rely on their secrecy. Apprehension made her dangerous when a group of soldiers invaded the kitchens a few months later. What the soldiers were looking for, Clara could not tell – there had been so many arrests all over the city – but they opened cupboards, rifled shelves, and forced one or two of the kitchen girls to lift their skirts, which they did without much giggling since there was nothing playful in the men's expressions. When they left, Clara found the cook standing over her.

'Someone has been up to something here, and I know what it is,' she said. 'It's what you read. They're after your kind.'

She thrust a hand brutally down the front of Clara's bodice, to see if she had a book concealed there. There was nothing to find but she continued to clutch Clara's arm, until the girl cried out in pain.

'Stop picking on her,' shouted Lily. 'She's not done anything.'

The cook's gaze swivelled and darkened, and she let Clara drop to the floor.

'Don't you bully us,' said Lily, rashly. 'Or we'll tell.'

'What's that?' said the cook dangerously. 'What will you tell?'

'We'll tell what we saw you take!' shouted Lily.

The cook backed off for a moment, and then said, 'A couple of lying girls like you. They'd have more sense than to take any notice.'

'I'll tell them whether they believe me or not,' said Lily defiantly.

The cook took Lily's left ear between her thumb and first finger and tweaked it so that tears ran down Lily's face.

'We'll see about that,' she said.

Then she picked up a wooden, three-legged stool, and led Lily into the adjoining room. From there came shouts of pain from Lily and the noise of blows from the wooden stool.

When the cook returned, she advanced on Clara.

'You were the other one,' she said.

Clara stared up at her.

'Hm,' said the cook, indecisively. 'Has she been telling you things?' she demanded of the other girls.

They hastened to bear witness to Clara's total failure to speak.

'That's because the other one was a liar,' said the cook, satisfied. 'She'll be gone by the morning.'

Lily's face was disfigured with bruises, and there was a cake of blood under her nose when she came into their bedroom that evening to collect her meagre possessions.

'Where will you go?' asked Clara.

'On the streets, I should think. But I'll have to wait to get my looks back,' said Lily, with a pathetic attempt at a laugh.

'How shall I ever find you?' cried Clara.

She could already feel the loneliness that must follow the loss of her protector. She had a sense, too, that as soon as Lily was gone, she would become the target of the cook's suspicion and spleen. Lily shook her head.

'I'll try and let you know where I am.'

She put her hot, wet face against Clara's smooth cheek, and Clara flung both arms around her neck.

When Lily had gone, Clara walked down the back stairs and looked out of the small window that gave on to the street. She felt helpless. If the same thing happened to me, she thought, I should not know what to do. She did not cry as she faced the possibility, but stared into the blankness of the street ahead. It was cold, and she shivered.

Chapter Eight

NATAN SHASSNER RETURNED from the Tyrol with undiminished energy. Young Franz Joseph on the Imperial throne sent out ambiguous signals, but it seemed likely that he would favour the expansion of his economy and Shassner had every intention of helping him to do so. For this, rail links were essential, as Salomon Rothschild had seen long ago.

Early in April, a little over a year after the Revolution, Natan Shassner planned to entertain two English visitors. He was in an ebullient mood; bossy, argumentative and cheerful. He easily overruled Anton's objections that his presence was not necessary.

Anton had spent the morning riding in the woods, and was feeling particularly healthy and alert, as Natan saw with a mixture of impatience and pleasure. As always, Anton had taken great care to match the copper tones of his waistcoat against the green sheen of his cravat. There was a golden shine to his brown hair and the fairness made a charming contrast to his lively brown eyes. His face lit up when he laughed. He still kept his hand in his pocket to disguise his crippling, but he was a handsome boy, and Natan was proud of his looks.

'You will practise your English,' he suggested.

The English had been viewed with suspicion in Metternich's day, since they were known to be overly tolerant of dissent in their own country.

'It is a language I don't know well,' admitted Anton.

Natan explained to his son the importance of the visitors. The husband was attached to the English Embassy. He was not a senior diplomat, but he had an area of expertise that interested Natan. He was an engineer, and he knew about railways. Anton frowned at the mention of railways. His eagerness for progress ran counter to a romantic distrust of mechanization, and he had not altogether brought his ideas together on the point.

'Surely we don't want those abominable steam trains destroying our lovely Austrian countryside?'

Natan explained the social advantages patiently.

'I still prefer to think of the countryside unspoilt,' said Anton. 'Von Mayerberg says . . .'

The vein in Natan's forehead began to beat again as he heard the name of the playwright.

'Austria needs these things if it is to hold its place in the world,' said Natan. 'Of course it is a risk to make such an investment when the political situation remains so uncertain.'

Perhaps fortunately, the arrival of the English couple put paid to discussion of any such possibility. The Englishman was red-faced and heavy, and wore an unfashionably casual beard, but his wife Jane was a lively woman in her late twenties and, if not exactly pretty, she was decidedly animated.

'I didn't want to come to Vienna,' she confided in Anton, as Natan engaged her husband in talk. 'I can't speak German. Anyway, it's so provincial compared to Paris.'

Anton's eyebrows rose at such a description of the centre of the Habsburg Empire.

'Oh, I grant you it is a centre of government,' she said with a glance over at her husband.

'We have dismissed the worst of our government,' said Anton proudly.

'For a freethinker like myself, all government is questionable,' she laughed.

Such ideas, though he might have heard them late at night in crowded coffee houses where music and noise cover everything, came as a surprise to Anton, who looked over instinctively at his father.

'A freethinker?' he enquired cautiously. 'About what do you think?'

'Have you read Mary Wollstonecraft?' she asked him.

Anton had not. Though he knew the title of *The Rights of Women*, the thought of the book had not hitherto excited him. Now he leaned forward eagerly, fascinated by this blue-eyed, thin-lipped woman, with her long face too pale and angular for beauty, whose enthusiasm was so much aroused. Her ready speech meant he learnt a great deal about her in a short time. She was a lover of the poetry of Shelley and had a passionate interest in the music of Mozart and Schubert. He also discovered that she had two small children and lamented the absence of a young girl to look after them.

'One might find a severe nanny well enough here,' she said. 'Or an Austrian peasant. But what I want is a warm-hearted girl of intelligence who could give them loving care.'

By the end of the afternoon she had an earnest admirer in Anton Shassner. She knew as much, and pressed his hand warmly as she left. Natan, whose own concerns had not prevented him glancing across from time to time at his son, was not altogether pleased.

In retreat from his father's sharp eye, and a little frustrated by his encounter, Anton made his excuses and left to go to his own room. He had only recently been troubled by the desire for love. His old friend Max, resplendent now in the uniform of the regiment he had joined after university, teased

him for his shyness, but he had never yet made any use of
the pretty women who frequented the cafés of the Graben.
This English Jane had not been flirting with him, he decided
sadly. She was simply a woman who needed friendship.
Nevertheless, his blood was on fire as he ran up the back
stairs, where he nearly tripped over Clara, sitting with a
book in the half-dark.

She was there to make use of the gas light that came in
from a small, round window at the side of the house, and she
was startled at being discovered. Her cheeks went scarlet and
she bit her lips in anxiety. It was not that these stairs had
ever been forbidden to her, but if either the cook or the
housekeeper heard of her venturing there, she feared it would
be more than her job was worth.

Anton begged her pardon and would have passed on,
when he was struck by the strangeness of her situation. Her
dress and manner proclaimed her someone from the kitchens,
yet there she sat, absorbed in a book.

Clara was still a child, altogether without coquetry. Her
only wish was to escape attention, back along the servants'
stairs to her own part of the house. With this in mind, she
kept her eyes downcast, but just for that reason Anton put a
hand beneath her chin to look into her face.

'What are you reading with such concentration?'

The question seemed to confuse her and, rather than reply,
she showed him the book. He was astonished to make out
the name of Heinrich Heine.

'What's this? Do you understand what you read?' he
challenged her, half suspiciously.

'Not altogether,' she replied, and saying so brought a half-
smile and a dimple to her face.

As Clara saw an answering smile in the handsome young
face of the man who held her arm, she threw herself on his
mercy in a rush of words.

'Don't ask my name,' she begged him. 'Let me go back where I belong. It was only the light. I needed the light . . .'

His hand released her immediately.

'I won't give away your secret,' he promised. 'But I think you could trust me with your name.'

Chapter Nine

ANTON, AS HE READILY ADMITTED to Minna, had no intention of going into his father's bank when he finished his studies.

'I will speak to your father,' said Minna, apprehensively.

As she feared, her husband was far from pleased.

'And what *will* he do?' asked Shassner.

'Let him explore,' urged Minna.

'And where will he do that? He cannot spend the rest of his life in a café,' exclaimed Shassner.

At supper he made the same point forcefully to his son. 'The Revolution is over. Vienna is back to normal. What are your plans?'

Anton's plans involved becoming a poet, a novelist or a playwright, with Rudolf von Mayerberg as guide and friend, but of this, he knew, his father would not approve. He understood why not. As he well knew, Rudolf von Mayerberg was not a self-denying man. He began the day with croissants dipped into creamy coffee and stuffed himself with sausages before going to Mass. He took cherry wine at midday and at five went off to play skittles. Anton often went with him to discuss the nature of art over a dish of fried snails or the oysters which were never served in the Shassner household. To share in such a life was not an ambition he could easily confess to his father.

'How can you be so complacent about the failure of the Revolution?' he therefore challenged him.

'Because it was bound to fail,' said Shassner.

'Was it? Prince Schwarzenberg had to call in the forces of the Tsar and fire cannons on Vienna to defeat it,' said Anton.

'Nevertheless, the revolt has been put down,' said Shassner mildly. 'There have been some gains. The new Emperor Franz Joseph is young. Let us see what happens. He may grant more liberal measures.'

'He seems rather more interested in re-establishing authority.'

'Your head has only just healed,' said Shassner pointedly as a servant entered to remove the soup dishes from the gleaming white table.

Anton fell into a brooding silence. When the servant had gone and the door was shut behind him, he burst out:

'This is what you want? To be spied on in your own house?'

'He is not a spy,' said Shassner, 'or I should not employ him. Still, it seems foolish to speak so rashly in front of him, don't you think?'

'Certainly I have no desire to be shot by one of the General Windischgrätz tribunals,' said Anton.

Minna sighed. 'Dear Anton, put your faith in the liberalism of German culture,' she said. 'That is how all of us will have freedom and progress.'

Anton gave her a faint smile and returned to his conversation with his father.

'Do your friends in the police have any news yet of my friend Efraim Jacob?'

'He is not on the list of executed,' said Shassner.

'In gaol, then,' said Anton gloomily.

'What has happened to Rudolf von Mayerberg, by the way?' asked Shassner.

'He went away,' said Anton, 'before we did. He comes back next week.'

Shassner frowned. 'Von Mayerberg makes no pretence to heroism, which is something. But I cannot like the man.'

'They say his mother will have influence at the court of Franz Joseph,' said Minna. She uttered the name of the new Emperor with great respect.

'It may be,' said Shassner indifferently. 'I rather doubt it. Now that the Archduchess Sophie is mother of an emperor, she will not be inclined to tittle-tattle with minor aristocracy like Rudolf's mother.'

'How cynical you are,' sighed Minna.

'It is fortunate we are not seeking preferment there,' said Shassner.

These days Anton usually got up in time for the early lecture on Roman or Contract Law, to which he listened with fair attention, but soon after lunch he went over to the chemistry laboratory, where his friend Max Kallman was already idling. Max had little interest in study, although his father was determined his son should follow a career in medicine.

Max had a nose for adventure. He liked to eat with a group of musical clowns, or a lovely leading lady of the latest comedy, and he sometimes took Anton to breakfast in the early hours of the morning at a tavern opposite the theatre, where they could watch the girls who played the smaller parts eating sausage sandwiches. Sometimes they spent their afternoons playing chess in a café, but usually Anton went home before three or four – avowedly to study, but customarily to write a few lines of an epic poem about the seventeenth-century defeat of the Turks at Vienna.

Anton had very little experience with any girls, more than playing tag and forfeits with some of his pretty cousins while on visits to his mother's family, when there had sometimes been occasions for embraces and kisses. Max, however, had already made the acquaintance of the young ladies of the inner city, and he bore himself like a man of the world. It was with Max that Anton had his first encounter that spring with one of the ladies whose furnished rooms lay above the Graben. They had been dining at a favourite restaurant and were walking back towards Spiegelgasse when Max drew his attention to a young woman signalling to them from the first floor. Above a small French cake shop with a pretty green awning sat a girl leaning gently against the iron railing of her balcony. She smiled and waved. She looked very young and very friendly as she stood up to catch his attention, her waist absurdly small in contrast to her full hips and breasts. Anton stared up at her so intently that the coachman of one of the carriages going by had to warn him to get out of the way. There he stood, a charming young man of little more than eighteen, in a pale gold cravat and silky green waistcoat shot through with golden brown. And the girl who beckoned to him was certainly smiling with an invitation slightly more generous than she usually offered her clients.

Anton, a little dizzy, even a little queasy from the brandy he had taken after the meal, hesitated, but the mockery in Max's eyes made him feel the situation was a challenge. As boldly as he could, therefore, he waved a hand back to the girl, who motioned him to make his way through the back of the shop.

'I'll wait for you if you like,' said Max. 'They make excellent coffee here.'

Anton's heart banged uncomfortably as he made his way up the narrow stairs, wondering if he would find the right room and half hoping he would not. But, as he turned on to the first landing, the girl was there to welcome him. She led him into a darkened room which smelled of a sweet, musky perfume and something else he could not place.

'I can't see where I am,' he stammered, and she answered with a giggling laugh. Gradually he made out the frills of the curtains at the window and the huge bed with shiny satin pillows and a flounced bedspread thrown carelessly to one side.

The girl herself, now he looked at her closely, was pretty enough, though she had a slight cast in one eye. As she began to take off first her bodice and then her elaborate skirt, he could see that her body was as voluptuously curved as he had guessed. She was barely laced in and, as her stays slid to the floor, he marvelled at the white skin and full breasts that appeared to him.

Nevertheless, he was suddenly without the least desire for her. He had responded to her invitation largely to impress Max. Now he regretted it.

Without any sense of this, she stood before him and said, provocatively, 'Money first!'

Anton nodded, rather tempted to hand over the money and make his way down the stairs without any further dealings with the girl.

As he counted the coins into her palm, however, she looked up at him wistfully.

'We don't often get nice-looking young fellows like you.'

Something in the softness of her voice brought a flicker of desire and he began to take off his clothes, beginning with his jacket, which she lay over a chair for him while he stiffly unbuttoned his waistcoat. He had almost forgotten his crippled fingers.

'Like a little boy,' she said as he put all his clothes in a pile. 'What's your name?'

'Max,' he lied quickly.

'Mine's Ulla. I'm a country girl, you see,' she said, and began to pull him towards the bed, smiling and apparently eager herself, though he imagined that was a trick of her profession. 'Don't be shy, Max,' she said, and she lay before him naked on the pink bed as he took off his lower garments.

He could see the opening of her sex as he had so often imagined it, and his body responded to that, but there was something in him that made it impossible to do more without some human acquaintance, so that instead of plunging into her, he lay down at her side.

At this, she propped herself up on one elbow to look at him, as if impatient. Then, seeing again how young he was, she put out a friendly hand to stroke his face.

'It's never your first time, is it?'

He nodded, ashamed, but already more excited by the words than the sight of her naked body. She stroked his arms, then his ribs, and he felt his penis stiffen at the caress: not at the eroticism of it but the human contact and the words of endearment. Her hands fondled his hips.

'Neat and thin as a blade,' she said approvingly.

Then her hands ran down his thighs, and the certainty of sweetness flooded him as her hands found their expert way between his legs to his crotch and at last to the heavy groin.

'Ulla,' he sighed, to prolong the sense of someone else there, someone who knew and liked him.

Her hand found his penis then and she gave a little, almost immediately repressed, exclamation. He ignored her gasp because his body was so ready to press inside her. In a moment their encounter was over.

As he lay there, drained with pleasure, her exclamation as she fondled his penis came back to his mind, and he raised himself to look into her face and enquire about it, intending at the same time to apologize for the brevity of the experience. He was quite unprepared to find all the friendliness gone out of her expression.

'All right,' she said. 'I'll wash now, if you don't mind.'

She got up from the bed and began to towel herself vigorously.

'And you can go,' she said. 'Just take yourself out the way you came.'

The change in her attitude was so hurtful that he cried out, 'What's wrong?'

He couldn't believe she treated all her customers so cruelly.

She was putting on her clothes now, her face closed to him and he had to repeat his question before she turned on him to say, 'You're a filthy Jew, aren't you? I didn't know that. Couldn't have guessed. I mean, you haven't got red hair or a Turkish nose or anything.'

'I would have told you if you had asked. I had no idea you made such distinctions among your clientele,' said Anton coldly.

The girl turned her back on him and in a moment he could hear her washing in the other room as he pulled on his own clothes vigorously. He could not get out of the room quickly enough now. He wanted to ask her, what does it mean to you which God I serve? You who sell your body every day. But he was too disturbed.

When she came towards him again he could see that she too was alarmed.

'I come from a small village,' she explained. 'We all learnt about Jews there. There aren't many in Vienna. But that is what it means, doesn't it? When you don't have a foreskin?'

'How does it matter to you? My Jewishness?' he asked.

'It's like not being human,' she said. 'Not having a foreskin.'

He could have explained. That all Jews began with fore-skins like the rest of the human race. That at the age of eight days these were removed as a sacrifice to God, to put Abraham's sign in their flesh, but he said nothing. She was staring at him with a kind of fascinated curiosity.

'Now I've done it with one of the Devil's children. The priest told us.' She shivered. 'Even when you look nice, you're still the Devil's children.'

Max had waited for his friend as he had promised, and Anton was relieved that, although his friend looked up enquiringly, he did not question him deeply. Anton himself gave only a cursory nod of recognition. Seeing that Max misunderstood his pallor, he made clear that he had managed to fulfil his part of the encounter without disgrace. Still amused, Max said, 'I know how you feel. The body degrades us.'

Pondering this, Max ordered a steaming hot coffee with whipped cream for both of them, as if the bodily satisfactions of eating and drinking were in a different category.

Max had few ambitions that were not encompassed by a pleasant drive to Doblin, a gay dinner al fresco and some intimate acquaintance with those pretty milliners and girls in flower shops who took his eye. He despaired of Anton's shyness, which continued until one evening he was able to introduce him to Charlotte, the wife of an army surgeon.

'An elegant woman,' said Max as they first observed the couple taking hot chocolate and apple cakes at a nearby table in Grinzing.

'Look at those marvellous grey eyes. Look at the way she moves her white hands.'

Anton agreed. Charlotte's face, framed in golden hair under a wide hat, was the very oval of a Florentine fresco.

'Lonely, too, I should think,' said Max.

'Why do you say that?' asked Anton, surprised.

'She is twenty years younger than her husband,' observed Max, 'and she has time on her hands.'

Anton was doubtful.

'You think every woman has nothing to do but make herself available for sexual pleasure.'

'That's my experience,' said Max, cheerfully. 'Shall I introduce you?'

'You know them?' asked Anton, surprised.

'Not well,' admitted Max, 'but the good doctor was once a colleague of my father and will be happy to be remembered.'

In this spirit, he approached the surgeon boldly, and the introductions were soon effected.

Charlotte was a graceful woman, who gave her hand in turn to the two young men who approached her with a faint smile.

'So, you are still at the University?' she enquired, her grey eyes going over Anton's face as she spoke.

She had a low, growling voice, which suggested intimacy and amusement at the same time.

'Yes, I am,' he said. 'For the moment. I read Law.'

'And what will you do after the moment is over?' she mocked him.

'I shall do *something* in the world,' he said.

'Men,' she sighed. 'They care for nothing but to make a dash. Women have more sense.'

'I should have thought too sensible a life was very boring,' said Anton.

Her eyes, which had been idle, suddenly sharpened.

'You have to learn not to confuse tranquillity with boredom, young man,' she said.

Anton had not meant to be impudent and withdrew from the conversation with red ears and a sense of bruised vanity.

'She thought I was an insolent young cub,' he said glumly to his friend in the carriage back to Vienna.

'You are wrong. She was most taken with you,' laughed Max. 'Getting into these relationships is a good deal easier than getting out of them, you will find.'

A few days later, Anton happened to meet Charlotte in the street outside a department store. He helped her to mount her waiting carriage with a great number of packages.

'Come and have tea with me tomorrow afternoon,' she murmured, bending out of her window.

He accepted the invitation eagerly.

Her husband was not at home, her child was at the park with his nurse, and Charlotte soon made it plain to Anton that he was a most welcome visitor. The whole adventure went far more easily than he had anticipated. Quite soon, he was on his knees beside her, incoherent with protestations of love which she received dreamily. She took his crippled hand in her own and studied it thoughtfully.

'Poor hand,' she said, first stroking it and then putting her soft lips to it, before turning it over to lick the centre of his palm. Excitement flared up in his groin as her tongue licked his flesh. Seeing as much, she held out her own hand and led him to her bedroom, which was still alight with the afternoon sun and smelled sweetly.

'Has there been another woman before me?' Charlotte asked him.

'Certainly not,' said Anton.

Within a week, they were scheming how they might meet away from the house and so be in less danger of interruption.

'Well?' said Max, when these events were described to him.

'Well enough,' agreed Anton.

He was infatuated and happy, and reluctant to give his friend any more details, though he accepted his help in borrowing a room for their further meetings.

Soon, Anton learned how to take the hatpins out of Charlotte's hat and the shawl from her shoulders, and was leading her into the bedroom like a lover of twice his years. He found her sadness particularly seductive.

'I've been very unhappy,' she admitted, 'most of my life.'

'Life is so empty and so short,' he agreed.

'Ah, but you don't love me,' she coaxed him. 'Do you? These afternoons don't mean anything to you.'

He protested his passion earnestly enough.

'I don't believe you,' she said, kissing his eyes. 'But I seem to need those words more than anything else.'

'Doesn't your husband utter them, then?'

'Oh, my husband – I think he hates me.'

'It isn't possible!'

'Yes. He finds me dull because I have no interest in what he cares about. Indeed, he makes me miserable every day for an hour, trying to improve me.'

'Monstrous!' said Anton, stroking her cheek.

She sighed. 'I sometimes think I don't really like people.'

'Are you still seeing Charlotte?' Max asked him one day.

'From time to time,' admitted Anton. He had no wish to be teased by his friend as overly faithful.

'I thought as much,' said Max. 'Poor Anton. You will have to be ruthless.'

'Perhaps I have no desire to be,' said Anton, defensively.

But the truth was he had begun to find their encounters less compelling. On one occasion, indeed, after a night spent talking into the early hours with Rudolf von Mayerberg, he had disgracefully fallen asleep in her bed.

'You will have to find a reason to end this,' said Max, judiciously.

'Please don't take it upon yourself to discover one,' said Anton. 'I am quite capable of extracting myself from the relationship when I am ready.'

In the event, the ruthlessness he lacked proved unnecessary, as Charlotte's husband was transferred to a provincial posting in Eastern Galicia. Charlotte received the news miserably. On the last evening they spent together, she repeated several times, 'Galicia! What will become of me?'

Anton forbore to insist on more personal aspects of her regret.

They kissed tenderly, and he was once again free.

Chapter Ten

A YEAR LATER, Anton took a walk through the Prater, a tract of woods between the Danube and the Danube Canal which had been an Imperial hunting ground until Joseph II opened it to the public. There were booths that sold wine, lemonade or gingerbread; amusements on every hand: jugglers, fire-eaters, dancing bears, and ballad singers. The sky was blue and the air seemed to glow in the sunlight. Anton's spirits were high. He paused to join the crowd around a puppet show for a moment. A little further on, he saw a group of Viennese gathered about another entertainment: two fierce dogs set upon an enfeebled donkey. Animal baiting was not to his taste, and he would have walked hastily away had he not made out startled cries in English. A tall woman dressed in fine, brown wool was showing vehement disapproval. To his surprise, he recognized Jane Newall, the wife of the English engineer. Her face was pale, and tears streamed down her cheeks.

Anton had not given much thought to Jane since their first meeting. In December she had sent him a card from London, to which she and her husband had retreated rather earlier than the usual break for Christmas, and he had seen nothing of her since.

He paused now, solicitously. She seemed quite alone and, since she was clearly unaware of anything but the snarls of the dogs and the shrill scream of the donkey, he put a hand on her arm to attract her attention. She turned and then made out who he was.

'Make them stop!' she cried. 'Make them stop!'

'Oh, that's impossible,' said Anton. 'You'd better leave. Don't watch it.'

'And if I stop watching, will that help the donkey?' she asked.

'Let me take you home,' said Anton. 'I have a carriage waiting at the edge of the park.'

She burst into fresh tears, but he urged her away and she yielded, still overpowered by the barbarity of the experience.

'This horrible city,' she shuddered. 'The people seem so kind and cheerful, but they actually enjoy cruelty.'

Jane now lived in Anolfstrasse in several darkly furnished rooms upon which she had taken little trouble to impress her own personality. Their dinginess surprised Anton, who would have expected her husband to have arranged better accommodation.

'They're vile,' Jane agreed as she saw his eyes go over the hunting scenes on her walls. 'The first year we managed to live in some style, but Anthony has difficulties at the moment.'

Her eyes were so frank and open that Anton was tempted to ask her what difficulties she meant, but instead he accepted the glass of wine she pressed on him, touched with a sense of his own chivalry. There was a burst of childish laughter from another room, and Jane's face softened.

'The children are being looked after by a huge peasant woman who cannot speak English, but I teach them to read myself,' she said proudly. 'Would you like to meet them?'

Anton politely agreed that he would, and two small girls shyly appeared.

Jane put her hand on the shining fair hair of the elder child and introduced her as Diana. She had a smiling, healthy face with round blue eyes and flushed cheeks. The younger girl had a darker face, and stared at Anton with a direct gaze, making no attempt to ingratiate herself.

'Their characters are very different,' said Jane. 'Diana has all the straightforward energy of my mother. The younger is exciting, isn't she?'

Even as she spoke with enthusiasm of her children, she was clearly distressed by something else. Her husband? Money? Anton speculated on what might be troubling her, as she sent the children away into the bare arms of their brawny nursemaid.

'You have found Vienna frightening?' suggested Anton.

She agreed, her lips tremulous. He watched her delicate hands as she cut a cake for him.

'I should like to be of some help,' he offered.

She smiled and secured a wisp of her hair more firmly into place.

'Do you know Byron's "Hebrew Melodies"?' she asked him. He did not, and she read one for him. For all his uncertain English, he was moved and was thanking her warmly when her husband appeared.

Anthony Newall reminded Anton of Holbein's portrait of Wyatt of which his father owned a Viennese copy: a stockily built man, with a body in perfect health and the sullen expression of a spoilt child. His mouth made a red, sensuous circle.

He recognized Anton and welcomed him at once in excellent German.

'Are you enjoying Vienna?' Anton asked him courteously.

'Very much,' said Newall. 'Now that things have settled down.'

Anton politely agreed that the situation seemed much more stable, but Jane broke in:

'Oh, you should not say that as if this repression must be approved. I know you cannot feel so.'

Anton cautiously pointed out that all Viennese were glad to walk the streets without fear again. Jane saw his caution and was impatient with it.

'Oh, you cannot think we are spies, people who would report your opinions to the authorities. I shall feel you do not trust us if you talk like that.'

'Nonsense, my dear. You assume more than you should,' said Newall. 'You know nothing of Herr Shassner's political opinions. The truth is' – he bent forward to Anton, confidentially – 'women have no feeling for politics.'

Jane's eyes flashed at the implication. 'I don't know why you should say that. I read as much as you do.'

'Reading,' said Newall, 'is only part of any story.'

Jane made an impatient grimace, and turned hopefully again to Anton.

'You must know what has been happening. The arrests. The executions. I believe the brother of your rabbi was among them. How can a Jew welcome the re-establishing of such a tyranny?'

'Now really,' said Newall, 'we should not subject our guest to such an inquisition. For my part, Vienna has been a city of discovery. You can teach us a great deal about the pleasures of living.'

'We guzzle,' admitted Anton. 'We eat sometimes as many as five times a day.'

Newall's eyes were smiling, and his face had an insinuating expression which led Anton to wonder if the pleasures he had in mind included the ladies of easy virtue in the Graben.

Jane had bitten her lip at Newall's words and both her pallor and the ferocity of the glare she directed towards her husband alarmed Anton. Nevertheless, as he rose to leave some of Jane's earlier warmth returned to her long face. 'You must come again.'

Anton promised that he would, for all his uneasy sense of nervous crisis in the household.

Over the next few months he visited the Newalls regularly, with a mounting respect for Jane's subtlety and a growing awareness of Newall's financial problems.

Chapter Eleven

CLARA DID NOT OFTEN set foot outside the servants' part of the house. At night in bed she lay reading for as long as she could before fatigue brought her to sleep; for the rest, she did what was required of her in the cook's domain.

One day, when there was a pleasant expectancy in the May sunshine, Clara was sent upstairs to help with the changing of beds.

'Do what the housekeeper tells you,' said the cook. 'You'll not be missed here.'

And she sent her through the door that separated guests from domestic quarters. Clara went obediently along a thickly carpeted corridor into Shassner's vast entrance hall. This atrium had been much refurbished according to Natan's taste, with sparkling chandeliers, oval mirrors and a statue of a naked cherub in bronze. The floor was marble, on which lay woven Turkish rugs in reds and blues.

'Follow me,' said the housekeeper impatiently, as Clara stood marvelling at this sudden splendour, and led the girl by the back stairs to the mysteries of a linen cupboard filled with soft pillows, silken duvets and sheets smelling of rose petals.

When Clara and the housekeeper had changed the embroidered coverlets and put out fresh towels in several rooms, the housekeeper thought of some other tasks for which Clara could be helpful.

'Wait there,' she said. 'And don't sit on the bed.'

Clara sat carefully on a low stool and waited as she was told.

To have absolutely nothing to do seemed a wonderful luxury. There was never time to herself in the kitchens. For a while, she took pleasure in her own thoughts, while observing the precise matching of the dark blue flowers on the curtains with the lighter patterns on the wallpaper but, after a quarter of an hour, she became uneasy that she had misunderstood the housekeeper's instructions.

Opening the door of the bedroom, she took a long look into the corridor. There was no sign of anyone. Facing her on the wall was a huge painting of a gentleman looking rather uncomfortable on a horse. The brilliant colours and sheer size of the portrait captured her attention for several moments and she was still staring up at it when Anton found her.

'If it isn't my little reader of Heine,' he observed. 'I haven't seen you for months.'

'More than a year,' she corrected him, softly.

He looked down at her vivid young face, observing in the half-light that she was growing into a young woman.

'So much has happened since,' he observed.

'You were kind enough then,' she reminded him, 'to make nothing of that other meeting.'

'It was a remarkable one, however,' he remembered. 'What are you reading now? Or have you lost that passion?'

She shook her head and would not be drawn.

'Schiller? Goethe?' he teased her.

She confessed to reading a play about Mary Stuart of England.

He stared down at her seriously. 'Are you happy here?' he asked her.

'I don't know what more I could hope for,' she replied.

Anton was taken aback by her words.

'You can't be content in the kitchens,' he said.

'I'm as content as I'm likely to be,' she said.

'What would you do if you could choose?' he asked her.

She gave the matter serious thought.

'Perhaps I could look after some lady's children,' she said.

Anton had been expecting her to imagine marriage to someone wealthy and grand.

'That isn't so fanciful a dream, surely?' he rebuked her.

A melancholy filled her face. 'Those who have such employment to offer do not often look in kitchens,' she said gravely. And then she flushed at making so considered a comment. Out of the corner of her eye she was aware of the housekeeper approaching.

'There are things I must be doing.'

Anton stared after her as she made her escape.

Just before Christmas, Anton called on Jane and Anthony Newall with presents for their children. He found Jane too preoccupied to make conversation. Anton commented on the beauty of her younger child.

'She resembles me as I was,' said Jane. 'But she will be less unhappy, I hope. Her features are finer, and more regular.'

'She will be a beauty,' said Anton, taking her hand on an impulse. 'But you must tell me, Jane. Why are you so unhappy? It cannot be necessary.'

She thrust him away, colouring, but far from displeased, and at that moment her husband entered the room.

'You see my wife's condition,' he said, carelessly.

Anton had not, until that moment, but now he did and a flush rose to his own cheeks. Jane was impatient with his mild embarrassment.

'I am so exhausted. I cannot welcome another child.

Otherwise, I should be pleased. Oh, if only I had a sensible English girl to help with the others,' she said.

Her husband grimaced. 'We cannot possibly afford such expense.'

'I know,' said Jane.

'I think,' said Anton impulsively, 'I know a very young girl who would serve you well, if you were prepared to educate her a little.'

A few weeks later, Clara moved from kitchen drudgery to a position in the household of the impecunious Newalls.

Part Two

1854

Chapter Twelve

A FEW YEARS AFTER the excitements of the 1848 uprising, a handsome young boy of fifteen stood at the window of a train looking out over Alpine slopes. It was late autumn and a fall of snow glittered in the stony hollows. It was a new railway line, and railways themselves were new enough to be distrusted. It would be a foolish traveller who did not recognize the risks as the train hesitated on the curves and braked on the steeper inclines, creaking at both ends as it adjusted speed. It was rather like flying on the wings of a cumbrous and jerky bird. The inexperienced often shrieked with vertigo; some insisted on having the blinds down in their carriages rather than look down on the landscape moving below them.

Joseph, however, enjoyed the flashing snows on the crags and gorges beneath. There was a carelessness in the way he stood at the window rail that suggested a physical confidence, such as perhaps a circus performer might have. He was dressed in well-cut clothes, with a flash of red at his neck that brought out the blackness of his hair and eyes, and he had a bold, broad forehead. His skin was white and clear. For all his confidence and prosperous clothes, it was not an aristocratic face. It was too mobile, too expressive. When he smiled, as he did to let a young woman pass down the train, his eyes were too bold. When his face was in repose, however, his eyes were melancholy. Except for that, there was little in his figure as it balanced against the rail of the moving train to recall the skinny, eager boy from Vienna's Haidgasse.

At fifteen, Joseph was used to thinking of himself as a violinist. Indeed, over the last two years he had not only supported himself but earned enough money to buy a small hat shop for Hannah. Hannah's wits had made the shop such a success that she and Peretz were now living in a much larger flat in another part of Leopoldstadt.

Some time in the preceding year Becker had declared he had nothing further to teach him, since Joseph by now was the finer musician. Nevertheless, Becker continued to travel with him as his manager. He was even now asleep in his comfortable bunk, blinds drawn against a vision of moving scenery with a bottle of good brandy for his further comfort. He did not travel out of the love of it, he claimed, but to protect Joseph and make sure he was accorded respectful treatment. That it was also a way of making sure all Joseph's fees passed directly into his hands was abundantly clear. Joseph understood, and did not object: he was glad to leave Becker responsible for arranging tours and negotiating payments.

The focus of Vienna's night life in the eighteen fifties was the creation of Franz Morawetz, a poor Jewish tailor who had once tried to set up steam baths in Vienna. When these had not proved a commercial success, he had taken out the water, put in parquet and gilding and created Sophiensaal. There, tiers of loggias, like those of a Renaissance palace, surrounded a glittering dance floor. Elegant spectators dined in private boxes amid palm fronds, to watch the dancing throng below. Under that great vaulting roof, which turned out to be an acoustic wonder, Becker went to arrange what had to be arranged, and Joseph had no wish to involve himself in the detail of these transactions, though he did sometimes wonder whether other managers took such a heavy percentage of their artists' earnings.

'Is that right?' demanded Peretz when Joseph incautiously mentioned the details of his contract.

'I don't know,' said the boy. 'Without him, I would still be scraping away at the Hungarian café.'

'And now you are an itinerant fiddler,' said Peretz. 'That's all. All right, be grateful. I'm grateful, your mother is delighted. I'm only asking – why should this man take fifty per cent of your earnings?'

'He needs the money,' said Joseph.

Joseph had long since understood that Becker's continuing financial problems arose from his extravagance. Whatever he earned, he spent; bills always surprised him as outrageous impositions.

'Have some sense,' pleaded Peretz. 'Ask your friends. What does this Becker do with his time?'

'I told you. He composes music,' said Joseph.

Joseph was far from certain about the merits of Becker's music. And he was well aware that Becker wrote very little these days. He travelled with manuscript paper wherever they went; he spread it out in every hotel bedroom they stopped in. But he often fell asleep over his first glass of wine when he began writing.

'Think of me as a father,' Becker had said to him. And so, in a way, Joseph did, though he could not help reflecting he had not been fortunate in his fathers. Peretz, for all his intelligence, would always have too much bitterness to be easily affectionate. And now Becker. Joseph often felt resentful of Becker. Not because he was greedy and extravagant but because the boy could see there were musical giants in the world and that Becker was not one of them: he envied those who had the chance to work in the presence of

greatness. Coming from where he had, he knew he was lucky
to have found Becker. Yet he could have been luckier. And
something in him felt he deserved to be luckier.

Looking out of the window on this train that was taking
him to Paris, he was thinking of the gay assembly in furs and
feathers that had made its way on to the train as they left
Vienna. Becker had said it was a small opera company, and
this was interesting enough to Joseph but, when the bustling
crowd had parted to reveal the unmistakable face of Johannes
Brahms, Joseph was excited. The thought of travelling on the
same train as a man Schumann had called a genius disturbed
Joseph so much that he was unable to settle down in the
carriage for all Becker's supplications.

'You will be tired. You will lose the edge of your
performance tomorrow. Brahms is a man like any other,'
said Becker.

'Perhaps Joachim is with him,' wondered Joseph.

'And how would that help us? I'm tired. If you want to
stay awake, go and stand in the corridor.'

Becker retired to his couch and lowered the blind, the
better to ignore the Alpine landscape.

And now Joseph was standing in the corridor as the train
lumbered towards France. Perhaps, Joseph wondered, if he
walked down the train he might catch a glimpse of the
composer. He jerked a little to this side and that as he went,
too shy to peer into windows for the people he was longing
to meet.

When he reached the baggage car, which was half way
along the train, he saw an elaborately dressed woman with
blonde ringlets arguing with the baggage car attendant.

'Of course I know how many cases I had. Do you take me
for a fool?' she demanded, her passion so visible that Joseph
could see her breasts heaving where they pushed up under
the blue dress. As Joseph paused to look at her angry face,

he saw that she was very beautiful and guessed at once that she was part of the opera company.

'Can I help?' he asked.

She turned her blue and furious eyes on him for a moment but, as she saw her questioner was a handsome young boy, her expression softened.

'I don't need help. I need my fifth suitcase. He has lost my bag with all my favourite dresses.'

At this the attendant began to protest. 'There *were* only four cases. I put them on myself. Four cases, not—'

'Don't interrupt.' Her eyes were flashing again. Joseph had never seen anyone so proud, or so little in need of assistance, but he remained at her side to help all he could. She was Austrian; that much he could tell from her voice, and no more than twenty, he judged, though in this he was mistaken by five years.

'Will you kindly go and search the other baggage car,' she demanded.

As soon as the man had left, she began to smile at Joseph.

'I have lots of other dresses. Do you think I am being unkind?'

'I think you are amusing yourself,' said Joseph without hesitating, since with a woman like this there was clearly no point in being polite.

She was startled by his reply but, before he could say anything more, the attendant returned full of apologies and with the fifth case. Joseph registered his astonishment.

'You see!' she crowed. 'You thought I was just making a fuss.'

He looked at the label on the case, trying to make out her name and the name of the hotel she would be staying in, but she saw as much and mischievously moved the bag from his eye.

'I know you. You play the violin,' she said.

'I do,' he said, surprised.

'Well, I thought so. You don't know how lucky you are,' she sighed. 'For us, who work with the opera, things have never been worse. No one understands what we need in order to do anything. All you need is a small room and another musician or two . . .' Her eyes teased him with the modesty of his success.

'I prefer chamber music,' he said awkwardly.

'You don't like opera?' she asked, with mock horror. 'Where do you play in Paris?'

He told her. It was a small hall, and she did not know it. Round her neck hung the huge silver cross favoured by devout Catholics. Her blue eyes were dancing. To Joseph she seemed the most beautiful girl he had ever seen.

'I hate Paris,' she said. 'I hate the French altogether. Well,' she shrugged, 'I must go back to my seat.'

'Shall I see you in Paris?' he asked with enormous daring.

'I don't see why,' she said. 'Why do you stare at me so intently? I don't like to be stared at.'

He flushed at the rebuff. 'Good day, then,' he said stiffly.

Any thought he might have had of asking her about Brahms and Joachim left his mind. He could feel the blood hot in his cheeks. Seeing as much, she seemed to regret her severity.

'I don't mean to be rude. It's only my manner. You are very young.' She came close to apologizing.

'I understand,' he replied, cool again and angry with her. To be fifteen, he thought, was in many ways terrible, but it would not last. By the time he was twenty, she would be twenty-five or thirty and he could treat her the same way as she was treating him now.

'My name is Sophie,' she said then, and smiled.

He looked into her blue eyes and was lost in enchantment. That night, as he lay on the swaying bunk, he thought about nothing else but those glittering eyes. Her presence recalled the ladies who had looked down on him as he stood behind his mother's stall. She might be an aristocrat, or she might be, as Becker told him when he returned to the carriage, no more than a minor singer who gave herself airs. But he wanted to conquer her, and he would, he told himself, one day. That night he dreamed of pressing himself against her in pleasure and woke up still angry and a little bewildered.

In the other bunk, Becker snored. For the first time, Joseph lay and thought about his prospects in life. What did he want, and was Becker going to get it for him? As he pondered, Becker turned over, shifted, and let out a long, hopeless snort. It seemed exceedingly unlikely.

Joseph lifted the curtain and stared outside. The Alps were no longer visible. Moonlight filled the whole sky, and the trees made one solid, furry covering for the mild French hills. The world seemed still and peaceful but his thoughts went on racing. When at last Joseph fell asleep he had made up his mind to look again at Becker's arrangements for the year ahead, so that, he thought as he slipped off to sleep, in the morning light everything might be different.

Joseph expected little from Paris. Among the small audience, however, happened to be Franz Hellman, the violinist who had played with Becker long ago in Vienna. Always more direct, less grudging and more friendly than Rubin, he came back to congratulate Joseph after the performance and explained something of his own fate. He seemed to have prospered. His grey, faun eyes were wide open as he praised Joseph for his treatment of his last sonata. His dislike of Becker, however, was palpable and his fine, short nose wrinkled with something like disgust. Later, in a small bar near Joseph's hotel, he voiced some of his reasons.

'He was always a clown. You cannot still be taught by him?'

'No,' Joseph admitted. 'Though I still have much to learn.'

'But not from him,' cried Hellman, calling for more wine, and clearly with more to say. 'You will have to detach yourself. He represents you badly. If I had not heard you play first, I would have had nothing to do with you.' The cat-shaped eyes looked deeply into Joseph's own. 'Will you come back to Paris, soon?'

'Yes, next month, as it happens,' said Joseph.

'Then perhaps you might play at a friend's party? You must be used to that, but this would be a special occasion.'

'If you can arrange it.'

'The friend in question is the Baron James de Rothschild. Does that alarm you?'

'How is such an invitation possible?' cried Joseph. 'They say only kings and nobles dine with him.'

'He also admires artists. And he is a great collector of them. It is my brief to keep him in touch with the young and talented. So, if you will give me the address of your hotel, I will see you have a formal invitation.'

'Do you mean to invite the whole of Becker's group?'

'No. I shall arrange a pianist and let you have the programme at least two weeks in advance.'

'I shall need to rehearse with the pianist.'

'Of course. Probably at my studio.'

'Perfect,' said Joseph.

The following day, over coffee and rolls, Becker looked at the thick, gilt-edged invitation card sourly.

'They say his wealth is greater than all the other financiers of France put together.'

Joseph could see that Becker was considerably put out by the invitation, which had been brought by the Baron's personal flunkey and had caused something of a stir at the modest hotel's reception desk.

'I shall put his riches out of my mind,' he said to Becker with a smile.

'Well, I hope you can carry it off,' said Becker, without much conviction.

A month later, Joseph wondered as much himself as he stepped out of the cab that brought him to the Baron's palace on rue Lafitte. The white marble and glittering chandeliers, the tailcoats of the servants who brought in the guests, the apparel of the guests themselves, all had an intimidating splendour. The Baron, a dignified figure quite unlike the cartoons of the family which Joseph had seen in Vienna, welcomed him courteously and his beautiful wife took the boy's arm and led him to meet some of the guests before the time came to play. Joseph would have preferred to go to another room and prepare his mind for the music; instead, he found himself introduced to a succession of smiling men and women whom he could hardly understand. At last he was offered a chair, into which he sank with gratitude. He refused the wine and delicate food brought to him. Somewhere in the assembly was Joachim; he had been assured as much; but Joachim would not make himself known until after he had heard Joseph play.

As he sat there, silent and to all outward appearances calm, Joseph's youth and good looks attracted favourable attention from a group of women clustered nearby around a man in a wheelchair.

'He is a young Byron.'

'But not English.'

'Austrian, I think.'

'Shall we meet him?'

'He is to play to us. Be patient,' said the invalid. He was

at first sight rather alarming: his eyelid hung down over his left eye and one side of his face looked immobile.

Presently, the pianist and Joseph went forward to play to the assembled guests, who fell more or less silent in expectation. Joseph had been asked to play Mendelssohn. The moment he lifted his instrument the tenderness and erotic power of the music filled his spirit, and he felt the nerves of the audience joining his own in the pleasure of it. For all the glitter of the occasion, the music was more powerful than any of the people there. When he had finished playing, people pressed forward to thank him, and he bowed and smiled. It was a strange magic.

The invalid was among the first to come forward, rolled in his chair, to compliment him.

'We can be grateful to the Baron,' he said. 'Would it not be a great blessing if all the kings in the world were removed and the family Rothschild put on their thrones? They know how to support culture.'

Joseph smiled, though his French was uneven and he could not reply.

Now that the formal entertainment was over, there was a burst of laughter from a group at the centre of the parquet floor and Joseph saw that it rose from a group of women in colourful dresses.

'Don't you like the way the French laugh?' said the invalid. 'There's nothing like it in Germany.'

'In Austria,' said Joseph, 'there's a good deal of laughter.'

'An Austrian, are you?' said the man in his clipped Northern German. 'There was a time Metternich's shadows came over here in hundreds to sound me out, but those villainous days are over.'

'We have Franz Joseph on the throne now,' said Joseph, wondering a little why Metternich's police should regard the man as so singular an enemy.

'And things are different?'

'Everyone knows that,' said Joseph, though he had an uneasy feeling his father would not have agreed with him. 'And Vienna is the best place for music in the whole of Europe. I love it.'

'Do you now?' said the invalid.

The strange but oddly charming gentleman laughed and began to cough. He accepted a handkerchief from the beautiful young woman at his side. 'But then you are young.'

Joseph began to wish he had expressed himself less forcefully.

'So you feel you belong in Austria?' asked the invalid, with a certain irony.

'Yes. I don't know where else. May I ask where you feel you belong?' asked Joseph, doubtfully.

'Exactly what I've often asked myself, young man. Born in Hamburg. Then exile in Paris. I suppose I belong to the disinherited,' said the invalid. 'I'll be a patriot when they have a place of their own.'

'You may wait a while for that, Herr Heine,' said another German voice at Joseph's side. It was Joachim himself. 'Come and see me tomorrow morning,' said the great violinist to the boy.

Joseph stammered something in reply, and Joachim smiled at his confusion.

'Here is my card,' he said. 'Will you find me?'

Joseph assured him that he would, and then looked back to the invalid.

'Is that Heinrich Heine, the poet?' he asked Joachim in a whisper.

'Certainly it is.'

'Then I must kiss his hand.'

Turning back impulsively to do so, Joseph bent low over the wheelchair.

The gesture charmed Heine, who stroked the curly hair of the young boy bent before him. 'Your music has a true lyric power,' he said. 'You cheer my heart.'

Joseph would have risen to go, but Heine seemed to have something he wished to say to him.

'Where does your mother live?' he asked.

Joseph had not seen Hannah for some time, and said as much with a pang of guilt. Heine nodded.

'Fifteen, are you? Well, it is the way. When I saw my mother after many years, she sat me down with a whole goose and oranges from Portugal and said, "You must be hungry." It is the nature of Jewish mothers: she thought I hadn't eaten since we last met.' Joseph was surprised, for he had not absorbed that Heine, too, was a Jew. The invalid saw as much.

'I did my best to escape,' he smiled, 'but I only succeeded in having the Jews dislike me as much as the Christians. So much for conversion. You are a fine young musician, and your generation – unlike mine – may be luckier.'

'Is your illness very serious?' asked Joseph.

Heine smiled at the innocence of the enquiry.

'My malady has been somewhat long drawn out. I don't recover from it, but it appears I don't die of it either.' He saw that Joseph's question had been completely sincere, and repented his frivolity. 'Some days I am very tired,' he said. 'I can hardly see out of my right eye.' He patted Joseph's hand. 'What will you do now?'

'Joachim will talk to me tomorrow.' Joseph's face lit up with happiness at the prospect.

'Have you more to learn?' Heine asked. 'I suppose it is so. Well, go now. And enjoy your life.'

A week or so later, back in Vienna, Joseph arranged to meet Becker at a café where Becker made a habit of eating in the early evening. He awaited Joseph at a table close to the dance floor, looking morose; he danced very little these days. He was sitting over a bottle of brandy, his face redder than usual. His hair was thinning over his scalp. There was a fat, rich cake on the table in front of him, which he had not attempted to eat.

'So, you want to leave me,' said Becker. 'Have you thought what that means? I have devoted these last five years to making you the violinist you are.'

'You have been very good to me,' said Joseph.

A waiter, hovering nearby, came to see if the boy wanted anything and Joseph ordered a glass of wine. He sat very upright on his chair, looking far more composed than he felt, and, as Becker was crouched over his brandy, Joseph seemed much the taller. Becker looked up at the boy slyly.

'Do you think you will make more money?'

Joseph flushed.

'It isn't the point. There is so much I need to learn. If I am to become the violinist I could be,' said Joseph.

Becker shook his head and poured himself another brandy.

The boy was fighting to keep a note of pleading out of his voice. Surely Becker, if he wished him well, must see what an opportunity it was to study with Joachim. He had been hoping to find some encouragement to take up his good fortune. But Becker was brooding along other lines.

'And what of the benefits I have given you?'

'In these last five years,' said Joseph directly, 'we have benefited each other, haven't we?'

'Very nicely put,' said Becker. 'Very nice.' He shrugged mournfully. 'I have laboured to no great end. Your success is the only fruit of these last five years.'

Joseph knew this to be true and, though he could have flattered Becker by reminding him of a few charming pieces he had written, instead said tactlessly, 'At least you have had the leisure for it.'

Becker's face purpled with fury. 'You ungrateful Jewish whelp,' he said. 'They say you should never trust a Jew. And now you give the story proof.'

'How is my religion relevant?' asked Joseph.

'I don't speak of religion,' said Becker. 'I have never seen any religion in you. I speak of race. You Jews are given the freedom of Vienna and, as soon as you can make your own way, you kick away the backs you have climbed on.'

Joseph was too startled by the attack to speak for a moment, and Becker's eyes sharpened with a sense of his advantage.

'Why do you think our tradesmen gather together to protest against the Jews? They take over their means of livelihood. You have as little scruple.'

Joseph thought of his mother in her hat shop, labouring every hour of the day either to please customers or to think of new designs, soothing Peretz when he came home.

'Jews work hard,' he said at last. 'They do well for that reason.'

'You make too much of a virtue of work.' Becker shook his head. 'There is more to life than work. We know that in Vienna.'

These words went home, and for some reason the laughing face of Sophie flashed across Joseph's mind.

'For a musician,' he said, 'there's no gap.'

'We Viennese understand how to live,' said Becker. 'Work is for the day time. You Jews do nothing else.'

Joseph flushed with anger. 'Then you may as well let me go. I want to be with people who love to work, not people who only work to live.'

'Go, go,' said Becker. 'Who is arguing?'

He sounded tired and defeated suddenly.

'Have you brought our contract?' asked Joseph.

Becker made a wry face, felt in an inner pocket and brought it out. 'Tear it up if you like,' he said.

'No,' replied Joseph. 'I want to do whatever is fairest. Isn't there a clause of release?'

'What rotten lawyers have you been talking to?' asked Becker, looking surly and still clutching the document in his hand.

'It is common sense. I am not a serf. No one can be tied for life, can they, in a civilized society?'

Joseph watched as Becker, thinking perhaps of his tailor's bill, paused and considered the matter.

'You must buy yourself out of it.'

Joseph had reached this point in his thoughts before their meeting, and had fixed upon a sum that would cover a year's earnings. Raised eyebrows immediately confirmed his guess that this was far higher than anything Becker had expected. Joseph did not care, even though he might now have to take help from Hannah and Peretz. He had pitched the sum high quite deliberately, not only to make sure that Becker's greed would lead him to agree, but also to make sure in advance that he need feel no guilt.

'You must be very confident in your future success,' said Becker, glaring.

Joseph bit his lip. He was gambling on himself, and he knew he was taking a risk. What he was doing might easily be a mistake. He was an artist, after all, not a business man. Only a surge of fury at Becker's sneering gave him the courage to press through with his plan. Anything was better than such humiliation, he thought defiantly. It was better to be free, whatever happened. Now one of Peretz's favourite sayings of Hillel helped him: 'If not now, when?'

'Young whelp,' said Becker again, but he opened out the contract and said, 'Write the sum for quittance here and when it is paid we will make an end.'

'Let us do it now,' said Joseph.

Becker stared at the cool, proud boy. Then he took the purse of money that was offered and tore the contract through with a single gesture.

Chapter Thirteen

ANTHONY NEWALL had been ungracious at first about his wife's decision to employ as a nanny the shy young girl introduced by Anton, but a week after Clara's arrival he was called away to Prague to advise the Embassy there on the practicalities of new railway contracts.

'I should be uneasy about leaving you in this condition,' he said to his wife as he prepared to mount the Embassy carriage, 'if you had no help.'

Jane received this mark of concern with a scowl. 'Well, I suppose you have your own business in Prague, too?'

'I cannot imagine what you mean,' said Anthony, kissing her lightly on the forehead.

For the rest of Jane's pregnancy, he was more often in Prague than Vienna.

Clara's presence in the household was therefore fortunate in many ways. Since Jane could afford little pocket money, she felt the least she could do in return for Clara's loving attention to the children was to help in her education. By this, Jane initially meant no more than a few social graces, but she soon recognized a mind as eager as her own. The girl learned English without effort, and Jane was soon teaching her French so that she could read Georges Sand. Jane also observed, as she struggled to practise the harpsichord, that Clara found it much easier than Jane did herself to count the rhythms as she turned the pages. Encouraged by Jane's puzzled persistence, Clara was soon trying her own hands at the instrument and Jane, who had no vanity about her own musical talents, was delighted to praise Clara's.

'You have more facility than I do,' she said, without a taint of envy in her fine face.

Almost without noticing, Jane and Clara became intimate friends.

Clara took her meals with the children for the most part but, as Jane's pregnancy grew heavier, she liked to have Clara join her for the evening meal. They ate simply and without fuss, and Jane vigorously expounded the importance of female education.

'My own mother thought of nothing but embroidery,' she said. 'And, in return, her husband neglected her shamefully.' She sighed. 'Which is not to say that cultivating one's mind is a way to ensure attention from a husband. What matters is to make life more than simply a matter of endurance.'

Clara drank in these ideas eagerly. Her first months with the Newalls were pure happiness. Not only had she been saved from kitchen drudgery, she was beginning to feel there was something valuable in her that was important to keep alive.

Jane was ill with childbirth fever after the birth of the child and, when she recovered, she was very weak. Clara pushed her daily in a wheelchair to the park, and read to her, too, as well as looking after the children. One evening, in some agitation, Jane suggested that Clara let one of the other servants put the children to bed.

'I want to talk to you,' she said. 'Will you take a glass of wine? I'm so unhappy. Do you know, you are the sweetest friend I have made in the whole city of Vienna?'

'You haven't tried very hard to make friends, then,' suggested Clara, pleased nevertheless.

'It's impossible to do it,' protested Jane. 'The local English ladies treat me as hopelessly bookish, and the Viennese think me some kind of freak because I don't take lovers. And I suppose they may be right, for never was a woman lonelier than I am.'

Clara wondered what to say to this, but she need not have hesitated, as Jane rapidly followed her own thoughts.

'Do you know I have never loved my husband?'

'Never?' laughed Clara. 'Then why did you marry him?'

The girl's laughter brought a faint half-smile to Jane's face in turn, and she tried to reply lightly.

'Well, I couldn't have Byron, could I? He was dead.' But her dark eyes and pale face soon resumed an alarming intensity. 'Look at me,' she said.

Clara looked at the long, aquiline face of her friend.

'I'm a little old for my husband. Or for any,' said Jane. 'And my father had no great lands or dowry. I wanted children.'

'These must often be considerations,' replied Clara.

'Now I don't know what to do,' said Jane, fretfully. 'If I were alone, I should leave and become a governess. But I cannot leave the children. Do you see what I mean?'

Clara saw clearly enough that Jane's agitation related to her husband, but her distress made no sense in the terms she was presenting it. After a moment's hesitation, she determined to speak frankly.

'I see you're lonely, and that your husband spends far too much time away from Vienna. But can this be a reason for leaving home? After all, if he's not here, he can't disturb you.'

'He *should* be here!' cried Jane.

'That's the trouble, really, isn't it?' said Clara, gently. She wasn't trying to be clever, only speaking her own thoughts. She was puzzled to know why Jane felt as she did.

Jane stared at her. 'You are right. I am deceiving myself. I want him to come back to me. What a hideous, humiliating business.' She laid a caressing hand on Clara's. 'Ah, my dear, what a wise head you have. I don't know how I managed without you. Even Anton no longer calls. I don't know why.'

'Wasn't there a card to say he was in Berlin?' asked Clara.

'Something of the kind. Well,' Jane sighed. She shook her head and pulled herself together briskly. 'Enough of myself. Your life has been so much harsher than mine. I'm quite ashamed to be so full of complaints.'

Clara smiled and her face lit up. 'There is a Hebrew prayer I remember. It is said at the Festival of Passover. It means—' She hesitated. '*It is enough*. Something like that. The Jews sang it when they crossed the Red Sea.'

'Goodness,' said Jane, intrigued. 'They were grateful even though they still had the desert to cross?'

'I can't remember exactly. I think the feeling was that one ought not to be greedy when there have been a series of miracles.'

'I am glad you are happy here,' said Jane quietly. And indeed she comforted herself for a moment with the thought that she had been able to offer refuge to her young friend. Exactly what life she had taken her away from had never preoccupied her much, but now she was curious.

'You have never discussed your childhood,' she therefore began.

'I can't,' Clara faltered. 'There is a strange blank . . . like a white cloud . . . over most of it.'

'Oh, not the details,' said Jane. 'But when did you come to Vienna? These days Jews pour in from every corner of the Empire.'

'I can't remember coming to Vienna. The Passover songs I overheard in Herr Shassner's house.'

'Did you live in one of those quaint wooden villages? And what language did you speak there? Did your father wear one of those strange fur hats and caftans which religious Jews preserve even through a Viennese summer?'

'It's not just the details,' said Clara flatly. 'I can remember nothing.'

Jane stared at her, but the open, direct look without the slightest attempt at ingratiation convinced her of the truth of Clara's words.

'Sometimes great shocks *can* have that effect,' Jane reflected. 'I lost my own mother when I was very young, and all I remember are the stories I was told about her. Were you not told anything?'

'The only relative I knew is dead,' said Clara.

'But your mother? The lady in the locket?'

Clara shook her head.

'There must be something.'

'Nothing. Nothing,' said Clara. 'My memories begin with Taborstrasse.'

'Be glad you escaped, then,' said Jane vigorously.

Some time after this, Anthony returned to Vienna, announcing that his tour of duty in Prague was over. Clara saw that Jane immediately began to look much happier.

Late one evening, when Jane had gone to bed, Clara happened to be in the hallway of the apartment as Newall came in through the door. It was immediately apparent, both in his face and voice, that he had been drinking. As she made to go up the stairs, he put out an arm to bar her way.

'What are you running away from? Not me, I hope?'

His hot, blue eyes and the smell of brandy on his breath set her heart beating with alarm.

'Let me go, please,' she said.

'You really are a pretty little thing,' he said, without

releasing her. 'Do you know some of you Austrian women are quite extraordinary. Indolent and at the same time as alert as greyhounds. Let me see . . .' With one hand he held her upper arm and with the other he traced the outline of her cheekbone with his forefinger. His flushed face, with its open, red circle of a mouth, was close to her own.

'I wonder what kind of creature you are,' he speculated.

'Please,' she begged him. 'Your fingers are bruising me.'

He laughed, and released her.

Clara rushed up the stairs as soon as he dropped her arm. She was in some confusion. Rather than going to her own room, she went softly into the nursery where the children lay asleep. The room was blue, with soft velvet curtains. The younger girl had fallen asleep with her thumb in her mouth. Clara bent over the child and kissed her. The sweet smell of the child's hair and the warm breathing which she hoped would comfort her instead stirred a further rush of panic. She was conscious of a terror which seemed to rise from some buried part of herself. She pushed the feeling away. In doing so, she had a sense of many times having pushed it away.

After a while, she went back to her own room. There, as she lay on her own cot, she determined to tell Jane nothing of what had happened – Jane was once again expecting a child, and terrified at the prospect of another confinement. Gradually, as Clara put the episode out of her mind, she drifted off to sleep. It was as if a huge, white featherbed had settled back into place.

A few days after this encounter on the stairs, an invitation for the Newalls came from the English Embassy. Clara brought the fine, square envelope into Jane as she sat drinking the lemon tea which had been recommended by a local doctor for flatulence. Jane opened the invitation, sighed, and shook her head.

'No, my dear. I cannot bear the thought of such an occasion.'

Anthony Newall lifted the heavily embossed card and smiled thoughtfully. 'Perhaps Clara would like to go?' he suggested.

Clara replied at once, 'I should not dare to go into such fine company.'

'Nonsense,' said Jane, with something of a return to her usual vigour. 'You are as well educated by now as any of the ladies likely to be there. Better than some. I can give you a dress that will suit.' She placed the silver-edged card before Clara on the small table. 'There will be music,' she said. 'Do go.'

It occurred to Clara in a flash that Jane imagined her presence might act as a brake upon her husband's activities, and that she was to be there in some sense as a chaperon.

'Yes, do, Clara, do,' persuaded Anthony Newall, without any hint of irony. 'I should like it very much.'

Clara looked down at the card before her. On it she saw that, to celebrate the end of the Crimean War, the Embassy was offering to entertain them with music of Brahms, played by a young violinist called Joseph Kovacs. Clara stared at the name. Could that really be the same young violinist who had lived close by in those sad slum flats in Leopoldstadt? She was very curious.

'Thank you,' she agreed. 'If you think it will be acceptable, I should very much like to go.'

'You shall count as an adopted member of the family. An adopted daughter,' said Jane.

And, indeed, Jane took a nearly maternal pleasure in dressing Clara for the occasion. She had a grey silk dress with light grey frills which she declared it was unlikely she would ever have the shape to wear again, and, when Clara put it on, exclaimed that she had never in any case looked so well in it as Clara now did.

The girl had a very slender waist and fashion plumped up her breasts so that their shape was clearly visible. The sombre thread of the bodice made Clara's skin look even whiter and her complexion clearer than ever. To complete the effect, Jane lent her a tortoiseshell comb so that some of Clara's hair was led to curl forward on her forehead, while the rest was caught up into a shining black coil on the top of her head. As Clara marvelled at the effect, Jane threw a black velvet cloak over her.

'You are Cinderella tonight,' said Anthony, as he offered her an arm and led her to the carriage.

Clara was excited and nervous as he handed her into the carriage and the coachman shut the door on them. They both sat back to be driven to the Inner City.

'Here's a jaunt,' said Anthony, rubbing his hands with the enjoyment of it, rather like a small boy at the prospect of fireworks. There was something engaging in the gesture, and Clara could not forbear to give him an enchanting smile, which brought out the dimples in both cheeks and made her black eyes sparkle.

'My God, you're a pretty witch,' he said, staring.

His gaze shifted to the place where her breasts showed under the new dress. Clara flushed and drew back into the corner of the carriage.

She was glad enough of his arm, however, at the entrance to the Embassy, where Vienna's notables made their way up the staircase to meet their own eyes in the huge Venetian mirror. Many of the men were in military dress, and their ladies, in deeply coloured velvets and silks, carried themselves like princesses.

If Clara was in awe of the audience assembled to hear this festival concert, there was one person there that night whose excitement was even more intense: Joseph's mother, Hannah. She had not been present before at so grand an occasion.

These days she dressed with style. She knew how to do so as elegantly as any lady there; some of them she might even have sold a hat or a handbag. Nevertheless, the occasion intimidated her, and she had avoided any hint of flamboyance. She had chosen to wear a pair of long kid gloves and a black cloak trimmed with lace. Yet she was unused to such company and there was a certain defiance in her carriage. Only the mad English, in Peretz's opinion, would let a street trader into their Embassy.

Peretz was pleased that his son should be invited to entertain these foreign gentiles, but he could see no pleasure in dressing up and trying to join in their celebrations. The concert hall was one thing; he could go there with his Taborstrasse friends. The English Embassy was another. He preferred to stay at home with his books, and have Hannah report on the occasion.

Joseph had arranged a seat for her, rather to one side and at the front. As Anthony led Clara to one of the rows reserved for Embassy staff, she passed Hannah and recognized her at once: her face was unchanged. Seeing her dispelled any doubt that it was her childhood friend Joseph about to play before this fine audience. Hannah, however, did not return her smile. There was little to connect the assured young lady who stood for a moment before her with the girl she had known. Hannah went on clutching her hands in her lap, with all her energies concentrated on the moment when the musicians would appear. Clara would have liked to remind her who she was, but instead some of the woman's tension transferred itself to her. Looking behind at the crowded hall, looking up at the columns and the chandeliers, her heart began to beat very fast, imagining the difficulty of performing before such a splendid audience.

Carrying their instruments, the musicians came out and took their places, to polite applause. The violinist was dressed with scrupulous care. His cravat was white, and his waistcoat charcoal brown. His hair was still as curly; his dark eyes sad; his mouth thin and wide. He bowed, and then smiled – not to the audience but to his fellow musicians. His face was transformed when he smiled. All melancholy left it then, and there was no mistaking the child that Clara remembered.

During the first movement of the Brahms quartet there was an odd stilling in the audience, as their casual pleasure deepened into excitement. The young soloist, for all a certain awkwardness in his stance, had such charm and gaiety. And then, as he began the slow, dark second movement, Clara felt tears coming to her eyes. The world was a beautiful and tragic place, and the music affirmed that knowledge. Joseph's fingers throbbed on the strings and released both beauty and sadness together.

With the last notes there was a moment's silence, as the audience took a measure of itself, and then applause broke out in which Clara joined so unselfconsciously that she beat her hands together until they hurt.

Joseph bowed formally and then looked up at the audience, recognizing their enthusiasm. Then he bowed again and acknowledged his fellow players with another shy smile.

Clara continued to clap her hands happily. Several of the audience had risen to their feet. At her side Anthony Newall shifted uncomfortably. Would this performance never stop? To his astonishment he saw that Clara's cheeks were wet with tears. He was even more surprised when she brushed them away and asked his permission to greet someone she knew. Newall could not imagine whom she could know in such an assembly, and watched with a frown as she went up to Hannah to introduce herself. Incredulously, Hannah's eyes went over the young girl as she received her congratulations.

'You must see Joseph,' she said.

The musicians were drinking in a little antechamber, their cravats undone. A certain jollity, very different from the mood in the decorous audience, pervaded the room. There was nothing in Clara's poised beauty to recall the child whom he had once befriended, but her good looks won Joseph's attention.

'My name is Clara,' she said and then bit her lip and dropped her eyes.

As he saw those dropped eyelids, suddenly he did remember the scruffy young girl whose unhappiness he had more than once comforted in Leopoldstadt.

'Of course I remember you. How good you are here. Did you enjoy the music?'

'It was the most beautiful I have heard,' she said. And she said it so directly, so simply, that he believed her.

'But how do you come to be at the English Embassy?'

'It would take a long time to explain,' she said ruefully, but at his insistence she began to do so.

As Hannah watched the two young people she experienced a quiver of jealousy. Together they looked like children and their interest in one another's lives excluded anyone else. Anthony Newall, too, was disappointed as he waited for Clara to return. With an ill grace he went home early to his wife, and left the carriage for Clara to follow him.

Chapter Fourteen

'WHY ARE YOU SO SAD, FRÄULEIN?'
Jane's younger daughter put one soft hand on Clara's hair, as Clara tied the big satin bow at the waist of her party dress. Clara met the serious grey eyes without a ready answer.

Ever since the evening she had heard Joseph play, melodies from the quartet had run through her mind, always with a certain melancholy. She could not say why. It was as if some hope she had not allowed herself before now ran in her veins; the hope of happiness. The beauty of the music itself warned her that such a hope was unlikely to come to fruition. And she could not even have said exactly what it was she was longing for, or whether her certainty of frustration made her miserable. Sad, yes; miserable, no. All this she could not explain to the intent face of the little girl who stared into her eyes.

'I am only dreaming,' she said.

Joseph had been wafted out of her sight. He was touring. To Venice, she heard. Then Rome. His life had an excitement she could barely imagine. In a way it was the excitement of his life, as much as anything else, that stirred her. Ungratefully, as she combed the little girl's hair, she knew her own life was dull and lustreless in comparison. Remembering the cold streets and the savage cook was no help. She was safe, she was comfortable, but she longed for something much more.

One evening, when Jane had gone to bed early, Clara sat at the harpsichord in the sitting room and tried to recall the painful beauty of what Joseph had played. The melody came easily enough, but the accompaniment was too difficult for her, and she settled into playing one of Schubert's songs, singing the while in a low voice. Almost unknown to herself, tears formed as she played. She was roused from her singing by a hand on her neck, and she started like a wild creature.

'No, no, don't stop,' said Anthony Newall, who had come in unobserved. 'You sing very prettily. I was enjoying it.'

He did not take his hand away from her neck. Her hands hung by her side. Her heart was pounding. She could not lift her fingers to the keys.

'You are so shy,' he said, and sat himself on the piano stool beside her.

She sat hypnotized, as a rabbit might be in the eye of an owl. When he put a hand to her hair, she flinched. He chuckled, and drew a line down the side of her face with his forefinger.

'Still so pretty,' he mused, his eyes fixed the while on the gap in her nightdress, where it was possible to make out the young, pert mounds of her breasts.

She drew her night garments closer around her.

'Anthony?'

There was a questioning call from the room above, and Anthony frowned. Clara jumped to her feet.

'Your wife heard you come in,' she pointed out rapidly.

He held the silk of the nightdress in his hands, and pulled at it roughly, almost without thinking, so that she could not make good her escape.

'You must not leave me so unsatisfied,' he muttered thickly.

'Anthony?'

Jane's voice came again, querulous now, even petulant. There were footsteps, too. Anthony released the garment.

'I am coming, dear,' he called back. 'Remember,' he said to Clara, 'next week we set off for Wiesbaden.'

The Wiesbaden trip was nominally for Jane's health. Doctors had advised the spa waters, and she was willing to give them a try, as long as it did not mean leaving Anthony behind, or her children, to whom she was much attached. Anthony put up less resistance to the trip than she had expected, and Jane admitted to Clara that she knew he had chosen that particular spa because there was a casino there.

'He may gamble a little,' she said, with shining eyes – she often had a light fever – 'but at least it will give him something to do. And these days he has learnt to be much more prudent.'

Clara privately feared that her own presence, necessary in order to give Jane any rest at all, might provide another danger which had not entered Jane's calculations. Once or twice she was on the verge of confessing as much.

Chapter Fifteen

WHEN RUDOLF VON MAYERBERG returned to Vienna, Anton expected him to make his presence felt at once in the Viennese theatre. Like the great Viennese playwright Franz Grillparzer, Rudolf had once been troubled by Metternich's censors. Anton attributed his silence of recent years to that brush with the police. Yet, although Rudolf continued to delight those who drank coffee at Neuners and the Central Café, no new work for the theatre had yet gone into production. Anton himself had industriously written several botched plays without being shown any of his friend's work.

One bright October day, when the sky shone sharp and blue behind St Stephen's Cathedral, Anton walked to his friend's house on Spiegelgasse and pulled the long brass bell on the wall. He was carrying two acts of his latest drama, and hoping for some encouragement to continue it.

Rudolf had just woken up.

'Can't read anything now, Anton. I'm late. I have to meet the manager of the Theatre on the Wien.'

'Is he going to put on your new play?' asked Anton excitedly.

'I haven't got a new play,' said Rudolf with an engaging smile.

Anton stared round his friend's crowded room, still

perfumed with the Turkish coffee that stood on the table. Every surface was covered with objects: candles, painted china, black and gold sculpture. There was a sombre green wallpaper and far too much furniture, mostly heavy walnut, but the ceilings were very prettily painted with pink and green flowers.

'Why don't you find a more convenient set of rooms?' he asked his friend.

'Exactly what my mother says,' replied Rudolf. 'She would like me to move back to the Herrengasse with her. But a man has to have some independence. Do you think this shirt will do?'

Anton said that it certainly would, and pressed his friend for more details of his appointment with the manager of the theatre.

'I hope he'll do something,' said Rudolf. 'I don't know what their plans are. You can come with me if you like.'

The offer was made carelessly. Rudolf could not imagine Anton putting the manager out by his presence; he was too docile, too full of admiration. The offer was made as a sign of favour, and Anton accepted it as such.

The Theatre on the Wien had belonged to Mozart's librettist, Emanuel Schikaneder, and though the first performance of *The Magic Flute* had actually taken place at another theatre, it was for Schikaneder that the present building had been built. The façade still showed him immortalized as Papageno. Beethoven's *Fidelio* had first been presented on that very stage, and some of the best drama of the years before the Revolution. To enter now, in the late morning when only those whose work was connected with the theatre were about their daily lives, was intoxicating.

The man whom Rudolf was to see was a bustling, energetic man, a Hungarian, Anton guessed, and he treated Rudolf without particular respect as he brought them into his office.

'You asked to see me,' he began. 'I haven't much time this morning. We are in rehearsal in fifteen minutes.'

'When we spoke yesterday at Demel's,' began Rudolf, 'you said you were interested in my work.'

The manager pointed to the wall, at a schedule for the coming year. 'This is our plan for the next season,' he said. 'You see how it is. What have you got for me?'

'I could have a new play,' began Rudolf. 'In a month or so.'

'Could?'

'It is not yet in its final draft,' admitted Rudolf. 'It is in my head, for the most part. But you spoke with some affection of *The Crippled Girl*.'

'Yes, as I said, very nice in its time,' said the manager. 'And we may do one of Franz Grillparzer's old plays. He is, after all, our greatest dramatist. But, otherwise, Rudolf, as a director, I'm not interested in revivals. What I want is the new, the young, the fresh.'

His eyes went over Anton speculatively for a moment, and Anton felt the colour come into his face.

'And if we can find them,' said the manager, 'we want operetta.'

'Operetta?' repeated Rudolf, stupefied.

'There is a wonderful new man in Paris, Offenbach. Have you heard his work?'

Rudolf said nothing. Then the manager stood up, and Rudolf and Anton stood also.

In a matter of moments they were outside, close to the fruit market from which came the heavy odours of autumn fruits in the October sunshine. Rudolf was shaking with humiliation.

'The little upstart. What does he know of Austria?

Offenbach is a little Jewish monkey. Only the French could enjoy him. What does this manager know of serious comedy? He's homosexual, of course.'

'Do you think so?' stammered Anton. He had not altogether absorbed the gibe at Offenbach's origins.

'Couldn't you see the way he looked at you? Damn you, Anton,' he said. 'I wish I had not asked you to accompany me.'

They took a carriage back to the First District and Rudolf continued to express his own sense of snub and rejection. After the first glass of wine, however, his anger had spread out more comfortably against foreigners controlling the arts and the press. And by the time they had reached their fried chicken and had begun to drink a second bottle of dry white wine, his animosity was entirely aimed at the introduction of new machinery into the textile industry which was putting good Austrians out of work.

He had forgotten to bring his wallet, and Anton paid for the meal.

It was something of a surprise to Anton when Rudolf von Mayerberg, after nearly forty years as a bachelor, determined on marriage. Rumour had it that the bride was not yet twenty and at the wedding Anton discovered her to be thin and pale, with a myopic appearance. She wore her hair very chastely in a bun. No one could have thought her pretty. There were whispers that she had once longed to enter the Church, and that her father had consented to the unsuitable marriage only through fear of never having grandchildren. No doubt Rudolf's ancient name had been another factor. For Rudolf, however, gossip could find no discreditable motive: Anna had little money of her own.

'Mother found her for me,' he told Anton. 'There's no mystery. I am marrying Anna because she loves me.'

His voice and face, so habitually ironic, made it impossible to read his words.

Married, however, he soon was, and after a time Anton visited the couple at their new apartment. Rudolf had moved into an old cobbled square near Fleischmarkt. The one redeeming feature of the square, as he pointed out to Anton, was the cherry tree that came into heavy blossom at the corner; it was the only sign of the seasons Anton could discern from the four panes of glass that overlooked the street.

His young wife ran the simple apartment in a plain, sensible fashion. There were leather chairs, firm tables and few ornaments, aside from relics of the country house which had once belonged to the Mayerberg family. Among these treasures was an ebony cross with a silver hanging Christ figure.

Anna was a believing Christian who wanted to live a good life and had always been convinced that Catholicism was the only true Church. Rudolf, for all his usual cynicism, was quite unperturbed by her innocent piety. Once or twice she even tried to convert Anton.

'Tell me,' she said one day, 'why don't you baptize? Is it some obstinate adherence to the beliefs of your fathers? I see no sign of it.'

Anton reddened and pointed out that he had no belief in Christianity either.

'Heine saw it as the ticket to Europe,' said Rudolf mildly.

'I hope he is mistaken,' Anton responded. 'I should prefer to enter Europe as a secular human being. It is a secular century.'

'But what of heaven? How will you enter there?' asked Anna.

Her low, persistent voice, plain face and obvious adoration of her husband all embarrassed Anton.

'I have no such aspiration,' said Anton shortly, 'having no belief in the existence of the place.'

'You may feel differently when the time comes,' said Anna.

For all her apparent softness, there was a steeliness in her response. She was a frail, bony woman, who had not shown signs of giving von Mayerberg a child, and Anton found something in her awkwardness alarming. It was Rudolf who changed the subject.

In most ways, Rudolf's life was not much altered by his marriage.

'Anna doesn't object to your spending so much time at Neuners Café?' asked Anton once as his friend escorted him to the door of the apartment.

'Anna understands me,' said Rudolf. 'And, by the way, I am thinking of a little holiday from Vienna. Would you care to join me?'

It seemed an unusual proposition from a recently married man, and Anton was not entirely sure what could lead Anna to be tolerant of it. Nevertheless, he found the suggestion flattering. They settled dates and as he left he received two contrary impressions: that his friend had come to depend very much on his young wife and at the same time needed desperately to get away from her. The girl reminded him strongly of someone, but it was not until he was climbing into his carriage the week before the spring trip that he suddenly succeeded in placing the elusive resemblance. Once he did, he was surprised he had not observed it immediately. Anna's voice and style, if not her actual appearance, recalled von Mayerberg's mother.

About the same time as Jane and Clara began to pack their bags and boxes for a week at the Hôtel de l'Angleterre, Anton and von Mayerberg set off in a carriage towards the same town. For all Anton's pleasure in Rudolf's conversation, the journey towards Wiesbaden was far from cheerful, however. Von Mayerberg was preoccupied, and inclined to respond rudely to questions. The weather was oppressive, and though it was spring there was something heavy in the air. Anton could not guess what it was that made his usually lively friend so sullen, but he supposed it had something to do with the letters that followed them daily from his wife Anna.

Their arrival in Wiesbaden suggested they were not likely to enjoy fine weather during their stay. The sky was heavy with unshed rain; Anton could feel the pressure of the rumbling thunder and longed for the release of a shower. As the carriage brought them to the entrance of their hotel, a song floated into his mind, a French song about a treacherous comrade in arms which he had heard on his trip to Paris. He, too, began to feel irritable.

Rudolf had booked rooms at the Hôtel de l'Angleterre, but, once he saw the guests, he was disenchanted.

'What have I come to?' he kept saying. 'How I hate the bourgeoisie.'

Anton could only remember his own relations, and wondered if Rudolf intended some comment on his family. Any sense of adventure began to evaporate.

'We're all bourgeoisie now,' he said. 'Let us find a good restaurant.'

Von Mayerberg's gloom deepened. 'I'm not hungry,' he said. 'You eat if you want to, but I have no stomach for it.'

Such indifference to food was unusual in von Mayerberg, and Anton wondered if his friend was ill.

'Let's see how you feel when you approach the tables,' he suggested without much optimism. He had only been in a casino once or twice himself, and had always found it a deeply dispiriting experience.

Rudolf's mood, however, changed from a brooding

unfriendliness to a kind of snappy lightness as soon as their carriage stopped in front of the casino. As they passed the doorman, he nodded as if Rudolf were a familiar figure. Rudolf showed none of Anton's curiosity about the seedy grandeur of the building. Nor did he spend time investigating the many salons. Instead, he walked directly to the room where roulette was being played. He moved with his usual heavy-footed nonchalance but Anton could not miss his mounting excitement as they approached the tables.

Clustered around these were about a hundred and fifty people, squeezed tightly together, the second and third rows pressing against those who were close enough to make bets. Von Mayerberg paused and surveyed the table before deciding where to take up a position. Two well-dressed men, who seemed to know him, made a space at the table, but he shook his head and moved on.

'They are police,' he told Anton, who had thought them merely spectators.

'Theft must be very easy here,' Anton supposed. The atmosphere did not please him. There was a peculiar reverence in it, almost a religious intensity, a devoted attention on the little bouncing ball, and the croupiers' cries. He disliked it. It was worse than any religion, this poor worship of Chance which denied all the ordinary laws of cause and effect. He said as much to his friend.

'Yes, it *is* foolery,' frowned Rudolf. 'Why do people do this? I don't think I will play tonight.'

But he sat down just the same. Casually, and just before the ball could stop in any hole, Anton watched him put a single coin on red. Rather to his surprise, von Mayerberg's bet was successful.

'Well, that's nothing,' said von Mayerberg. 'No damage done yet.'

Carelessly, he left both coins for another turn of the wheel, and won again.

Anton was already bored. 'Play these for me,' he suggested to his friend.

'Perhaps I shall lose them.'

'No matter,' said Anton, 'whether you lose them or I do.'

He preferred to walk about the room in search of some pretty young woman to liven up the proceedings, but though there were many ladies in silk crinolines, their elegant hair piled about their heads, none engaged his attention.

It was the voice of Anthony Newall that woke him from his mooching promenade around the salon.

'I didn't know you shared the vice,' he said, with a laugh, clapping his young friend on the shoulder.

'I'm only visiting,' said Anton, smiling.

'Jane is sitting in the other room,' said Anthony. 'Why don't you go and say hello? We've missed you.'

Seated at a small table he saw his English friend Jane, and another woman, dressed in dark green, whom he half recognized. Anton was delighted to pause and ask if he could join them.

'My dear, what a pleasant surprise,' said Jane.

She looked rather unwell. Her neck had a faint mottling, and her colour had risen uncomfortably in her cheeks. Nevertheless, the smile that she turned on him was still charming.

'So, you still have the same helper,' said Anton in his best English, confirming after a moment's scrutiny that the girl at Jane's side was indeed Clara. 'I see she has grown into a beauty.'

Clara smiled and suggested that she had been in service so long that she was in danger of becoming an old maid.

The turn of phrase, and the rapidity of the English – which

he had not guessed she would follow – astonished Anton, and he looked at her closely. He had spoken no more than the truth, though he had uttered it lightly. Clara's face would have taken his attention even if he had known neither woman.

'And where are your children?' he enquired of Jane, puzzled.

'They're asleep in the hotel. They'll be well enough for an hour or so. And I wanted Clara to keep me company. I am here for the waters,' explained Jane. 'It's my husband who is here for the tables.'

'And is he a fortunate gambler?' asked Anton.

'Are there such gamblers?'

'My friend,' said Anton, 'is winning at the moment.'

'Oh, poor man,' said Jane.

Anton was puzzled.

'Luckily, my husband always loses the amount he allows himself very quickly,' said Jane, 'and that's that. Winning at first can be fatal. Is your friend wealthy?'

'Not really,' admitted Anton. 'He comes from an important family, but their wealth has dispersed over the generations.'

'Then in all conscience you should intervene,' said Jane. 'But I doubt if you will be successful. Urge him away from the tables while there is still time.'

'Come and help me do so,' suggested Anton politely, his eyes the while on Clara.

'I can hardly move these days,' said Jane, a little petulantly. Anton guessed she had intercepted his look.

'Go with Clara. See if you can perform some kind of rescue,' suggested Jane.

Clara smiled and shook her head. Seeing her reluctance, Anton said that he would return after inspecting his friend's case.

He found von Mayerberg had moved to a comfortable armchair hard up against the table. To Anton's surprise, he seemed to have a considerable pile of winnings, in both gold coins and bank notes, in front of him. His forehead was white and sweaty, and he made no sign of observing his friend's return.

The little ball flew round the wheel, began to bounce over the notches and at last the croupier called out coolly, 'Zero.' Von Mayerberg had won again.

A little cheer rose from a group of people pressing around him and following his bets.

'Well,' Anton said, 'you do seem to have done well. Perhaps you should gather your winnings and we could have something to eat?'

His friend turned a blind face up to him. 'I can't leave yet.'

Anton frowned and said, 'Surely this is the time to leave, when you are winning.'

'You're right, of course,' muttered von Mayerberg. 'I will certainly do so.' But he continued to sit where he was, and as the little ball flew past he put on another bet. This time he lost.

'You see?' said Anton, depressed. 'Look. Count what you have, and when you see how much it is you will be pleased to leave with it.'

'Go away,' said von Mayerberg hoarsely. 'You don't bring me luck. I can feel it.'

As soon as he said those words the crowd pressing round them turned towards Anton with hostility.

'You heard what he said.'

'You are spoiling his chances.'

'All right,' said Anton, surprised by this, and faintly hurt. He wandered back to Jane and Clara, and wryly reported the failure of his intervention. They laughed at his crestfallen air.

'Your charm will have to do the trick,' he suggested, holding out a hand to the girl.

She did not take his hand, but she stood up, apparently still reluctant to leave Jane's side.

'Don't be afraid,' he reassured her, amused at her hesitation. 'We shall do no more than walk across to the tables and then I will bring you back.'

'I don't like to leave Jane,' said Clara, and her eyes met his with so unfrightened a directness that he saw her concern was genuine.

'Is she very ill, then?' he said, with a little pang, as they walked away together.

'She's in danger,' said Clara gravely. 'She should not, of course, be having this child at all.'

'Is it due?' asked Anton nervously.

'Not until next month,' said Clara.

'Do you know a lot about such matters?' he asked.

'Only what I've seen since I've been with the family.'

'It must be three years,' he calculated.

'Yes. And Jane has three times carried a child.'

Again Anton was struck by the naturalness and the air of equality she assumed without any kind of affectation.

Bearing in mind his reputation for ill-luck, Anton approached the table this time from the opposite side to his friend. At first glance, he was relieved to see that von Mayerberg's winnings appeared to have increased rather than diminished. He also saw that his friend's manner had changed, and that he now seemed to be betting much more wildly. Even as he watched, von Mayerberg pushed half of his pile in a flutter of conviction on to the black. He kept his face downwards, hardly looking at the ball as he did so. The ball clattered its way round, and then a little cry went up from the table. Von Mayerberg had won again.

'Rudolf,' called Anton urgently.

There was no response. Indeed, von Mayerberg gave no sign even of having grasped his good fortune, except that he gave out two gold coins to young men at each side. Even to do this, he did not raise his head from its dropped position. It was as if he feared any movement would break the spell.

'Rudolf,' said Anton again, irritably.

Blank-faced with inner concentration, his friend at last raised his head and looked across the table, responding to the voice but without any sense of his friend's presence. As he did so, a startled look went across Clara's face, and she said, 'But I know him.' Her young face had gone ashen pale.

'Really?' asked Anton, intrigued.

There was no recognition in von Mayerberg's face.

'How could your paths have crossed, I wonder?'

Clara made no reply.

'I can't remember,' she said, after a pause.

Anton made a little impatient noise of incredulity. 'You cannot recognize and not recognize at the same time, can you now?' he asked.

'It must have been a long while ago,' she said hesitantly.

'Perhaps you are mistaken?'

Once again he met the full force of those dark eyes, and he was struck by her inability to say what was convenient.

Another little cry went round the table and distracted him. Von Mayerberg was staring down with stunned disbelief. His next stake had removed half of his winnings at a turn. It was as if he had woken from a dream. He looked up as if suddenly aware of Anton at the other side of the table.

'My dear friend,' he said. 'You cannot imagine what a night this has been.'

'Let me come and speak with you,' said Anton, and the crowd parted to let him join his friend.

In that moment, Clara was gone.

*

'Is something wrong?' asked Jane, as the girl returned to her side.

'I'll be all right,' said Clara, shaking her head.

'I should be more at ease myself if we were at the hotel listening for the children,' sighed Jane. 'And I confess I am tired.'

Clara saw that she was, even as she tried to fathom the source of her own distress. She did not understand why the sight of von Mayerberg's huge, sweaty face had set her heart beating so uncomfortably. There was an inexplicable sickness just under her ribs. Yet, try as she might, she could not recall the man; she racked her brain to remember if he had been a visitor at the Shassners' house. He could hardly have entered her tenement life in Leopoldstadt.

'He is charming, the young Shassner boy, don't you think?' asked Jane.

'I had hardly thought of him,' said Clara, with some surprise.

And indeed she had not. Falteringly, she began to try and explain to Jane what preoccupied her, but Jane was looking round for her husband and eager to leave the room.

'You really don't look well,' she agreed. 'Let's go now. My shawl? There. Did you say Anton's friend was still winning?'

Clara's colour had begun to come back to her face, and she adjusted herself to putting Jane's needs first.

'Let me carry your bag,' she said firmly.

The Newall family had taken several adjoining rooms in the hotel, and after Jane and Clara had gone in to confirm the maid's primly voiced opinion that the children slept like angels, Jane decided to go to bed almost immediately, although it was not yet nine in the evening. Clara helped her to undress, since her heaviness made her clumsy, and at last she tucked Jane beneath the covers as if she were a child herself. The exertions of the day had tired Jane, but she seemed disposed to talk of Clara's troubles as she settled back into her bed.

'I have never seen you so pale,' she observed, her grey eyes going over the girl's face.

'I think I shall be well enough when I am resting and reading,' said Clara, forcing herself to laugh.

She took Jane's hand to reassure her, and Jane smiled gratefully.

'You know,' said Jane, 'I hardly think of you as a servant. More as a sister. If anything worries you, it concerns me too.'

'I know,' said Clara, softly.

'You should take some brandy as a cordial.'

Her friend was lying deep in her pillow, and even as she offered help she looked far more in need of it herself.

'Rest now,' said Clara, holding Jane's hand as her eyes closed.

In a moment or two, and without any further requests for confidence from Clara, Jane was asleep.

Undressed herself, and ready for sleep, Clara did not find it easy to settle down to the English book she had left open by her bed. She would have liked to soothe herself with music. Instead she opened the curtains of the bedroom and stared out at the dark, wet trees. These were black and twiggy against the sky. A watery moon travelled through fast-moving clouds. As she watched, she was surprised to hear a tap on her bedroom door.

Opening it, she made out the figure of Anthony Newall. He looked perfectly sober, however, and after a moment's alarm she was relieved to hear him say:

'Jane said you had been unwell. She sent me to bring you a nightcap.'

'Thank you, but I need nothing,' said Clara.

She shook her head in a smiling refusal, but he entered the room nevertheless, carrying a bottle of Armagnac and two glasses.

'You look unaccountably fragile,' he said cheerfully. 'You have had some shock, Jane says.'

Clara pulled the lace gown around her more closely.

'Will you confide in me?' His face looked open and friendly. 'It may be with my rakish, worldly ways I can help,' he said. He had set down the tray and poured two glasses before she could complain further.

'Now drink this,' he insisted. 'Don't look so suspicious. You will sleep the better for it.'

'There is really nothing to tell,' she said. 'If you want to help, the best thing would be to leave me to recover.'

'Come now,' he said. 'If I had found you asleep that might make sense, but something clearly continues to disturb you or you would hardly be out of your bed and wakeful when the children have you up at an unconscionably early hour every morning. What is there to recover from?'

'The absurdity,' said Clara, 'is that I hardly know.'

She took up the glass he had poured, gratefully, and the liquid soothed her the more quickly since she had eaten almost nothing all evening.

'I promise not to behave like a horrified employer,' he said. 'You recognized Anton's friend, Jane says?'

'Yes,' said Clara.

'Well, I gather he lost all the money he has in the world and is in another corridor of the hotel being calmed by poor Anton.' He laughed. 'Tell me how you know him.'

'I don't really *know* him,' said Clara. 'At least I don't know why his face is so familiar.'

'If it were anyone but you,' said Anthony, 'I should laugh,

but I doubt if you have been earning a little money on the side by peddling your beauty in the Graben.'

He put his hand affectionately on her arm, and Clara shifted slightly away from him.

'You say Jane sent you?'

'Of course,' he said. 'She was sorry not to be able to help more herself.'

Clara sank into the chaise-longue which filled one side of her small room, and allowed him to refill her glass.

'Now,' he said, his sharp blue eyes watching her intently. 'Tell me everything. He seems quite old.'

'Almost forty,' she said.

'An aristocrat, I gather.'

'Yes.'

He burst out laughing. 'Anton tells me he is one of the finest writers in Austria, that Goethe or someone similar praised his work.' He came and sat next to her on the chaise-longue. 'Well, now,' he said, 'are you feeling a little better?'

In truth, the brandy had helped, and as it worked it was as if some kind of shutter began to close over the blackness she feared. She began to wonder whether Anton was right after all, and that she had only imagined an acquaintance.

'Perhaps I am disturbed for nothing,' she smiled.

He perceived the change in her mood, and the return of the elusive dimple to her cheek.

'Ah, my dear, if you only knew how I admire you,' he said suddenly, seizing her shoulders and staring into her eyes. 'It isn't only your beauty – I'm not the brute you think me. I have listened to you play the music poor Jane stumbles over. Can't I persuade you to give me a chance to look after you?' His breath was hot upon her cheek.

'Let me go,' she said.

But he held her fast, and the wrap fell from her shoulders.

'You mistake me, you know,' he said wistfully. 'I mean you no harm. All I want is a chance to look after you as you deserve.'

'You are hurting me,' Clara pointed out, remaining as still as she could, and hoping to dart away from him as soon as he released her. He slackened the grip of his fingers, without allowing her to move away.

'Won't you let me love you?' he begged. 'You will do Jane no harm by it; she has no interest in loving me herself; I always feel our intimacy is an invasion she cannot welcome.'

'Please don't tell me anything about such matters,' said Clara angrily, struggling a little now, and afraid of the blank black look growing in the eyes he fixed upon her. Her anger fired him, and he bent to kiss her deeply on the lips. Clara tore her mouth away, but her resistance seemed to destroy what remained of Newall's self-control, and he kissed her again, first on her neck and then on her throat, and began to fumble at her night clothes, mumbling the while, 'so lovely, so lovely'. His full weight now pinned her so that she was powerless to move, and his hands tore at her night garments while his leg forced its way between her own. His breathing became stertorous as he felt for the hem of her nightgown. An involuntary cry of alarm left her lips, as he began to open his own garments.

'Please don't, please!'

'You will wake her,' he muttered. 'Don't scream. Just let me—'

He had managed to jerk her nightdress upwards and she could feel the warmth of his naked body against her stomach as he forced her legs apart. But even as she struggled she became aware of another presence above his shoulders. Jane stood in the doorway. For a moment Clara felt relief, but the fury in her friend's face soon dispelled any sense of rescue.

'You slut!' shouted Jane. 'You treacherous and disgusting

slut. After all the goodness I have shown you. You take your drunken pleasure at night, do you? And how long has this been going on, while I treated you as a sister?'

Clara turned wildly to Anthony for defence, but he was shamefacedly adjusting his clothes.

'Tell her,' she demanded. 'Tell her!'

But Anthony only hung his head like a guilty thing.

'Pack your things,' said Jane, her voice bright with hatred. 'I have been very foolish. Pack your things and leave in the morning. I do not want to set eyes on you again.'

'This is cruelly unfair,' said Clara.

The thought of losing her only friend for the moment outweighed the threat of lost employment. Jane laughed bitterly.

'I shall give you a fair reference,' she said.

Then she left the room and, after a moment's pause, Anthony followed her.

Von Mayerberg lay on his back on the hotel bed. He had not undressed, but all his clothes were unbuttoned: he simply lay on the top of the coverlet with his clothes open, looking fat and out of control.

'It is over,' he muttered. 'I don't want to talk. I don't want to move.'

Perplexed, Anton came and stood by his bed.

'I am finished,' von Mayerberg repeated. 'And I deserve to be. I am a waster. A waster of my substance.'

It seemed impossible either to reply to the muttering or to ignore it and, after a time, Anton sat down on a chair and drew it up to his friend's bed.

'This has happened before, then?' he asked.

The question was voiced without any thought of reproach, but the words made his friend's huge body squirm into a new position as if salt had been thrown on to a worm.

'Yes. To my shame. It has happened, but never on such a scale. Now I am ruined.'

Anton, not knowing what else to do, continued to sit and watch. He was exhausted himself, but sleep seemed impossible in such a crisis. 'Shall I find you a glass of cold water?' he asked.

Von Mayerberg shuddered and tossed. Anton frowned. He still had no idea how large a sum was involved. Tentatively, and not wishing to cause pain, he enquired. The question seemed to calm his friend immediately. His eyes opened, and he replied at once.

'I pledged what is left of the family estate. It is gone. Now I have nothing. We have nothing. Anna. Poor Anna.'

At the thought of this, his eyes closed again. He turned on his side and began to sob uncontrollably into the pillow.

'But, in practical terms,' said Anton as quietly as he could, so as not to distress his friend further, 'what is the amount?'

Von Mayerberg named the sum. Anton paused, in some surprise. It was a great deal more than his own father allowed him to spend in a year.

'You see? I am ruined,' said von Mayerberg 'And there is nothing I can do.'

'Perhaps,' began Anton, 'if you began to work again.'

'Don't say it,' begged von Mayerberg. 'I haven't written a play in ten years, as everyone knows. If I had the courage of my ancestors, I would take my own life.'

'I suppose I could raise the money,' Anton said after a moment. 'But it's not very clear to me how you could ever repay it.'

Von Mayerberg's eyes opened again. 'Well, I could let you have the revenue of my estates in the East. Since I did not own them, I haven't lost that money. It would take some years, but I suppose . . .'

'Yes. I see,' said Anton.

He had no wish to enter into any such transaction. He had always loathed the lending of money, and most of the anti-Semitic remarks he had heard in his life had been directed against that practice. Nevertheless, he could hardly let his friend down in his troubles.

'I will take no interest,' he said, more to himself than to von Mayerberg.

Von Mayerberg looked incredulous, not at this proposed restraint but at the possibility of rescue.

'You mean you can really find so much money?'

'Yes,' said Anton wearily. 'I can redeem the pledge for you when we return to Vienna. And if you make over your revenues at the same time, that will be an end to the matter.'

'I can't thank you enough,' said von Mayerberg.

Anton felt a brooding sense of doom about the whole arrangement, as if the whole tenor of their friendship had changed.

The next morning, early, Anton paid the hotel bill, sent a reassuring note to Anna von Mayerberg and was just sending the porters up to the bedroom when he became aware of Clara standing by two small cases in the hall.

'Are you leaving so soon?' he asked in surprise.

'Yes,' she said. She looked as if she had been crying.

'Alone?' he asked.

She nodded.

'Where are you going?'

She looked him frankly in the eyes, her head held proudly, even though there were evident signs of distress.

'You will hear soon enough,' she said. 'So I may as well tell you. I have been dismissed.'

He was astonished. 'But I thought you were so close to Jane?' he enquired.

Her lip trembled. 'Yes.'

Anton's curiosity was aroused and he felt a little responsible too, though it was nearly three years since he had brought the young girl to his friends for refuge.

'Have you had breakfast?' he asked therefore.

'No,' she said.

'Let me buy you a bowl of coffee before you go,' he suggested.

His spirits, which had been much lowered by his dealings with von Mayerberg, had begun to revive a little. Over breakfast, Clara told him her story. She told it without drama, almost as if the shock had numbed her responses, but the blackness of her eyes told another story. All night she had wept over losing Jane's friendship, her mind turning over plans and possibilities without a thought of sleep. She drank the coffee now but, although she accepted the golden bread for which the hotel was famous, she only crumbled it on her plate as she talked.

Anton listened politely. He did not believe her story and supposed Newall to have been making love to her for some considerable time. It was surprising in an Englishman, but then he had heard hints of such behaviour in other connections many times from Jane, and Clara was certainly a beauty. Men had lost their heads over far less interesting prey.

'Don't look so anxious,' he reassured her, for all his scepticism about her tale. 'I will find you a room and you will manage very well.'

His friendly words, and perhaps even more his smiling acceptance of her situation, seemed to go some way to restoring a more normal expression to her pale face. Blood came back into her cheeks and to her lips.

'I thought I could give language lessons,' she faltered.

'So you shall,' said Anton.

Privately, he thought she would have no need to do anything so arduous. The girl was beautiful and reasonably

well educated and would soon be courted in Vienna, he had
no doubt of it. He began to think it would be very pleasant
to have such a pretty young friend in Vienna.

'You will find a prince,' he smiled.

Her own mouth was not yet ready to smile, though it was
a relief to feel she was not, after all, to starve in the streets.
Her full underlip trembled as she tried to thank him. Seeing
as much, Anton felt an unexpected flicker of desire at the
very core of his being. I must have her, he thought to
himself.

Chapter Sixteen

ANTON HAD DETERMINED to raise the money for his friend's debts by selling Dutch property that had come to him through a legacy of an aunt in Amsterdam. It was the only way he could hope to escape the vigilance of his father's professional eye, and he was well aware that his father would not approve of the transaction. He was far from happy about it himself. Von Mayerberg's wife Anna, in complete ignorance of how very much she ought to be grateful to him, had become instead remote and even a little hostile.

Meanwhile, Minna's Uncle Elias came to stay with the Shassners on a visit from Berlin. Elias was a little younger than Minna's dead father, fashionably dressed in charcoal grey with a single diamond tie pin in his green cravat, and always scented with lavender. A bachelor himself, Elias was particularly fond of his only nephew. In his youth he had taken aromatic Chinese tea at the salon of the hostess Rahel Varnhagen and there met Humboldt and imbibed a respect for Goethe. On this visit to Vienna he rose early, looked round the art galleries with great seriousness and marvelled at the fecklessness of the Viennese. He was first and foremost a shrewd businessman, but he liked talking to Anton.

'Did you hear of the meeting between Goethe and Heine?' Anton asked one day. 'I believe Goethe behaved pompously.'

'Heine had the temerity to address him as an equal. They say he even claimed to be writing another version of Faust,' said Elias. 'Of course the meeting went badly.'

'My sympathies are all with Heine.'

'Naturally,' said Elias. 'In that story he is the son and Goethe is the father. I should be surprised if you thought differently at your age.'

Emboldened by Elias's interest, Anton shyly confessed the literary aspirations he had not confided in his mother. He even showed him articles he had written under an assumed name. Elias was surprised to find them so outspoken.

'Is there no more censorship, then, in Vienna?'

'Oh, there is,' said Anton. 'But it is like everything else in Vienna: totally inefficient. Some days the censor kills a story in one paper, but it appears in another. You soon get the hang of what attracts attention and what does not.'

'The newspaper is an art form, then,' said Elias.

When Elias left, Natan Shassner was mildly relieved, though he could not have said exactly why. That morning he took breakfast with his wife on the balcony of their bedroom rather later than usual.

'There's something I want to discuss with you,' said Minna.

Natan looked up from his copy of *Neue Freie Presse* and smiled encouragement. 'What's that?'

'There are many newspapers in Vienna now,' she said.

'Certainly there are. And I see no sign that the Emperor is planning to close them down,' said Natan mildly.

'You must have noticed that several newspapers have owners who made their money in industry.'

'I have, and indeed we know some of them.'

Minna guessed that by now her husband had a shrewd idea of her tack. 'Not all of them are successful. I know of at least one that would be happy to sell out to a new owner. Could we purchase it?'

'This is a strange fancy. You don't usually take an interest in business affairs,' he pointed out.

'It would give Anton a purpose in life,' she said, her eyes shining. 'He would work so hard if he could find something he cared about.'

'You need experience to run a newspaper,' said Natan. 'What experience does Anton have, other than drinking in a coffee house? What makes you think he would be even ordinarily competent?'

'He writes well,' said Minna. 'He has serious convictions.'

'Has he? We must hope he keeps the most dangerous to himself.'

'He has great enthusiasm,' said Minna.

Natan doubted it, and wondered if it were his own fault. He was unsure. He had wanted to give his son a set of principles but knew he had failed to do so. Anton dislikes what I do, he thought glumly, and yet he does not know what to do himself. More resentfully, he thought of Minna. You have made him into a boy, he thought with distaste. A charming boy, perhaps, but one who may never become a man. No doubt Anton's crippled hand had made her over-protective, but Natan knew that she took from her son as much as she gave.

'A newspaper can lose a great deal of money if it goes wrong,' he said now. 'At the moment I'm developing textile mills in Bohemia. One can't do everything at once.'

Minna leant forward, as if she had been expecting as much. 'I don't want to burden your resources. I know you are committed. But I could go to Uncle Elias for capital. He likes Anton. And he has no children of his own.'

'You have talked to Elias about this plan? Before talking to me?' Natan was angry at what he felt as disloyalty. For a moment the history of their marriage lay between them.

'It's not appropriate to go behind my back like that. And

I won't be bullied, even if your family is wealthy. You must understand: I need to make up my own mind.'

'Please, Natan,' she murmured. 'I would not ask except for Anton. The boy needs you to believe in him.'

'How can I do so?' growled Natan. 'What does he do? He travels about the world in search of entertainment.'

'He needs something to put his hand to, that's all. It won't be such a risk. Look – put in an editor. Let me find half the backing.'

'I will talk to Anton about it,' said Natan. 'These things should be arranged face to face between father and son.'

'Yes, Natan,' said Minna. 'Talk to him.'

So Anton and his father talked, and a deal was arranged. Anton had no wish to have his father's eye on the protection he wished to offer Clara just at this juncture. Accordingly, he found her rooms in the Sixth District, just outside the wall of the city, some way from the area of gay young ladies kept as pets by Viennese men of means. This decision, though entirely self-interested, Clara found both tactful and considerate: to Anton's consternation, she expressed her gratitude by kissing him on the cheek and calling him her elder brother. He received the compliment rather sourly.

Chapter Seventeen

CLARA'S ROOMS WERE soberly furnished but spacious and light. She woke early to the sound of birds, and brilliant sunshine flooded her bed, since she liked to leave her curtains open. From her window she could see the first green leaves on the birch trees, and clouds of white apple blossom. After she had eaten her modest breakfast, she enjoyed walking through the washed streets.

Workmen, then pulling down the walls that separated the inner city from the Sixth District and shoring up the buildings on either side, looked curiously after the eager, pretty girl who seemed without coquetry and yet had none of the protection of the daughter of a respectable family. Her position was, as she knew, anomalous. What she needed was a livelihood.

From her kitchen window, since the apartment ran from the front of the building to the back, she could see the street where men in the early morning sunshine, well dressed and careless, looked into the windows of the shops beneath her. She could see the flowers being set out in the flower shop opposite. There were women, too, young ones, elaborately dressed, and others more dour: a lady in black walked by sometimes with a stick and paused to glare at a group of the younger women.

For all Clara's loneliness, she was too badly shaken by her sudden dismissal to look for friends. She missed the children. She missed the eager conversations she had enjoyed with Jane, and the books they had shared. In her three years with the Newall family she had unconsciously picked up the aspirations of a young English woman who longed for equality, and had no idea where to look for similar attitudes in the Viennese society around her. Anton's offer of assistance seemed her one piece of good fortune.

Once Anton had grasped how readily Clara responded to English literature, he saw it might be easy to help her. He had a young cousin, Sarah, who, as he could not but be aware, had always admired him. She had deep-set eyes, a narrow face and imperfect skin, but her voice was warm and she was intelligent and good-natured. So far, for all the likely size of her dowry, she had attracted no suitor who interested her. Her passion in life was English literature – Sir Walter Scott above all – and she wanted to learn a more colloquial English which would help her to read the authors she loved. Anton directed her to Clara, and found other young ladies willing to pay well for lessons, which they took in the comfort of their own homes. Anton had reckoned this would be a clever way of subsidizing Clara's living expenses without directly offering her money. To his astonishment, she took the work exceptionally seriously, putting so much care into it that the girls began to suggest her as a tutor to other families. She was soon able to pay her own rent, and even to invite Anton to take an occasional supper with her.

Anton was drawn to Clara sexually in a way he did not altogether understand. She was entirely frank and trusting, and without the slightest hint of coquetry, but her very glance stirred his desire. It was not only her voluptuous beauty: there was something erotic even in the childlike perfection of her skin. The brotherly and affectionate relationship that had grown up between them was far from the one he had intended.

'The truth is,' said one of his friends, 'you are becoming sentimental.'

Anton flushed and denied it vigorously.

For her part, Clara would have been happy enough but for one thing. About once a week, for no apparent reason, she had begun to wake from a recurrent nightmare with her limbs wet and her heart pounding.

The dream began in many different ways. Sometimes she would find herself in a dark street between tenement buildings, near a canal. There was a smell of weeds and something fouler. Sometimes she would be led up stone stairs, listening to the click of heels on the steps like the clicking of a clock. As she approached, there was a heavy mahogany door and a brass handle, then a richly coloured room. That was when her blood would begin to bang in her ears with terror and she would wake with a shriek to find herself in her own bed. The extremity of the terror, which left her pale young limbs running with sweat, was hard to explain. After a time she would get up and walk around the room, and the fear would pass.

Once, over an early supper with Anton in a restaurant near the Graben, she tried to explain her troubled nights, and he was pleased to be taken so intimately into her confidence. He remembered his own fevered dreams of the preceding night, in which, shamefully, Clara's pale and beautiful face had bent to his thighs.

'Does nothing more happen?' he probed.

'Nothing. I look down and see my own body.'

'Naked?' he enquired, his own excitement mounting as he tried to enter her imagination.

'A child's body,' she said, shaking her head.

'You should not live alone,' he said then, putting a hand over hers.

She did not withdraw her hand but she gave no sign of being comforted. She stared straight ahead of her.

'You cannot have company in your dreams,' she pointed out. 'I should still be alone in my sleep.'

'But perhaps you are afraid because there is no one to protect you?' he suggested. 'Dreams must tell us something.'

'Must they?' Her sprightliness returned. 'Perhaps they are warnings, then, as poets and seers have always told us. But, of course, we cannot understand their language.'

'You are being warned,' he said severely, 'not to remain a child.'

She understood well enough, he decided, but he felt the unresponsiveness of her hand and took away his own. He abandoned his attempts to enter her thoughts.

'Would you like to go to a theatre?' he asked her.

'Oh, yes,' she said, her face coming to life at once. 'I should like that very much.'

Anton thought how very much he would like to see her lovely face light up with another kind of pleasure.

Chapter Eighteen

ANTON WAS SITTING WITH a pretty young
actress under the trees at his favourite Grinzing restaurant on a warm evening in late August when a figure in
full dress uniform strode towards him. After a moment's
surprise, Anton recognized his old friend Max Kallman,
whom he had not seen since his student days.

Max was dressed in a blue tunic over white trousers; a
uniform which made him look as brilliant as a kingfisher: the
colour of the tunic brought out the icy sharpness of his eyes.
He was also wearing the compulsory hedgehog haircut,
which suited his small, neat features admirably. The army
was not a career Anton would have expected Max to follow
after his conscription for a year when University studies
ended, but his enlistment explained why he had not been
seen around the cafés of Vienna.

'Join us,' said Anton, and Max did so, his eyes running
appreciatively over the actress at Anton's side, who dropped
her eyes under his bold stare.

Max held the rank of Major, no doubt as a result of his
family connections.

'You abandoned University life, I see.'

'That was hardly difficult,' said Max cheerfully. 'The
Faculty of Science was not pressing its invitations upon me,
for all my father's eminence.'

'And the theatre did not tempt you?'

'Endlessly,' said Max, his eyes once again on the actress, who coloured prettily. 'But most of what I loved in the theatre remains available. Girls like to see a man in uniform.'

Max's broad shoulders and shining face were indeed arousing a good deal of interest in the actress at Anton's side, who bent forward to ask impudently:

'Well, and have you been decorated for bravery?'

'I was fortunate enough to escape death on the battlefield once or twice,' Max replied carelessly. 'Let us order some more wine.'

The small orchestra had begun to play one of the favourite Strauss waltzes of the season. Anton waved to a waiter and then said mildly:

'You are very sanguine about the dangers of a military life. I am told the Emperor himself was appalled by the battle of Solferino.'

'I am part of a peacetime army,' said Max, grinning. 'It's a wonderful life. In Vienna everybody loves us. What are you doing these days?'

'I am a scribbler,' said Anton.

'Ah yes, I think I heard as much,' said Max. 'Strange, isn't it, how the shape of our lives seems to be waiting for us? I think I must always have known I would swagger as a soldier.'

'You won't swagger so much if you have to fight the Prussians,' said Anton with a hint of malice.

'It may be so,' said Max indifferently. 'We put down some agitation among the Ruthenians in Bukovina but for the most part life is uneventful. We may not be too much of an army on the battlefields of Europe but we do help to keep the Emperor on his throne.'

'And there are no misfits? Bullies?'

'For people like us the worst fate is to be sent to Galicia.

I've heard life is so boring there that some officers end up having half their pay docked every month to pay their gambling debts. Well, one must have some vice, I suppose.'

'And what is your vice?' asked Anton.

Max's bright eyes went over the actress again speculatively. 'Beautiful women,' he said. 'I haven't changed.'

The waltz started up again, sweetly, seductively, and Max bent over to beg the girl's hand. 'May I ask your companion for a dance?'

Anton shrugged. He was far from deeply involved and had, indeed, contemplated slipping off home rather earlier than usual. When his companions returned, laughing and delighted with one another, he stood up to make his excuses.

Max looked disappointed but not, Anton observed, the actress. He was not altogether pleased to see the rapidity of Max's conquest, but these days he found it difficult to maintain an interest in any woman other than Clara. It was not a situation he welcomed, since Clara kept him quietly at a distance, but it brought him a certain immunity.

'I have heard that married women can be very dangerous for Army officers,' he said to Max mischievously.

Max smiled. He had a duelling scar on his left cheekbone that women saw and found instantly attractive, suggesting as it did both recklessness and sexual misdemeanour.

'Shall I call you tomorrow?' Max asked.

'If you have time,' said Anton politely.

Chapter Nineteen

THE SEAMSTRESS WHO LIVED below Clara was a charming girl of eighteen, with a sweet face; sometimes they exchanged smiles on the stairs. One afternoon she came to knock timidly on Clara's door to suggest an outing.

Mitzi, as she was called, had a small dark room, with poorly papered walls she had decorated with one or two cheap engravings. There was a lamp suspended over the table, with a pink shade, and the whole room had an odour of perfume and curling tongs, for Mitzi had spent most of the day preparing to meet a young officer in the dragoons. He had a friend, it seemed, and she wondered if Clara would like to join them that evening.

After her years with Jane, who was so much more interested in literature than sexual adventure, Clara was intrigued by Mitzi's unashamed relish at the thought of meeting two handsome young men.

'My Fritz – wait till you see him. He has the curliest black hair and the sweetest lips. And he lives in a fine flat, with soft lights and a piano.'

'And his friend?' enquired Clara, dubiously.

'He's much younger, but handsome enough. See what you think. You can flirt a bit, can't you? Tell me about yourself, though. How do you come to be here?'

Clara described the difficulties with Anthony Newall that had led to her dismissal.

'Well, never mind him,' said Mitzi, misunderstanding Clara's sadness. 'There are plenty of men in Vienna, I can tell you. Look at all this!'

And she showed Clara a drawer of trophies: dried flowers, letters, locks of hair and photographs. She selected a little casket with three perfumes: Patchouli, Chypre and Autumn Rose.

'Look,' said Mitzi. 'This is what Fritz bought me. And he takes me to eat oysters. I adore oysters.'

Her simplicity touched Clara. 'How did you meet this Fritz?' she asked.

'On the street. Sharing an umbrella. How does one meet people? We talked about all sorts of things right away. How he was thrown out of school, how his father wanted him to go into the army, how he'd always loved the theatre.'

Mitzi's voice flew onwards with gaiety and her eyes sparkled with a roguish expression, so that Clara found herself smiling easily in response.

'Will you come? He is sad and handsome, Fritz's friend.'

'All right,' said Clara.

'We're to be ready in an hour.'

'What shall I wear?' asked Clara, suddenly quite excited at the prospect.

'I've seen you in a black velvet dress. Wear that. And you can have one of these red roses to decorate it.'

Mitzi broke off one of the buds, and smiled as she did so.

'My Fritz is very devoted,' she said. 'He brought me these. All he thinks about is love.'

When Clara came downstairs again, Mitzi took a short inward breath and shook her head. 'You are a beauty,' she said. 'And no mistake.'

Fritz, for all the description Mitzi had given of him,

seemed a very ordinary young man, with honest, rather
knobbly features. He laughed a great deal. His friend was
decidedly melancholy. Together the four young people
walked through the park, paused to drink a raspberry juice,
and decided on a place to dance. Fritz and Mitzi were soon
giggling happily together, while Clara and her young soldier
found little to say. His name, she learned, was Theo, but he
was too shy or too cautious to tell her anything else about
himself without prompting.

'Are you unhappy about something?' Clara asked after a
time.

He gave a sardonic grunt. 'I am.'

'Do you want to talk about why?'

'There's no point,' he said.

Nevertheless, his face regained some animation at the
possibility.

'I have lost the love of my life to another man,' he said, as
she seemed reluctant to question him further.

'No wonder you are sad,' said Clara, softly.

'Sad? I shall never shake off the misery,' he said, giving a
bark of bitter laughter.

It was a warm night. Outside, under the trees, there were
tables where town notables ate with their children. A band
was loudly playing a polka.

'Shall we sit here?' suggested Fritz.

'Oh yes. We can drink wine and sing, and dance under the
trees,' cried Mitzi.

Theo and Clara agreed.

'Can we have champagne?' asked Mitzi.

Fritz tilted her chin with one finger.

'You see, Theo? Mitzi enjoys life so much. It makes me
happy just to be with her. Of course we can have champagne.' Mitzi clapped her hands. 'And sweet cakes. And
everything you want.'

When the waiter brought the wine, they all drank to one another quite solemnly, and Clara's spirits lifted in the warm, scented air. After the first glass of wine, Theo took off his hat and unfastened the top button of his uniform.

'Tell me about your unhappy love,' Clara suggested, since he seemed unable to talk about anything else.

His young, pink cheeks lengthened at the question. 'She is married already. To a horrid, vulgar man. Unworthy of her.'

'Sometimes that happens,' said Clara.

It occurred to her that he was very young to have lost his heart so irrevocably, and she wondered if his tragic affair had been either as intimate or as reciprocal as he implied.

'It was her soul I loved,' he said, almost as if in answer to her doubts, pouring them both another glass of wine. 'I shall never find anyone like her.'

'You don't know till you look,' said Clara, encouragingly.

At this he took her hand and looked urgently into her eyes. 'Will you help me? To forget her?'

'If I can,' said Clara, uncertainly.

A third glass of wine emboldened him even further. 'Let's dance,' he said abruptly, and offered her his hand.

Soon they were moving around the floor alongside the other dancers. Theo danced with great enthusiasm. He clearly much preferred it to talking. There were stars overhead, and lights in the trees.

'She was not as beautiful as you,' said Theo hoarsely.

For a moment, she hardly knew what he meant. She had forgotten his story, or indeed his individuality, in the pleasure of the dance and the excitement of the summer night. When the music stopped, he continued to clutch her to him, and his hands trembled.

'Let us go back and sit down,' she suggested.

'Your friend Mitzi is no virgin, is she?' he whispered, as they made their way back to the table.

Clara coloured and said she did not know.

'Not very intelligent, either, but that's no matter. All one wants is a pretty, warm girl. Nothing interesting. Women aren't meant to be interesting.'

Clara drew away at that, but as they sat down again, and she looked at his flushed, youthful face, she softened towards him and said, as kindly as she could, that women varied as much as men. He laughed at the idea.

'Do you know so many women, then?' she asked sharply.

'Of course I do.'

'From the villages?' she teased him.

'No. From all over Vienna. From theatre dressing rooms and little flower shops . . .'

Clara, whose blood was enlivened by the dancing quite as much as the wine, laughed at his indignation, and forbore to remind him of his lost love. They had another glass of the champagne and danced again, and Clara was happy, though she could not afterwards have repeated a word of what had been said. She was alone in the world, and the knowledge of that gave her gaiety an odd poignancy.

As they returned to the table this last time, Clara's hair tumbling about her face, her young admirer now rather drunk, they passed a table of finely dressed young people who were sitting quietly, enjoying the summer night. These people, unmistakably, were both noble and wealthy. It was clear not only from their careful dress, but from their personal bearing.

Seeing as much, Clara gathered her skirts decorously about her, and was preparing to pass by when, with a pang, she recognized a young man sitting amongst them, a little apart from his friends.

A half-smile of recognition came to Clara's lips. It was Joseph. But as she met his gaze she realized he was unaware of her presence. She dropped her eyes at once, embarrassed to think her readiness to speak to him owed something to champagne. She paused for a moment, nevertheless, wondering whether to greet him, but he seemed preoccupied and, even as she hesitated, the elegant young lady at his side grasped one of his hands between her white-gloved ones and pressed a kiss upon it. The gesture appeared to waken him from his reverie for a moment and he patted the girl's hair gently. He seemed otherwise lost in his own thoughts.

Clara shivered. He was altogether at ease among these wealthy friends. His whole being had changed; he was no longer a struggling musician but someone rare and privileged. The girl at his side was looking up at him with something closer to reverence than affection. It came to Clara that she had seen his name on posters and perhaps in newspapers, and that the glamour of that fame hung around his person.

Theo dragged at her hand clumsily, in an effort to get her to come back to their own place, and she was suddenly conscious that she was staring like a beggar at her betters. Crestfallen, she turned and let Theo lead her away.

Back at their own table, she found herself impatient both with the jollity of the young men and the innocent cheerfulness of her friend. Their ordinariness, their complete unpretentiousness, no longer had the slightest charm. No doubt this pleasure was the best she could expect, yet it seemed a poor thing now. She could hardly bring herself to smile, and had no desire to drink another glass of wine.

'What is it, Clara?' asked Mitzi. She followed Clara's gaze. 'Who is he?'

'A friend. Not even that, it seems,' said Clara, shaking her head, annoyed with herself.

Determinedly, she returned to her flirtation with the young man at her side.

As they walked home together under the trees, Theo put

an arm tentatively round Clara's waist and at last risked a
gentle pressure of her lips. His shyness confirmed her earlier
suspicion that he had had little experience of love.

Rather clumsily, he attempted a few not entirely harmless
caresses. She permitted them. Why not? Who would care,
whatever she did? He hesitated to risk anything alarming.
When his fingers felt for an entry to her clothes, she pulled
away, and he stopped at once, perhaps relieved.

'How old are you?' she asked him.

'Twenty-one,' he said.

She wondered if he was telling the truth.

'I must see you again,' he said as they reached her door.

'I don't know about that,' she said, shaking her head.

'Yes. Come to Fritz's flat on Friday. He has rooms in a
little lane in the Strohgasse. We shall have a marvellous
evening.'

Mitzi, holding Fritz's hand and pink in the face from
rolling in the bushes, joined her invitation to Theo's as they
reached Ebonstrasse.

'You must come. You will see. The rooms are lit by pretty
green candles and we always have cakes and champagne.'

Clara shook hands cordially with both young men, but
made her excuses.

That Sunday she walked on her own through the Vienna
woods, picking wild anemones. When she came home, she
put them in a little glass Mitzi had given her. In a few hours
they were pale brown.

'This is what will happen to you,' said Mitzi. 'Young girls
are like flowers, and none of us stay young for ever.'

However, it was Mitzi herself who needed consolation a
few weeks later, when she heard Fritz's regiment was leaving
Vienna.

'He says his regiment is being sent to the East but I know

better,' said Mitzi, crying a little as she told her story, but then bravely shaking her head. Clara listened and patted her hand.

'Of course, he wasn't the first. I was quite honest. I told him I'd had other lovers.'

'Does that matter now?' asked Clara.

'What matters is he is the first man I've really loved,' said Mitzi.

Her handkerchief, wet with tears, was balled into her fist.

'And what about him? Does he feel the same?' asked Clara, curiously. Mitzi's passions were strange to her. She did not know how to think about them.

'Oh, as to that—' Mitzi shrugged. 'Fidelity doesn't mean much to a man.'

'You sound so wise. As if all this had happened before,' said Clara, softly. 'So, perhaps . . .'

'I know what you want to say,' said Mitzi. 'Perhaps I shall be all right.'

'Yes,' said Clara.

'Pretty girls always have lovers,' said Mitzi.

Clara nodded. Mitzi's sadness deepened, for all her attempts to encourage herself.

'You aren't angry with him,' Clara observed.

Mitzi sighed. 'All men decide when they don't want to see you again.'

Clara tried to think of something that would make Mitzi feel better. 'Perhaps he will write to you from wherever he's posted?' she suggested. 'Maybe he will be able to come back and visit you?'

Mitzi shrugged. 'It wouldn't matter how near it was, he won't come back. You become just a memory to them, if that.'

'There'll be another soldier soon,' said Clara, partly

because she felt it was the comforting thing to say, and partly because she guessed it was true.

Mitzi looked up rather bitterly at the consolation. 'Perhaps you are the clever one, after all.'

Sometimes, when there was a full moon and it sat above the trees in magical, solid completeness, Clara sat on her own and gazed up entranced. She loved the trees, the darkness in the cypress or the wind stirring the lime trees. She observed the way the new arc lights made the birch hedges look heavy. She read Byron now and at night the voice of his lyrics went with her as she walked through the streets.

'I am a voyeur,' she wrote in her notebook. 'I look on at the great, exciting world which I do not know how to join. Perhaps I shall never join it. Women may do so in England and France, but not in Vienna. I am not unhappy. There are things I cannot afford but I am lucky not to need them. I could not afford to be ill, of course, or even to need a dentist, but I am young and for the moment I eat well enough. Sometimes I feel so lonely that I might be living on a steep mountainside, but then I find a kind of strength inside myself. I don't know where it comes from. I look sometimes at the pretty face of my mother in the locket and it almost seems as if I could remember her. Sometimes I think I must have invented her, and that she was as fierce and careless as Rebekka herself.

'Sometimes, when I hear music that speaks of happiness as well as pain, I am scalded with longing, though I cannot exactly say for what.'

In her notebook she wrote honestly. She longed for love, but not for a husband. If she had, she might have smiled more knowingly at the young men who surveyed her in the Café Central on a drizzly afternoon and found more than one who would have been willing to take on their scandalized family to make her a respectable woman.

She went boldly into the Café Central just for the pleasure of seeing the writers who liked to gather there. Under the Moorish ceiling, she sat at a marble table and watched the men with their silvered trays, drinking small cups of black coffee and glasses of water. She loved the exotic decorations in browns and blues and the hanging lights in bronze. Mostly she simply listened to the voices raised in excitement. Once she had a chance to overhear the ageing Grillparzer; once a young man, taken with her dark eyes and pretty face, invited her to his table, but she did not give him her attention.

'Why do you sit and look with those huge eyes at what is going on at the other table?' he grumbled jealously.

There was one very young man, an aspirant writer himself, who mooned after her for weeks. His family was both old and rich and would have been horrified to see that their son was in danger of involving himself with a girl of no family whatsoever. But Clara had no more thoughts of attaching the young man to her seriously than she had of flying to the moon she watched. She didn't want to marry into a good family. She did not even want a sensible, practical marriage to a man who would look after her. And the poets themselves were shabby, pale, often drunken creatures; happy to show her their verses, uninterested in what she might say about them.

Was it possible, she wondered, to become a complete human being in the strange situation in which she found herself – without family, without home, without any baggage from her past? She was unsure.

One of her pupils took her on a horse-drawn tram to the wooded hills of Kahlenberg for a picnic, and that summer she learned to swim. At Anton's insistence, she accepted the loan of a small, upright piano which enabled her to sing

Schubert songs to herself. Sometimes, as she sang, one of Mitzi's visitors would look up from her couch and break off his endearments to enquire into the owner of the lovely voice.

Clara knew her good fortune; in an earlier period she would never have been given a licence to teach in Vienna. Now teachers of English were much in demand. She was a good teacher and her pupils made progress; she could take pride in them. Sometimes they forgot to pay: like rich, spoilt girls, they had spent the money given by trusting parents on a new pair of gloves or a scarf, and were unaware that their defection could leave Clara literally hungry, though food was cheap in Vienna.

'Do you have a young man?' asked one of the girls, giggling a little since she had just announced her own engagement.

Clara said that she did not, and smiled.

Part Three

1864

Chapter Twenty

THE WALLS AROUND the First District were coming down on the order of the Emperor, and a new Vienna was spilling over the trench where they had been. Money, flowing in from textile mills, machine shops, mines and ironworks, was shaping a new city: there was a ring-road of baroque opulence, two hundred feet wide; the central route for wheeled traffic, with two tree-shaded lanes for gentlemen riders. There were arches, towers and sculptured vistas; scented flower gardens, green with the leaves of lime and plane trees. There were freedoms, too, although the young Emperor, Franz Joseph, could still revoke the constitution should he feel like it. A sense of optimism and confidence infused everyone.

Hannah and Peretz had moved to another flat, with larger rooms and fine windows. Hannah had taken a bigger shop, too, and sold clothes now as well as shoes, handbags and hats. She had a fleet of nimble-fingered seamstresses and cutters from Poland to work for her, and the wives of newly prosperous lawyers and doctors preferred her styles to those that could be purchased in the First District. Still thin, still ginger-haired, Hannah had come into her own. And so had Peretz, who had grown into a traditional, scholarly Jew, who left all practical matters to his wife. There was a fortunate tradition into which he fell; that of learned man, whose job was the study of the Torah. When Joseph visited his parents, he observed that, although they still quarrelled, the rancour had gone out of their arguments.

They lived in an area in which there were many new immigrants to Vienna, and Hannah's easy, sociable manner made friends. One October, she decided to celebrate her birthday with a small party and asked her son to join them.

Peretz's friends had, by and large, done well for themselves. Those who had been his neighbours in Taborstrasse had branched out into every form of economic activity. In explaining as much to Joseph, Peretz pointed to their worldly success as a sign of God's favour.

'Look at Moritz,' said Peretz. 'One generation out of the ghetto and he owns a huge store. And Levi. Do you remember him, Joseph? He used to give you potato cakes from his stall when you came home from school. Now he is buying a coal mine.'

Joseph anticipated little pleasure from his mother's party, though he was glad to have her happy. As he expected, the flat was packed with her new friends. Many of them were Jews who had flooded into Vienna since the Revolution; their heavier features recalled the caricature of the anti-Semitic Viennese press and put his own dark, good looks into a context he did not altogether like. He was disturbed at recognizing a kinship to a wider family than he had realized.

He saw his mother's face, too, among them. The women were strong, independent creatures whose mothers had run mills and breweries in the villages from which they came; it was their pleasure now to dwindle into domestic creatures with nothing more to do than run a family, in evidence of their husband's success. Yet the new privilege of leisure left them with too much energy. They were easily carried away by impatience. Even their flirtatious manners were a little alarming.

The men were not peasants. They were sensible, cautious people who had come to Vienna with a vivid memory of the humiliations of Galicia, Bohemia and Hungary. They might go to Joseph's concerts, but they had no desire for the risks or the rewards of a musical life. What they wanted for their own children was the profession of a physician, or a dentist, or a lawyer. A good living, a sensible life: that was what they craved. In their presence Joseph always felt reduced. Jews recognize success, he thought, in terms of money. In no other way does one Jew have respect for another, any more than prisoners in a hostile country. Admiration, perhaps, even envy. But not respect.

Standing about moodily among them, Joseph let himself be introduced to an academic from the Medical Faculty, to whom even Peretz spoke with some deference.

'It is not easy to be appointed a professor if you are a Jew,' he was lamenting. 'It is very strange. They let us in to the University to study and to teach. Why not? But they don't feel such honours are appropriate. Professors must come from the old families of Vienna. You are the violinist Kovacs, aren't you?' he asked.

Joseph said that he was and took another of Hannah's excellent cakes and a sip of the wine which Peretz preferred and was far sweeter than the usual dry wine of the Viennese.

His words turned the head of a rather heavier man with a flushed, surly face who might have been a butcher. Peretz introduced him.

'I would be happier if my son had fewer ambitions in that direction,' he said, without preamble.

'Well, and what does your son play?' asked Joseph with a little sigh.

'The piano. He studies with a good teacher.' He named the man, who was indeed among the very best in Vienna.

'How old is he?'

'Seven.'

Joseph remembered his own childhood struggles – the Hungarian café, the first years with Becker – and could not help smiling at the change in expectations of this new generation. The man, however, seemed unaware of any of these thoughts.

'Would you listen to him?' he begged. 'I want to know if he really has talent. Or, better still, if he has not, you can discourage him.'

Joseph explained that he had little expertise on the piano, but the man would not be put off.

'He knows your name. He will believe you. You are busy, but we can wait. Come next month, if you like. You will know,' said the man vigorously. 'Surely you will know. He is intelligent. The school says he might do anything. Why should he set his heart so firmly on that?'

At length, though still reluctant, Joseph agreed.

The following week, at an apartment in a road off Jaegerzeile, Joseph listened to a small child not much older than the boy Mozart, his feet swinging many inches away from the pedals. The parents, he now perceived, were far less wealthy than he had expected, and there were many other children – six or seven, he guessed – who came out solemnly to be introduced to him. Most of them were at the Gymnasium. Schooling was expensive, but where an Austrian with the same income might hesitate, Jews saw education as their only chance of advancement.

The child played well, though not flawlessly. Probably he was very nervous. Joseph pursed his lips, and was wondering how best to advise the father, when the boy, a small-featured child with big, liquid eyes, said suddenly, 'I don't want to be a performer, Herr Kovacs.'

'No?' asked Joseph, astonished.

'No. My teacher knows that. I want to compose music.'

Joseph looked down at the serious, unfrightened face.

'What makes you think you can do so?' he asked with a pang.

He was still only twenty-four himself, yet the boy's expectations were decidedly those of a newer generation. Joseph had been through a harsher struggle.

'I have composed some pieces already,' said the child. 'Will you hear them?'

With an uneasy sense that he was doing far more than the father intended, Joseph agreed. He didn't know what he was expecting. The first piece was little more than an exercise on a theme of Mozart, but the second took him by surprise. It had a long, slow melody that grew under the boy's fingers as if it had always been in the world. The boy did not ask what he thought of the piece.

'Will you talk to my father?' he asked. 'Will you try to persuade him that music is worth giving your life to?'

'I will certainly try,' said Joseph.

The little boy's face, with his amber eyes and delicate lips, remained in his memory along with the poignant melody.

Anton had not expected to devote himself with such intensity to his newspaper. At first, though he carried the name of Editor, his assistant had to advise him on everything from layout to the price of printers. Over the years, however, he had learned every skill, and now he took every decision himself. He read all the other newspapers in Vienna, admiring some, castigating others; he was determined to open the columns of his own newspaper to liberals of every nationality. But most of all he wanted to find the lost poets, the wittiest essayists, the sharpest cartoonists, who had been hidden in Metternich's day.

One morning, just before lunch, Anton was walking down Kärntnerstrasse when he saw a familiar, thin figure. It was

Efraim Jacob; a little more stooped, but still black-haired.
Anton was not entirely astonished to see him in the streets
of Vienna since he had recently seen his name in *Neue Freie
Presse* and had wondered about him.

'Jacob!' he called out, catching up with his friend at a run.

Jacob turned and Anton was disconcerted to meet a flash
of hostility from the liquid black eyes and see that deep lines
had bitten into his face from the nose to the mouth.

'Anton Shassner,' Jacob nodded. 'Well?'

Anton dropped his extended arm a little awkwardly. The
years fell away from him as he felt Jacob's disapproval.

'I heard you were back in Vienna,' he said, with as much
cordiality as he could muster.

Jacob nodded sombrely. 'You seem unchanged,' he said,
after a moment's prolonged scrutiny.

'Will you have a glass of wine?'

'I'm in a hurry,' said Jacob.

'It's been so long,' said Anton. 'Let's talk a little, if only
to arrange another meeting.'

A little sullenly, Jacob followed Anton into a nearby café.
It was not a fashionable place; rather dark and smoky, with
several working men in shirt sleeves eating soup at the only
occupied table.

'Will this do?' asked Anton.

'Let us sit. It's fine,' said Jacob impatiently, pulling out a
chair.

'I suppose it will serve,' said Anton, joining him. 'I've so
much to ask you. Where have you been all these years?'

'I spent a month in gaol,' said Jacob, with a sudden,
flashing smile. 'Then I left for Paris.'

'Was it—?' Anton hesitated. 'Hard to bear?'

'Gaol was brutal,' said Jacob, as if the memory amused
him, 'but exile was a delight.'

'Yet you returned?'

'My father fell ill,' said Jacob. 'I came back to see him through his dying.'

'And then?'

'I became a wine merchant.'

Anton laughed.

'It was not such a bad life,' said Jacob thoughtfully. 'But I didn't have much time for myself. When Mother died I sold up. Now I try to make my way as a journalist.'

'You did not complete your studies?'

'After so many years away? No. I had no inclination,' shrugged Jacob. His eyes examined Anton. 'Your father has been kinder to you than mine was to me.'

Anton accepted the comment.

'I have seen your journal, by the way,' said Jacob. 'It is interesting enough, though it lacks bite.'

Anton flushed. 'I suppose you feel I should spend more time attacking the government? Jacob, things have improved. For most people.'

'For the people you know, perhaps,' said Jacob. He nodded in the direction of the man eating at the other table. 'He wouldn't agree, for one.'

'But, Jacob, things are never going to be good for everyone,' protested Anton. 'We are a liberal, progressive paper. Our position is close to *Neue Freie Presse*.'

Jacob laughed. *Neue Freie Presse* was the most important newspaper in the Empire. Owned, and for the most part written, by Jews, it was edited by the ebullient Moritz Benedikt. The anti-Semitic populist press were fond of publishing caricatures of Benedikt, sometimes as a swollen tentacle on some blatantly Jewish spider. So far, Anton's paper had not attracted the same venom.

'Moritz,' said Jacob, 'thinks himself only a little less important than the Emperor. So he's hardly an aggressive critic of the powerful. I take it you approve of Franz Joseph?'

'I approve of his liberal measures, certainly.'

Jacob laughed again.

'You mean equal rights?'

'It was one of the earliest acts of his regime, wasn't it?'

'It came about as a result of a revolution he hated,' said Jacob. 'Or don't you remember that? But to talk of *Neue Freie Presse* – do you really believe Benedikt's paper helps the workers in this city?'

'Indirectly, yes.'

'The only interests he serves are those of the bankers and manufacturers,' said Jacob.

'I don't think his liberalism is just a mask for his own interests,' argued Anton. 'For the moment, and it may only be for a moment, some consensus exists. About how to develop industries in this backward country.'

Jacob sighed and rose to his feet. 'I was always to the radical left of you, Shassner.'

Anton looked at the black-eyed, fervent face. Jacob seemed as fiercely young as ever. 'Have you read Sebastian Brunner's newspaper?' he asked quietly.

'That vile rag?'

'Yes. It was begun in the Revolution itself. I'd have thought liberalism has enough enemies on the right, without people like you joining in from the radical left.'

'I'm interested in ordinary people. What a man takes home to his wife at the end of a working week. If he has found work.'

'Are you married yourself?' Anton asked.

'Luckily, I have no one to look after but myself,' said Jacob, rising to his feet.

'Let me see your work. Send me some,' said Anton, as his friend seemed ready to leave.

'Why not?' said Jacob. 'I send my stuff to all the other newspapers in Vienna.'

When Anton read the short pieces delivered by hand a few days later, he flushed with excitement. That evening he made his way eagerly across town to the lodgings where Jacob lived to tell him that he would accept every one of the articles and would commission more on a weekly basis.

Jacob had returned to Taborstrasse and Anton, who did not often go to that district, was surprised to see so many Jews there dressed in Hasidic garments. He disapproved of the fashion, seeing those who wore such clothes as a superstitious remnant refusing to take part in the new opportunities of the glorious enlightenment. Saying as much to Jacob, he expected immediate agreement since his friend wrote so angrily of the continuing power of irrational prejudice.

'Don't you think they should cultivate Austrian civility and politeness?' Anton asked him.

'To guard against ill feeling?'

'Yes.'

Jacob laughed, but Anton noticed that the amusement did not reach the edges of eyes that remained open and watchful.

'I think all our misfortunes come from our wish to be acceptable. It is always a mistake to try for it. I think a caftan-wearing Jew with sidelocks deserves the same opportunities as any other Austrian citizen.'

'There must be a payment for becoming a citizen,' said Anton, mildly enough.

'Meaning Jews must become as German as possible?'

'I think so.'

Jacob shrugged.

'Why do you live in this neighbourhood, anyway? Nostalgia?' enquired Anton. 'Don't you find this flat uncomfortable?' He stared round at Jacob's bare walls, piled books and the broken door of a cupboard that hung open.

'It's cheap,' said Jacob. 'If I want to live independently I have to economize.'

'You sold a profitable wine business. You could afford to live somewhere better.'

'I admit it's not my only reason. I like these Galician Jews. I prefer them to the ones moving up in the world, if you want to know. Why should I move? It is always lively round here. I enjoy the variety.'

'Do you? But can you speak to them? Don't they only know a barbaric tongue?'

'Yiddish is not a barbaric language. They have their own ironic storytellers. My father spoke Yiddish for preference.'

'Tell me, where do they all come from?' asked Anton.

'The villages in the east,' shrugged Jacob.

'From the land?'

'When they were fortunate.'

'Did they live as manual labourers there?'

'Not commonly. They once had a useful role in the countryside. The peasants made use of their talents as distributors. We have unbalanced all that.'

'I suppose it is the price of modernity,' said Anton. 'But what will they do here? Won't they be in competition with the Viennese for the same jobs?'

'They will try to find a niche. I don't know. They are industrious. They will urge their children to study. Probably they will become like yourself as soon as they can.'

'But I am completely Austrian,' said Anton, surprised. 'Don't you feel the same?'

'What is an Austrian? I can understand what is meant by Germans, Czechs, Hungarians. But Austrians?' Once again, Jacob gave the troubling smile that did not reach his eyes. 'What has happened to our friend von Mayerberg, by the way?' he asked.

'He is not doing much,' admitted Anton.

As far as he knew, Rudolf was not doing anything at all. That year, Anna had finally become pregnant and he had responded as a devoted husband, making her favourite tisanes and carrying home delicacies to tempt her uncertain appetite. The child had died soon after birth. These days Rudolf came rarely to a coffee house and, when he did, he could hardly be drawn into animation. With Anton, in any case, there had been an unease ever since their trip to Wiesbaden had left him so heavily indebted, and Anton did not know how to repair their friendship. He would have liked to bring him back into the literary life of the city, but he did not know how to do that either. One morning, after not seeing each other for months, they met casually in the street, and Anton took him for lunch in a new Hungarian restaurant to try to persuade him to write for his newspaper. But von Mayerberg had absolutely no wish to contribute to *New Vienna*. He was not a journalist, he pointed out. Anton knew as much.

'But I want something in the style of your plays. You can be sarcastic, even hurtful. You can write about incompetent cabinet ministers, deputies who take bribes, bad poets or fraudulent bankers,' said Anton. 'Whatever you like, as long as it is sharp.'

'These are matters for your coffee house literati,' said von Mayerberg. 'I am not a journalist.'

He smiled as though well aware of sounding pompous. He plied his knife and fork with a great vigour, however, and Anton filled his glass with wine.

'Then write about simple folk,' said Anton. 'No one can do it better: the musical bands of the Prater; the funfair on the fringe of town; the people running the sideshows.'

'I don't think so,' said von Mayerberg. 'I am about to become a father, and the prospect leads me to meditate on my own sins.' Again, his smile belied his words.

'You can't preach at the Viennese like Jeremiah,' said Anton. 'You have to make them laugh.'

Von Mayerberg looked up helplessly. 'If I could, my dear Anton, I would. I *can't* and that is that. You know what Grillparzer calls the curse of the House of Habsburg? "The half-trodden path and the half-finished act". For me, it is worse than leaving what I can do unfinished – I have not even *begun* for a very long time.'

'Then let me encourage you to make a beginning,' said Anton.

'I'm a man of the theatre, not a newspaper columnist. Not an essayist, either. I cannot think on my own as the Germans do,' said von Mayerberg. 'We Viennese need interaction. And what is there to say? We take liberalism for granted now.'

Anton reflected that those of his own origin could never speak so casually of their emancipation.

'I suppose I might have something to say about Austrian pride,' said von Mayerberg. 'This is a Habsburg realm, and people lose sight of it in all this nonsense of becoming more and more of a multi-ethnic state.'

'Isn't that an incomparable gain?' Anton asked, surprised.

Von Mayerberg shrugged. 'The Croats peddle kitchen ware. The Czechs are cobblers, and pastry cooks, too. I'm not sure we need any of them.'

Anton ordered another bottle of wine. These were not opinions he wanted to give space to in his newspaper.

'You are a very determined bachelor,' said von Mayerberg, after munching in silence for some time. 'I'm surprised your family don't try to marry you off.'

'They do,' said Anton impatiently. 'Luckily, I'm no longer entirely dependent on them.'

'Are you still involved with the girl on Ebonstrasse?' von Mayerberg asked.

Anton coloured at this. He had not introduced Clara to von Mayerberg, and the casual remark suggested that too many people speculated about the relationship. He knew his situation was bizarre. For all his efforts, he had failed over the years to make Clara his mistress, yet he had been completely unable to put her out of his mind.

'She's an unusual girl,' he said guardedly. 'I've undertaken her education.'

Von Mayerberg raised his eyebrows at this, which he thought a pompous euphemism.

'And is she an eager pupil?'

'Yes,' said Anton.

Indeed she was. They went to concerts of new music and he showed her the paintings in the Kunsthistorische Museum. Her responses were always fresh and surprising. He took her to the Augustinerkirche, the wedding church of the Habsburgs, to see the Canova marble sculptures put up in memory of the Archduchess Marie Christine. Clara stood silently for a long time before the mourning figures trooping towards the open door of the pyramid tomb.

'How chilling,' she said. 'It is as if they are only *performing* their grief, with all those urns and torches. Only the lion looks warm-blooded.'

Anton looked again at the sleeping animal, and the allegorical figures of Charity and the Blind Beggar.

'I have heard that said,' he murmured, 'but still I admire the sculpture.'

'It's very graceful,' she agreed.

As they left the church and found themselves on the cobbles of the square outside, with an August sun baking down, he put a hand on her arm, which was bare at the elbow. The rounded moulding of her elbow was as graceful as any of the Canova statues, but he could feel the warmth of the flesh, with just the slight, intoxicating moisture produced by the heat.

'They say you are besottedly in love with her,' said von Mayerberg.

'So I am,' said Anton, smiling to remove any weight from his utterance.

Clara was, and he knew she was, the reason he could not seriously involve himself with any other woman, still less entertain the thought of marriage.

He thought of her as a girl, because her skin was so fresh and her face as perfectly unlined as when she was eighteen. The child-like, untouched quality was something he found particularly seductive, and sometimes he marvelled at how she had preserved it.

Mitzi, who continued to live in the same building and sometimes made dresses for Clara, made the same observation one day as she looked at her own reflection above Clara's in a long mirror. Her own skin was dry, and there were tiny lines at the edges of her eyes.

'You still look young,' said Mitzi, 'because nothing has happened to you. You don't let anything happen. I tell you, for all your beauty, I wouldn't change places.'

Clara smiled, a little sadly. She did not understand herself why she could not respond to the many offers of love she had turned away. She wondered about her own behaviour.

'Something is wrong,' she admitted in the journal she now kept assiduously. 'When a man touches me, I feel none of the desires that Mitzi tells me about. There is a kind of excitement, but I don't enjoy it. I can't. It frightens me. Does any other woman feel the same way? I'm twenty-five. Soon I shall be too old for any man to care about.'

Clara rarely thought of Anton, but more often than she wished she thought about Joseph. She had tried to put him out of her mind, but whenever she saw posters for concerts she scoured them eagerly. The lettering of Joseph's name had grown larger of late, and she took a peculiar pleasure in his success, almost as if it were her own.

Chapter Twenty-One

JOSEPH ENJOYED the new shape of his life, which he had not yet begun to take for granted. As he stood at the windows of the Hotel Lafayette on the Seine one sharp autumn day, he remembered his early, stammering encounter with Joachim, the first concerts in Paris, the miraculous change in his expectations since. The sun lit up the gilt rococo decorations of the room behind him. The management of the hotel had sent up a huge basket of early fruit from the south of France and a complimentary bottle of fine champagne in a bucket of ice.

He looked out at the flecks of light on the river, at the blue sky and the carriages glinting beneath. Perhaps there was a touch of vanity in his bearing. He liked to dress well and he had cultivated a luxuriant black moustache, which gave his face an Italianate, dangerous look. He enjoyed his long, elegant coat, his buckled shoes, his fine linen. His silk handkerchiefs were perfumed with roses. When he called to the young woman who prepared herself in the sumptuous dressing room, he did so in an easy, caressing voice.

'Marie, my love. I'm hungry. Let's go and eat.'

'I'm nearly ready,' she called back in her bird-like voice. 'Don't be impatient, darling.'

The truth was, he was preoccupied. He had travelled towards Paris with a sweet Austrian girl called Mouche, with brown curls and an upturned nose. In conversation, Joseph had learned that she had once carried music from an Austrian composer to Heinrich Heine in Paris and there became his last love. Joseph had been much taken with her soft presence and had spoken at some length of his own first encounter with the poet. It was not the girl herself who disturbed him but the evidence her story offered of a sweeter and more intimate way of relating to a woman than any he had so far discovered; a love closer to the emotions he felt when he responded to music.

As Marie emerged at last from the bathroom, a line of Heine came to his mind, and Schubert's setting of it. He hummed it softly.

'What's that, darling?' Marie called brightly.

'The greatest German poet since Goethe,' he said. 'Did you know he died not very far from Paris?'

She was looking in the mirror and said, abstractedly, 'Is it important where you die?'

'Not very,' he agreed. 'I am a little melancholy today.'

Privately, he decided that the time had come to end this particular affair. He would dine that day in the Boeuf à la Mode in the rue des Bons Enfants with an impresario who was trying to persuade him to visit England. He was in two minds about the possibility, but England loved German musicians and the Queen had adored Mendelssohn. Well, he would see.

The decision was made that lunchtime, but it had nothing to do with the delights of England. For the impresario had invited one or two people to brighten the lunch and among them was the vivacious singer Sophie von Briesen, whom he had met long ago on a train from Vienna to France and had never forgotten.

She gave no sign of recalling their earlier meeting. She was dressed in a deep purple robe, which clung to a figure still as splendidly full as he remembered it, though it was clear now that she was closer to thirty-five than twenty-five. Her neck was decorated by a fine string of diamonds. I wonder who bought those for her, he thought to himself.

The impresario was squat with great, hunched shoulders and a shiny cravat. He placed Joseph next to Sophie, as if guessing what would please him most, and Marie at the far end of the table. Sophie was intently studying the menu.

'Do they not have oysters?' she demanded. 'I want nothing but seafood. I particularly like those red, prickly creatures. What are they called?'

'Sea urchins,' said Joseph.

She looked up at him gravely. 'Thank you. I have been told I must seduce you into an English tour,' she said. 'But I cannot find it in my heart to do it. You are, after all, Viennese, as I am, and will find London grey and dull.'

'Please, Sophie,' begged the impresario. 'If you won't do what I ask, at least do not put him against England.'

'England is a cold, wet country,' she said. 'I say no more than the truth.'

'But he will be there in high summer,' pleaded the impresario. 'In any case, he will be playing in such splendid halls that he will not notice the rain. Joseph, take no notice of her; she is being mischievous.'

Joseph guessed that to be frequently the case. 'You have just returned?' he asked.

'I sang at their Opera House,' said Sophie, indifferently.

'Was that not a splendid building?' demanded the impresario. 'And the audience, too. Didn't you find it enthusiastic?'

'Of course.' Her eyes flashed blue as chipped sapphires, and the jewellery at her neck glinted.

'But then encourage him,' begged the impresario.

'I prefer the theatre in Vienna.'

The impresario shook his finger at her, only half in play, and Joseph felt sympathetic, and bent close to Sophie.

'What an old tyrant,' he whispered to her. 'Does he work for you? You can't need him.'

'Have you heard me sing, then?' she demanded.

'No,' admitted Joseph.

'That somewhat reduces your compliment,' she said tartly, a little disappointed.

'Do you remember when we met before?'

'Have we?'

'Yes,' he said.

She shook her head. 'I would have remembered.'

'We were much younger then,' he said, taking a spoonful of red salmon eggs on to his plate and smiling. 'This is the only seafood I really enjoy,' he explained.

'You are not polite,' she murmured, 'to remind me of my age.'

'I am not polite,' he agreed with cool amusement.

A startled look crossed her face and for a moment he thought she would stand up and leave her place at the table. He put a hand on her knee to check her, and their eyes met again.

'Don't get up,' he said.

She seemed nonplussed by his hand, which she made no effort to remove.

'You seem to think you have some rights over me,' she said.

'I do,' he said. 'When I was only a boy, I dreamed of you.'

She laughed.

'Yes, that gives me a kind of right,' he insisted. His teeth flashed white under the black moustache.

A waiter came over to bring oysters on a silver plate of ice, and she stared at them for a moment before announcing, 'These are not what I wanted.'

'I am sorry,' said the waiter. 'Today we do not have fresh urchins. It is very important that they should be absolutely fresh from the coast.'

'Well, I am not hungry,' she said. 'Let the others eat these.'

'Is it true?' asked Joseph, 'that you are not hungry?'

'Yes,' she said.

'Then why not,' he suggested impulsively, 'leave with me now? I won't go to England as he wants and you . . .'

'Yes?'

'You can come back to Vienna tomorrow with me.'

'Do you mean you're here alone?'

'I'm not,' he admitted, 'but I shall make arrangements to be alone by tomorrow morning.'

She looked him full in the eye, and an electric wave of desire ran between them. It was fár removed from the tenderness he had longed for earlier that morning, but Sophie's presence had exploded any such thoughts.

'Till tomorrow, then,' she said slowly.

A month later, watching her sing a small part in an unimportant operetta with great verve, Joseph had the intoxicating sense that his life was beginning again. Sophie was witty and impudent, and if she were rather older than he had first guessed, it mattered nothing to him. She was the very spirit of Vienna and, in loving her, he was loving the world he was happy to join.

Soon after his return to Vienna, Joseph changed his apartment and Sophie helped him to furnish his new rooms, which were on a street near the Freyung, close to the new Ring. On the wall outside was a cameo portrait of a woman and child in painted plaster, their limbs tangled charmingly with two putti holding flutes. Legend gave the house to three girls that Schubert had loved in vain. Joseph enjoyed the thought, even if there were almost as many houses claimed for Schubert as for Beethoven in a city where both men had moved their lodgings so many times. This was only a two-storey house, with an attic floor. The rooms were small but very bright. Sophie wanted to cover the walls with brocaded silk, and he agreed to her choice of emerald in the piano room and a deep, sultry red for the bedroom, and he let her choose wine-red stripes to match the velvet upholstery of the sofas and chairs. For all his infatuation, however, Joseph resisted her love of dark, elaborately carved chests and tables.

He was aware that not all his friends liked either Sophie or her taste. Hellman, who had returned from Paris to live in Vienna, was particularly hostile to Joseph's new attachment.

'Don't take Sophie so seriously!' was his advice. 'These actresses and singers behave like royalty. They think themselves good enough to be the mistress of the Emperor, but really they are just little bits of things.'

'But she is charming, isn't she? I like her frills and lace,' said Joseph, smiling.

'She knows how to use her fan and parasol,' agreed his friend sourly. 'But do you trust her?'

'Not in the least,' said Joseph, as if it were a matter of complete indifference to him. 'She wants to marry a diplomat, or at least a needy younger son. And so she will, when she finds one that suits her.'

'Or perhaps a brilliant violinist?'

'No, certainly not. I am not interested in marrying her,' said Joseph, laughing. 'She knows as much.'

'That is why she will torment you,' said Hellman quietly. 'Be careful, my friend.'

Except in bed, Joseph found there were many ways in which he and Sophie disagreed.

'I should like to live in the country,' she often sighed.

'We have cherry blossom in Vienna,' he teased her. 'And parks as fine as in Paris.'

'I mean the real countryside. With fields of corn, and cows and horses.'

'To work on the land, perhaps?' he mocked her.

'Why not? People are happy doing so,' she said. 'Their lives are more natural. I was brought up in the mountain air and I know.'

'And where would you find an opera house to mount a production of your favourite music?' he asked.

'I wouldn't need such satisfactions.'

'Well, why did you leave, then?'

'My family had to give up their land. To a moneylender. Or I should still live where I grew up as a child.'

'Why did your family borrow the money?' asked Joseph rebelliously.

'It was the railways,' she said. 'They destroyed everything.'

One Sunday, she raised her lovely head from the pillows and announced, 'We ought to go to church.'

'Why ought we?' said Joseph lazily, stroking her pretty white shoulders.

'People do.'

He laughed.

'Sometimes I go. I believe I should, anyway,' she said.

She sat up in bed and he could see the splendid curve of her full bosom. He put his hand on one of her breasts but she pushed him away, frowning.

'I am being serious,' she said.

'But what effect does your Christian belief have on your life?' he asked.

'The effect is that sometimes I go to church,' she said.

'Well, it seems meaningless to me. Anyway, I am a Jew,' said Joseph.

'Don't say it! Don't say it!' she screamed. 'I don't want to believe it. No one like you can be such a cursed thing.'

'You know I am. Have I ever pretended otherwise? Anyway, what is the curse?'

'You killed Christ,' she moaned. 'You know that. You took his blood on your head.'

'I don't remember it,' he teased her.

'Your forefathers, stupid.'

'And you believe all that happened, just like it says in the book?'

'Of course I believe it. That's what my religion tells me.'

She threw a pillow at him, crossly, but he caught it away from her and was soon lying across her body with his mouth on hers. For the moment their passion resolved all difficulties.

Chapter Twenty-Two

SOPHIE HAD A SMALL PART in Offenbach's *Orpheus in the Underworld*, which was playing to packed audiences in the Opera House on Kärntnerstrasse, and one hot evening Joseph took a horse tram to Grinzing with a double bass player from Germany.

The air was warm and heavy. The skies were clear and high, and there was only a white sliver of a moon so that a great many stars filled the dark arch above them. As they travelled gently towards Grinzing, Joseph's friend, Fritz Schultz, a large-boned, plain Bavarian, argued over Joseph's choice of programme for Princess Metternich, for whom they were playing the following week.

'You are stuck in your ways. All that admiration for old, traditional men. You can't *see* what is going to be the new, important German music. Wagner, Bruckner, Liszt.'

'Not Brahms?'

'Not all the time, anyway,' said Fritz.

As they walked through the dark streets, the noise of their footsteps was magically softened in the summer air. Joseph pointed out the bush of vine leaves that hung against the door of the *heurigen*. This showed that the owners of the vineyard had wine to sell, and allowed them some dispensation from the licensing laws of Vienna. The dry white wine that grew on the slopes of the local hills was excellent. The heurigen Joseph had chosen was a particular favourite of musicians: it was said that both Beethoven and Schubert had loved to drink there. The tables stood in the garden at the back of the house under trees and were lit by candles. That evening, in the flickering light, Joseph made out, at one end of one of the long tables, the huge, grey-bearded face of Johannes Brahms, who had come as a conductor to the Viennese Singakademie for the season.

Although Joseph had met the composer on several occasions, neither he nor his friend would have thought of joining the table if they had not been waved to do so by Eduard Hanslick, the powerful critic who had recently written favourably of Joseph's performance in the *Neue Freie Presse*.

The conversation along the table was quiet and good humoured, until Joseph heard a voice declaring:

'I admit I am obsessed with *Tristan*. It's the harmony. It is simply the most beautiful sound I have ever heard.'

Another voice, whose owner could only be guessed at in the warm darkness, replied, 'I happen to know you listen to Wagner's operas with your eyes shut. You haven't the faintest idea what they are about.'

'I know as much as Strauss does.'

Joseph knew then what was under discussion. Johann Strauss was conducting the orchestral version of *Tristan and Isolde* in the Volksgarten the following week. As Brahms, who was expected elsewhere, made his apologies and left, the conversation became more general.

'Isn't Strauss a surprising choice as a conductor of Wagner?' asked Fritz.

'He once called Strauss the most musical mind in Europe,' offered Joseph.

'How much of *Tristan* can be played?' asked another voice.

'I think there will be an orchestral version of the love-duet in Act Three,' came the unmistakably authoritative voice of Hanslick.

'Isn't it a disgrace that Vienna cannot offer to stage the whole opera?' asked Fritz.

'The Vienna Opera considered it last year,' said Hanslick. 'It was thought unperformable.'

Then the critic leant forward to discuss with Joseph a new composition of Brahms that Joseph had begun to rehearse. Flattered, Joseph gave the critic all his attention.

'The poems Brahms sets are the impulses to a tune, not a psychological experience,' Hanslick at length concluded.

Fritz frowned at this, which he rightly perceived to be a criticism of Richard Wagner. Joseph, emboldened by his second flask of wine, bent forward to ask Hanslick whether the world of music would always be so divided.

'There's a story in Brahms's music, too, even if the heart of it is less dramatic,' he said. 'Must I prefer one to the other?'

Hanslick smiled gently at his open, eager face.

'The contempt and the claims come all from the other side,' he replied. 'I agree with you, young man – the heaven of music has many mansions. There was a time when Wagner could even see the genius of Mendelssohn, until he blamed him for the bad notices he got in Leipzig.'

'And do you admire Wagner yourself?' asked Joseph, with great daring.

'I admire his energy, and indeed his tenacity. Moreover, I was an early champion of *Tannhäuser*,' said Hanslick mildly. 'But musical structure is what matters, not the expression of poetic content.'

Fritz was a good deal less in awe of Hanslick than Joseph, partly because he was not a native of Vienna, and he wondered aloud whether there were not personal reasons for so much antagonism towards Wagner. Hanslick frowned at this. Joseph kicked his friend under the table. He knew, as everyone did, that Hanslick had reason to resent his portrait as Beckmesser in *Die Meistersinger*.

'Wagner has always been very civil to me,' said Hanslick, still frowning at the ungainly young German. 'My friend the Director of the Burgtheater invited us both to a dinner party only last year and there was no ill feeling.'

He turned away from the two young musicians to talk to his neighbour.

'I'm sorry. Was that tactless?' Fritz asked Joseph.

'I hope not. He doesn't have a mean spirit,' said Joseph judiciously.

'And will you go to the outdoor performance of *Tristan*?' asked Fritz.

'If I'm not playing myself, certainly,' said Joseph. 'Sophie is an enthusiast.'

Anton, too, had noted the outdoor concert in the Volksgarten and, indeed, planned to take Clara to it. His hopes were not entirely musical. In his fantasy, the informality of the occasion would allow him to put an arm around Clara's bare shoulder, and perhaps touch her white flesh. His dreams offered bolder possibilities. He did not altogether understand why she had so captured his erotic imagination, but he knew he was almost ready to commit himself to marrying her.

Marriage, he well knew, was very much part of his mother's plans for him. She had in mind the younger sister of his cousin Sarah.

'Be fair. I can't live for ever. You must give me grand-children,' Minna pleaded.

'I'm not going to marry a girl I don't find attractive.'

'And how many girls are still attractive after their first

child? For marriage, it is the soul that matters. The
intelligence.'

'Sarah is the most intelligent member of that family, but I
still don't want to marry her.'

Minna frowned.

'Leave the boy alone,' Natan intervened. As Minna turned
to him, rather put out, he growled in part explanation, 'Not
all arranged marriages work out, do they?'

As the day of the concert approached, Clara felt herself
confused by unusual emotions. She often woke in the bright,
early hours of the morning and the sharpness of the dawn
light filled her with its beauty. In the evenings, when the sky
was pale blue and the light faded slowly, she felt a longing
for someone to share her feelings. And yet Anton could not
be that person. As she tried to explain these feelings, Mitzi
could only make a gurgling sound of disapproval. She was
impressed with Anton and thought Clara was foolish not to
accept him as a lover. She admired everything about him,
from his carriage to his clothes.

'I don't know what you could expect more,' she said.

'I cannot explain,' said Clara.

Now Clara sat in the quiet of the park and let Wagner's
music enfold her. It seemed as if the long melodies spoke out
of her own longing and sang her own needs. She was
hypnotized by the harmonies. Seeing her rapt, lovely face,
Anton took her hand stealthily and she did not protest. She
hardly noticed. As they rose in the interval, he saw she was
pale as ivory.

'Are you well?' he asked with concern.

She nodded. 'It was the music,' she said.

He squeezed her hand, his own ardour rising in response
to the sight of her emotion, but she pulled herself away and

stood up. As they walked together under the arc lights, she drew the eye of every man she passed in the half-lit dark.

Among these, she was suddenly aware, was Joseph, with a handsome woman on his arm. She had quite stopped expecting him to take any notice of her and so was surprised to find him smiling in her direction. When he tentatively approached her, her heart leapt so violently she thought she must be ill. There was a suffocating pressure in her chest.

'Forgive me if I am mistaken—' he began.

'You are not mistaken,' Clara said quickly. 'Anton, this is Joseph Kovacs. He is my friend from childhood.'

Anton bowed formally. He had heard the violinist play and was surprised to hear that his childhood was linked in any way to Clara's.

Clara guessed that Joseph had not yet placed exactly where he had met her before. He introduced Sophie carefully to Anton, whom he knew by sight, and then turned interrogatively to Clara.

'I travel a good deal these days,' said Joseph. 'I am not always in Vienna. Where, I wonder—?'

'It has been many years,' said Clara, seeing sadly that he had altogether forgotten their last encounter. 'Do you remember Taborstrasse?' She saw the flicker of recognition. 'How is your mother?' she asked quickly, before he could move away, disappointed in the nature of their connection.

'She is well enough,' he said, his eyes on her face and showing no inclination to move away.

Anton saw some of Clara's feelings even as he observed that Sophie was holding Joseph's arm a little too tightly.

'I have often heard your concerts,' said Clara.

'Have you?' Joseph's eyes went over her thoughtfully.

'Too many give you their admiration, or I should have joined them afterwards,' she said frankly.

Sophie's eyes narrowed at this. The girl's candour was more seductive than any attempt at flirtation.

'Are you a musician, then?' she asked, with a little edge to her voice.

'I love music,' said Clara. 'That is all.'

'I see,' said Sophie, her little nose tilting. She pulled on Joseph's arm in a proprietorial way. 'Aren't we going to have a glass of champagne?' she asked.

Anton held up his hand for waiters to bring what they needed, and Sophie's lips tightened. She had mainly intended to move away from the girl. Joseph gently released his arm, then turned back to Clara.

'I remember perfectly now,' he said in a low voice.

Anton frowned to see the handsome young man bending over Clara, whose face seemed transformed with light and life in his presence.

Clara reminded Joseph of their encounter at the English Embassy, and he shook his head.

'Didn't I teach you to read one cold, winter afternoon?' he asked her.

'You were my earliest education,' she agreed, laughing. 'Your books, your words, your music.'

'You have changed,' he observed, his eyes flickering over her delicate white skin. He looked then with a little frown at Anton, clearly disliking what he took to be the nature of their relationship.

'Are you enjoying the music?' asked Anton, making polite conversation with Sophie.

Sophie threw up her arms in despair. 'How can you ask? He is the greatest composer Germany has ever produced.'

Anton and Sophie talked for a while, perhaps to conceal the animation of their companions' conversation.

'That young man took a great deal of interest in you,' commented Anton as they left the park much later.

'Do you think so?'

'You must have seen as much,' said Anton.

'I don't think he approved of my way of life,' she said with a little laugh.

'You called him a childhood friend?' he pressed.

'Not close,' she said. 'He hardly remembered me.'

'He asked for your address,' observed Anton. 'I don't think the singer who accompanied him was best pleased.'

'Perhaps it was improper of me to give it to him,' she said. 'I saw as much myself.'

Although Clara looked for some message from Joseph over the succeeding weeks, none came, and at length she ceased to hope for it. He was travelling, certainly, and most likely in the company of his beautiful friend.

However, Joseph had not forgotten Clara. Her intelligent black eyes looking up at him had aroused a protective tenderness he had not felt before. Sophie, who had observed the pleasure he took from the encounter, mocked him bitterly for his interest the following day.

'Poor Joseph. She is not as young as she looks, you know.'

'There's no need to be jealous—' began Joseph, who had no wish to be plunged into one of the furious quarrels Sophie often precipitated these days.

'Jealous? Don't be absurd. Do you imagine I could feel jealous of one of Shassner's women?'

Sophie, who was adjusting the clasp on a new dress, turned from the mirror to stare at him haughtily. The summer light from the window fell without flattery across her face and Joseph made out, guiltily, the first signs of her ageing.

'Don't be so sure about their relationship,' he said with a teasing smile.

Seeing what she took to be affection in his face, Sophie sidled up to put one velvety arm round his neck.

'Are you tired of me?' she murmured in his ear.

'No,' he said, 'no.'

He held her in his arms. She was still a beautiful woman.

All the same, Joseph was not altogether sorry to leave Sophie behind when he took the train for St Petersburg at the end of the week, and he carried with him a half-written letter to Clara. The letter was never sent, since he was not sure what he intended or what he could offer. Yet in the Baltic light of the radiant northern city, as he marvelled at the golden dome of St Isaac's and the deep blue walls of the palace in which he played, Clara's sensitive face continued to haunt him.

Chapter Twenty-Three

NATAN SHASSNER did not often go to the races, but some time in April 1866 Baron Hess, a close friend of Prince Schwarzenberg and an important figure in the administration, invited him to do so. Something in the Baron's tone suggested that there were matters of importance he wished to discuss and, as Shassner well knew, he was not a frivolous man.

The days of Metternich might be over, but the new regime remained inordinately interested in its citizens' opinions. Both the Prince and the Baron were Catholics: for both, the preservation of the existing order was the most important thing. What the Baron might want with him Shassner did not yet know.

So it was, in formal top hat and carefully tie-pinned cravat, pretending to an enjoyment he did not feel, that Shassner stepped into the shiny carriage the Baron had sent for him and set off for the races.

The Baron came from an old family which had managed its estates with care over the years. He had a box of his own at the races which commanded an excellent view of the course, but he suggested Shassner might like to walk and look at the paddock where the horses paraded before the race began.

As they strolled through the crowds towards the paddock,

a light wind fluttered the leaves. The girls' skirts, too, fluttered at the ankles and Shassner found the spring air brought back feelings that rarely troubled him these days. As he remembered, he looked about at the great poplars and willows on the Danube banks, and admired the fresh green lawn and the white grandstand. Together, he and the Baron surveyed the clean lines of the horses. Shassner admired the gleaming coats and the assurance of their riders.

'Do you have any intuitions?' enquired the Baron.

'I am not a gambling man,' admitted Shassner.

All horses looked the same to him, but this he did not say.

'Nevertheless, it is the custom,' said the Baron quietly.

'Then perhaps number seven will be lucky,' said Shassner, rather irritated to find himself falling back on the number magic of the ghetto.

'You look melancholy today,' said the Baron, as they took their seats in the box.

'Not so. Or not exactly. Memories disturb me,' said Shassner.

'It is the weather,' said his companion with an unexpected smile.

Shassner waited for the conversation to take whatever serious direction his host might wish. He was not altogether surprised to find that the Baron was concerned about articles that had appeared in Anton's newspaper.

'Even the *Neue Freie Presse* is not so impudent,' said Baron Hess, as if hurt.

A cry went up from the crowd and the horses were off. The Baron offered Shassner his binoculars. Number seven, its jockey in vivid green, was lying behind a bunch of other horses at the rear, he saw without much surprise, offering the binoculars back to his host. Hess took them, and then gave a muffled grunt of surprise.

'Well, I'm damned!'

Shassner peered at the course. It looked as though an animal mounted by a vivid green jockey was edging into the forward group of horses.

'I do believe,' said the Baron, 'you have chosen the winner.'

In a moment a cry from the whole crowd confirmed this was so.

'Fortune favours the foolish,' said Shassner with a smile.

It was a distraction, and he was quite surprised both at the Baron's excitement and the eagerness with which he collected his winnings.

'You have an eye for it, that is clear,' Hess insisted, urging Shassner to place another bet. 'An eye.'

Shassner sighed. He knew he had shown neither intelligence nor skill in choosing the winning horse and, though he reluctantly now chose number three, he was glad to get back to the Baron's uncomfortable seats. His leg was beginning to hurt, and the crowds disturbed him.

Once sitting down again, the Baron came back to the point.

'Your son makes fun of the army.'

'Why consult me?' demanded Shassner.

'Do you no longer have a controlling financial interest?'

'My son was able to buy me out,' said Shassner, with a smile of rare pleasure.

'I heard of some transfer of control,' admitted Baron Hess. 'But you must have some influence over your son, and we have dealt with one another for many years.'

Baron Hess was smiling, but he was clearly put out.

'Anton wanted complete independence,' Shassner said evenly.

'He's been successful, I know. A great many people read his newspaper.'

'He has excellent coverage of the arts,' Shassner agreed. 'Hanslick writes for him now.'

'Not only the arts,' muttered Baron Hess. 'The press love venality. *Neue Freie Presse* even writes scurrilously about the police. There was a case recently about officers who chose not to prosecute a brothel. They dared to claim it was because some of the force were making use of it. An absurdity.'

'I heard something of that.'

'These are things we dislike, but they are not serious. But would you say this was a moment to be writing satirically about the army? With line-drawings?' demanded Baron Hess. 'You know what Grillparzer says: the army *is* Austria.'

'The army is very popular in Vienna,' said Shassner. 'Surely the laughter is innocent enough. Like operetta.'

The Baron leant forward very seriously. 'Perhaps. But you know the difficulties the Emperor has with King William of Prussia and Bismarck?'

'Naturally.'

'Bismarck has plans,' said Baron Hess, 'to take over the whole of the German Federation. Austria is the only power that could stop him. He should be afraid of us. I don't think he has a sense of humour.'

Shassner nodded.

'When his Imperial Majesty,' said Baron Hess, 'has appointed a General who is pleased to question his own appointment, that is not a matter for the press. Is it?'

'I suppose not,' said Shassner carefully.

'Can't you persuade your son to have the interests of Austria in mind?'

Shassner murmured that these days there were too many newspapers for one to have much importance in itself.

That remark set Baron Hess on another tack.

'Many newspapers, yes. But isn't it strange, it sometimes seems that only Jews write for them?'

'Should this alarm you?' asked Shassner. 'Why?'

The moment after he spoke, he regretted the question. I must be quite tired or old, he thought, to treat an old wolf like Hess as if he were a friendly dog. But Hess nodded, as if the question were entirely reasonable.

'Your people control the finance of Vienna,' he said.

'You exaggerate,' said Shassner. 'The feudal influence and power of the great landowners is far greater.'

'The princes of the world go into liquidation,' said Baron Hess. 'But the Rothschilds remain where they are.'

'Not all Jews are Rothschilds,' said Shassner, patiently. 'I hope you don't mistake my own resources, Baron.'

'Sugar, coal, steel, beer, lignite. Your people are very bold these days. You develop them all,' pointed out Hess. 'It isn't only banking. It's leather goods, furniture, ready-to-wear clothing. And now the press is in your hands. Your people pour in because of the kindness with which Vienna receives them,' continued the Baron. 'Not everyone is so pleased. There are complaints every day from the good tradesfolk of Vienna. We choose to ignore them.'

'I understand,' said Shassner.

There was a threat in the Baron's voice, and Shassner did indeed understand it. He remembered a land where pogroms had been organized at the nod of an aristocratic head. What the Baron was telling him was that the present security of the Jews in Vienna was no more solid than that his father had enjoyed in the stetl. Things could change. He had learnt that lesson long ago. For a moment he was angry with himself for failing to pass that knowledge on to his son. It was the responsibility of successful Jews not to bring trouble on the rest. The lesson Shassner had learnt was to keep his head down; Anton was holding his own head too proudly, because he had no feeling for that terrible history.

'We are all loyal to the Habsburgs,' said Shassner, directly.

'And with reason. The Emperor is above petty nationalism. Austrian Jews are Austrians first and last.'

'Your own loyalty to the Habsburgs is well known,' said Baron Hess. 'I come to you, Shassner, as a representative of your people as a whole. I am sure you know as well as I do that your son has radical friends.'

'The apple doesn't fall very far from the tree, however.'

'I am not sure any vegetable metaphor is suitable for the Jews. They have no roots, and they move from country to country,' said Hess sharply.

'They are drawn to the greatness of Vienna,' murmured Shassner.

'Some things may seem irreversible,' said the Baron, musing, 'when they are not.'

'We are grateful to the Imperial dispensation,' said Shassner. His heart lurched uneasily when the Baron took his leave.

A few months later, as the Viennese were celebrating on a fine evening with wine and bratwurst in the Prater, the battle of Königgrätz was fought between Prussia and Austria. It proved an unequal trial of strength. The highly disciplined Prussian military machine, armed with breech-loading rifles, defeated the Austrians completely. Twenty thousand Austrians were taken prisoner, and thirty thousand men who had for so many years enjoyed the role of operetta soldiers now paid for their handsome uniforms with their lives.

Natan Shassner, returning home in his carriage in sombre mood, observed that people in the Prater went on dancing even after they had heard the news.

Chapter Twenty-Four

THESE DAYS SHASSNER often visited Budapest. Some time after the disaster of Königgrätz had been absorbed and accommodated, he returned from such a trip and appeared at the offices of Anton's newspaper with only the most cursory of warnings. Anton, who had watched the shiny black carriage approach with some foreboding, welcomed Shassner into the editorial office with his usual dislike of his father's appraising eye. There was, however, a marked change in his father's appearance.

'You do not look well,' said Anton.

'No,' said Shassner, shortly.

'Have you seen a doctor?'

'Those heavy Hungarian meals give me indigestion,' said Shassner, with a little movement of his mouth that suggested pain.

'Too much goose fat,' agreed Anton.

For a moment, he looked at his father with concern. At sixty-two, Shassner looked strong enough. His hair was grey but his face was unlined and his eyes were sharp. Still, he could hardly be immortal, and Anton felt a pang of compassion for him which he nevertheless suppressed, as he had always done since childhood. Shassner did too much: he was incapable of leisure. For that, no doubt, there was a price to be paid. He could hear his mother's grave voice saying as much.

'How is Mother?' asked Anton, a little guiltily.

These days he saw Minna only at weekends. She seemed frail and a little pathetic when he called. His father's travels left her too much alone, he decided.

'Minna is well enough,' said Shassner, frowning.

Shassner saw that his son was buoyant and cheerful. Military disaster, which had occupied his newspaper for weeks after the battle with Prussia, had given way to other stories. There had been rumours that the Prussians had learnt of defence plans ahead of time from the Austrian Defence Ministry, and General Benedek, who had been in charge of the campaign, was relieved of his commission, and severely interrogated. Anton seemed altogether at ease. He had found his niche, Shassner acknowledged.

At last Anton dismissed everyone else and swivelled in his chair to talk to his father.

'There are more riots in Budapest, I hear.'

Shassner nodded gloomily. 'Two factories were attacked, too. There will have to be some accommodation with the Hungarians. Things can't go on as they are. The tide is running against Austria.'

'Don't look so unhappy about it. Wherever I look,' said Anton, 'I see the opening of a new era, a better one, with more people able to enjoy prosperity.'

'You think that because the Stock Exchange is rising for the moment. People are optimistic because they believe Austria cannot risk any more excursions into Germany.'

'But that's a good thing, isn't it?' said Anton. 'Let's not be sentimental about the Empire. It may be for the best to see the end of it.'

'I was far from cheered by the loss of Lombardy to the Italians.'

'Think of the changes in Vienna,' said Anton, laughing. 'Look how people dress and play now. They enjoy their money here.'

'Well, I am pleased of course that my physician can afford to drive a pair-drawn fiacre these days,' said Shassner with some irony. 'But I'm surprised to hear you place so much value on material welfare.'

'One thing leads to another,' said Anton. 'There is far greater freedom everywhere.'

'Licence, too,' said Shassner crisply.

'You are not so sympathetic as I am to national aspirations.'

'No. I have seen what comes of them.'

'My newspaper offers both points of view to our readers. The rise of nationalism is important to them.'

'It may be very important, but I think you mistake its likely results,' said Shassner.

Anton shrugged. 'If you mean I don't understand the virtues of the Habsburgs . . .'

'I mean what I say,' said Shassner. 'When every language has its own nation, will that be better? When every people is behind its own frontier, will that be better?'

'That choice is their right.'

'Their right? Perhaps. But it will hardly benefit them. You campaign as a radical,' said Shassner, 'from a very comfortable position.'

Shassner's blood pressure had risen, and the pulse in his temple was beating visibly.

'None of this is what I came here to discuss,' he said. 'Yes, things are going well. Some people feel prosperous. But must you give space in your newspaper to our enemies? We have a duty to be thoughtful. And, if things go wrong, there will be many who conclude the emancipation of the Jews is responsible.'

'I must give space to radicals because it's my business to explain how things really are,' said Anton.

'And how are they?' Shassner's eyebrows went up.

'It's an age of transition. I don't approve of the way everything is going. For instance, I can see no particular virtue in the mass production of a capitalist society,' said Anton.

This observation incensed Shassner. 'Can't you? And what do you suggest in its stead?' he asked. 'Efraim Jacob's socialism?'

'The artisans in the Guilds want a breathing space.'

'A very popular position,' said Shassner, coming to the point. 'But how do you justify your liberal attitude towards this mad cleric?'

A man had been gaoled for breach of the peace: he had been shouting insults outside a textile factory recently opened by an enterprising businessman from Budapest. The man who caused the affray was a one-time priest, and evidently a little crazed, but some of the Viennese citizens who joined in with enthusiasm were decent tradesfolk who found themselves without jobs. Their anger was directed against the new machinery, so Anton was as sympathetic as Jacob. What was confusing was the shape that hatred had taken over the past week.

'I know he denounces Jewish capital,' said Anton slowly, 'but that is irrelevant since the particular factory owner happens to be a gentile Hungarian.'

'He is also claiming that Jews murder Christian children. It's the oldest lie in the book, but the men who shouted and threw stones in the streets yesterday believed him. They clamoured for an enquiry into some missing boy. You should use your paper to make the sensible point, not show sympathy for what has sent him mad.'

'No one who reads our paper will believe his tale,' said

Anton. 'This is Vienna, not some superstitious little village under the Tsar. For God's sake, we are nearly three-quarters of the way through the nineteenth century.'

'You may be right,' said Shassner. 'But yesterday we came close to having a street riot in Taborstrasse. A few workshops had bricks thrown through their windows. People think the new technologies are depriving them of their livelihood and they think the Jews brought them in. What's he like, this man who hates Jews so much?'

'Son of a shoemaker. Came from a big family. A retarded child, they say.'

'He seems fluent enough now,' said Shassner with a touch of bitterness.

'I sometimes wonder,' said Anton, 'why secular Jews don't convert. If we believe in nothing, why go to so much trouble to be hated by everyone.'

Shassner smiled. 'It's a kind of obstinacy. And a kind of honesty. Converting or not converting is part of another age.'

'I am not much tempted by another religion,' Anton admitted wryly. 'The temptation is to be like other people. I don't want to think about any of it. There are people who still have to haul their drinking water out to the suburbs. I'd rather campaign about that.'

Against his intentions, Shassner found himself raising a matter which was altogether irrelevant to their discussion.

'And what exactly are your intentions towards the young woman in Ebonstrasse?'

'She is a friend,' said Anton, rather awkwardly. He did not ask what his father had heard of Clara.

'Please don't be so pious with me. I'm quite aware of how young men think it appropriate to behave in this city.'

Anton was angry now, all the more so since he had spoken the simple truth.

'Don't lecture me,' he said. He looked at the reddening face of his father and unbidden memories from his own childhood came back to him: his mother's tense and beautiful face, weeping; her careworn, gracious mantle of womanhood.

'You used to pretend saintliness, but I know better.'

'What do you mean?' asked his father, dangerously.

'There were other women in your own life when I was young. I always suspected it. My mother confided as much to me. I see no reason to be answerable to you on moral grounds.'

'Your mother confided in you?' repeated Shassner, stupidly. He sat down.

'Yes, she told me,' said Anton. His satisfaction mounted at his father's discomfiture.

'I did not think her so treacherous,' said Shassner. 'When did she tell you this?'

'Long ago,' said Anton, rather disconcerted to see his father so shaken.

'What did she tell you?'

'Very little,' Anton admitted.

Shassner absorbed this. 'There was little to tell,' he said at length. 'It was when your mother was ill. There was no real love in it. A wild girl.'

'What became of her?'

'How can it matter to you? I don't know,' said Shassner.

'What a hypocrite you are,' said Anton. 'How dare you bully me about a friendship which is, little as you might imagine it, perfectly chaste.'

'Please, Anton,' said Shassner, 'it's not necessary to explain any more.'

'Are you calling me a liar?'

'I am calling you a fool,' said Shassner. 'And, if you are lying, it is no more than I would have expected of you.'

Anton flushed. 'If you were not my father—' he began.

'What then? You would call me to a duel like your fine aristocratic friends, would you?'

Even now, old and squat and ugly, Shassner looked unafraid and powerful.

'I have nothing more to say to you,' he said, breathing heavily as he rose to his feet.

'The carriage is outside,' said Anton.

Shassner picked up his hat and gloves and strode out of the office.

Chapter Twenty-Five

THAT SAME AFTERNOON, Clara was walking back from the home of one of her pupils along the Graben when a woman dressed in shiny black stopped in front of her and exclaimed, 'Clara, isn't it?'

Clara stared into a broad, pasty face, jauntily capped with a red straw hat, and doubtfully made out a friend from her first days in Shassner's kitchens.

'Lily?' she enquired uncertainly.

'The same. Lord, I've aged, I know, but I hope I'm still recognizable.'

Clara let herself be drawn into Lily's arms, and smelled a mix of sweet and musty scents which made her shiver uneasily.

'You've become a beauty,' said Lily. 'You'll be one of the lucky ones, I expect. Married with a fine husband, is that the story?'

'Not married,' said Clara, 'but I've been lucky enough. There are other kinds of good fortune.'

'Don't say it,' begged Lily. 'I'd have said that once, but I know better now. Marriage is the only fortune for a girl, let me tell you straight. When I see the old dears walking round the street, all safely married and nothing to worry about, I could spit with envy.'

Clara laughed.

'Marry while you can,' said Lily, shaking her head. 'I've been out in this cruel city and I know what *fun* is worth.'

'I wasn't thinking of what you mean by fun,' said Clara.

'I should think not, a prim little thing like you. Well, I never thought to see you on Ebonstrasse, but nothing is certain in this life. And you seem to have done well enough for yourself.'

'I work for my living,' said Clara, rather proudly.

'And who doesn't?' said Lily with a throaty laugh. 'I work hard, even if I'm convalescent these last few days. Look, I live just up here.' Lily drew Clara into a doorway and up some shabby stairs as she went on talking. 'You may think they aren't loved, the respectable women. That's what all the men tell us, but who's to know what goes on when the curtains are drawn?'

Clara stared round Lily's bare room with its big bed and poor furniture, and Lily read the pity in her expression.

'It's not much,' she said. 'Still, I'm not short of a bottle to celebrate. Will you take a glass?'

Clara sat on the bed and nodded politely.

'What has happened to you, Lily?'

'Well, you can see. It might be worse. I've a protector, which is more than some have, so I'm happy enough. Only trouble—' Lily stared urgently into the mirror. 'I'm not so healthy as I was. I've been to the hospital but there's no getting away with it. You have to be careful on this game. Well, we can still drink, can't we?' She poured Clara a glass and looked at the girl's clear skin and bright eyes. 'You *have* looked after yourself.'

Clara explained something of her life since she left Shassner's house. Lily listened, giving several interjections and often pouring herself a glass of wine without remembering to do as much for Clara.

'You can't tell me,' she said at last. 'This latest is the one, isn't he? This Anton of yours. That's why you look so well, I should think.'

Clara explained that Anton was no more than a friend. Lily burst into a laugh of raucous scepticism.

'He paid your rent all that time for nothing, then, I suppose?'

Clara explained about the lessons and Lily laughed again.

'If it was anyone else, I'd tell you what I thought of that as an explanation but, if that's your line, so be it. He sounds a fine gentleman, and good luck to you while you can hold on to him.' She shook her head in bewilderment as Clara described Anton's charming manners and elegant clothes, adding that he was a handsome young man. 'You can't choose who you love, and that's for certain,' said Lily. 'But look at the girl. There must be someone else, and that's dangerous.'

Clara shook her head. Lily peered into her face, more than a little drunk now and with perspiration running down her cheeks.

Clara said, 'There isn't anybody.'

'You always were a funny little thing. What's the matter? Haven't you ever?'

Clara dropped her gaze.

'You telling me you're a virgin?' demanded Lily. Then she gave a hoot of laughter. 'Well, I'm damned. Now I've seen everything. Looking like you do in the middle of Vienna? Well, there's a strange thing. Oh, you'll be holding out for marriage, I suppose. Well, whatever I said before, don't go thinking marriage is such a picnic, either. Have a little love first, at least, is my advice. I'm married. Had two babies, as a matter of fact, though I couldn't keep them. Didn't have the money for it. Still, until I was ill things were well enough.'

'And your protector?' asked Clara.

'He'll be here, he'll be here for supper, I hope. Do you want to meet him? He's no gentleman, mind,' said Lily. 'But I love him. And that's what matters, isn't it? All that matters to a girl is love.'

Clara said, 'I don't know that I feel like that.'

'You have to have a man,' said Lily. 'Every girl wants a man. Don't pretend to me. You're the same as everyone else.'

Clara shook her head.

'There must have been men after you?'

'I'm not saying there haven't,' said Clara, remembering the last young, eager face, not much older than her own.

'You don't know till you try,' said Lily.

Clara shrugged. 'I've thought about it, Lily.'

'Oh, there must be someone,' said Lily. 'You always wanted a prince, that's your trouble.'

'Not a prince,' said Clara, stung out of her reticence.

'Who, then? Who, then?' clamoured Lily. Her face had blotched with drinking and she pulled at Clara's dress. 'There's someone you've met,' she encouraged.

'A musician,' said Clara. 'I suppose.'

Lily was incredulous. 'Musicians! They're everywhere. Bad as gypsies, most of them. And when do you see him?'

'I don't,' said Clara.

'Well, what's the use of that to a girl?' asked Lily. 'You're off in a dream again. Might as well be a prince in one of your books as that.'

Clara was sorry she had said as much as she had.

'I'll go now,' she said. 'Look after your health.'

'I will,' said Lily, pouring herself another glass of wine and lying back abruptly on the bed.

Clara made a note of Lily's address and Lily did not try to detain her.

Chapter Twenty-Six

FROM HANNAH'S WINDOWS in her new flat on the Jaegerzeile, the elegant world could be seen coming back from the races in their carriages. Close by, there was a public garden with a well-kept lawn, flowerbeds and fragile tables and chairs in front of a low, white building with long windows. Women in long dresses sat there under parasols watching children playing.

Yet Joseph still did not take Sophie to meet his mother. He knew exactly why. For all the commercial success of Hannah's two shops and the prosperity that now brought comfort to her flat and elegance to Hannah's dress, there was something ineluctably foreign about her. And he had no wish to have Sophie sniff at it. He could not bear to think of his mother hurt by the scorn in Sophie's fine nostrils. And in her turn, he reflected, Hannah would not be impressed. Why should she be? Sophie, though she was a piquant actress, was no great singer. She might aspire to the role of Susanna in Mozart's *Marriage of Figaro*, for which her personality fitted her admirably, but she had neither the musical intelligence nor the vocal clarity for it. He visited home, therefore, on his own.

On one such visit, Joseph was surprised to be met with solemn looks. The musical son of their friends had been taken into hospital.

'Will you visit him?' asked Hannah.

The boy had been taken ill with sudden appendicitis. He had just been accepted at the Conservatory, too, and his mother was beside herself with misery.

'Is he home again?' asked Joseph, by no means eager to visit the hospital.

'Yes.'

'And he wants me to visit him?'

'He particularly asked. And his mother, you know, is very decent. A poor Jewish woman who does her best to keep the family going,' said Hannah. 'She comes from a village in Galicia not far from ours. Please, Joseph?'

'Perhaps next week, then,' said Joseph.

It was not the butcher's wife who answered the door of the small flat to Joseph this time, but the boy's elder sister, skinny, black-eyed and long-faced, who welcomed Joseph with an embarrassing reverence.

'Mother looks after the shop these days,' she explained. 'My father is in the countryside. He arranges the deliveries of meat.'

This girl, too, it seemed, had musical ambitions, but had put them aside in favour of her younger brother. There were other children rushing around, including two boys a year or two younger than the sick child. It was not an orderly household.

As soon as Joseph saw the boy lying in his pile of white pillows, he realized how sick he was. He was deathly pale and his eyes, always large, seemed now to fill his tiny face. He must have lost a great deal of blood at the time of the operation, Joseph judged, wondering if he were not still running a fever.

The boy could hardly raise his head, and held out his hand to beckon Joseph close to the bed.

'Here's a piece of ill luck,' said Joseph, with as much good cheer as he could muster. 'But you'll soon be well again. You must eat good chicken broth and noodles.'

'He has no appetite,' said his sister, shaking her head.

'You need no appetite for broth,' said Joseph. 'It slips down like a drink.'

At the boy's insistence, Joseph sat down on the coverlet and waited for him to speak.

'I wanted to see you again,' the child whispered.

'And I am here,' said Joseph. 'I hope all your wishes will be so easily satisfied. Is there anything else you would like?'

'I can't work,' the boy whispered again. 'I have no strength even to hold a pen.'

Joseph felt a sudden prickle of tears at the back of his eyes as memory, unbidden, recalled the lovely melody the boy had played him at their first meeting.

'I still remember your piece,' he said. 'It went like this . . .' He hummed the air to the boy, who gave a little smile of recognition. 'Do I have it right?'

'Perfectly.' The boy swallowed with difficulty.

'Would you like a drink?' asked his sister.

'Yes,' he murmured.

The girl went off to get one.

'I hear you won a place at the Conservatory. That will be a fine opportunity,' said Joseph.

'Yes. If I live to take it up.'

'But you must,' said Joseph, startled. He put his hand on the boy's forehead, which seemed to him exceedingly hot. 'When does the doctor say you will be better?'

'He says he does not know,' said the child.

'Sooner than you think. See if that isn't so,' said Joseph, though his voice sounded a little hollow to his own ears.

'It wouldn't be fair, would it? To die without doing what I want to do,' said the child.

'Have you written any more pieces?'

'One is for you,' whispered the child.

He gestured towards the table but, as far as Joseph could see, there was no manuscript on it. His sister had returned now and was giving him a glass of lemon juice to drink.

'May I see the piece that was left on the table?' Joseph asked, turning to the girl.

She bit her lips in some distress.

'She says I imagine it,' said the child. 'She says it is only a dream of mine. But I wrote it out the other day and showed it to Papa, and he left it on the table for me to give to you.' The effort of saying so much seemed to have exhausted him and his eyes closed.

'Perhaps your father knows where it is?' asked Joseph. The girl shook her head. 'There is no such piece of paper. Everything is in his head.'

Joseph saw that there were tears on her cheeks, and he believed her. His own thoughts were painful. He was moved by the boy's passion. His own good fortune seemed clear, hard-edged, incontrovertible in comparison; yet the boy had perhaps the finer gift. His breathing was stertorous, and he seemed to have fallen into a heavy sleep.

Everything remained in his head.

'Have you brought your violin?' asked the girl. 'You could play to him.'

'No. I will come back,' promised Joseph. 'Early next week.'

But the next day Hannah sent him a message with the news he had half expected. The child was dead. Nothing that remained in his head would ever be heard now.

Chapter Twenty-Seven

SOME TIME AFTER the child's death, a letter arrived asking Joseph to play at Baron von Presser's castle in his country home in the Tyrol.

'It's very short notice,' commented Joseph. 'Someone must have fallen ill.'

'But you are free that weekend?' Sophie pointed out.

'How do you know that I am free without looking at my diary?' Joseph was booked a year ahead and had no memory of free days himself.

'Because I looked,' Sophie smiled.

'Why did you bother?' Joseph was far from pleased.

'Von Presser asked me to. He has important guests.'

'Which guests are so important?' Joseph enquired, with a little acid in his voice since he had recently given a concert for the daughter of Prince Metternich.

'You'll have a chance to meet Richard Wagner,' said Sophie, with thrilled reverence in her voice.

All the rumours suggested that this would be far from an unequivocal pleasure but of late Joseph had experienced a wish to test himself, a spiritual urge which not even an invitation to the Imperial Palace could assuage. His spirit seemed to open out and expand at the prospect of such a meeting, though he perversely opposed Sophie's urging.

'I wonder what Wagner needs from von Presser?' he speculated. 'Is he a new patron?'

Sophie rebuked him for his cynicism.

'Wagner is richly supported these days by the King of Bavaria,' she said. 'Those dreadful months in Vienna when he owed everyone money and had to live on someone else's kept woman are over.'

'He has expensive tastes,' said Joseph.

'But von Presser's invitation?' she interrupted impatiently. 'Will you accept?'

'I suppose to meet Wagner might be something.'

'How can you hesitate?'

'His dislike of Jews is well known.'

'Stupid! He surrounds himself with Jews,' said Sophie. 'Virtuosos flock to his court. I happen to know the singer Angelo Neumann is a Jew. I don't understand you. I would give my arm and leg for such an opportunity. You should embrace it.'

Joseph said irritably, 'I have already said I will accept.'

'But so grudgingly, without any joy. Perhaps you're spoiled by too much success. Von Presser said as much the other day.'

Joseph frowned at this additional intimation that the arrangement had been made with Sophie's assistance.

'Do you intend to accompany me?' he asked.

'Of course!'

Joseph had a number of reasons for disliking von Presser: among them his military bearing, his high rank in the diplomatic service and the scorn with which he treated musicians while purporting to revere music. Above all this, however, was Joseph's suspicion that von Presser had been one of Sophie's earlier lovers. It was not that Joseph was jealous exactly: what he disliked was the way Sophie became more snobbish in von Presser's presence.

That vitality and self-confidence Joseph so much admired

in Sophie rested on the reality of her good health and good
looks. She had begun, recently, to make other claims. An
ancient connection to a noble family, for instance, which she
insisted lay behind her own humble village origin. This was
the inheritance that gave her rights on the Austrian stage,
and she raged against half-Czech or half-Magyar singers who
were given roles she coveted. She particularly resented the
huge salaries given to Italian prima donnas. In this, she was
expressing no more than a general exasperation the talented
Viennese felt about the invasion of their city. In von Presser's
company, she often went further.

'Why must you always agree with him?' he said.

'I do not change.'

'Oh yes,' he insisted. 'You become as flirtatious as a bit-
part actress flirting with a man who has brought flowers
after the show.'

'A bit-part actress!' she said, furiously. 'My God! What
arrogance! My father would turn in his grave to hear me
spoken to as you do. How can you dare? Only because your
violin brings you everything.'

Joseph stirred his breakfast coffee quietly, and agreed.
His violin had brought him most of what he needed.
But something in him craved more. An acceptance which
was more than applause, more than praise, more than
fees.

'We should all like to create great music,' he said.

'But you can't, and nor can your friends,' she flashed.
'Not even Brahms. They can create nothing of any size.
Wagner is a revolutionary: he knows how European society
must be regenerated.'

'Size is not everything.'

'The Austrian press are against him, and the French and
English are worse. Surely any musician knows that Wagner
is the greatest composer in Europe?'

'Are you hoping he will offer you a role in his new opera?' suggested Joseph.

He thought it unlikely: Sophie's light voice and flighty manner hardly fitted her for Wagner's grand heroines.

'I want to set eyes on him. Shake his hand. That's all.'

For all his apparent hesitation, Joseph shared some of the same excitement at the prospect of having Wagner in his audience; the more so as it occurred to him that his host must have asked so important a guest to choose both music and musicians. After all, he thought, it was good of Sophie to arrange such an encounter, even if she had only herself in mind.

As he rose, he looked down at Sophie's fair hair, downy skin and provocatively curved body. She was very beautiful and, as he registered as much, she smiled up at him teasingly.

'Let us by all means have a pleasant weekend in the hills,' he said lightly. He no longer altogether liked Sophie, but he still desired her. She saw as much and lay back like a powerful cat and opened her legs.

It was a vile, windy afternoon in late March as Joseph set out on his own towards von Presser's castle. Von Presser had invited him to join the family for dinner on the Friday evening, so that Joseph would be able to relax and prepare himself for the concert on the Saturday night. Sophie was to join him the following day.

A black, sleety rain struck at the carriage, and the hills dissolved into great black shapes in the darkness. From time to time, a shaft of lightning illumined the conifer trees and revealed slopes with a scattering of snow. The road was poor and Joseph's carriage creaked on its springs.

As evening came on and he travelled further into the mountains, the storm grew more alarming. The crack of trees and the noise of the wind made it impossible to doze. Quite suddenly a jolt signalled that one of the wheels had caught in a rut. The coachman had to clamber down from his box and guide the wheel so that the horses could draw the carriage safely. It took nearly an hour and subsequently the carriage proceeded at a modest pace towards the next village so as not to risk damaging the axle further. There, Joseph was forced to negotiate the hire of a new vehicle. This took time and he began to fear he would be too late to enjoy a civilized meal when he arrived and might find his host seriously put out. He toyed with the thought of sending a wire to explain his delay.

He was already tired from the uncomfortable journey and wished nothing more than a bed and the recovery of a blank night's sleep. His last visit to the Tyrol had been all sunshine; his memory of the landscape had given a tinge of pleasure to von Presser's invitation. Now he was only conscious of the noisy thunder, the driving rain and a sense of displacement. He was used to travelling alone, but on this rainy evening every bush and tree seemed to be filled with darkness and the patches of sky that were visible between the clouds were coloured so strangely that he felt ill at ease.

It was long past eleven before he arrived at von Presser's castle. His host and hostess had already retired to bed, as he had half expected. The servant who came out to help the coachman unpack Joseph's cases was a short, gnome-like fellow with a beard cut to expose his chin: he seemed taciturn and obscurely hostile. Joseph wondered at his closed expression and found a coin for the man, but the nod with which it was received remained unfriendly. The house itself was in darkness.

Joseph was abandoned for a time in what seemed to be the dining room where several dishes of cold food were set out, though he had no appetite. By the light of the single candle he made out that the room was papered in a dark brown with little rosebuds and that the velvet curtains were the colour of garnets. On one of the tables he observed an ornate snuff box which he guessed was solid gold. If creditors were still pursuing Richard Wagner, he thought, they must be at a safe range. In Vienna they had taken everything, and many of his friends' knick-knacks had disappeared in the confusion. The room smelled of snuff and a strong perfume.

Suddenly he became aware of the woman. She sat in the darkness at a window that commanded a view of the road he had taken. As the gnome returned, having stowed Joseph's luggage, the man addressed the woman at the window rather than Joseph.

Even sitting down, the woman was taller than the servant. She was also, Joseph conjectured, pregnant. She had a profile which reminded him of his mother, with a pronounced and bony nose, but as the servant approached her with more light Joseph could see that, for all the apparent severity, her mouth was tender and her eyebrows generous. She wore a black cloak secured at the neck by two fluted buttons and a snake of bronze caught into a knot.

'You said to bring any message in here,' said the servant, as if speaking to the mistress of the house, although Joseph knew she must be another guest.

The woman addressed all her words to the servant, seeming too distressed even to notice Joseph.

'Has an answer come to my letter?'

'Nothing, madam.'

The woman now glanced briefly at Joseph, as if trying to make out who he could be.

'Are you certain my letter reached the King?' she asked.

'Yes, madam.'

The lantern he was carrying illuminated the woman's face more clearly now. She looked a little like a madonna by Correggio that Joseph had seen in a museum in Florence – with blue eyes, a tanned face and her blonde hair glistening

in a coil at the back of her head. Getting up from her chair
by the window, she began to pace the carpet in agitation.
After a few turns she paused and asked:

'Now who is this? I can't possibly attend to him now.'

The servant saw that he had mistaken his instructions.

'Shall I take him up to his room?'

She paused and looked at Joseph suspiciously. 'What is he
doing here?'

'It is the young violinist from Vienna. The master particularly said he was to be cared for,' said the servant.

'Not very young,' she said, looking Joseph over with
sudden alertness. 'Twenty-two? How old are you?'

'Twenty-seven,' said Joseph, angered by her tone. 'My
name is Joseph Kovacs.'

'I believe I have heard of you.'

At that a little more anger rose in Joseph.

'I have come at von Presser's invitation—' he began.

'Oh, I cannot attend to this now,' she interrupted.

Joseph bowed formally. If she speaks to me again in that
abstracted, condescending voice, he told himself, I shall leave.
It will be quite easy. I shall get back into my carriage and
whip the horses back into the town myself and stay at any
hotel I find. It is insufferable to come all this way at such
inconvenience for such a reception. But suddenly she was
extending her hand, and her face was all warmth and blessing.

'I remember now. Richard wanted to hear you. Forgive
me, I have many matters on my mind.'

For all this new friendliness, something in Joseph shrank
as he watched her turn her pent-up fury against the servant.

'Can't you see how tired he is? Why don't you look after
him?' she demanded. 'He is a musician of talent and deserves
attention.'

As the servant guided him upstairs, it occurred to Joseph

that no introductions had been made and, though the woman's imperious presence made it easy to guess her identity, he enquired into it delicately.

'That is Cosima von Bülow,' said the servant. 'She is the conductor's wife. And, of course, a loyal servant and secretary to Herr Wagner.'

'Is von Bülow here?' asked Joseph.

'The conductor went back to Berlin,' said the man phlegmatically.

As they reached the top of the stairs, a gust of wind sent a scurry of leaves from the landing across the hallway.

'And the other musicians?'

'The storm delayed everyone, but they will be here by lunchtime. They're coming from Munich.'

'But we must rehearse together at least once tomorrow,' said Joseph, dismayed. This was not how he had imagined playing before Richard Wagner.

'Everything will be looked after. You must rest. This house is full of beds,' said the servant. 'I'll bring you hot water.'

The wardrobe in Joseph's room was stuffed with dressing gowns and silk suits lined with fur which might well, Joseph conjectured, belong to Richard Wagner. He was clearly a frequent guest in von Presser's house and no doubt enjoyed many privileges in this friendship as he had in others. Joseph had no great urge to unpack for himself. Through the window, he could see that the rain had slackened and that the sky had cleared a little.

'Do you want anything to eat?'

Joseph suddenly felt altogether exhausted.

'I think I will go straight to sleep.'

He had been travelling with a Guarneri violin and, with a little touch of panic, he could not remember having carried it into the house.

'Where is my violin?' he asked.

'Safely in your room.'

Joseph was asleep as soon as he had undressed and fallen on his bed but he was woken at about three a.m. by the brilliant moonlight that poured into the room. The weather outside had altogether changed, and there was now a huge white moon outside his window which seemed to float in the darkness, flooding the whole room with silver light. He got up to close the curtains but was hypnotized by the beauty of what he saw: a single mountain gleamed whitely ahead, and a lake shared the pale glimmer of a sky which was silent and high above it, filled with a profusion of stars. Tired as he was, Joseph was reluctant to shut out so much splendour. He left the curtains undrawn and went back to bed, where he fell again into a dreamless sleep.

Breakfast, or at least rolls and coffee, appeared in his bedroom shortly after eight. Joseph prepared himself briskly for his usual morning practice. He had hardly begun when his embarrassed host, who had heard of his difficulties the night before, came to apologize for not being awake to receive him. The second violinist had arrived in the afternoon. The other musicians, having travelled through the night from Munich, were downstairs but would need some sleep before they played. Joseph went down to greet them.

He had played in a group many times with the second violinist and the cellist Ehrenstein; indeed they had shared a platform at the Theatre on the Wien the previous summer. They hugged one another cordially.

The viola player Joseph did not know, except by reputation. He was a gaunt, dark-haired man with deep lines in his cheeks and sadly hooded eyes. Perhaps because of his difficult journey, he was markedly less talkative than Ehrenstein. His name was Meyer, and Joseph remembered having heard him play. He recalled the occasion with some pleasure.

'I know you, too,' said Meyer, without reciprocating the compliment.

'I have a sense of crisis,' said Ehrenstein, 'They say Wagner left during the night.'

'That would be disappointing,' cried Joseph. 'What is this crisis?'

'They say there is some scandal in Bavaria about Wagner and the wife of von Bülow,' said Ehrenstein.

'I thought their relationship was common knowledge,' said Joseph, a little bewildered.

'Ah, but close relations, even idolatry, is one thing, and adultery is another,' said Ehrenstein. 'They say King Ludwig will not put up with it.'

Instinctively, all their voices had fallen into whispers, and Joseph drew away from the scandal.

'Cosima has been living here with her children, and Wagner is trying to make his peace with King Ludwig.'

'Not a good time to meet him, then,' said Joseph, with a slant smile.

'Is there a good time?' asked Meyer with an ambiguous shrug, in which Joseph recognized something of his own father.

'Can we play after lunch? I'd like to rest and bathe,' said Ehrenstein.

Back in his room, Joseph looked out at the garden. The weird cry of peacocks broke the quiet. The rain had left all the trees wet and glistening, but the sky was bright. His spirits were calm.

The guests for von Presser's weekend had already begun to arrive. He could see the shining carriages as they turned into the park, and hear the loudest of the cries of welcome from the hall below. About noon, von Presser sent a message to invite him to join them, but Joseph politely declined: he liked to prepare for a concert on his own; it was his custom;

he hoped von Presser would understand. When Sophie arrived, he knew she would join the other guests. If Wagner was there, thought Joseph, he would meet him after the music and, if not, it was no great matter. Sophie might be disappointed but he could endure it well enough.

After they had played through, Joseph smiled across to the viola player and said gruffly, 'You play like an angel.'

'Oh,' said Meyer, 'I play well enough.'

'It doesn't seem to please you.'

'What is it to be an executant musician?' asked Meyer with a melancholy smile.

Joseph had never asked himself the question and paused at it. 'You aspire to composition?'

'It is impossible,' said Meyer. 'How can we contribute to German music? We are not part of the culture.'

'How do you mean *we*, exactly?'

Even as he asked the question, Joseph observed that all of the musicians were Jews. Meyer saw he had no need to make the point, but he said, 'As Jews we can never fully enter European culture because we have no part in its heritage.'

'Please don't just mouth Wagner's words,' said Joseph.

'When I first read his books,' said Meyer quietly, 'I thought the only way out was to kill myself.'

'Well,' said Joseph, laughing rather nervously, 'you're still here.'

'I was a coward,' said Meyer. 'Even there I failed.'

Joseph put that conversation out of his mind as he entered the small, yellow-ochre room where the glittering audience expected them to play that evening. As he looked around, he found Sophie's pretty face three or four rows back, next to von Presser. He also saw Cosima, magnificent in purple, in the front row. There was no sign of Wagner. Was he sorry? A little, but, as he felt the spirit of Beethoven's music descending into him, he knew that whether or not Wagner heard him was finally unimportant. In the front row, Cosima was amongst the most enthusiastic of applauders, even standing up to register her pleasure. The rest of the audience, including von Presser and Sophie, followed her lead.

Afterwards, Cosima came up to him and took his hand seriously.

'In your playing, I regained my own soul,' she said. 'I had forgotten. Great music calms and cures all ills. If Richard had heard you play he would have felt as I do. Forgive him for being away?'

'I do,' Joseph said, inescapably flattered by a response so plainly genuine.

'You have come at a bad time,' she said.

Joseph nodded guardedly and waited to see what else might be told to him.

'Richard has other problems, I fear,' she said.

'I heard so,' said Joseph.

'Yes,' she sighed. 'The gossip is everywhere. It is unkind. But we have friends. Come, join us.' She took Joseph's arm.

The musicians followed von Presser and his guests into the dining room where supper had been laid out. Von Presser bent low over Sophie's hand and brought her over to Joseph in a way that Joseph found unpleasantly proprietorial, so that he accepted her congratulations rather coldly.

'Well,' said Sophie, 'I hope you are pleased that you came. Cosima von Bülow speaks well of you!'

'It is pleasant enough,' said Joseph, 'even without the gentleman in the Dürer hat.'

The other musicians withdrew fairly early in the proceedings but Joseph stood around to receive plaudits and friendly words from the audience, who pressed up to praise him. He also drank a great deal of the excellent red wine which von

Presser plied him with, though he was usually a fairly moderate drinker. Something in the occasion, for all its apparent success, had disturbed him – perhaps Meyer's uneasy words at the rehearsal. Sophie was urging him to withdraw but he shook himself free of her arm, obscurely and unfairly identifying his unease with her presence.

The guests, too, had now drunk freely and the conversation had taken off in directions far removed from Beethoven. With something of a shock, Joseph heard his host say, in a hearty voice:

'I am not against Jews. Well, there's no point. Is there? Once all society is permeated by the money ethic, there is no reason to exclude them.'

This remark brought laughter from the rest of the guests. Sophie pulled at Joseph's arm, obviously afraid that he, who had taken exception to such remarks before, would take the matter up with his host in an undignified fashion. Von Presser himself, suddenly aware of his guest's likely reaction, made a deprecating noise.

'Those who do not approve of the industrialization of Europe commonly blame us for it,' said Joseph mildly. 'It coincides very neatly with our emancipation.'

The other guests, who had thought of him as a musician staying a little later than might be expected, now identified him as a Jew. They looked to Cosima, who had been so fulsome in her congratulations, for some kind of lead. Joseph saw her great, aquiline profile turning itself in the direction of the speakers, and he remembered the rumours of her own birth: there were said to be Jewish bankers in her own history, and not so remotely, either.

'Do you really feel,' he then asked courteously, 'that Jews can make no contribution to German culture?'

'They make the contribution they can,' said Cosima. That

she said no more was a tribute perhaps to the pleasure she had taken in Joseph's rendering of Beethoven, or perhaps the high regard Wagner had expressed himself.

'Isn't Heine the greatest lyric poet of the age?' he persisted, since he knew Heine had been a friend of Wagner in Paris.

Sophie exchanged a glance with von Presser, and Joseph saw as much. It incensed him further, though his voice remained low. She tugged again at his arm.

'In anything but an age like this, he could not so impress,' said von Presser. 'Even if he duped two of our own composers.'

'How can a Jew make any contribution to the German language?' said another guest, perhaps too drunk to be alert to Joseph's own position. 'He has no mother tongue.'

The gloom of that exclusion filled Joseph's spirit. He looked to Cosima for support but none was forthcoming, and he steeled himself to the knowledge of being among enemies. Releasing his arm from Sophie's, he bowed and quietly left the room. As he did so, he heard a voice behind him saying, 'The cultured Jew is the worst.'

Upstairs in the bedroom, he packed with speed and anger in silence. He would not stay another night there. He should not have come. It was Brahms and Joachim who had shown him friendship. These were the enemies of his friends. Sophie joined him and watched as he flung his clothes together.

'You cannot expect to leave at this hour?'

'Why not? I arrived in the middle of the night and can leave when I choose.'

'But I am tired,' she said sullenly.

She went to the bed and lay back on it in a pose clearly intended to be seductive. His body did not respond.

'You let von Presser paw your hand,' he said unexpectedly.

'Are you jealous?' she asked. Her face lit up with relief at his words for, if that was all that lay behind this new blackness in his face, she could put it right. Von Presser was nothing to her. She found his paunchiness repulsive and she longed to be lying in Joseph's arms. 'There is no need,' she smiled, 'my dear love.'

'You bitch,' he said then, quite unfairly. 'You brought me to a house of enemies.'

She was as astonished as if he had struck her.

'They aren't *your* enemies!'

'Yes,' he said.

'You think such thoughts are spoken nowhere else?'

'I know they are. They are muttered in the streets. But to find them here is another matter.'

The poor, white face of the dead boy in Taborstrasse, who had never had a chance to do what he wanted, came suddenly into his mind. How pathetic his trust seemed now. Even if he had written what he had to write, how would these people have received it? And what of poor Meyer, who believed what these people said?

'I can't afford to listen,' said Joseph. 'That's why I'm going.'

'Everyone hears these things,' she pleaded. 'They don't matter.'

'They are evil,' he said.

'But these are not evil people. Maybe there *are* too many Jews in Vienna,' said Sophie, 'and that is the cause.'

'Too many,' he said. 'I see.'

'Yes. Too many in the arts and sciences and journalism. All too eager to send their children to the best schools.'

'And what is wrong with educating children into the Viennese way of life?'

She hesitated. She could see his fury. She wanted to conciliate him, but the way he framed his questions drove her to make the situation worse and worse.

'Maybe they are too ambitious for success?'

'Is that a wicked aspiration?'

'The Viennese want their own intelligentsia,' said Sophie baldly. 'It's natural enough.'

He had finished packing.

'You are going, then?' she said. 'I hope you don't expect me to come with you?'

'I don't,' he replied.

Proud as she was, she came close to pleading.

'If you leave now,' she said, 'I shall be completely humiliated.'

He gave a wry laugh. 'It's all right for me to stay and be humbled, I suppose?'

'What is it to you, if people utter a few fashionable prejudices?' she cried, wildly. 'It is impersonal; it is nothing to do with you.'

'It enters the soul,' he said again. And once more he thought of Meyer.

'If you go now,' she said proudly, 'that is the end of our relationship.'

He looked at her strangely. It came to him that he had been waiting for this for some time but before, whenever the idea had crossed his mind, it had been accompanied by great pain. Now he felt nothing.

'Let it be so, then,' he said.

A week later found Joseph at his mother's apartment. He usually ate his mother's Polish cucumbers and sliced fish with pleasure; now he pushed them round his plate, with an abstracted and moody air.

'You seem low today,' said Hannah. 'What is it?'

He could not explain. 'Sometimes I wonder what I am doing with my life,' he said instead. He smiled, to reduce the impact of his words, but Hannah came and sat next to him and he was sorry he had said as much.

'Is it a small thing to be such a wonderful musician?'

'To be a composer might be something,' he said.

'Another thing,' she agreed, puzzled and waiting for him to spell out what he meant. 'What would be a better life?' she asked him. 'Don't you live like a gentleman?'

'You only mean I have the money to dress well,' he said impatiently.

'What else do you want? To own a house on the Ring, to eat with the Emperor?'

'I don't need more luxuries,' he said, his face still dark.

'I don't understand,' she said.

He gave a bitter laugh. He had no belief that she could help him. What could Hannah, without education or breeding, living off a hat shop with a stetl husband, know about his spirit?

'Listen,' she said. 'You are the first generation to have the chance.'

'A chance of what? To see the world?' he mocked bitterly. 'I see hotels, trains, countryside.'

'A chance to excel,' she said quietly. 'That is something. You did not have to dream of what might have been, or wonder what the life of a musician might be. You are doing what you wanted. Isn't that a great thing?'

'My uncle was a musician,' he said doggedly.

'Yes,' she agreed. 'He had a fine talent, too. But where did he have the chance to use it? Russian weddings, taverns, country inns. He played dance music and old songs. You play the music you love. Don't you?'

During this conversation, Peretz had come in, unobserved, and had listened to this last exchange with his usual sardonic expression.

Peretz had been ill for some months with an ailment of the kidneys which had brought a yellow tone to his skin and the whites of his eyes. In his convalescence, he had begun to teach young boys in preparation for their bar mitzvah; more commonly, he studied for his own pleasure. As Hannah began to expound the legal gains of the last few years in Vienna, he broke in, scoffing.

'Legal gains? Popularity? What does emancipation mean for Jews? Some of us buy fine horses and carriages—'

'Nonsense. It means opportunity,' Hannah broke in vigorously. 'Now we are citizens like anyone else.'

Peretz gave a scornful laugh. 'You believe that, you'll believe anything! Your mother imagines that all the Viennese ladies who come into her shop do so because they like her. In fact they come because she has stylish hats more cheaply than anywhere else in Vienna. These are our opportunities.'

'But for Joseph it is different,' said Hannah. 'He is part of another world. A liberal world. Among people of culture.' Peretz gave a snort of amusement.

'We are outsiders in any Christian country. It's in their book. We are meant to be outside. And I don't mind. A Jew's homeland is other Jews,' said Peretz. 'That's the only place we can live happily.'

'You want to be separated off into ghettoes again?' asked Hannah.

'There were some advantages,' said Peretz.

'You see what he is like?' said Hannah to Joseph. 'What he wants back?'

'I am only saying it's not paradise now,' said Peretz. 'And our children have to go into the army, where they are generally tormented.'

'All the same, it is a time of opportunity. Isn't it, Joseph?' pleaded Hannah.

Joseph would have liked to give his mother the reassurance she craved but for once his father's words did not seem so foolish.

Chapter Twenty-Eight

HOWEVER LONG a working day Anton imposed on himself, Clara's face, with its childlike, mischievous smile and perfect skin, was there in his thoughts as soon as he lay down in his bed. Some nights he dreamt of her with the grossest abandon. He might use other women in his efforts to rid himself of his obsession: former mistresses, young country girls, occasional prostitutes. None could generate the tingling lust he experienced in Clara's presence.

There was only one real bond between them. Clara took an interest in whatever Anton wrote, particularly the stories and satires he wrote under an assumed name. She read attentively everything he brought her, questioning a word here or there, sometimes suggesting another. He brought one of his most successful essays to show her the day before he planned to put it in *New Vienna*.

'I shall publish it tomorrow,' he said. 'With line-drawings by a good Hungarian artist. Will you celebrate with me at the Gay Pig?'

She hesitated for a moment at that. 'In one of the private rooms?'

'Certainly,' he said. 'With Beluga caviar and champagne, and all that is fitting to mark such a triumphant occasion.'

Her hesitation pleased him. It suggested she knew of the use that was often made of the private rooms beyond and that, if she accepted, there might be some chance of pushing their relationship into the one he desired.

Their private room was painted an elegant, pale green with the famous trompe l'œil paintings of windows between columns and a curved oval ceiling. Through the windows, Cupid delicately pricked with his arrows the naked women who sported on the grass or lay under trees. The room itself was quite small, its furniture gilt like a stage set. Cold food had been laid out for them, and champagne in a silver bucket. The candles, too, were green, and Clara drew in her breath with pleasure at the beauty of the display. Anton's breathing changed to hear as much, but for another reason: ever since the quarrel with his father, he had determined to make his love known to Clara. She must know how he felt about her, but this evening he would make sure she understood the seriousness of his commitment. He did not even rule out matrimony, if she responded favourably.

As she bent over him to offer the first dish, he longed to bend so that his lips touched her white breast, but she smiled at him without guile and moved back to take her own portion.

'I shall never be used to such splendour,' she said.

He found it difficult to listen to what she was saying. Her dress was chaste enough, but in his imagination the body beneath was warm and eager.

Clara was unaware of his excitement. Her own concerns were all connected to her meeting with Lily.

'She looks like an old woman. Today I tried to write about it, but I could not find the words.'

'The right words,' he repeated stupidly.

'She is ill from drink and the diseases of her trade. Yet she simply accepts what has happened to her as natural. Poor Lily, she was so much in need of love.'

Anton leaned forward hopefully. 'Surely that is a natural instinct? She has simply been unlucky.'

'Well, I don't feel that instinct,' said Clara, frowning.

'Have you never felt any such thing?' asked Anton.

She shook her head.

'Not even for Newall?'

She stared at him. 'I hated him.'

'Even at first?' suggested Anton. 'I know how brutally he treated you at the end, but I thought you must have been attracted. He behaved desperately. Badly. But he was a handsome man.' He hesitated. 'Another man would be gentler with you. If you would let him.'

'I have thought about it,' she said, in a low voice.

'And?' His excitement hardened almost painfully.

'Perhaps there is something wrong with me,' she said simply. 'I feel so frightened at the thought of it.'

'*It?*' he asked slowly. 'The act itself, do you mean?'

'It must be too much of an invasion,' she said.

'You only think so because you do not know the pleasure it would bring.' He spoke urgently. 'Think of the poets.'

'They are men for the most part who write as they do,' she said. 'Perhaps it is a male pleasure, and women only pretend to feel any such thing.'

'Well, what of your Lily, then?'

'Can you recommend her fate to me?' she cried.

'Of course not. But consider,' he wheedled. 'Even in marriage you would have to consent to be loved. How else would there be children?'

'I have no wish to be married.'

'You want to live as a spinster?'

'I see nothing wrong with it.'

'To be so afraid of the greatest pleasure in the world,' he burst out. 'It is irrational. There may be a little pain at first.'

'I don't believe in the pleasure,' she said. 'And it's not the pain I fear.'

'You madden me,' he said. 'Have you no experience of desire?'

She hesitated. 'Perhaps,' she admitted.

He was incensed and jealous at once.

'No one you know,' she assured him. 'No one I see nowadays.'

She was a little ashamed to have referred to Joseph again after so recently betraying herself to Lily. It was such a doomed attachment. He forgot her as soon as she was out of sight. She had once sent him a card after a concert he gave at the Konzerthalle but he had never replied to her note.

'Has there really been no one you could love?' Anton asked her.

'No,' she said.

As she leant her head on one hand, without the slightest coquetry, her wrap slid away to reveal a bare arm. She continued quietly and ruminatively to eat her cold fish, looking up as she did so at the suggestive paintings that decorated the walls of the little room.

'You said you would like to read what I have been writing,' she said, after a time.

'Yes,' said Anton, suppressing a certain irritability since it was far from what he wanted to be doing at that moment.

She nodded, and bent to her bag from which she took several neat, handwritten sheaves.

'See what you think,' she said.

He took the papers in his hand with as much generosity as he could muster. His head was already buzzing, yet before he began he took a glass of wine. He could concentrate on nothing.

'You should write under a man's name,' he suggested, out of habit. 'Not many women publish in Vienna.'

'I don't like the idea of pretending,' she said doubtfully. 'Would you pretend, in my place? Would you pretend not to be a Jew, for instance?'

'Isn't that different?' Anton paused. For all his liberal convictions, he could not think of the resistance to women contributing to the arts as a prejudice of the same kind.

'It isn't vanity,' she said. 'I don't object to a pseudonym. But I should pick a woman's name.'

'People expect different things of a woman,' he tried to explain, 'and for the most part they are right to do so.'

'Jane used to say things were changing in England and France,' said Clara rebelliously.

'Even in England, even in France, women still write under men's names. And here—' He hesitated. 'Things are caught in a warp of time.'

Unexpectedly there came a little tinkling bell which indicated that a servant was at the door of their hidden room.

'I am sorry,' said Anton with surprise. 'They have strict instructions not to disturb us.'

'You could hardly compromise me more than I am,' she said, with a certain gaiety. 'I have altogether fallen out of society.'

She looked at him with a humour he would have liked to believe was flirtatious. He went to the door and, opening the heavy velvet curtain no more than a crack, shouted angrily, 'Have I not told you I was not to be disturbed?'

'But, sir, oh, sir—'

'What is it?'

'Your father,' said the servant. 'Your father is dead.'

'Oh, my God,' said Anton.

Once again he saw his father's reddening face, and the beating vein in his forehead.

'He was found in his study just an hour ago. Your mother asks you to return.'

Chapter Twenty-Nine

'MOTHER,' SAID ANTON, 'I came the moment I heard.'

Minna had been awoken from her bed, but even in such distress she had put her hair in order and looked magnificent in grey lace. She embraced her son, and he smelled the sweet rose perfume he could remember from his childhood as she folded him in her arms.

'It is a terrible story. You quarrelled with him?'

'How do you know?'

'The servants. The servants hear everything,' she said.

'We can talk about it in the morning,' he said, kissing her cheek tenderly.

'I cannot sleep,' she replied. 'There is so much to organize. Tomorrow all our relatives will be here. Do you think we should cover the mirrors in preparation?'

'No,' he said. 'Or, if we do, it can be done tomorrow.'

He did not want to talk to his mother at that moment, but she seemed to need his presence: she held his hand tightly and went on with her own thoughts.

'It is such a strange custom,' she said. 'As if we might see the spirits of the dead in the glass. Or perhaps as if we might be drawn out to follow them? Do you know which it is?'

'No,' he said.

'All I remember when my own father died,' she said, 'were

the huge glass mirrors covered with black silk. And the stools close to the floor. How strange our Christian friends will find the Hebrew. Do you still read the language?'

'I never learnt it well,' he said. For all her calm demeanour, Minna looked very pale. 'You must look after yourself,' he said. 'Or, you know . . .' His voice trailed off.

Suddenly, to Anton's horror, her control broke and she wept frantically. He tried to comfort her, without any success.

At last he asked, 'Must you grieve for him so intensely? I did not think you were close.'

'He was unhappy. He had a fine soul,' sobbed his mother.

'Really?'

'Yes, he had a sensitive, delicate soul. People did not know him. He growled like a bear, but inside he was as gentle and sweet as . . .'

The rest of the comparison was drowned in a flood of tears.

Anton looked impatient. 'You have no reason to feel guilty. You were good to him.'

'Ah no, I was not,' she said, beginning to quieten. Her eyes were red as she thought about her loss. 'I did not give him what he wanted. I did not know how to love him as he wanted to be loved.'

Anton sighed and looked at his little gold watch.

'I shall be lonely now,' Minna said, drying her eyes.

Anton wondered if she was hoping he would come back to live with her; he even thought of it. Yet he knew he could not. It was enough for him to take on his father's role at the bank.

'I was always the sick one,' she said. 'All our lives together he was in rude health until this last year. And then, sud-denly— Why did you quarrel?'

'Something political,' said Anton. He decided it was hardly the time to mention any other issue.

'I wish you had been friends,' she said. 'He had so many worries.'

'Did he?'

'Nothing he could not have coped with if he had been alive.' She looked directly at Anton. 'You must take over now. There will be decisions to make.' She laughed a little. 'You have no idea how complicated it will be to run his affairs.'

'I had not intended to become a banker,' said Anton. It came to him that the decisions he was forced to make daily on the newspaper had perhaps fitted him for it, but he had no desire for the responsibility.

'You will have to face enquiries, of course,' said his mother. 'The family will want to know if you can manage everything. Anton—' Her eyes found his, and she clutched his arm nervously. 'Don't give it away. You have a right to your inheritance. It is what your father would have wanted. You mustn't listen to anyone who tells you differently.'

Anton said he would not.

'You sold your Dutch property?'

Anton remembered von Mayerberg, and flushed.

'Your aunt told me. Oh, why did you not come to me?' she cried.

'It wasn't necessary to worry you,' said Anton.

'What has become of your friend, von Mayerberg, since the death of his child?' Minna asked him, without any attempt to make the connection.

'I don't know,' said Anton shortly.

The funeral was arranged without much need for Anton's intervention; Shassner was a valued member of the First District synagogue. It was a brilliant autumn day; the sun shone as though no one in the world had to die. To the burial grounds came a representative of the house of Rothschild, members of the new Reichstag, nobles, industrialists, bankers. Anton, still stunned by the change in his fortunes, greeted the notable members of the Jewish community, who pressed his hand and wished him long life, at the same time as he registered the many Viennese who had come to show their respects at the funeral. Whether or not their concern at the death of his father was genuine, their attitude to Anton was unmistakable: as the man who was the heir apparent to Shassner's bank he was going to be treated with a different courtesy.

His uncle from Berlin shook his hand with a Prussian formality.

'Terrible times,' he said. 'The family must hold together.'

Anton nodded, though he thought it was a foolish hope after Königgrätz. If his father's ghost was aware of anything, Anton reflected, it would be aware of the need for coolness towards the Prussian branch of the family. He felt two green eyes on him, as he gave his own formal bow: they belonged to Baron Hess.

As the mourners followed the coffin on its barrow towards the grave, Anton kept a little distance from his uncle. When the coffin had been placed in the grave, and the mourners had begun to stream towards the waiting carriages, his aunt from Amsterdam approached him. Not too many women of the family came to the grounds; it was not the custom; they were supposed to wait at the house and prepare the traditional food, or, since that was hardly necessary at Minna's, comfort the widow. He liked his aunt, and remembered her help and care when he had needed to sell his Dutch property.

When they returned, the drawing room had been draped in black crêpe, the table set with chopped herring and boiled eggs. Anton could not face eating a morsel. He did not like the change in his fortunes, he decided. He would be prevented from living as he liked. He felt too young to have such a mantle of respectability descend upon him. Couldn't he throw it off? Appoint someone to deal with his affairs? Any one of these men would be better at what needed to be done. Even as the thought entered his head, he found himself looking into his mother's eyes.

'Remember,' she said to him as he kissed her.

He nodded. Formal men he had known since childhood crowded about him, confident, prosperous and curious. He steeled himself to resist the pressure of their enquiries.

The most uncomfortable presences in the room were those of Minna's Christian relations. They were handsome women, much about Minna's age, who had married into the Austrian aristocracy, and carried themselves accordingly. One of them, a Countess in her own right, approached Anton as he stood by his mother. She had green eyes, with smiling lines at the corner of them, carefully dressed hair and black satin elegantly ruched over her sloping bosom. It was not the custom of Jews to wear black at funerals but by now she was used to the Christian behaviour in the face of death. Anton remembered her from his childhood. Then, in an ornate garden with her children on the grass around her, he had heard her laugh and overheard her whisper, 'A handsome boy. A shame about his crippled hand.' Even now, he found the memory hurtful.

Now she stood before them. His mother, usually so poised and graceful, seemed uneasy under her inspection. He wondered at her unease. That evening in his childhood, when he had blurted out his story to Minna, it seemed to him, even as she comforted him, she had not been displeased to hear he hated these formidable relations. Certainly she had not reproached him for his response. Of course, he had hardly described his true emotions. He found the family teasing and fun, particularly the younger girls he chased round the topiary in the maze at the back of their country mansion.

They giggled and flirted with him. He enjoyed their gaiety. Now the low voice of his second cousin commiserated with them both.

'Poor Minna,' she said. 'What will you do now?'

'My circumstances are hardly reduced,' said Minna, with quiet irony.

'But was there not some talk of an honour for your husband which he has not lived to enjoy?'

'These things are not important,' said Minna.

'Ah, you are brave to say so,' sighed her cousin.

Anton had been told of no such impending honour, but many bankers who had been useful to the Court were rewarded in this way by the Emperor, and he fancied, without much respect, that his father would have earned his title.

His attention wandered. Even on such a solemn occasion, when he wanted to think what the loss of his father might mean to him, he could not help his thoughts running back to Clara, and the last evening they had spent together. In his memory, her mouth opened sweetly and she looked at him with a certain invitation. Next week he was taking her to the opera. It was not an occasion that lent itself so easily to proposing a new form for their relationship, but he was determined to take the opportunity. He was thinking how best to phrase his offer, when he became aware of a bright and uncomfortable gaze upon him. Baron Hess was listening and looking with particular attention, and at that moment he approached. Anton bowed formally. Hess, he saw, was a military man. There was even a duelling scar on his cheek. He was a strange friend for his father to have had.

'Dreaming, young man?' said Hess.

'I am ashamed to confess I was thinking of my box at the opera,' Anton admitted. 'I hope my father would forgive me. He was no great fan of the opera himself.'

Hess allowed himself a charming smile. 'Do you admire what is being done under the new management? They say to hear the chorus properly you need to reduce it by half. The people in the back just go through the motions.'

'I was last there for Gounod's *Faust*,' said Anton. 'I thought it a fine production.'

'They put on more French operas than German and Italian together,' grumbled Hess. 'Who is singing this week?'

'Louise Dustmann-Meyer.'

'Well, she is wonderful.'

'And Karl Meyerhofer.'

'Wasn't he a soloist last year at the Theatre on the Wien?'

'Yes. He used to be an actor, which makes a great difference,' said Anton enthusiastically. 'I saw him in Offenbach's *Orpheus* a couple of years ago.'

'How the Viennese love Offenbach,' mused Hess. 'They recognize his light heart.'

'And his impudent spirit,' said Anton. 'Of course, there is still censorship of a kind in our own theatre. I remember not so long ago they wouldn't let the management have the word "Rome" in a production of *Tannhäuser*.'

Hess, who had warmed during the brief discussion to the point of friendliness, drew back with some irony at the mention of censorship.

'Times change. And circumstances!' he observed. 'Your own, also. Will you combine the roles of banker and newspaper editor?'

'I have not yet made plans,' said Anton.

For the moment, though he did not mention this to Hess, he had put Efraim Jacob in charge of the paper. He was well aware of Hess's likely attitude to Jacob.

'It is very moving when sons step into their fathers' shoes,' said Baron Hess.

Anton bowed again.

'Has there been a post-mortem?' Hess gleamed through a monocle.

'Certainly not,' Anton answered curtly. 'It was quite unnecessary.'

'The doctor who issued the death certificate is no doubt a close friend of the family?' said the Baron. 'I should like to question him. Your father was a good friend of mine. There have been rumours.'

'What rumours?'

His throat had dried. Baron Hess shrugged.

'People say so many things. But then you understand that, since you work for the newspapers yourself.'

Anton put a hand to the Baron's sleeve as he turned away, and for a moment he thought that the Baron was so incensed by the familiarity of the gesture that he would brush his hand away. However, the solemnity of the occasion had him check the impulse which only flared for a second in his blue eyes.

'I should like you to tell me what you mean.'

'We can talk next week,' said the Baron. 'This is not an appropriate time.'

Anton stood where he was while another aunt pressed his hand and flirted with him, as was often the way with elderly members of the family in the presence of a young and attractive relation. 'He has the looks of his mother,' she said, to nobody in particular.

Her voice had a penetration that made her clearly audible at the other side of the room, where Baron Hess and his Prussian uncle were standing mutely in one another's presence, both in their different ways getting ready to leave the occasion.

With some affection, Anton greeted a rabbi from his childhood, who began, after a few words of sympathy, to solicit his assistance for the city's poor.

'Now you are such a wealthy man,' he was saying, 'I am sure you will be as generous as your father.'

Am I wealthy? wondered Anton. He felt no different. Yet people certainly treated him differently. To be the son of a wealthy man was one thing; evidently to enter into his kingdom was another. Almost without understanding it, everyone's attitude to him had changed. It came to him that it would be for him to decide on what would happen to the steel mills of Czechoslovakia, and the rail links in Transylvania equally. That was why these gentlemen no longer treated him like a boy, but with respect.

Chapter Thirty

THE JUNE AFTERNOON before the opera was sultry and dark; the trees moved uneasily and the air itself was heavy. Clara was filled with foreboding. There were several rumbles of thunder and a few splashes of violent rain, but no sign of the downpour that would have washed the air clean and left the city fresh again; not enough even to settle the dust in the streets.

She began to get ready, a little wearily, for her excursion. She peered into the mirror. A great loneliness possessed her. Not the loneliness of being solitary – for that morning she had taught two charming pupils and they had laughed together, and that evening she was dining with Anton. It was another kind of loneliness. As she looked into the glass, it seemed to her the signs of her inner unhappiness were visible in the darkness of her eyes. She guessed that Anton intended to make her some definite proposal that evening, and that their friendship might not survive a refusal. She sighed. Why could she not love Anton? What, after all, could she expect, more than to become the mistress of someone like Anton, who liked her and would provide for her after their love affair was finished? She felt no physical desire for him, but Mitzi had said some women were like that, and maybe she was one of them.

Her face in the mirror stared back, dark-eyed and beautiful

although she had slept badly, thinking of the urgency in Anton's eyes. It was a long while since she had been troubled by strange dreams. Now, as she stared into her reflection, she remembered waking once again early that morning from her old nightmare: the steps, the door, the brass handle, the red cushion. She put the puzzle away from her.

The Imperial Opera House stood on Kärntnerstrasse and, as Anton and Clara walked towards it, a girl ran from one of the adjoining houses and greeted Anton. Several of the houses had been acquired over the years by the Opera House and actresses and singers looking for work commonly hung around hoping to be talent-spotted. In this case the young girl, a friend of Max Kallman, was only concerned to discover his whereabouts. Anton gave her what friendly help he could, and steered Clara into the theatre.

The theatre was an intimate one, and Anton had a great affection for it. It was here, when stone deaf, that Beethoven had first conducted his Ninth Symphony. In the revolutionary year the building had been damaged, but Franz Joseph had made it a court theatre again, and now it was flourishing. It was a narrow building with five tiers of boxes. Naturally, Anton had one of the best.

'I don't know how this will be,' said Anton, registering Clara's silence. 'The new director has the unfortunate nickname of "Snob". There will be a good deal of pretence about the performance, I imagine. But the music will be fine.'

'I am sure,' she murmured, as the orchestra took their places.

'You do not care for Mozart tonight?' Anton asked her during the interval.

'I was brooding,' she confessed.

Then she became aware that two people were at Anton's elbow.

Anton had never introduced Clara to von Mayerberg. For a number of reasons, it had always seemed to him a poor idea to do so. He had no wish to see the raised eyebrows and knowing sneer with which he felt his relationship to Clara would be regarded. Now he had no choice but to make the introduction formally. Anton was proud of Clara's appearance, which he knew attracted the attention of all the young men in the room. She was so very much a beauty now, with her black hair dressed carefully and in the silks and finery Mitzi had sewn for her. He watched his friend's eyes go up and down Clara's handsome figure.

'I am delighted to meet you at last,' murmured von Mayerberg, bending caressingly over Clara's long white fingers.

As Clara met his gaze, she gave a little cry.

'What is it?' asked Anton.

Then he remembered that Clara had once before, long ago, seemed to know something of his friend. Her face had gone very pale, but she said nothing. Conversation continued between Rudolf and Anton, without any contribution from Clara.

Clara's mind blazed. She sat in her seat again when the bell called them back but heard nothing of the action on the stage when the curtain rose on the second act.

She was once again a small child in a forgotten house, sitting on a red cushion and staring up at the face of a man. That man she was now convinced was von Mayerberg. He was part of her dream, and part of her past; her heart beat so loudly that she thought Anton must surely hear it. Perturbed by the expression on her face, though far from guessing the cause, Anton whispered something in her ear which she did not even try to make out. The irrelevance of the action on the stage made sitting still a torture, and her head ached with the effort of ordinary civility. Until the curtain came down she was trapped in an agony of impatience to be out of the theatre. She could not have given any account of the thoughts that agitated her limbs. As soon as the curtain went down on the act, she jumped to her feet.

'Are you ill?' enquired Anton, who had been enjoying the opera and was not best pleased to leave before the third act.

'I am likely to faint,' she said. 'Will you forgive me? I must go home.'

For a moment, Anton thought of sending her home in a carriage but a glance at her face changed his mind.

'I will take you home.'

'It isn't necessary.'

'I think it is.'

And, indeed, she was shivering uncontrollably as he gave her his arm to get into the carriage. The air was hot and damp with unshed rain.

Once in the carriage, he took her hand and she clutched his fingers hard.

'Tell me what so distresses you,' he said, stirred against his will by her beauty even as he was curious about this sudden outburst.

'The dream,' she said. 'And the memory.'

'What memory?'

'He was the one.'

She knew he could not understand. She hardly understood herself. The words had blurted from some buried part of her.

'Take me home,' she said. 'Leave me.'

'I cannot leave you like this,' he pointed out, sensibly enough.

She shuddered. Anton bent out of the window to signal the coachman to extend the drive through the woods.

'Tell me,' he said. 'You can tell me anything.' He had both of her hands now. 'You know that I love you.'

'Oh, that word all Vienna uses,' she said passionately. Then she fell silent and he stroked her hand.

'I will tell you,' she said presently. 'I must share this or die, I think. That face belongs to my childhood.'

'What do you mean?'

'The house near the Danube. The house of my dreams, with the stairs and the mahogany door. Do you remember my story?'

'I do,' said Anton.

'I recognize his face; the way his lips open.'

Her hands trembled.

'What are you remembering, exactly?' asked Anton slowly.

'My aunt. And the other girls.'

'Girls? What girls?'

'Pretty girls. They gave me sweet cakes and dolls.'

Her voice faltered and the years fell away from it. She sounded like a child, and it felt cruel to press her further. Yet he did.

'Go on.'

'The men gave me presents sometimes. The ones who came to the house. Someone played music.'

'All right,' said Anton. 'That's the house. Now, about von Mayerberg?'

'He was the one,' she said again. 'They laughed at him and teased him, because he couldn't do anything, they said. I didn't know what they meant.'

'Didn't you?' said Anton.

'But I wasn't puzzled either. I liked him. Sometimes he came and played with me. He got down on his knees on the rug to build my bricks. He liked to stroke my hair.'

As she fell silent, Anton urged her again.

'Go on.'

'One day Rebekka took me by the hand. Up the stairs. We went up the stairs of my dream. Through the redwood door. And he was there.'

'Von Mayerberg?'

'Yes. He was smiling at me. But he looked strange, and I wanted to go away. My aunt said I should take off my clothes. She had to help me. First the dress, then the woollen underclothes. It wasn't cold – there was a big fire at the other side of the room – but I began to shiver.'

Clara was shivering even then, as she remembered.

'Go on,' said Anton.

'"Go close to the fire," she said. "You'll be warmer. He won't hurt you. I won't let him touch you." "Sit down on the cushion," he said in a funny voice. Then he said, "No, not like that. I want to see you properly." And he turned me round to face him. I was clutching my arms hard round my knees to keep myself from shaking, but he put out a hand gently and said, "Unclasp your hands." So I did, and my knees fell open.'

'And did he . . .' asked Anton, 'touch you?'

'Not then.'

Clara was lost in the past, clutching Anton's hand as she remembered.

'What did you—?' He hesitated. 'How did you feel? Were you afraid?'

'I was curious,' she answered. 'But next time . . .'

'It happened again?'

'Yes. The next time it wasn't enough for him just to look. He said, "I have to feel you." And he put his hand between my legs.'

Her voice had dropped so that Anton could not hear what she was saying, but now he could not urge her to speak more loudly. He simply held her hand tightly and waited.

'I tried to keep my legs closed,' she said. 'And suddenly he let out a huge sigh and said, "That's enough. That's it."'

'And then? And then?'

'Don't push me, Anton. I know what you are asking, but I only remember in patches.'

Anton pressed her shoulder again. 'How old do you think you were?'

'Perhaps seven,' said Clara, whispering now. 'Not more. I didn't yet reach Rebekka's middle.'

'And did von Mayerberg pay your aunt?'

'No, another woman, in a stiff Dutch cap, whose house it was. I cannot remember everything.' Clara had begun to weep. 'How can you expect it?'

'What a horror story,' said Anton. 'But von Mayerberg? How can you be sure?'

'It was him,' said Clara, clutching Anton's hand now, so that it was deliciously painful to him as he watched her white bosom rise and fall with emotion. 'It was because of him that the memory of all this came back. He was part of it. I remember a particular day, a hot and sticky day much like this afternoon, and my aunt had been angry with me. She had to hit me many times before I came to sit on the cushion as she wished. And I cried. I remember the tears which I could not prevent coming into my nose and down my throat. I think I had a slight fever. When the gentleman came into the room—'

'Do you mean von Mayerberg?'

'He saw my tears and he covered his face. But he couldn't resist doing what he wanted. Afterwards, when we were going home, he was standing outside and he seized my aunt's arm. I looked up at him, full in the face. That's what I remember. "You are a monster," he said to my aunt. "You will rot in hell." My aunt just laughed. I have never forgotten his face, or my own terror.' She shivered.

'You will feel better now you have told me all this,' said Anton. Privately, he thought there was much more to her story. He was sure now that her prudery did not come from innocence. How could a child be innocent, coming from such a background? She had been a prostitute. Not of her

own volition, it was true, but a prostitute none the less
and he had been altogether too reticent in his pursuit of
her.

'I will see you to your room,' he said.

Clara squeezed his hand again, gratefully. She was more
afraid of what might still be waiting in the deep waters of her
mind than concerned for any impression she might have
made on her friend. She was glad to have his reassuring
presence, and to enter the familiar passageway with Anton's
hand on her neck, guiding her up the steps, pausing protec-
tively as she opened the front door with her key and helping
her into the small vestibule.

As they entered her sitting room, he bent to light the oil
lamp, which threw a flickering glow over the familiar room,
and he paused to breathe in the scent of her soaps and
clothes.

'You will rest and feel better.'

'Yes,' she said.

'Let me help you,' he suggested.

Something in his voice surprised her and she turned to
look at him. At once she saw that her story had inflamed
him grossly. His face was dark and blind, and he seemed to
be breathing with difficulty. Even as she saw as much, he
came forward and took her roughly in his arms.

'What are you doing?' she cried, trying to break free. But
he was stronger than she realized and, without a word, he
lifted her up and into the bedroom. One of his feet was on
the hem of her dress, and the skirt ripped as he lifted her.

'Let us have this dress off,' he said.

She could hardly recognize his swollen face. His eyes were
half-closed.

'I've been waiting so stupidly, and all the while you have
been laughing at me,' he said.

'No, Anton. That's not so,' she whispered.

She fell across the bed and, with one movement, he had her skirt up and was parting the voluminous petticoats.

'How can you be so crude?' she begged him.

He was past caring and in a moment she felt his full weight upon her and his body thrusting into her. When his body stopped moving, a silence filled the room.

Clara lay where she was, feeling no more than a small, remote pain. There was a wetness between her legs. After a long pause, Anton lifted himself from her and lay for a few minutes at her side, breathing in the scent of her hair and her flesh, exhausted by the rush of sensation. Then, gradually, he sat up, and she watched him smooth his hair automatically and adjust his own clothes. He bent over to light the lamp at the bedside and look down on her where she lay, exactly as the violent movement had left her, stunned and without any apparent will of her own. He was startled at what he saw. Blood was trickling down her thigh.

She continued to lie where she was. Her eyes were dry. There was nothing in her mind, only a great lake of silence. She could hear his voice as if from a distance, tired now, rather than passionate.

'A virgin,' he said, stupidly. 'Clara—'

She did not reply.

'Did I hurt you?' he asked.

Still she did not answer.

'Will you forgive me?'

She could think of nothing to say to him.

'I wanted to love you,' he pleaded. Sadness and self-disgust overwhelmed him. He had behaved like a brute. Now only desolation lay between them.

Chapter Thirty-One

CLARA WOKE the next morning with a sense that some enormity had occurred. Then the knowledge came back to her. She did not move. Nor did she fall back into sleep. Her face was aflame, her body wet with sweat. After a while, she got up to be sick in a basin, and stumbled back to her bed. The day went strangely fast, between sickness and sleep, and she had no thought of getting out of bed.

The second morning, she heard knocking on the door and could not bring herself to answer it. She could not imagine whom she would want to see. The light made a bright patch on the wall, and then disappeared. When the room was completely dark again, there was more knocking; louder and more urgent. She made no attempt to answer it.

At length, on the third day, she felt a twinge of appetite, not for food, but for coffee. She got out of bed and went to the window. There she sat in the sunlight, doing nothing for herself and brooding over what had happened. Women are destroyed, she thought, if they let themselves be destroyed. It's up to them; it's how they think about themselves. But then the memory of a body forcing itself into her returned, and she felt sick and faint again.

She did not want to be a woman. Perhaps, she thought, I can dress up and live as a man? She had read of such things. Jane had told her of a Russian woman who lived as a soldier for twenty-five years and was only exposed as a woman on her death. She would like that, she thought, shuddering.

After a time, she bathed and went to look at herself in the mirror. Her face was flushed as if she had a fever, but she was otherwise unchanged. She touched the familiar contours of her face and picked up a brush to straighten her hair into shape. Then she went back and lay down on her bed.

By evening, she felt a little better. She was able to look in her purse for some coins, and contemplate going outside to buy a loaf of bread and some fresh coffee. She was still shaken. But she had a sense of her own physical resilience.

So, she told herself, I shall recover. Or my body will. It was as if, even though her body did not belong to her, there was something else in her, still silent, that was her own.

At the doorway, she paused. There was a letter on the carpet. Someone, perhaps whoever had been eagerly banging the day before, must have pushed it underneath the door. The letter was addressed to her. She did not recognize the hand. Everything, she found, had to be done very slowly, as though she were recovering from a long illness. As she opened the letter even the noise of the tearing paper went through her nervous system like a rasping saw.

It was signed Joseph. 'I have been thinking about you. I don't know why. My life has taken a knock, I suppose. And I was ill for a while. Nothing serious, but I have been out of spirits, and your lovely face keeps coming to my mind. If you have a free moment to spare, I should much like to see you again. I am in Vienna until Saturday. You could leave a message for me, and I will send a carriage for you.' Remotely, the good news of his interest reached the outer edges of her mind, but her thoughts were still blank and white. Coffee first, she thought. Then bread. And she would see. The effort of doing something, even something she wanted, still seemed too much for her. Her will seemed to have broken like a spring. Perhaps if I walk outside a while, she thought, the air will revive me.

She could not have said how she reached the nearby park but she was soon walking, almost blindly, under the trees. At last she flung herself full length on the grass, where she lay dry-eyed as it grew darker. It was raining.

'I say! You'll get pneumonia if you don't take shelter,' said an English voice.

She did not respond. She could not have said what she had been thinking.

She was soaked through as she opened the door and saw Mitzi on the stairs.

'Where have you been?' called her friend. 'You look dreadful. And so many people asking for you.'

'So many?'

'Well, two. Both men, of course.' Mitzi took her arm and looked into her face. 'Are you ill?'

'Yes,' said Clara, swaying a little. 'I think I am.'

'Let me look after you,' cried Mitzi good-heartedly. And she brought Clara into her own room where she at once collapsed across the bed.

Mitzi observed the wet clothes, the torn dress and the white face and clucked cheerfully, 'You'll recover. As long as it's not cholera. What a fool you are to go out in this rain.'

'But that's not it,' said Clara. 'I'll tell you what happened.'

Mitzi heard her out in silence.

'Men!' she said. 'They're all the same, poor dears. But don't make too much of it. Are you religious?'

Clara shook her head.

'Well, then. It happens to all of us.'

Clara's spirits began to recover a little under Mitzi's gentle tuition. 'I would love a glass of chocolate. And a slice of bread. I meant to buy them.'

'You shall have both. And a coddled egg, too,' cried Mitzi.

'Don't move. But go on talking. Talking always helps. There's hardly a trouble in the world that isn't less if you tell it out to a friend.'

Clara began to eat and drink gratefully, while Mitzi's voice pattered on. For all the advice to talk, she left Clara little enough time to speak.

'Don't take it too seriously,' said Mitzi. 'Or not more than you have to.'

'It's not what happened last night,' said Clara. 'It's my childhood.'

'Well, and what about mine?' demanded Mitzi. 'I'm another orphan, though I don't talk about it. The poor are always victims, one way or another. I could tell you such stories!'

But Clara shook her head. 'You don't feel defiled.'

'These grand words!' said Mitzi.

'And what if I'm pregnant?' said Clara, more practically.

'If you are, don't do anything by yourself,' said Mitzi. 'I know a very good woman who's helped another friend of mine. It's not very likely, dear,' she scoffed reassuringly. 'The streets of Vienna would be crawling with little bastards if that was likely.'

'I wonder . . .' said Clara, and stopped.

'What's that?' asked Mitzi.

'I must have been just such a little child,' said Clara sadly. 'Somewhere in my memory there is a sweet woman, and some father I do not know.'

'Forget them,' said Mitzi. 'You won't find them now, will you? And, if you did, ten to one they wouldn't want to have anything to do with you.'

'They can't have been very loving,' Clara agreed, 'or they would not have abandoned me.'

'They'll be dead,' said Mitzi. 'People die. That's usually the story. Now you go to sleep.'

'Here? On your bed?'

'Yes.'

'Where will you sleep?'

'Don't you worry. You just lie back. I wouldn't feel happy leaving you alone.'

As Clara drifted off to sleep, she remembered Joseph's letter, but she did not mention it. I'll be better in the morning, she told herself.

But in the morning she was not better. Her fever had returned, and Mitzi wondered whether she should call a doctor. 'They don't know much, but they can give you drops to soothe your head,' she said.

On the third day she borrowed some valerian from a girl in Stock-in-Eisenplatz but by then Clara was well enough to sit up normally. At once, Clara remembered Joseph's letter.

'I have to send a message,' she said rapidly.

'Oh, I'll do that, don't worry. You look better today,' said Mitzi.

'Is it Friday?' asked Clara.

'No, Saturday,' said Mitzi.

Clara bit her underlip. 'He'll have left,' she said. 'He'll have left Vienna. I've missed my chance.'

And for the first time she put her head down on the pillow and sobbed bitterly.

Chapter Thirty-Two

ANTON SPENT THE WEEK AFTER his assault on Clara in Budapest, dealing with a strike at the new textile mills. He had chosen the hotel on the Danube where his father had always stayed and, for that reason, the manager was effusively welcoming. Anton found it difficult to respond. He stared moodily at the fat, green pillars in the foyer and the elaborate bronze fountain with its statue of the boy Cupid at the centre. What was it to him that he could make out a frog, a lizard, a duck and a tortoise in the water?

He would drink a good deal, he told himself, make as sensible a business decision as he could, and sleep alone. He was not a wicked man and he found it difficult to believe he could have behaved with such criminal brutality. It made him loathe himself, even though he continued selfishly to wonder if his act had destroyed any chance of her loving him as he wanted to be loved. Before leaving Vienna, he had arranged for flowers to be delivered to Clara's apartment; now he could think of no appropriate note of apology that would not make matters worse.

He slept poorly, but the next morning sunlight flooded the balcony early and he awoke with a resurgence of interest in what he had to do. Before he tackled the business affairs of the day, however, he determined to try out the thermal baths for which the hotel was famous.

The pool was fed by aromatic water through the mouths of stone lions; the water was clear and warm and bubbled gently around him. As he lay in the waters, he let their gentle warmth and the prettiness of the dark blues and terracotta decorations soothe him. It was possible to feel a pagan, he mused, staring at the gracious statues from which the curative waters poured so gently. After ten minutes or so, he left the pool and let skilled masseurs wash his body and stretch and pound his limbs.

During the day he met a French industrialist who was interested in buying up a famous Hungarian chocolate factory. His eyes twinkling, his voice ironic, he suggested to Anton that the French and Austrians had a great deal in common. Particularly in their civilized attitude to sexuality. Anton found it more difficult than usual to mock the straitlaced English. The general tone of the conversation was male, worldly, conspiratorial. The assumptions were those he was used to sharing, yet the thought of Clara prevented him joining in.

That evening he met two Hungarian politicians, who took some pride in showing him the great cathedral and the evidence for the role the Magyars had played in turning back the invasion of the Turks. They dined at a restaurant that looked down from Castle Hill, ate sour cherry soup and Hortobagi pancakes and drank good wine. Anton took an open carriage back to his hotel so that he could savour the dark blue sky over the river and the moonlit green domes. The beauty was poisoned by his unhappiness. I shall never forgive myself, he thought bleakly.

Returning home in the carriage which had collected him from the railway station in Vienna, his mood darkened still further. His servants took his travelling clothes and brought in his baggage, which contained pieces of porcelain, some paintings and bottles of fine wine that had been given to him by his Magyar hosts.

'I shall read my post over coffee in my study,' he announced, almost as his father would have done. 'After I have bathed.'

'And will you take an evening meal?'

'Later,' he said.

Again he heard the echo of his father's heavy, sardonic voice in his own. Passing the long, ornate mirrors of the vestibule, he satisfied himself, as he often did these days, that at least in appearance he did not yet resemble his father. None of the messages, he saw at a glance, were from Clara, but one was from von Mayerberg to request an urgent meeting.

There were several embarrassments in meeting von Mayerberg, of which Clara's disclosures formed only a part, and Anton frowned to recall them. He opened the other personal letters, which included a rather melancholy page from his mother, who was staying with her cousins in Berlin and finding their company oppressive. Then he returned to von Mayerberg's note. Von Mayerberg was very far from clearing his original debt, and Anton would have long ago forgiven him the whole amount if that offer had not instantly produced a desperate plea for a further loan. Whatever urgency von Mayerberg might have in mind himself, however, it was Clara's story which now troubled Anton most. Yet he was not sure he would have the courage to raise so offensive an accusation.

At length he picked up his favourite quill and wrote to von Mayerberg in his most precise handwriting that they should meet for half an hour the next day at Grienstiedl Café, a choice of meeting place which more or less ruled out any such intimate conversation.

Grienstiedl was on the ground floor of the Palais Herberstein, a stone's throw from the Imperial castle. Writers loved the café even more than Neuners. The familiar piles of newspapers, brocaded décor and the animated faces of journalists, actors and poets restored Anton to a sense of all that was worldly and acceptable. He arrived a little before his friend, and was soon engaged in animated disagreement with Jacob, on the matter of the Hungarian strikers. Anton ordered himself a chocolate torte, quite as good as those which Sacher had prepared for Prince Metternich in the days before the Revolution, and found the frivolity and excitement of Vienna was beginning to wash his mind free. By the time von Mayerberg arrived, Anton found it possible to greet him affably.

Von Mayerberg was a lumbering figure these days. His face was puffy and the lines in it were those of deep melancholy. Yet, when he saw Anton, his blue eyes gleamed with wit and malice much as they always had.

'Ah, the editor has returned, and the literati gather about him for crumbs.'

'I am as lazy as you could wish me,' said Anton. 'I do all my best editing over coffee and cake.'

'For myself, I should prefer a brandy,' said von Mayerberg.

Nevertheless, he chose a large apple strudel and asked for whipped cream. Anton ordered him a brandy and, as his friend appeared to be puffing a little, asked with some concern:

'Are you short of breath these days?'

'Of breath and everything else,' said von Mayerberg. 'May I have your ear in private for a moment?'

Reluctantly, Anton let himself be steered towards a table a little removed from the general area of conversation.

'I'm sorry. You can guess my problem.'

Anton supposed he was once again pushed for money.

'Are you any further forward with your Tyrolese sketches?' he temporized.

Von Mayerberg swallowed down his Cognac without the least attempt to savour it.

'I don't blame you for pretending not to understand. But you can see how it is. There are as many kinds of sin, my friend, as there are stones in the sea. I am completely strapped for money.'

Anton nodded, and ordered another coffee for himself. As he did so, he felt once again something of his father's gesture. I don't want to be doing this, he told himself. I should like to give him as many florins as he needs and never see him again.

Von Mayerberg stared moodily down at the table and seemed reluctant to say more.

'You have been gambling?' enquired Anton.

'Yes.'

It was not going to be possible to escape, thought Anton. He waited, as he knew his father would have waited.

'I must beg you, above all, not to tell my wife.'

At this, a smile came to Anton's lips. On the few occasions he had met Anna at his mother's soirées she had drawn her skirts away from him.

'We are not intimate,' Anton said mildly.

'I know. She is bitter.'

'I can see as much.'

'She blames you for my defection.'

This was more startling.

'How does she make that out, I wonder?'

'You are the new world, and she hates everything about it. The way land no longer counts, and the aristocracy have to go cap in hand to industrial capital . . .'

'I am hardly responsible for that.'

'For my debts, too.'

'I see. I should not have lent you money?'

'It is an argument.'

'Yes,' said Anton quietly.

'The Viennese,' said von Mayerberg, 'have never admired the ability to look after money providently.'

A wish to be free of his present role filled Anton savagely.

'As to those debts,' said von Mayerberg, 'it was to put them right, above all, that I returned to the tables.'

Anton sighed. 'I understand. You are about to tell me you cannot pay me the quarter's interest? Is that it?'

'If you look in your accounts, you will see I have failed to do so for three succeeding quarters.'

'I know that,' said Anton.

His brown eyes met his friend's bright blue ones steadily. Does he imagine me a fool? he thought with sudden irritation. Once again he waved to the waiter, this time to ask for his coat.

'Let us leave this matter for a moment. I want to take you to supper.'

Von Mayerberg looked startled. 'You do?'

'Yes. I have some questions to put to you.'

Anton chose a quiet restaurant, run by an eccentric member of the Sacher family whose quirks were ill-judged to attract a fashionable clientele. She was always happy to give a penniless charmer whatever he wanted, while refusing to serve an ugly millionaire. Anton expected to see none of his friends there.

'The menu is very good,' he suggested.

Agitated though he was, von Mayerberg's eyes wandered greedily over the delights he was offered.

'Pheasant,' he said. 'I have had no pheasant this year.'

When the orders had been conveyed to the waiter, however, Anton felt no relish for the approaching feast. Von Mayerberg was too moody and preoccupied to notice.

'This will be embarrassing,' said Anton. 'You may even get up and leave the table. I shall understand. Nor hold it against you. I promise you it will in no way affect our arrangements. But, if you can keep your temper and answer two questions, I shall be very grateful.'

Von Mayerberg shifted uncomfortably. 'Your preamble is somewhat alarming. However, go on.'

'You have not had much interest in women, as I remember.'

Von Mayerberg looked puzzled. 'That vice at least I have been spared.'

'Even in youth? Do you, did you, know anything of Vienna's brothels?'

Von Mayerberg shook his head.

'A little, naturally, but I have not been their visitor for twenty years.'

'Before you married, perhaps?'

Von Mayerberg fell silent for a moment and then he put down his glass and stared honestly into his friend's face.

'Anton, Anton, now why do you question me about brothels? Brothels are innocent in comparison to the true monstrosities of human behaviour.'

'No doubt,' said Anton. 'Nevertheless—'

'Let me explain something to you, Anton. I am not myself much excited by lust. Sex with a woman has to be spiced, to have an additional element. Or I feel nothing of it.' Anton waited. 'Luckily, my wife has little interest in these games. She is a pure spirit.'

'Go on,' said Anton.

Von Mayerberg cast his eyes up to heaven. 'How do you bear it, Anton? Not to believe in Christ? To imagine meeting a God without some kind of mediation? All the evidence I need for Christianity comes from the twisted desires of my own heart.'

'Explain,' said Anton. His own heart had begun to beat rather faster than he liked.

'Do you feel yourself so innocent?'

Anton thought suddenly of his assault on Clara, and shook his head.

'Is there not some wish to humiliate, some cruelty even, in all kinds of sexuality?'

Again, Anton thought of Clara. He denied the wish to hurt; what he had wanted was an erotic tenderness, a delight she had denied him.

'We can be sentimental, romantic,' said Anton.

'Don't you think it is there? In all male sexuality? Don't you find it yourself?' von Mayerberg pleaded.

'No,' said Anton harshly.

'We cannot choose the shape of our sins,' said von Mayerberg quietly. 'I have never found myself capable of desire without that element.'

There was no mistaking his bald honesty.

'And you can feel so towards your wife?' cried Anton.

'You must see what I am saying! I can feel no lust for her.'

He fell silent as the waiter began to set down the birds before them. Anton had chosen a good wine; now he had not the slightest desire for it. Von Mayerberg, too, for all the eagerness he had evinced when they ordered the pheasants, was hardly toying with the food.

'I cannot imagine why you should need this confession,' he said. 'Whatever the reason, please do not speak of it to my wife.'

'Once again, then,' said Anton, 'let me say that the possibility does not arise.'

An uneasy sense of male complicity filled him. His knife slid off the heavily sauced, skinned flesh of the bird.

'The strange thing about the devil,' said von Mayerberg, 'is the way he mixes our best impulses and our temptations. There is a crippled girl who sits in the doorway of my block of flats. She will never walk without limping. No one could pass her without pity.'

'Go on,' said Anton.

'I feel pity, like everyone else. I stop and talk to her. I give her sweet cakes. Her condition and the thought of the life she will never have fill me with pity. Yet for the first time in years I feel a flow of desire. You see what a monster I am? And you talk to me of brothels! What could I do in a brothel that would be as wicked as that frisson of desire? That lust mingled with pity?'

'I remember now,' said Anton slowly. 'In your first play.'

'Yes, there was a twelve-year-old crippled girl there, too. Her sadness fired my lust.'

Anton took a drink of wine without tasting it. He was ashamed of what he had learnt.

Von Mayerberg continued to drink moodily, preoccupied.

'When I lie in Anna's bed,' he said, 'there is nothing erotic in it. Can you understand? I lie at her side like a child by a mother.'

Anton nodded.

'The Church knows,' said von Mayerberg. 'The only good sex is for the conception of children. And there I am the greatest villain of all. You know Anna lost a baby?'

Anton remembered hearing as much years earlier.

'You can't imagine the pain she endured,' said von Mayerberg. 'Or the happiness she felt before. It was when we came back from Wiesbaden. Do you remember? I had to tell her of my gambling, and she soothed me as she always did.

And forgave me. "Anna, we have lost everything. We might have to leave Vienna," I said. "I know," she said, sleepily. "Your earrings and your brooch. Your mother's china. All have gone," I said. "I know," she said again. "It doesn't matter. Go to sleep." I could not understand. "You forgive me so easily?" "Of course," she said. "But your mother's things," I reminded her, recalling her red and angry face on other occasions, unable completely to accept her reassurance. "Why are you suddenly so indifferent?"

' "Something had happened to make me happy, and it will make you happy, too," she told me serenely. And I knew what she was going to say before she spoke. "We are having a child. At last. God is good. Maybe he could not answer one set of prayers like this without taking away something else." But how could we manage? I thought. What a monster I was. How stupid and egotistical. "I will go to my mother's family," she reassured me. "They will not abandon me altogether. You will see." I will never gamble again, I promised. She is so good. I wanted to bless her. But God knew what he was doing. The child died.'

Anton could say nothing.

'You see how it is,' said von Mayerberg. 'I seem frivolous, but I have death inside me all the time I eat.'

Anton cleared his throat and began to tell Clara's story. At the end of it, von Mayerberg pushed his plate and the uneaten bird away.

'I know the street,' he said. 'I know the house. But I swear I have never entered it.'

Chapter Thirty-Three

CLARA MADE NO RESPONSE to Anton's letters and, after a month, he ceased to write them. His old friend Max Kallman had returned to Vienna and, although Anton no longer had much patience for the lazy, drifting life Max preferred, he hoped an evening or two in his company might assuage his sense of guilt. And Max shook his head over Anton's late-night confession.

'Dear Anton, you have no sense of the female spirit.'

'Not all women are the creatures you imagine,' said Anton.

'Yes,' insisted Max. 'They are liars from birth.' Anton shook his head. 'Yes. Some are romantic, sweet things but they all have to defend themselves in a male world. Deceit is their only option. We demand it from them.'

'Do we?'

'Yes. They make up stories to please us. We have taught them to behave as they do. We make them so.'

'Except that Clara did not have to please me, and she knew as much.'

'She has kept you at bay, hasn't she?' Max tapped his nostrils, knowingly. 'She is thinking of marriage, mark my words.'

Anton shook his head again. 'You mistake her. She is altogether without calculation of that kind.'

'There are no such women,' said Max.

'Supposing I am in love with her?'

'What could be more natural? She sends you away. If she pursued you, that would be another matter.'

Max's cynicism did not succeed in restoring Anton's self-esteem, but there were a press of other matters needing his attention. The day-to-day running of the newspaper now belonged to Jacob, since Anton had no time to deal with that alongside his father's affairs in Budapest and Prague. For a time, he kept a finger on the literary section, but literature, which had once been the essential purpose of his life, had moved to the edge of it. It felt like an image for all his efforts. His father's spirit had taken over the central push of his life, and all those things he thought of as quintessentially his own had been displaced. From now on, he thought gloomily, I am more or less a businessman.

It was not, as he had once imagined, merely a matter of lending money and taking profits. Every day brought a moral question. And a political one. While Efraim Jacob campaigned for better wages and conditions for miners and mill workers, Anton, who saw their exploitation, tried to arrange the necessary Austrian capital. He could no longer simply applaud the angry strikers on the streets, though he was happy for Jacob to present their case. He could no longer see any easy solutions.

One morning, while he was sorting impatiently through his desk in preparation for Jacob, he came across the folder of writing which Clara had given him earlier in the year. The sight of her neat, black hand gave a little knock to his heart and, though there was absolutely no need for it, he opened the folder and began to read greedily, though he could not have said what he was looking for. There was no mention of love, no thoughts of men; she was writing about the women of the streets and what they could hope for. The savagery and intelligence of her attack stunned him. What she hated most, it seemed, was the acceptance of being helpless. Against his will and however he tried to conjure up Max's blue-eyed, mocking face, the biting honesty evoked Clara so strongly that for a moment he was overpowered by his memory of her. Then he put the thought away. There was a good deal to do. For one thing, he had to prepare for a meeting with Baron Hess that evening.

Anton scribbled a note for Jacob, replaced his baroque silver pen into the holder with a charming model of two young cupids, and left the office.

That evening Baron Hess called upon him and, with some misgivings, Anton admitted him to the small room that had once been his father's study. Only the painting of Joseph II remained to recall his father's time there. He saw the Baron taking in the changes of furnishing and the gentler ambience.

'Let me come to the point,' said the Baron. 'You have taken over the reins of your father's affairs. That gives you a certain voice in the affairs of the State.'

'And no doubt the State is concerned in what decisions I make,' replied Anton cautiously.

'We are pleased with your dealings,' said the Baron. 'The growth of industry has been important.'

'I shall not neglect it.'

'I gather you have given over the editorship of *New Vienna* into other hands?'

'Yes,' said Anton.

'I have to confess we should have preferred someone less radical.'

'These days,' shrugged Anton, 'everyone is radical.'

Baron Hess, his eyeglass twinkling, did not disagree.

'In the main, your interests coincide with ours.'

'I suppose all of us depend on the prosperity of Austria,' said Anton gracefully.

The Baron chose to accept those words as agreement.

'We shall be grateful, suitably grateful,' he said. 'Before your father died, we had already considered that his substantial contribution to the welfare of the Austrian people needed some acknowledgement. The Emperor will be delighted to do so now, in the person of his son.'

For a moment, Anton did not understand what Baron Hess intended. Then a wild desire to laugh afflicted him. If anyone had told him in his adolescence that he might enter the aristocracy himself, he would hardly have believed it. Now that he was less in awe of a coat of arms, he was being offered one of his own.

'Life is very surprising,' he said, bowing.

He wished the news made him happier. The honour seemed oddly hollow. Perhaps his mother would enjoy it.

That Friday he dined alone with his mother. She had re-established a ritual he remembered from his childhood: the ceremonial white cloth, the glitter of candles and silver. There was no prayer book, however, and no attempt to say the prayers his father had always spoken. He supposed the book showed a kind of nostalgia for the happiness of her married life, and he made no comment upon it. She was looking more frail these days; pale and thin; her translucent skin tight over her cheekbones, and framed by soft, white hair.

'You should go to Berlin,' he told her.

She shrugged. 'I am not ill, Anton,' she said.

He bent to touch her soft cheek with his lips.

'Perhaps you should go out more?'

'Don't reproach me,' she said. 'I am bored when I do.'

'There is a new operetta – everyone is talking about it,' he suggested. 'Perhaps we should go together?'

'If you like. Yes, get tickets. Why not?'

For a while they ate in silence. Then he told her the news

the Baron had brought him. She did not seem as delighted as
he had hoped, though she reached across to pat his hand.

'You have been very successful,' she said. 'Are you happy?'

He would have liked to please her by saying that he was.
So much that they had once decided together was important
in life was now his as of right. He was acceptable everywhere,
respected, even admired; now ennobled. He was working
hard. In his own way he was doing a great deal of good. He
should be happy. His mother wanted to hear that he was
happy. He could not say so.

'As this world goes,' he shrugged, 'happy enough.'

He saw that she was disappointed and he regretted the
words as soon as they were uttered.

'I miss your father,' she said then. 'His energy; the life in
him.'

He was stung by the criticism this implied of himself.

'Of course, I should rather have become a great poet,' he
said with an attempt at jocularity.

'Yes,' she nodded. 'I know.' The words were discomfort-
ing; she saw as much, and soothed him. 'We don't know one
another's inner feelings any more. Don't mind me, Anton. I
am often unhappy myself.'

The servant came in to clear their plates and set out cakes
and fruit pies that had been specially prepared for his visit.

'I am sorry,' he said. She smiled at the inadequacy of that
response. 'Is there anything I can do to help?'

'You could marry,' she said. 'Have children.'

He put down his napkin. He was not hungry, and this was
not what he had expected or wanted.

'There is no one suitable I want to marry,' he said baldly.

'Suitable? You don't have to worry about suitability,' she
said. 'A baron with lands and wealth can please himself.'

She spoke with such kindness, and with so little concern
for the social niceties which ordinarily preoccupied her, that

he was touched. Her words brought back the days when he had felt her sadness and beauty most intensely. She, at least, had loved him and he was tempted to confide in her. But her whole being had come from so protected a life, he did not know how to talk to her about his behaviour and his longings.

'Unfortunately, I seem to be obsessed with a woman who will not even receive my letters,' he said.

She nodded. 'It is not such an uncommon experience. I don't really understand why we often love most where we are scorned.'

'How could you understand such a stupidity?' he smiled.

'Go on about yourself. This girl – she is the beauty from the Ebonstrasse, I suppose?'

He was startled.

'Sometimes your father told me his worries. Not always,' she said evenly. 'You have known her for many years, I know. Has something new happened? A rival? What?'

He brooded. 'I did something to offend her. Forgive me if I don't talk about that.'

'What is her background?'

He gave an uncomfortable laugh as he imagined his mother's response to the facts of Clara's childhood.

'Too indecent even to describe to you.'

'Her parents?'

'She is an orphan.'

'No one is an orphan at birth,' she said quietly. 'However soon afterwards.'

The remark echoed in his heart that evening and the whole of the next day. Perhaps he had accepted Clara's story with too little question. And perhaps it was the mystery that haunted him. It would hardly bring him into her favour to probe, but it might allay his own unhappiness to find out something more precise.

Chapter Thirty-Four

'I WANT YOU TO HELP ME,' Anton said abruptly to Efraim Jacob the following morning in the offices of *New Vienna*.

'In what way?' Jacob's teeth flashed in a smile that acknowledged recent disagreements. 'Is there something you want me to tone down? Some client you want me to whitewash? I am not the man for it.'

'Nothing like that.'

'What, then?'

'It's a kind of research. You will know better than I how to pursue it.'

Anton might have gone for the help he wanted to Max Kallman, but he did not like the thought of Max as an emissary to Clara. He told himself this was because she would instinctively distrust his easy charm, but perhaps he also feared that, like so many women, she would fall under his spell.

As he explained something of what he wanted, Jacob shook his head.

'I haven't the time for it.'

'Don't do it for me,' said Anton. 'Go and meet her. Do it for her.'

Jacob looked up. 'For who?'

Anton would have been embarrassed to tell his own part

in Clara's story but in soliciting Jacob's help he was forced to confess that Clara had refused to see him. Miserably, he picked up an awakened interest in his friend's dark face.

'I know a man that's hanging around after you,' said Mitzi a few days later.

Clara had a lesson to give at the other side of Vienna and, though she had agreed to take coffee with Mitzi, she was in no mood for it. Only her gratitude for the way Mitzi had nursed her through her illness constrained her to sit and listen as the girl chattered on about her own hopes and fears.

'Please don't press me,' begged Clara.

'You've someone else on your mind,' guessed Mitzi.

'Something else, not someone else,' said Clara. 'And I don't like soldiers, Mitzi.'

'He isn't a soldier. He writes for the papers himself. He's another poet. Will you meet him?'

'How does he know me?'

'He says he works for *New Vienna*. His name is Efraim Jacob.'

'The socialist?' asked Clara.

'Whatever is a socialist?' asked Mitzi.

'He was one of the students imprisoned after the Revolution,' said Clara. 'How do you know him?'

'He was waiting here one night. He talked to me. Shall I arrange for you to meet him?'

'No,' said Clara.

'I promised,' said Mitzi. 'I thought you'd agree.'

'No,' said Clara.

But, two days later, as she came downstairs after a lesson, Mitzi was waiting and Jacob was with her, carrying the folder of Clara's writing.

'There aren't many women with your kind of intelligence,' he said immediately. 'I want to help you.'

She looked at Jacob warily. His beard was black and thick, curling without much discipline from a sallow skin. His eyes were the colour of a burnt candle wick, she thought, but liquid and very gleaming.

'I don't need help,' she said.

'Yes, you do,' he insisted. 'No one knows about you. How many articles do you have?'

'A few more.'

'You see! Of course you need help.'

'Has Anton sent you?' she asked directly.

He hesitated and, seeing as much, she moved to get up from her chair.

'Look, I am not intimate with Shassner,' said Jacob. 'I know nothing about his life or loves. I know nothing about you.'

Something in his fanatic eye, and the simplicity of his words, persuaded her of what he was saying.

'There was never a question of love between Anton and me,' she said contemptuously. 'But we used to be friends.'

'I just want to help you,' he said. 'Won't you believe me?'

She shrugged. 'It's not so important.'

'Perhaps I will publish your work in *New Vienna*.'

'Why?'

He smiled, his white teeth flashing like those of a healthy animal in his dark face.

'Your voice is gritty and harsh. It is important for women to read a voice like yours.'

'I am sorry if I was ungracious,' she said, suddenly liking him.

He put out his hand and she shook it.

'There,' he said. 'Please count me as a friend.'

Over the weeks his friendship gave Clara a measure of reassurance. She even found herself confiding some part of her story to him, and he responded quietly to all her uncertainties about memory and dream.

After this meeting, Jacob was exasperated by Anton's request to act on his behalf. He had never overcome his distrust of Anton as a rich man's son; now that he ran his father's affairs, Jacob's antipathy had a solid foundation. After talking to Clara, he was angry for another reason: he liked Clara, in her innocence and her eagerness, just as he liked what she wrote.

'I am too busy to act as your go-between,' Jacob told Anton abruptly the following day.

'The trouble with you,' said Anton without ill-feeling, 'is that you are only interested in social theory. You have no interest in human beings.'

'I can't imagine what you expect me to discover.'

'Whatever you can,' said Anton. 'You have worked as a journalist.'

'While you consider your investments in Moravia and Slovakia, or wherever you put your mines and railways?' jeered Jacob.

'Our political disagreements can be resolved on another occasion,' said Anton. 'Though let me explain something to you, Jacob. I've been thinking of selling the paper.'

His voice was more threatening than he intended and he saw the effect in Jacob's eyes. My father, he thought. I sound like my father.

'The main reason I've not sold already,' he explained more gently, 'is largely to continue your voice in this city, where it remains needed even if your views are often hopelessly simplistic.'

Jacob sat down as he absorbed the possibility of another owner, likely to be less open than Anton.

'I can protect the paper,' said Anton. 'We don't see eye to eye; I don't pretend we do. Our interests are not the same. But it is important a voice like yours should be heard. It's a problem we shall have to resolve. But, in this other matter – in which, of course, you can refuse all assistance . . .'

'It is hardly part of my job.'

'I ask only for your help. As a friend. And for Clara, too. She is a remarkable person. And there is a mystery hanging over her life. Can you imagine what it must be like not to know where you came from? Who your mother is?'

'I remember little enough of my own mother,' said Jacob, shrugging. 'These preoccupations have less weight in the working classes. However, I am interested in Clara, though I'm less interested in finding out who her parents were.'

'She might like to find out herself. See her from time to time. Ask her.'

'When I can. I'm very busy.'

'Ask her,' repeated Anton.

Dreams no longer woke Clara, but her daytime spirits were low. When her birthday came that October, she opened her journal and wrote: 'What can I hope for now? Why is it I feel I deserve more? As if there were something in me that might have come to fruition, and has not. It is difficult to accept that life will bring me no more happiness than teaching girls about literature, with reading and scribbling my only satisfactions. And yet many women can expect far less.' Then she sat gazing out of her window at the autumn trees in all their yellow and rusty splendour. Her mind was full of unanswered questions as she wondered how deeply her childhood had damaged her. Was she still capable of love? She set only one word on the next line: 'Joseph'.

In early November, when most of the leaves had fallen from the trees and the branches made sombre black patterns against the white sky, Jacob turned up unexpectedly and asked Clara without fuss whether she was curious about her mother. Clara was confused by the question.

'Poor woman! Her history is most likely to be the same as countless others, isn't it?'

'No,' said Jacob, categorically. He had thought about it a good deal. 'Women who came in from the ghettoes of Eastern Galicia came in as part of families. Everything in your story suggests isolation. Strangeness. A woman who had fallen out of the ordinary network completely. Do we even know if she was Jewish?'

'There is a locket,' she said, frowning. 'It is engraved with a Shield of David.'

'May I see it?'

'I keep it in my room,' she said.

Jacob made no great occasion of entering her room. He threw his coat over a chair but did not sit down as she brought the treasure out of one of the drawers and showed it to him. He was surprised to find the locket was solid gold.

'How have you preserved this? It must have been very tempting to sell it.' He turned it over several times, looking for some kind of mark, and at length said, 'Maybe the pawn shops can help us. I don't know.' He flicked it open. 'A pretty face,' he said, and smiled. 'What was the name of your aunt?'

'Rebekka Shönerer,' she said.

'I wonder when she came into Vienna? And from where? She may have registered with the police, I suppose. I will see what I can find out,' said Jacob. 'Let us go behind memory. Follow clues.'

Clara was excited by a sudden, enormous curiosity, a little mixed with anxiety.

*

At the first busy pawnshop, on Dorotheerstrasse, a man with a goatee beard, grey hair and a pince-nez which kept falling off his nose was impatient with Jacob's enquiries.

'I should say it was made around 1840 by a very good craftsman, but what do you expect me to say else?'

'You might have more help to offer,' said Jacob, uncertainly.

'Well, I haven't. Sorry,' he said, handing it back.

The second shop was empty, and the young man who ran it was intrigued by Clara's dark beauty.

'A pretty piece of work. I'll ask my father,' he said, then he clicked open the front and looked at the painting. 'She looks like a member of the von Arnstein family. Are you a relative?'

'Not at all,' said Clara, flushing at what she took to be an obvious attempt at flattery.

'You must have seen the likeness. We happen to have a painting. You might be interested to see it.'

'We are not purchasers,' said Jacob awkwardly.

'And this is not for sale,' the young man rebuked him. 'It sits here in store, not on pawn, with some articles my father cleared from a friend's house. The von Arnsteins have little use for pawnbrokers.'

'I can imagine,' smiled Jacob.

The painting they were shown was not really a very good portrait, and the resemblance to Clara was more marked than the likeness to the small picture of the lady in her locket.

'Disappointing,' said Jacob. 'Yet perhaps there is something in the eyes.'

A few days later Jacob appeared again without announcement. Clara knew at once he had news.

'May I come in?'

'Of course. What have you discovered?' she asked him.

'In some things Metternich's police were quite useful. This aunt of yours, this Rebekka Shönerer, she was a prostitute, as you might have guessed. So much I know from Court records. But she kept no bawdy house. Or was never so charged.'

'I see,' said Clara.

'And she wasn't involved in the paedophile brothels close by the Danube. You didn't imagine those, by the way. I have the address of two where such tastes are catered for. And one or two clients. But we do have one clue,' said Jacob. 'Rebekka registered with the police at an address near the Danube before she went to live in Taborstrasse. So it might be worth investigating there.'

'So many years ago? What could we find now?'

'There might be someone who would remember her.'

Clara stared at him, and her heart began to beat more quickly.

'Do you have the time to pursue this?'

'I have a carriage outside,' he said.

They left the carriage at the end of a small street which was half cobbled and evil-smelling.

'This is the street,' said Jacob, giving his hand to help Clara out of the carriage. For a moment they stared uneasily along the dark passageway. 'Are you sure you want to venture there?' asked Jacob.

'I'm not frightened,' said Clara.

In spite of her brave words, her heart banged uncomfortably as they walked between the poor houses with their numbers scratched on the brick. At length they found the number Jacob had been given.

'This is the house. Do you recognize anything?'

They stared up at the grey door in pitted stucco.

'I can't be sure,' said Clara.

It was a long while before anyone answered Jacob's knock.

The woman who opened the door was stringy-haired and unhappy-faced, and might have been fifty.

'What the hell do you want?' she demanded, glaring at them and easily making out they were from another district of the city. Jacob produced a few schillings.

'Information. I'm from *New Vienna*.'

'And what information would that be?' she asked suspiciously. 'This is a respectable lodging house, this is, and no news here that I'm aware of.'

'I'm sure none of the questions need make you anxious,' he said smoothly, watching her pocket the schillings.

'What do you want to know about?'

'Were you keeping a lodging house here thirty years ago?' he asked her.

'I was not,' she laughed. 'And that's not a flattering question. How old do you think I look? I'd better put my hair in curl before I talk to you.'

Jacob apologized, and consulted the paper in his hands.

'It says here one Rebekka Shönerer lodged here in 1840.'

The woman turned behind her and yelled up the stairs.

'Mother! There's some people here with questions.'

'Oh, is there?'

A woman with greying hair, rather shorter, much fatter and obscurely formidable came and stood in the doorway. A smell of poverty and cabbage soup came down the corridor after her.

'Yes?' she said truculently.

Jacob brought out another schilling from his pocket and repeated his question.

'Rebekka Shönerer? And what if she did? I know nothing of that,' she said, taking the schilling but remaining both hostile and suspicious.

'We were wanting your help,' said Clara.

For the first time the woman looked closely at the girl.

Jacob brought the locket out of his jacket and opened it before her.

'Do you remember a lady who looked like this?'

She looked at it, and then in a flash back to Clara, saying, 'Bless me. Poor lady. Yes.'

Clara felt her throat contract. 'You do?' she whispered.

'I'd only just taken the house when my man died. Yes. She took the front room. Oh, she was a pretty thing.'

'Was she alone?'

'No. She had a baby girl with her.'

Once again she stared at Clara, though if she saw a resemblance she was not to be drawn on it.

'Did she live here long?' asked Jacob.

'They lived here for about four years.'

'How did she live?'

'Well, she had some money at first. Not much, or she wouldn't have been living down here.'

'What happened to her?'

'Poor girl. Always waiting for letters, she was.'

'Where from?' asked Jacob.

'All over the place. Venice. Prague. Budapest. They stopped coming in the last year or so. She was very down then. But, whatever happened, she tended that baby. Always teaching it, she was. And playing with it.'

'Did she ever talk about the father?'

'No. I'm not even sure the letters came from him.'

'And why did she leave?'

'She never did leave. She died. I don't know what it was, more than poverty and grief.'

'And what happened to the baby girl?'

'What else? We put her in an orphanage.'

'Which one?'

'St Joseph and Mary. Down the street.'

Clara said, 'Thank you. Thank you very much.'

'There's something else,' said Jacob. 'This Rebekka. She must have been here at the same time.'

'We had a lot of girls. You understand?' She gave Jacob a little wink. 'I was used to them. But this one – I'm not saying she was a good girl – but she was different.'

She looked at Clara again, doubtfully.

'Thank you,' said Jacob again, and the woman closed the door without volunteering any other thoughts.

'Do we go to the orphanage?' asked Clara.

'If you have the strength,' said Jacob with a frown.

The street went downhill and smelt of dank, rotting wood and mould. Clara began to cough. At length, they came to a brick building with a cross marked out in the stonework which they recognized as the orphanage. A nun in black garments came to the door and ushered them into an unlit, whitewashed room.

'We need to see your Mother Superior,' began Jacob.

'I don't think she is free,' said the nun.

'We come from *New Vienna*.'

'That is no inducement to me to break into her prayers,' said the nun. 'It is a godless paper and no friend to the only true Church.'

'You are a friend to the children in your care, however,' said Jacob.

'It is our duty to look after as many as we can,' she replied. 'We are poorly endowed.'

The hostile black eyes were still not disposed to be helpful.

'Well, I imagine you have a record of those who have been in your charge,' he said. 'If only because it is your civic and legal responsibility to keep such records.'

'That's as may be.'

'Do they go back to 1840?'

'They do, naturally.'

'May we see them?'

'We don't let just anyone go poking about in our records.'

'Even relatives of one of the children?' Jacob hesitated, and at last decided to risk the offer of money. 'Do you accept charitable donations?'

He need not have worried. She took the schillings into the pockets of her black garments at once and said, with markedly less reluctance, 'How can I help?'

'We are looking for the records of a child brought to your care some time in 1845. From a nearby lodging house.'

He gave the address of the house from which they had come.

'It may be so.'

'Her name would be Clara.'

'Ever since the press was free we've had no peace,' the nun said. 'Pushing and probing. All right. Come and wait in here.'

Clara and Jacob followed her into a room which looked out on to an inner courtyard with the branches of an elm tree trying to grow in the centre. There was an overpowering smell of damp that caught in Clara's throat.

'Wait here,' said the nun. 'I'll find the book.'

Clara sat on a creaking chair and Jacob put a hand on her shoulder to comfort her. He did not ask her the question uppermost in his mind, but she answered his thoughts.

'I don't recognize this,' she said. 'Not really. Except for the smell.'

In about five minutes the nun came back with a large brown book.

'Yes,' she said. 'We did have such a girl from the address you mention.'

Clara could taste the blood in her mouth where she had bitten hard into her lower lip.

'But she left three months later.'

'With a Rebekka Shönerer?'

Something was wrong. Something the nun had discovered in the book embarrassed her.

'I was not in charge in those years. They were difficult times.'

'I must insist you tell me what you have discovered,' said Jacob.

'Yes, the woman came. She had known the mother, she said. We gave her Clara, and she paid us a little money. We exist on charity, you know. People are not so generous as they should be.' Jacob put his hand into his pocket, but she checked him.

'In those days we were careless: often children were given into most unsuitable hands.'

'And this Clara?'

'The most unsuitable hands!' she cried. 'They should be cursed for ever. I will not utter it. I can only say we did not know her designs. She was a friend of the mother, she said. Almost an aunt. And the girl seemed to recognize her. Well, it's not such a wonderful life here for orphans. We sent her off.'

'The memory troubles you.'

'Yes. I should have known what she was.'

'I am not here to blame you,' said Jacob.

'None of it was the wish of the orphanage.'

'I believe you,' he said quietly.

'It is shameful that such women should exist in our city. That brothels of any kind find customers is bad enough. If I prayed for the rest of my life I could not cleanse the city of such sins.'

As Jacob put out a hand to help Clara back into the carriage, he saw she was shaking.

'I'm sorry to have put you through all this to no end,' he said.

'It's not been altogether for nothing,' she said. 'I know at least my mother did not abandon me. Somehow I knew she would not throw me away. That makes me feel better.'

'It's cold,' said Jacob. He reached behind him for a woollen rug. 'Here. Put this over you.'

Chapter Thirty-Five

'AND THAT IS ALL I have been able to discover,' said Jacob. 'It is not much, I'm afraid.'

'Was Clara much affected?'

'She is curiously resilient,' said Jacob. 'For someone with so terrible a history.'

'There are some surprises in your story for me,' observed Anton thoughtfully. 'You remember my mother is related to the von Arnstein family.'

'You take a painted resemblance as a serious clue?'

'I must follow it up, certainly,' said Anton. 'But for that I shall need the locket.'

'She will not see you,' said Jacob flatly.

'But she trusts you, I suppose?'

'Correctly. I won't deceive her,' said Jacob, shaking his head. 'I'll tell her what you want and, if she agrees, I'll bring you the locket. She may not like to let it out of her hand. She may not like to think of your involvement. Or trust your motives.'

'You were wrong once before,' said Anton. 'Try.'

In the event, Clara was curious enough to let the precious golden object be given to Anton, and to await the outcome.

Minna had caught a chill, and the doctors were worried about the danger of pneumonia. When Anton visited her, she had taken to her bed. She looked much as she always did, sitting up in her pale grey lace and satin robes, trying to drink a little soup from a silver tray. The servants had lit a roaring fire in her bedroom which made the room a little oppressive, even though it was mid-December.

'Don't fuss,' she told her son. 'I shall stay in the warm and be perfectly all right.'

'And your lungs?'

'I no longer have anything wrong with my lungs. These doctors know nothing.'

The dark-lidded eyes brooded over her son. 'Now, what is this urgent matter you wish to discuss with me?'

'Time enough for that when I have assured myself you are well,' said Anton, smiling.

'You look pale yourself,' said Minna. 'I hope you are not being troubled by Hess and his minions?'

'No,' he said.

'Your father always came away from such meetings holding his heart and muttering. If it is not Hess, and not the newspaper, what is this excitement?'

'I want you to look at this,' he said. 'You were brought up with the von Arnsteins and may recognize the painted face. It would help me if you could.'

She took the locket into her hand and stared at it silently for a few moments. She did not open it.

'You seem to know the work,' said Anton.

His heart began to bang in his chest uneasily.

'Perhaps. I cannot be sure,' Minna said. 'I have some foreboding which makes me reluctant to look any further.'

'Come now,' said Anton.

She flicked open the neatly made locket. Then she let out a cry.

'You know the face!' cried Anton.

'I do.'

Anton was alarmed at her pallor.

'Where are your drops? Why do you look so pale?'

'Because I know her well,' said Minna. 'Give me a glass of water.'

'Is she a von Arnstein?' demanded Anton.

'No,' said Minna.

'Who, then?'

'She is my own cousin,' she said.

And, saying as much, her head fell back into the cushions in a faint.

Anton rang the bell, thoroughly alarmed, but even before the servant arrived his mother had recovered dramatically. She waved the servant away as the colour came back into her cheeks and an urgency came back into her eyes.

'You may go,' said Anton to the servant, and then added, 'But send for a doctor at the same time.'

'I don't need a doctor,' said Minna, waving the servant away vigorously. 'I am perfectly healthy. Half of my troubles come from boredom. I have no intention of dying, especially now this has arisen and needs sorting out.'

Anton nodded at the bewildered maidservant, who curtsied and left the room.

Sitting on the edge of the bed now, her thin legs were the only part of Minna that looked frail or old. She seemed quite ready to get out of bed.

'Now,' she said. 'Tell me where you found this piece.'

'It belongs to the girl called Clara,' said Anton. To his own ears, his voice sounded remote and strange.

'I see. The girl from Ebonstrasse? How strange life is! Well, perhaps this is my chance to right some injustice.'

'Does this concern our family, then?'

'Yes. A scandal from the past. This is a painting of my poor, mad cousin Elizabeth. She was once as pretty as the Empress herself, and almost as unlucky.'

'She was Viennese?'

'Yes. From the Christian side of the family. When she was eighteen, she went off to Italy against her father's wishes. There in Venice she lived with a group of English poets of some notoriety. They say Lord Byron was among them for a time before he went to Greece. She came from a wild family. Rebellious or fanatic, all of them. One or two became nuns, I remember. Not Liza, however. She lived exactly as she liked in Italy and at last simply disappeared. It was a tragedy of wilfulness. Now, where are my drops?'

Anton looked closely at his mother's face, which had begun to close into its familiar lines.

'They are here,' he said.

She nodded and took them quietly. Her face had lost some of the first eagerness and she looked wary, he thought.

'I will get up and sit close to the fire.'

He brought up a chair for her but she did not move, and he did not urge her to do so. The story, though he believed it, was incomplete. He knew as much. There was nothing in it so far to suggest a grave wrong that could be righted and for which his mother had responsibility.

'Do you think this Elizabeth may have returned to Vienna?' he prompted.

'What gives you such an idea?'

'She had a child here,' said Anton, flatly.

'No. She had no child,' said Minna.

'I think perhaps she did,' said Anton.

Minna's eyes, always deep-set, now seemed to disappear under their lids.

'I am tired,' she said.

Anton was tempted to withdraw, but he was teased by the certainty there was more to know.

'You mentioned a wrong that might be righted.'

She seemed to be weighing up how much to say.

'I suppose there is something you should know,' she said. 'Your father was involved with the girl. For a time.'

Anton seemed to know the truth before she spoke.

'You remember once, I told you, there was another woman. That was my cousin Elizabeth. They met in Venice, I think, or perhaps Prague; somewhere he travelled. He was lonely. He confessed to me. I cannot think what she saw in him, such a wild girl as she was. She cannot have loved him.'

Anton did not want to believe what he had heard. The anxiety made him brutal.

'And?'

'And nothing. Nothing. He told me, and I forgave him. What else should there be?'

'Then what was the *wrong*? You felt there was a *wrong*,' cried Anton.

'The wrong, my dear, was to him. To your *father*,' said Minna. 'The way I drew away from him. And in doing so turned you away from him. That was wrong.'

He believed her.

'You need not assume she is your sister,' said Minna, seeing suddenly that this was the nub of his concern.

Anton thought about that. 'Was the affair a matter of years?'

'A matter of weeks, I believe,' said Minna. 'Or so he told me.'

'Was there correspondence?'

'None that I know. I would not expect letters. She was a proud girl, Elizabeth.'

'Had she no money of her own?'

'My dear,' said Minna softly, 'you look frantic. Be calm. This Elizabeth had many lovers.'

'You must know more. You are concealing it. Was there nothing in the will? Was no provision made?'

'Nothing,' said Minna steadily. 'Your father knew of no

child. You cannot imagine he would have left the girl unprovided for had he known.'

'Nevertheless, we can hardly ignore the possibility. Or the girl. Can we?'

He could read in Minna's face how little she liked the thought of pushing the matter.

'Don't you see? Even if she is not my sister, she *must* be your cousin Elizabeth's daughter. So she is a relative.'

'A distant one. A second cousin of a family that always thought itself rather superior to ours. And, let me tell you, that particular family will take little note of the relationship,' said Minna. 'They don't even like to be reminded of their respectable poor connections. Elizabeth's behaviour led them to throw her out of their hearts long ago.'

'The family has not been particularly fertile, however,' observed Anton.

'There is a son. A grandson. They are satisfied.'

'Can you be so hard-hearted? Think of her mother as she was when she was young,' urged Anton. 'To die in such poverty, and leave her child uncared for. The story is so sad.'

'When she was young, her beauty made me feel dowdy. She was never a girl I liked,' muttered Minna.

'Nonsense. You must always have been lovely,' said Anton.

Minna remained mutinous. 'I am sorry for her. Very well. But why should we look after her child?'

'If only to ensure that our middle age is not haunted by our childhood.'

Minna patted his left hand, which lay without concealment on his chair.

'So many wounds. We carry them with us. You have endured yours more readily than most.'

'Have I?'

'That girl Elizabeth took disgraceful risks,' Minna said

reflectively. 'And she threw away one of the greatest fortunes of the age without a care, just to go her own way. Can you imagine such folly?'

'What happened to the inheritance?'

'Oh,' she shrugged, 'the family shared it. You need not imagine this child will get her hands on it now, even if she could prove her rights.'

'The more reason, then, for us to help her.'

Minna still hesitated. 'You are sentimental. Yes, we should help, but not perhaps bring her here. The thought frightens me. It might bring disrepute to your father's name.'

'I would see it did not,' said Anton.

'Who knows how many men her wanton mother had after your father left Venice? Aren't you disgusted at the thought?'

Anton shrugged. 'You will not find the girl herself disreputable, I promise you. I think, if you knew her, you would like her.'

'It is not to the point,' she said. 'I am old, and I should like a peaceful end to my life. She must be full of resentment. An angry girl. I feel her as a threat.' Her face darkened. 'When she learns her mother's story she will hate us all.'

'Mother, I am clear in my mind: to bring her here is the right thing to do,' said Anton.

A great calm filled him. It was in many ways despairing because he knew now that, whatever the truth of her parentage, these discoveries had distanced him from Clara for ever except as a brother. Unexpectedly, the extinction of all sexual hope had freed him and given him confidence; he could push through what had to be done even against his mother's opposition. And he would. Minna sensed as much.

'You must do what you think best,' she said.

It came to him that she had never sounded so resigned to his going his own way.

*

The first trial of Anton's new strength waited for him in Ebonstrasse. He had no fear that Clara would refuse to see him. He was no longer a suitor; he had information in his possession that would bring her a new life. He had no need now to approach her through Jacob.

As he reached the doorway, Mitzi was leaving the building and hesitated to close the door after herself, even while denying him the right of entry. He saw the uncertainty behind her assertive words.

'She will not see you. She's a silly girl, but I can't let you in. I'm sorry. I gave my word.'

'I have important news for her,' said Anton steadily. 'She will want to have it, I promise you.'

He looked down into Mitzi's impish face. At the corners of her bright eyes new lines signalled the dissipation of the previous nights.

'Give your news to me,' said Mitzi. 'I will take it to her.'

She had not yet shut the door behind her. Anton put his hand where her little gloved fingers clutched the doorknob. It was more like a caress than an attempt to make his point by force. He smiled winningly.

'She would not want to hear this from anyone else,' he said.

Mitzi shook her head reluctantly, while Anton pressed her fingers.

'I dare not. Please. Don't,' she whispered.

As their game proceeded, they were roused from it by a voice from upstairs.

'Mitzi?'

As Anton heard Clara's voice his heart responded awkwardly. Then his new serenity empowered him.

'Let me in, Clara,' he called back firmly. 'I have your locket and your news.'

Mitzi's arm no longer kept him out and he entered the small hallway just as Clara appeared at the banisters and looked down. It was a little shock to him to see she was pale and had lost weight. For a moment he thought she would send him away, and demand he deal with her only through Jacob, but she did not. With the locket in his hand, he made his way up the stairs towards her.

She was a little afraid of him, he saw, with a pang of remorse. It took some courage for her to allow him into her room but, having made her decision, her manner was cool and friendly. She led him into the silent flat.

'Why are you here?' she asked. 'I expected Jacob to bring any news there might be.'

He met her eyes bravely. It would perhaps never be possible to refer to what had happened between them.

'Please forgive me for coming myself against your express instructions . . .'

'May I have the locket?'

He gave it to her at once. 'When you hear what I have to say, you will understand why I have come.'

And then, before she could formulate any objection, he told her the story as far as he had pieced it together.

She sat for a long while, silently, so that he was almost afraid she had not grasped the enormity of it. When at last she spoke, however, she said thoughtfully:

'I see. But what is that to me? If the family cast off my mother, they will hardly be more friendly to her illegitimate daughter.'

'You are wrong,' he said eagerly. 'I am an important part of that family and I have come to take you home.'

Now indeed she looked at him warily. 'To your own home?' The thought of sleeping under the same roof as him frightened her. Her body distrusted him; he saw as much. 'I don't think I could do it, Anton.'

The strength he had felt surging into him when he confronted his mother returned to carry him.

'Yes,' he insisted. 'You can. I'm not stupid; I know what you feel. Take the risk. You have the courage. You must not refuse a life of splendour and opportunity.'

'The life my mother threw away?'

'I don't speak of money. These are different days,' he said. 'There will be opportunities for you she could never imagine.'

She shook her head. 'Anton, I need my independence.'

He looked impatient. 'That's just a word, isn't it? What does it really mean, for a woman? In Vienna?'

She shook her head again. 'I don't know. It seems to be all I have.'

'You can't forgive me. That's it, isn't it?' he cried out.

She looked at him wanly, and saw how wretched he was.

'I shall never forgive myself,' he muttered.

Clara tried to confront her confused feelings. There had been so much anger and hurt. All the gaiety of the city had darkened in the aftermath of the last months.

'I have forgiven you, Anton,' she said at last. 'What was done to me was no worse than other women endure every day in this city.'

He stared into her candid eyes. 'Every day?' he chided her gently.

'There are so many kinds of injustice. So many kinds of victim.'

He dared not put out a hand to touch her. 'Won't you at least let me help you?'

Her eyes met his gravely. 'I don't think you can.'

'Come and meet my mother. It's important for her.'

Clara thought about that. 'If you like. But I will return here.'

DREAMERS

Clara slept little that night but, though she seemed weary when Anton came to call for her the next morning, she kept her word. She looked at him doubtfully, but she gave him her hand to help her into his family carriage.

Chapter Thirty-Six

ABOUT TWO MONTHS LATER, Anna von Mayerberg called on Anton at home. The visit was a surprising one and, although he immediately asked for her to be shown into his study, he was not best pleased. He was in no mood to meet her hostility with politeness.

When she approached him, he smiled as cordially as he could and saw that she looked pale and tired.

'I will come to the point at once,' she said. 'Rudolf is ill and wishes to see you.'

Anton stared at her. Everything that once made her a figure of whom he was slightly apprehensive was disappearing in her middle age. Her blondeness was greying; her complexion, though still flawless, no longer shone with freshness. Only the steely carriage remained.

'Will you come and see him?'

'I don't know.'

He had a strong wish to keep away from the man he had once admired so intensely. He watched Anna's fingers go fluttering up to her lips to conceal both their pallor and her nervousness.

'He is dying,' she said.

Anton had heard Rudolf was ill. Drink, some said. There had been other rumours: tuberculosis, syphilis.

'What is his illness?' Anton enquired. His voice was cold, though he tried to look as sympathetic as he could.

'The doctors say it is his heart. He cannot last long. A month or two. Perhaps less.'

Anton wondered at the love his old friend had been able to inspire: so intense, he fancied, that Anna had actually aged into becoming the contemporary of a man twenty years older.

'Why does he want to see me?'

'I don't know. He was always much attached to you.'

For a moment he saw the old, bright gleam of dislike in her eyes.

'Very well,' he said. 'I will come.'

Anton had not seen his friend for some time and was shocked at his appearance. The flesh had peeled from him, leaving his body at once flabby and emaciated. Books lay piled about the bed on either side and there was an odd, sweet smell Anton could not place.

He made his apologies as politely as he could for the length of time that had elapsed since their last meeting, and came and sat at the bedside. He had often sat by Rudolf's bed and listened to him talk: in despair, or mockery. He had never taken his seat there with such a sense of miserable finality.

'Don't trouble yourself too much,' said Rudolf, wanly, reading the shock of his condition in Anton's expression.

'Are you receiving good treatment?' asked Anton, incapable of anything but the merest civilities.

'As to medicine,' shrugged Rudolf, 'I believe the best doctors these days understand there is little can be done to help the human body. The most important thing is not to harm it.'

'A point of view,' Anton nodded. 'I am not sure I altogether share it. May I send you my own physician?'

Rudolf smiled and shook his head. 'Please do not put yourself to the bother. I am well satisfied, believe me.'

Anton was not sure whether it was the quality of medical care that pleased Rudolf, or his own state.

'I have been brooding,' said Rudolf, 'about my father.'

'As I get older, I think far more kindly of my own.'

'Mine was a weak man, but oddly resilient. A child at heart. Did you know he is still alive? It was my mother who died.'

Anton murmured something consoling.

'His second wife lasted hardly two years. He saw them both out, for all his feebleness.'

'I didn't know he remarried,' said Anton. He had no wish to impart his own family secrets and hoped he would not be urged towards any such confession.

'Death cements the bond between generations,' said Rudolf. 'I should have stayed in the countryside and lived without all this taint of the arts.'

'No taint, surely? Your best work will be remembered.'

'Ah, it is the living we forget, not the dead. I never mattered much to anyone.'

'You matter to your wife.'

'She has her consolations,' said Rudolf. 'From my point of view, this collapse of the body hardly seems important. The Viennese like to honour genius when it is safely dead, and I have already benefited from their generosity. My talents died long ago and I have already enjoyed the good fortune of a little posthumous fame.'

Anton smiled wryly.

'Are you in pain?'

'Yes,' said Rudolf. 'It will not be for long, however. Well, I shall be a formidable ghost.'

'What is this, deathbed prophecy?' asked Anton as lightly as he could.

'I have seen the world change.' He coughed. 'And I am tired now. Goodbye, old friend.'

'Can nothing be done?' Anton asked Anna as he prepared to leave.

'Nothing,' she said. 'The doctor says it is a matter of days, perhaps hours. But I want your advice about his notebooks. He says I should not read his notebooks. That they should be burnt. He says they are wicked and that his immortal soul would be in danger if they see the light of day. What must I do?'

'Have you not consulted a priest?' he asked, ironically.

'I cannot!' she cried.

'Have you given him a promise?' he asked her, trying not to let his curiosity affect him.

'I could not do so.'

'If they are all that is left of him, you must not burn them,' said Anton awkwardly. 'Probably he does not intend you to do so. Think of Virgil.' He saw she had not heard the story. 'Virgil was displeased with his own work. If his friends had obeyed him, we should not now have had his great epic poem.'

She nodded. 'It is the kind of anxiety I felt. And yet, I have much less respect for literature than you do. I think it may deceive and persuade and lead men from the Church.'

'You don't want the responsibility.'

'You are right.' She hesitated again. 'May I entrust them to you?'

Anton was nonplussed. 'I thought you imagined me as some kind of villain?'

'It was never a personal distrust.'

'That is what I found so offensive.'

He remembered the charges that were being made by

people much like her, yet he was sorry for her in her loneliness. And he remembered the loss of her child.

'You are still a young woman,' he said awkwardly, though indeed she did not look it.

She shook her head. 'When the baby died, I lost my youth.'

He dropped his eyes, remembering what von Mayerberg had told him.

'Do you want to know how it happened? It was four in the morning. The birds were just beginning their song when the pains began. And I lay alone in my bed counting the time between pains. Rudolf was in his study. Writing. In his journal. He had fallen asleep across the desk. I went to whisper, "Rudolf, it is time to go for the midwife," but he was very deeply asleep. It was Sunday morning and there was neither maid nor cook. Rudolf would not stir. I shook his arm, first gently and then with panic. The last shaking woke him and he sat up blearily. "Hurry," I said urgently. "Hurry. There is not much time." He nodded as if he understood, and followed me back to the bedroom. As I lay down again, however, he lay beside me and was asleep in a moment. I realized he had not grasped the problem. Another pain took me, and another which followed quickly on the first. I shrieked. Then he was awake. "What? What shall I do to help?" "Fetch . . . her . . ." I said. "Where are my shoes?" he asked. "The bed," I gasped. "Under the bed." He found them and was gone. A first baby takes a long time, I thought in the silence that followed his going. My mother said that. If only my mother were here. It will take a long time. Twenty-four hours, my mother said it took her to have her first child. When I heard that story, I had not realized the pains would be so intense. They left me no time to pray, though I tried to do so in case I was about to die. The midwife was here in time to turn the baby's head. It was a small child. Under six pounds, and frail, but I clasped it to my stomach and turned a new gaze on my husband. "My dear, are you well? Are you well?" he asked me, tears streaming down his face. "My good one, my loyal one, how I have failed you!" But I said nothing, kissing the small, peaky face of the child and went to sleep.

'It was several days before my strength returned. I was far too feeble to feed the child. It was a week before I could sit upright. Oddly enough, when my strength returned, my first question was, "What is it you write in your study? Is it a novel?" "No. It is a prayer for forgiveness," he said. "My angel. And will you forgive me? That it took me so long to come to your help?" "I will forgive. I must. But where is the child? Bring her to me." As he hesitated, I read the terrible news in his face. My newborn child was dead. For the first time in my marriage I turned eyes of hatred upon him, and my shriek sent him from the room with his hands over his ears.'

Her story had stunned Anton but, whatever her motive in telling it – whether to excuse her own bitterness or to explain the ambivalence of her feeling towards the journal – she left the tale behind, and began to speak of other matters, of her friendship with the wife of Baron Hess, for instance, who had been enormously kind to her in recent weeks. As Anton well knew, the Baron was a close friend of Prince Schwartzenberg, and hardly a likely acquaintance for so modest a family, but it seemed that the two women had been friends since attending the same village church in their childhood, and that von Mayerberg's family was some kind of distant connection.

'We have found one another,' she said.

Anton speculated in what sense the Baroness could be said to have been looking for Anna, but supposed it was a kindness.

'Now will you help me?' she asked directly.

'What would you like me to do?'

'Think about his work. His immortal part will be in heaven this month,' she said softly.

Anton took away the only immortal part that he believed in, and put the volumes in his personal safe.

Two weeks later, Rudolf von Mayerberg was dead. In St Stephan's Cathedral his body lay in an open bronze casket and those who had known him went to look at the dead face in the candlelight. As Anton gazed down at his old friend he wondered silently, What do you really want me to do?

Above the altar, the blues and reds in the stained glass recalled a Catholic God that had frightened him in his school days. Less oppressively, the four faces of the Church Fathers on the pulpit were sly, worldly, altogether human. He realized there was no way he could make the correct decision without some form of transgression.

When he returned to his office, he took several volumes of the journal out of the safe. Each was locked very securely, but Anna had attached the key by a blue ribbon round the books and, after a little hesitation, he pushed the metal into the lock, which opened at once. He turned back the pages, not knowing exactly what to expect, half dreading a journal in which erotic exploits were recorded in explicit detail.

The pages were blank. Nonplussed, he unlocked the next volume, and the next. All the pages were blank. And then he understood. It was for that blankness that von Mayerberg imagined he would be damned.

Anton closed all the locks, put the blue ribbon round the heavy volumes, and placed them once again in the metal safe.

Chapter Thirty-Seven

IN HER JOURNAL, Clara noted the ways in which
her inner world was changing. She was no longer troubled
by dreams, and though she often woke to find memories
from childhood alive in her mind, the pain seemed to have
been drawn from them. Since she had given Anton the
forgiveness he asked for, her own sense of violation had
disappeared. It was as if she had been released from a spell,
and yet remained a princess woken out of her glass casket
without much expectation of happiness.

In the second week of December, when the sun was like a
red coal in the sky, and frozen air hurt her throat, Clara was
invited by one of her earliest pupils, Anton's cousin Sarah,
to celebrate the last night of the festival of Hanukkah at her
family home in Herrengasse. It was an unexpected invitation
and Clara was in two minds about accepting. She was fond
of Sarah, who was much her own age and shared many of
her own interests, but she had resolved to keep clear of the
Shassner family.

As the last candle of the ceremonial candlestick was lit by
Sarah's father with grave dignity, Clara felt very much an
outsider; she had never been taught the words of the songs,
though she dimly recognized the tunes from her days in the
Shassner household. Nevertheless, she liked the gentle flicker
of the candles in their silver holder. Seeing as much, Sarah's

father explained the story of the festival; the way holy oil had been miraculously renewed in the temple of the Maccabees. 'It's a story of faith and impossibility,' he explained.

After the meal, Sarah led her to the room in which the lessons had been given, and as Sarah began to speak in English, they regained something of their old relationship.

'What of your ambitions?' Sarah enquired.

'These days I have none,' said Clara.

This was a partial truth. A flood of creative energy had been released in her since the discoveries of the last weeks, but all her new work was filled with the violent images that had once haunted her thoughts, and few of her poems were suitable for *New Vienna*. She had little hope of seeing them published.

'Women delude themselves, don't they?' said Sarah with a melancholy smile. 'At least in Vienna. We are both old maids.'

Clara accepted the description politely, though it grated on her. 'From choice, at least,' she said.

'In a sense.' Sarah shrugged.

'Do you still enjoy English novels?' asked Clara, wishing to change the direction of the conversation.

Sarah's face lit up at once. 'There's a wonderful new one. Do you know it?' She took three leather volumes from her desk and pushed them eagerly into Clara's hands. 'I can't imagine anyone in Vienna writing of a plain heroine with such sympathy.'

Clara looked at Sarah's powerful features, which might have been handsome in a man.

'Is beauty so much more important here?'

'Certainly it is. In Vienna men don't even notice sensitive thoughts unless they're revealed on delicate features. No one will ever think of you and me in the same way, not in twenty years.'

Clara sighed. 'And will that make my life easier?'

She began to think it was time to return home, but Sarah frowned. She had intended the conversation to take another turn. Clumsily, she came to the point.

'Clara, I know something of your story.'

Her words gave Clara a jolt before she realized that Anton would only have spoken of her possible parentage.

'Please. I want you to think of me as a sister.'

'My dear Sarah,' said Clara awkwardly.

She did not want to be drawn into the Shassner family. Yet the generosity and affection in Sarah's eyes were undeniable. It would have been curmudgeonly to reject her offer of friendship.

Joseph sat in a café in Grinzing and looked down at the lights of Vienna. He was alone. A few musicians of his acquaintance hailed him, but he did no more than nod to them. His melancholy had hardly lifted since his affair with Sophie had come to an end. It was not that he regretted the decision to part from her: he had seen her on several occasions since and she had made it plain enough that the situation might be reversed. But he could not go back. Something had aged and grown bitter in him. And then he had been ill; an infection which brought him to cancel two weeks of concerts in Paris and Berlin, and led Hannah to bring him home to nurse him. His gloom distressed her.

'What is it? What has happened that's so terrible?' she pleaded with him. 'Something you didn't know? The gentiles don't like us? That particular bunch around Richard Wagner don't like us? You knew that already.'

Joseph tried to explain. 'But I was one of them. I was part of their world. All of us, all those musicians, we gave them the best of ourselves and they took it and judged it. *And it didn't make any difference.*'

'It's your mother's fault,' said Peretz. 'She makes the same mistake. She's invited to this one and that one. If you would take my advice . . .'

'Please,' said Hannah. 'It's different for him. I sell clothes. I know what that means. I have money now, but I don't delude myself. But our Joseph could go anywhere in the world. He is even invited to America.'

'If you would listen,' said Peretz. 'If you would listen while I finish my sentence.'

'Go on,' said Joseph, wearied and amused at the same time by the life-long battle between Hannah and Peretz which seemed set to continue into old age.

'Thank you. What I was going to say is exactly that. *America*. That is the answer. If you are invited there, go. We could all go. Why not? They don't care where you come from or who you are in America. It's the golden land. Everyone can pursue their own happiness. All people are the same there. So why do we have to stay in Europe? For all we know, Europe is finished. Finished or not, it was always bad for Jews, and always will be.'

'Listen to the man! What do you know about America?' demanded Hannah. 'Terrible stories come back from there. All right, they don't care so much whether you are Jewish, but Indians take your scalp because you are white.'

'There aren't any Indians in New York,' said Peretz. 'Where are you invited?'

'New York,' said Joseph. 'But I don't want to leave Vienna, anyway. I should feel defeated.'

Yet defeated was what Joseph continued to feel. Even though invitations to play poured in. Even though he could feel the eyes of a handsome woman in a huge hat surveying him that very moment with unmistakable speculation. He did not respond to her, or to a pretty young singer who paused and smiled, intending to break through Joseph's remoteness with good-natured affection. Joseph raised his eyes to stare at her implacably and she went off with a shrug.

Joseph ordered another bottle of wine, and a plate of Wiener Schnitzel for which he had no appetite. He gathered up the newspapers and began to read one of them without curiosity. What was it to him who married and who died, what lines were newly drawn about which municipality, what buildings went up?

There was an advertisement for a light opera at the Theatre on the Wien. For a moment he found himself scanning the cast list to see if Sophie had succeeded in winning the role she wanted; with an edge of malice he saw that she had not. Then his eyes were taken by a short lyric on the same page. He read it because it was filled with a loneliness like his own: a solitary bleakness. The first verse ran:

> The moon that floods the garden with its light
> Streams through my bedroom window this spring night
> And cuts the shadow of one branch across
> My silver bed, a quiet sign of loss.

Only that morning he had woken to find a sharp, leafy branch cutting a black shadow across his own bed, and had felt a similar melancholy. He glanced to see who had written the poem, for he knew most of the poets who published in *Neue Freie Presse*. To his surprise, he saw it was signed with a woman's name.

Did women, then, have such feelings? He realized that he had not imagined so. He had seen them only as figures to be desired, or escaped, as if they stopped being conscious as soon as they were alone. He was not sure he liked the idea of anything else. The idea of a woman filled with longing was almost uncomfortable to him. As he took a carriage back to the Ring, the little lyric sounded like a tune in his head.

A few days later, walking towards his favourite café in the sunshine, he stopped to look in the window of a bookshop. Remotely, at the corner of his eye, a lady with two or three parcels came out of a dress shop and began to climb into a carriage freshly painted with a coat of arms. At the edge of his attention, he made out the high spirits of the horses, the elegance of the coachman and the beauty of the woman who was getting into the carriage. Then he recognized her face, with its poignant dark eyes and perfect lips. It was Clara.

Joseph had thought of Clara many times since his impulsive note had met no reply, but he imagined himself resigned to the knowledge that she belonged to another man. Seeing her now was more of a shock than he could quite explain.

She gave the parcels to the coachman and turned, half-expectantly, towards him.

'Joseph?'

The softness and vulnerability in the voice touched him more than her apparel. His eyes went over her. The face was no longer as eager and young as he remembered it; it was easier now to make out the fine bones; the lips, though tender, had more irony in their shaping. The hair was hidden by a fashionable bonnet.

'You did not reply to my note,' he remembered. 'No reason why you should, I suppose, but I was disappointed.'

'I was ill,' she said, quickly, 'or I should have done so before anything.'

'I wrote at a bleak time for me,' he said. 'It seemed you could help. I don't know why. Perhaps because, meeting you, I remembered . . .' He stopped, a little embarrassed to realize that these words were almost the first unnecessary ones he had bothered to utter since his return from the Tyrol. 'Those days in Haidgasse seem far away to you, I expect,' he concluded lamely. 'I see you have prospered.'

'My life is much the same as it was,' she said. 'These days I teach less.'

For a time they exchanged civilities about Hannah and Peretz.

'Will you take a glass of tea with me?' he asked.

It was the first such invitation he had felt the least inclination to make for a long time.

'I should be glad.'

Then Joseph looked at the crest on the lacquered carriage.

'And which aristocrat is your patron these days?' he enquired, with an edge to his voice which brought the blood to her cheeks.

'The crest belongs to the Shassner family,' she said quietly. 'Anton was made a Baron. Sometimes, at his urging, I make use of the carriage.'

His eyebrows went up and he made her a little bow.

'Part of the family?'

'In a way, yes.'

Her eyes looked steadily into his own. Joseph's curiosity was aroused. He wanted to talk to her. To hear her story, certainly, but also to tell his own.

Afterwards, they walked in the woods together. The light wind stirred the tops of the dark trees; all around was the scent of pine resin. Clara had told more than she had intended, more than Anton would have liked. She knew it was folly, but there seemed no point in concealment. She had given no promise to Anton. Every womanly instinct told her it was unwise, that the sensible thing to do was to give away the Shassner part of the story and leave out her own history. She could not do it. With Joseph, she felt there was no sense in pretending, or playing a tactical game.

'So you see,' she concluded with a wry laugh, 'you occupy

a special place in my thoughts. You are the only untainted piece of my childhood.'

For a moment he was silent, and she could not read his expression.

'I don't see how you have survived this,' said Joseph.

'Women survive far worse,' she said. 'My friend Lily is horribly ill. Even before her illness she was in danger of starving. In comparison to Lily, I have been fortunate.'

'There is always the one-legged man in the street to console us,' said Joseph bitterly. 'And perhaps the totally blind to console him. You must have seen I was feeling sorry for myself when we met.'

She looked into his face, searchingly and with a measure of fear. 'You are not repelled by my history?'

'No,' he said. 'No.'

'There would be people who would be disgusted. Victims attract something of the opprobrium of the criminal.'

They walked on together in silence.

'So much violence. Can you forget it?' he asked.

'I no longer have terrifying dreams,' she said. 'But sometimes when I am awake I wonder . . .'

He stopped walking and looked into her face.

'You are very beautiful,' he said. He put a hand on her shoulder delicately. 'If I touch you, do I frighten you?'

'No,' she said steadily.

He lifted her chin for a moment, gently.

'I like your courage,' he said. 'You must be very strong.' He went on looking into her face.

'You said something had distressed you,' she said quickly, perhaps to protect herself from the intensity of his gaze. 'What could it be? Don't you have everything your younger self would have dreamed of?'

He shook his head.

'You have become famous since the day I first listened to

you in the English Embassy. I suppose it must be that a woman has disappointed you.'

His face darkened for a moment as he remembered the snubs of his Tyrol experience.

'I'm lonely,' he admitted. 'And disappointed. But my heart is unbroken.'

'What are your plans?' she asked him.

His thin lips widened into a smile under his moustache.

'I shall go on playing the violin, I suppose. That is all I can do.'

'You mean it isn't a joy? I should thank God every day if I could play as you do.'

'Let me tell you what makes me unhappy,' said Joseph. 'Or did, until I met you again . . .'

He said nothing more for a moment. As he stood, he was almost six inches taller than she was and to catch his words she had her face turned up to him. She could see he wanted to kiss her on the lips.

'You must hate all men after what has happened to you,' he said, wistfully.

'No. I don't hate you,' she said steadily.

Abruptly he bent to kiss her, his moustache hard against her upper lip; a hard, dry kiss. Then he raised his head to look into her eyes.

'You know what I feel. What all men feel in the presence of beauty. Do you mind that?'

She had not drawn away from him. Her eyes were open.

'I have loved you all my life,' she said.

These days there was a portrait of Franz Joseph in Anton's study, where his father had once hung Joseph II in sign of the loyal gratitude he felt for the Toleranzpatent which allowed a few families of notable Jews to enjoy a more liberal life. Now Franz Joseph stood in his stead, clad in the white uniform of a General, with a wide, blood-red sash across his chest and a Military Order at his throat. The blue eyes looked as hard as china. A black helmet with dark green heron's feathers lay on a table at his side. It was a strange pose, Anton reflected, for a rule whose troops had lost almost every battle his armies had entered, and who was himself notoriously squeamish in the face of slaughter.

As Anton sat in his study drinking the short cup of black coffee with which he liked to begin the morning, he pondered the day's news. There were urgent messages from Prague and Budapest, and rumours of war between Prussia and France. In Vienna a group of angry leatherworkers had thrown a Croat boy of twelve through a plate-glass window to protest some danger to their livelihood. He permitted himself a mirthless smile. Nothing changed.

And yet, he reflected, in the twenty years since he had been willing to mount the barricades himself, there *had* been changes. Important changes. And in his own life, too. He wasn't so proud of them all. He had grown heavier, and decidedly less radical. Only this week the smouldering, angry disagreement with Jacob had broken into flame:

'You can't run on both sides,' said Jacob. 'You can't be with the owners and the workers at the same time. It is impossible. Their interests are opposed.'

'I want what is fair. The only loyalty I feel is to Austria,' Anton tried to explain.

'There is no such entity,' said Jacob flatly. 'It isn't real. All that's real is the class war. And we are on opposite sides, Anton. You will close the paper. It's inevitable.'

'No,' said Anton. 'You will see.'

These days he often wished he had been friendlier to his father. It seemed now that the old quarrel between them had been altogether misconceived. These days, too, when he thought of marriage, he thought without antipathy of his cousin Sarah and wondered if his father had married in the same mood.

Clara's friendship with Sarah had eased Anton's relationship with her. Sometimes they all took tea together. He had wanted to help; to give her a better life; but she refused to allow him. Through Sarah, it became possible. Early in March, however, Anton was surprised to receive a note from Clara suggesting they meet at Neuners Café. Rather to his surprise, she took the initiative in the conversation at once and announced her engagement to Joseph Kovacs.

Anton knew something of the matter. Joseph and Clara had been seen together many times in the last few months. *Neue Freie Presse* had even written about the mysterious dark beauty who often took Kovacs' arm as he left his concerts. Anton had not let himself speculate about their sexual involvement. Now Clara's announcement took him by surprise. Against his will, he felt an intolerable rush of jealousy which was altogether inappropriate in a half-brother. She saw as much.

'Forgive me,' he muttered. 'Your happiness excludes me.'

'I thought you would want to be told.'

'Don't be angry,' he said feebly.

'I shall be married,' she said serenely, 'next month. In the synagogue in Leopoldstadt. It is arranged.'

His calm shattered. 'This is precipitate. Next month. Do you know his family? His mother has a hat shop or two in Spiegelgasse. His father used to be a pedlar. Is this suitable?'

'Let's not be silly, Anton,' she said quietly. 'Joseph needs no family connection to recommend him. What is this sudden access of snobbery? Joseph has played for the Emperor. When we go to England he will play for Queen Victoria. He belongs to the aristocracy of talent.'

337

'You are going to England?'

'First. Then New York. But we shall not stay there. Joseph is determined to make his home in Vienna.'

There were things Anton wanted to ask that were impossible to ask. She saw them in his eyes.

'Try to be happy for me,' she said softly, and put out a hand to touch the crippled fingers that for once lay unselfconsciously on the white cloth. 'Joseph and I love one another. It's a great fortune. Things might easily have ended very differently.'

'My mother will be pleased,' he said at last, with an effort. Clara smiled.

'She will be proud to count Joseph Kovacs among our family,' Anton added. 'And I'm glad you will stay in Vienna.'

The air was warm, the buds green under the new street lighting, the evening sky a dark and cloudless blue. A year later, Clara and Joseph were among the audience for the ceremonial opening of the Opera House on the Ringstrasse. As a mark of her favour, Minna had given Clara a string of diamonds. Even without them her face was radiant as she entered the red and pale gold auditorium to take a seat in the stalls.

The Emperor and the Archdukes were in the Imperial box. In the lowest tier at the other side sat Minna, Anton and Sarah. Baron Hess and his wife sat in an adjoining box. The orchestra arrived. The curtain went up to reveal an actress from Cologne carrying the Imperial flag, who spoke an unexpected Prologue: 'The true greatness of Vienna lies in its Opera House.'

The audience were not disposed to argue and Joseph observed as much, his face alight with amusement: 'Italy's lost, Hungary too, and Prussia runs the German Confederation but tonight all the Viennese care about is *Don Giovanni*,' said Joseph, his own spirits high.

Clara saw his exuberant mood and smiled. As the overture began she felt Joseph's hand take hers and let the music conquer her senses.

The streets that lay outside the Opera House pulsed with their own life; old waltzes in Sophiensaal, argument in Neuners Café. And in the districts further out the latest wave of children from Moravia, Bohemia and Galicia lay asleep: Sigmund Freud, Arthur Schnitzler and Gustav Mahler dreamed in their narrow beds. Far above the city, the woods rustled in the spring night air. The moon caught the glint of green on the dome of the Hofburg, and the earth turned towards the end of the century.

CHRIS O'BRIEN

0181 451 7377
Mobile: 0831 759042

Lauren

959 4184

Catherine
0171
372
2128